THINK BIG, THINK DIRTY

THINK BIG, THINK DIRTY

William Garner

ST. MARTIN'S PRESS
NEW YORK

Library of Congress Cataloging in Publication Data

Garner, William, 1920-
   Think big, think dirty.

   I. Title.
PR6057.A675T5   1983   823'.914   83-9757
ISBN 0-312-80014-2

First published in Great Britain by William Heinemann Ltd.

First U.S. Edition

10 9 8 7 6 5 4 3 2 1

For my wife,
as always

"The unofficial motto of space age
spying is think big and think dirty."
Time Magazine

"If a chap doesn't like a file kept
on him, he's a very good reason for not
liking it in my opinion, and that's
the very chap a file should be kept on."
A retired senior police
officer, *Panorama*, BBC
TV, February 1981.

"We do not believe any group of men
adequate enough or wise enough to
operate without scrutiny or without
criticism. We know that the only way
to avoid error is to detect it, that
the only way to detect it is to be
free to enquire. We know that in
secrecy error undetected will
flourish and subvert."
J. Robert Oppenheimer

I

Trigger

"Trigger! Hey, Trigger!"

Trigg registered the sound, but failing, as yet, to associate himself with it, went purposefully on his way.

An extraneous phenomenon intercepted him, ruffling his self-absorption. He found himself staring, at close quarters, into a face he found vaguely familiar.

"Trigger, you old so-and-so!" said the face, contorted in apparent pleasure. "Had me worried for a tick, knew I knew you, couldn't place you, had to think fast, cudgel the old grey cells. Got you though, didn't I? Not bad after . . . what? How many years? Don't tell me, doesn't bear thinking about, forget it, right? Well, how *are* you, Trigger? Listen, we absolutely must have a drink on this, won't take no for an answer, we're right outside my watering hole. Come on, treat's on me."

With no further ado the not totally strange stranger grabbed Trigg by the arm so that, for all his bulk, he was wheeled with something approaching main force through the open door of the Two Brewers.

It was crowded with lunchtime drinkers. Mechanically mumbling apologies to several people he cannoned into, Trigg eventually found himself up against the bar.

At its farther end the man on the stool was talking to the landlord about showing roses in competition. "The great thing," he was saying, "is you don't want to feel rushed, know what I mean? Turn up in plenty of time, blooms back in water first thing. What else you need is a good pair of secateurs and a nice lightweight little watering-can for topping up."

1

He stopped. The landlord said, "Got one, plastic it is, but . . ." The landlord stopped too, seeing that the man on the stool wasn't listening, was staring, in fact, at the end of the bar nearest the door.

"Something up, George?" The landlord knew George was some kind of a copper, not that he talked about it much.

Roses temporarily forgotten, George said softly, "Seen that one before, Arthur? Geezer with the sporty gent?"

* * *

"Never forgotten," Trigg's newfound friend was saying. "Guinness. Always Guinness. Some things never change, right?" A half of Guinness was rammed into Trigg's large but unprepared hand. Some of it found its way down his wrist and under his shirt-cuff. A glass holding a large Scotch chinked dangerously against his. "Cheers, old boy! Here's to us! Who's like us? Damn few! Remember? Course you do, memory like an elephant, am I right? Course I am." The pinkish, sagging face with its quasi-military moustache thrust itself at Trigg's wooden features yet again, breathing bonhomie and the warm fumes of whisky.

"Quiet as ever, eh, Trigger? Still waters running deep, always did. Trigger's a deep 'un, we used to say. Don't try any hanky-panky with old Trigger." There might have been a time, many years past, when this stranger in his hound's-tooth check jacket and cavalry twill trousers had been what used to be called dashing.

Trigg spoke for the first time, his Guinness untouched. "Just one thing, sunshine." His harsh north-country voice, flat, with the earpunching vowels, bored effortlessly through the din. "Who the heck are you when you're at home?"

The other man deflated. Baggy, Trigg thought brutally; baggy clothes, baggy face, baggy body, baggy mind. "Reckon I must have known you," he said grudgingly. "Long time ago. I don't forget faces that easy."

"*Trigger!*" The other, displaying exaggerated dismay, hunched himself toward Trigg in a kind of supplication. "It's me, Joliffe! Tony Joliffe! You remember *me*! Couldn't forget, couldn't *possibly* forget! Colchester barracks, exercises on the Plain, Singapore, Brunei, all that bloody stinking jungle! Here's to us! Who's like us? Damn few! The old mob, Trigger! The old mob!"

"Captain Joliffe," Trigg said slowly, enlightened but otherwise unmoved. He lifted his Guinness, apparently deciding that it had become relevant. As he drank, his pale grey eyes remained unwinkingly on Joliffe. "Captain Joliffe," he repeated eventually. "Who'd have thought?"

"All finished, that stuff, old man, years and years ago," Joliffe protested. "Captain Joliffe, Corporal Trigg, two other people, way, *way* back. Now it's Tony, and . . ." He snatched fretfully at one side of his badly trimmed moustache. "Jog me, Trigger, there's a good chap. First name's slipped my mind. Tony and . . . ?"

"Eustace Roland." Trigg put down his drained glass. "Corporal Trigg, ER, 5979261. Sir!" he added abruptly. A sardonic gleam flickered briefly at the back of his eyes.

"Eustace Roland," Joliffe repeated, faltering. "Course!" He bounced back from the ropes. "ER! That's why we called you Trigger."

"None of my choosing, Mr Joliffe," Trigg said ambiguously, continuing to study Joliffe as if running down a checklist. There was a slight excess of emphasis, Joliffe thought, on that 'Mister'.

"Tony," he coaxed. He leered, anguishedly desirous of being accepted as well as recalled. "After all, old man, what are we? Couple of ordinary blokes, one as good as the other. Or maybe," he revised hastily, "you're better than me now. All that single-minded purpose, eh? Used it to make yourself a millionaire or something, Trigger?"

"No," Trigg said flatly. "A millionaire is one of the things I'm not. Are you, Mr Joliffe?"

"Hah!" Joliffe deployed every muscle in a running display of gestures, twitches and general displacement activity. "Me? Ha! Ha-ha! Wish I was, Trigger, really wish I was. Got it there" – Joliffe knuckled his thinning hair vigorously – "when it comes to a scheme or wheeze, but not brains, old boy, not brains *exactly*, just low cunning. Fancy the other half?"

"Pint," Trigg corrected, his fixed gaze making Joliffe feel like a specimen in a bottle. "My shout." He reached sideways to capture the arm of a passing barmaid. "Pint of Guinness, love, and a Scotch." To Joliffe he said, "Phony Tony, that's what they used to call you. Sir."

"Know." Joliffe bared his teeth, grinning furiously. "Always did, old boy. Phony Tony and Tricky Dicky. Remember Dick

Travers? Dead now, car crash, something like that, always was a rotten driver. Or was that old Sloper Timms? Never mind, doesn't matter now. Quick, old man, table behind you."

* * *

The landlord finished serving a customer and returned to George. "No," he said again. "Never set eyes on him before. Get all types in here, you know that. See him off, should I?"

George shook his head, still watching, and took a pull at his pint of London. "Going to give someone a bell. Don't let my stool go." He slid down, worked his way through the noisy throng, a big, nondescript sort of man for whom people tended instinctively to make way. The switchboard operator put him through to Ramble's desk.

"Thought you were off, cock," Ramble said. "What's this then, social call?"

"You know me, always hungry. Listen, what's with the Bowman? Lost, is he?"

"Lost? Who says he's lost?"

"He's here, mate. In the Two Brewers."

"The Brewers? Get off! Here, how long have *you* been in the Brewers?"

"Knock if off, will you? I'm serious. He's here, just come in. What's Patton's lot doing?"

"Patton? He's . . . here, hang on a tick."

George held on for several ticks, catching a brief, reassuring glimpse of chummy each time someone passed through the door to the saloon.

"George?"

"Still here, darling. Me and the boy, clocked him again just now."

"Listen. We've just been on to Patton through the squawker. Him and his lot are out at the Gate, so's Bowman, still in bed, that's what they tell me. Hasn't shifted all morning. Stop scratching, George. The Bowman couldn't get from the Gate to the Brewers without being seen, not if he was Superman. Kick the booze, mate. Go home early and make your missus a happy woman."

"Are you sure? Are *they* sure?"

"Sure they're sure. On oath."

"Okay," George said patiently. "So it's a ringer. But listen,

4

I want it booked, pal. If they find chummy's shown them the back of his heels, I want it on the record I gave you a bell, right?"

"Right, my old mate, will do. Straight up, George, he's safe at home in Notting Hill. Go and take another butcher's at the ringer, only this time put your glasses on."

George held the receiver away from his ear until Ramble, ending his noisy laughter, said, "Your call booked in at 12.07, okay? Now go and have one for me."

"I'll do that." George went back for another look at chummy.

* * *

Joliffe slid hastily into the vacated seat. Trigg, after carefully checking his change, joined him. The crowd jostled thickly about him but his solidity, though he was not a particularly large man, seemed to create its own space, within which he moved freely.

"Neither of us getting any younger, eh, Trigger?" Joliffe was looking unhappily at his single whisky, wanting to do something about it but not daring, because Trigg had bought it. "Can't promote him, old boy," Joliffe remembered Tricky Dick Travers saying. "Beggar's just as likely to be huffy as grateful, take it as unspoken criticism of his performance as corporal, know what I mean?"

Joliffe knew, all over again, just what Travers had meant. Nothing had changed. Trigg was still Trigg, not to be tampered with in case his being, his very Triggishness, should be permanently disturbed.

"Well," he said, trying to make his Scotch last by picking it up and putting it down again untouched, "how's the world treating you, Trigger? Where's the family seat? Somewhere here in the Smoke, right?"

"Family seat?" Trigger echoed the words in the tone of a man whose ears are unable to credit what they have heard. "Where it always was. Went back the day I was demobbed, been there ever since."

"Cleethorpes!" Suddenly remembering, Joliffe stifled an insane and probably dangerous desire to laugh. A great many memories passed through his mind in a kind of disorganised stampede; Corporal Trigg contemplating Capetown, Colombo, Singapore, Brunei with the same unchangingly stony expression before saying, "Not a patch on Cleethorpes." No one in Trigg's company believed he was joking, especially as he might have had a point about Brunei.

Cleethorpes, about which Joliffe knew little and cared less, was a small, wildly unfashionable seaside resort somewhere on the East coast; Lincolnshire? Yorkshire? what did it matter? The very idea of comparing it with the fabled sights of the Orient had made Corporal Trigg a legend, not just in 'B' Company but throughout the theatre of operations. Old Sloper Timms, air-dropped with a handful of men into a Borneo jungle clearing with instructions to report on its possibilities as a staging post, had earned himself a brisk but not too serious reprimand from the GOC by radioing: 'Suitable in all respects but not a patch on Cleethorpes.'

*   *   *

"Okay, George? Everything all right?" The landlord looked at George curiously. No good publican minds having a copper as a regular, someone to speak up for him in time of trouble. Not that there ever was much trouble at the Two Brewers, barring the odd late-night drunk, but if the wooden-faced, lumpish character at the table next to the door meant trouble, the landed wanted to know.

George picked up his glass, drained it and pushed it across the bar. "Same again, Arthur, please."

"Or similar," the landlord said automatically.

"Or similar," George agreed. "No, it's all right, Arthur, no trouble. My mistake."

"Must have been two other blokes?"

"That's it, two other blokes. Know the other one, Arthur? Bookie's tout?"

"Checks and brothel creepers? Regular lunchtime, Monday to Friday, like a lot of 'em. Works round the corner, that big office block. Shows up at six o'clock now and then, but not often."

George nodded. It was funny, though, coming across a ringer, just like that.

*   *   *

"Cleethorpes," Joliffe repeated. "Seriously, Trigger? Never had an itch to move?" He peered earnestly, hoping to detect rudimentary humour. There was none. There never had been.

6

"See more of the world, that it? No," Trigg said. "Why should I? Folk are much the same everywhere."

Joliffe shook his head respectfully. "Haven't changed, not a bit. What about family, then? Married, are you? Family man? Little Triggers?" For some obscure reason the thought appalled him.

"Never felt the need."

About to ask him which need, Joliffe changed his mind. It was something he felt he would rather not know. "Family, though? Parents? Brothers? Sisters? Mean to say, must have some reason for staying in Cleethorpes."

"Reason is, I like it," Trigg said simply. "No sense in going somewhere else if you're no better off and might end up worse. Anyway, my mam's still there. And there's the work."

"Ah, yes, the work. Same old job, old man? What was it now? Something to do with . . . ?"

"With what, Mr Joliffe?" Trigg asked innocently. Or *was* it innocent? All Trigg's old habits began to loom in Joliffe's memory; innocent remarks that might not have been, if you visualised a crooked smile lodged somewhere behind that unchangingly wooden face. He took refuge in honesty. "Tell the truth, old son, can't remember."

"Rock, Mr Joliffe." Trigg finished his Guinness, dabbed his mouth with the back of his hand and turned his basilisk gaze upon Joliffe. "I'm in rock."

"Rock! Ha! Ha-ha! Yes! Course! Knew it was something of that sort, just couldn't fish it up. Rock! Course you were, remember now." He was sure now that Trigg was having him on, almost sure, though not quite, that rock had not been invented when he and Trigg were doing their military service.

"Not in those days," Trigg said, patient as if he were dealing with a half-wit. "Never took much interest in those days. There was my dad, then."

Joliffe gave up. "Anyway, what brings you to the Smoke? Something big, something important, I'll bet."

"Money," Trigg said. "If you call that important. There's some who don't."

"But you do, am I right, Trigger? Course I am."

"Wrong. Take it or leave it, that's me, Mr Joliffe."

"Tony," Joliffe said as a dying fling. "Try it for size, old man."

Hauling an old-fashioned silver hunter from his waistcoat

7

pocket and checking it against the pub clock, Trigg said, "Anyway, what do you do these days, Mr Joliffe? That clock's fast."

"Me?" Joliffe affected surprise. "Ha! Ha-ha! Yes, well, old man, nothing so very different, that's the answer. Still the old admin. lark. Notice the big office block just behind this place, did you? Well, that's where I am. Office manager. Not much difference from pushing around the bumf in the old days, eh?"

"Glad to hear you've made good, Mr Joliffe. Got to be off now. So long, sunshine." Ignoring Joliffe's outstretched hand, Trigg worked his way toward the door, and was gone.

Feeling like a squeezed lemon, Joliffe abandoned his seat, and struggled to the bar. "Excuse me." He looked behind him. A largish man with a city-smart face and inquisitive eyes was standing at his elbow. "Excuse me," he said again. "That bloke you were with, have a feeling I know him. Happen to know his name, do you?"

"Trigger," Joliffe said, then, "Ha! Ha-ha, no! Trigg. Trigger's his nickname. Eustace Roland Trigg," he added with a certain pressure-relieving malice.

The large man shook his head. "Must be mistaken. Thanks anyway."

"Pleasure's mine," Joliffe said. He caught the barmaid's eye. "Scotch, please, dear. Better make it a double."

2

Bowman

"Helga, it's me. Look, you really mustn't go on doing this."

"It's all right. I knew Steve wasn't there."

"Maybe, but sooner or later you'll be caught."

"For ringing my husband?"

"When he isn't there. When you know he isn't there."

"I want to talk to you. Where are you?"

"In a call box. You didn't think I'd call from Curzon Street? And I only have a minute or two."

"Not enough. I must see you."

"I don't think it would be a good idea."

"Why? Are you afraid of being followed?" She laughed. The laugh was unnatural, part forced, part not really laughter.

"You know it's not that, although . . ."

". . . although you do think we'll be caught. In the end."

"Not if we're sensible."

"But even if we're not caught, we shall be found out."

"Only if we're stupid." Give me patience, he thought, not that I deserve it. "Listen, Helga, I . . ."

"If we are not found out, I mean by Steve, it doesn't say very much for the safety of the country, all those undiscovered spies." Her voice was febrile, words somersaulting out. Did she begin this early, he wondered, drinking as soon as she got up? Or at any rate, as soon as Steve was out of the flat? "I mean," she was saying, "if Steve can't catch his wife with her lover, how should he be able" – In times of stress, her syntax tended to become unsettled – "to catch a spy?"

"Helga, I didn't call you to talk about things you know very

9

well shouldn't be discussed on an open line. I rang because your message said it was urgent."

"It is. I must see you. I know Steve will be away tonight. He told me he will go to The Other Place. And he will stay the night, isn't that so?"

"Possibly. Look, I've got to go."

"Possibly! Will you possibly tell me where The Other Place is?"

"You've been married to Steve all these years and he hasn't told you where it is, so you can hardly expect me to."

"Steve tells me nothing." A sharpness, but also something else, typically Helga; like Schubert, wandering from *freude* to *angst*, major to minor key; wistful, forlorn.

"I must go. I'm seeing the Minister in fifteen minutes."

"First tell me you love me."

"Helga, please."

"I know. You don't, not really, do you?"

"Dearest Helga, this isn't fair."

"Ah, the famous English fairness! All these years and I still don't learn to be fair. You must come tonight, Johnny. I insist you come tonight."

"It's no use. Don't you see, it's . . ." She had rung off.

He stood with the phone in his hand, wondering whether to ring her back, knowing he must not. Another man's wife. The other man his trusted deputy, his wife an incipient alcoholic. Or perhaps no longer incipient? Why had he let it begin? Or go on? How could he run it down before it eventually exploded like a time bomb?

He stepped out of the box, stood indecisively, receiving unwelcome messages from the hinterland of his mind. He became aware that someone on the other side of the street, where the sign that said NEW SCOTLAND YARD rotated slowly on its pivot, was gesturing, waiting for a break in the traffic.

Having finally braved the crossing, the someone said, "Paying for your own phone calls, Mr Morpurgo? I reckon we could just about have stood you one before you left."

Morpurgo smiled. "Kind of you, Chief Superintendent, but it was a personal call."

Chief Superintendent Placket chuckled dutifully. "If everyone at the Yard thought that, the phone bill'd drop by a half. Didn't want us to hear your secrets, more like." He took a deep, appreciative breath of air heavy with carbon monoxide and the toxic fumes of lead. "Beautiful morning. Which way are you going?"

"Smith Square. Nearly, anyway."

"Ah, we part then. I'm away to Horseferry Road. Can't be far from having them off now, right?"

"Depends," Morpurgo said vaguely. "Bring them in when we're ready."

"Sorry, sir." The Special Branch man's attitude changed instantly. "Wasn't fishing." He nodded curtly. "Be seeing you, Mr Morpurgo."

"Be seeing you," Morpurgo said. "Your chaps are doing a good job."

The compliment restored Placket's humour. "Good of you to say so, sir. Do our best, can't do better."

"Of course." Morpurgo stood gazing absently after the chief superintendent for a moment or two, then resumed his own way.

The Minister's town house was in one of the little streets just off Smith Square, within easy walking distance of the Palace of Westminster, linked to the straggling circuits of the division bell and comfortably close to Whitehall.

Admitted by the Minister's man, he was shown into a room that made abundantly plain the Minister's place in the political spectrum. The furniture was all the third and fourth Georges. The pictures, chiefly oils, ran from a Lely to the Edwardians, not least a Sargent of the Minister's wife's grandmother, but was significantly short on the twentieth century. The Minister himself was by Huntsman, his classic three-piece nicely setting off his Guards tie and a decorous shirt of the kind one ordered by the dozen in Jermyn Street. The Minister liked to think of himself as the voice of the man in the street, but the street would have had to resemble those around Smith Square.

"Come in, come in," he boomed at Morpurgo, who was already in. "Drink? What shall it be? Sherry? Scotch, a rather decent single malt? Or are you like the old Duke of Whatsisname, didn't believe in drinking before noon but was prepared to make an exception in the case of champagne?"

"Nothing, thank you, Minister." He was waved to one of the two high-backed chairs flanking an elegant fireplace in which stood a flower arrangement as unnaturally immaculate as a Tory

11

lady's coiffure. Morpurgo had no doubt that the flowers had been disciplined by the Minister's wife.

"Smoke?" Morpurgo shook his head. It was up to the Minister to make the running now. He watched his political master settle into the facing chair, and turn an amiable, pink-and-white expanse of face in Morpurgo's direction.

"Well now. Dare say Sir Hugh told you, willing to hear it from the horse's mouth. He agreed, mind you, likes his chaps to have a chance to show what they're made of, am I right? How's that wife of yours, by the way? Last time we met she was just about to have her new exhibition. Promised her I'd look in, didn't though, politician's promise, what? Tell her, there's a good chap, grovellingly apologetic, pressure of work, won't believe me naturally. How did it go?"

Identifying his target with some difficulty, Morpurgo said, "Very well, Minister. Good reviews, some high class commissions." He thought that was about right.

"Good, good! She has great talent. Or ought I to say genius?"

"She'd believe you if you said talent."

"But genius, politician's blarney, yes? Like kissing babies." The Minister laughed his booming laugh: *hyuk-hyuk-hyuk*.

"All right." He dismissed laughter as brusquely as he dismissed hecklers. "Tell me about Joseph Sattin." His big head came forward, miming concentration. He reminded Morpurgo just a little of a panda; large, slow and deceptively gentle-looking.

"You see all the summaries, Minister?"

The Minister nodded toward the table with its three dispatch boxes, two red, one yellow, the yellow spilling security reports over the lustrous table-top. "Be honest, can't say first priority, my own civil servants bung too much paper at me for that. But read them, yes, every day. Assure you, I don't take that particular responsibility lightly." Smile on, smile off, a glimpse of crooked teeth. "Your chaps seem to have been very skilful."

"I think so. But I'm still certain that the opposition's been warned. Sattin, Kagalov, I don't know which, but it went down the line to the Stringers."

"So you say." The Minister leaned far forward, eyes as friendly as glass marbles fixed on Morpurgo as if to stare him down. "Yes. That, I gather, is your line."

"It is, Minister."

"But you've more than enough to bring them in. Good solid stuff, chapter and verse, go down well at a trial?"

"On Sattin and the Stringers. Kagalov, too, of course, but we can't bring Kagalov in."

"Couldn't keep him, you mean. Embassy man, diplomat, so far as any of them are diplomats and not KGB snoopers. Best we could do is boot him out, not much mileage in that."

"Agreed. Time for a chat first though. And catching him red-handed, a nasty little knock for Moscow Centre. We would take pleasure in it, let's put it that way, Minister." He wanted Kagalov, wanted him badly.

The Minister flung himself back in his chair in slow motion, recoiling from something that had not yet put in an appearance. "Yes, of course, quite see that. Still, can't always have what we want, can we?"

Here we go, Morpurgo thought. "I'd willingly forego Kagalov if we could keep the ring running a little longer, Minister. Long enough to get a compass reading on the fifth man."

This was what the Minister had already retreated from. "Ah. Yes. Five. The fifth man." He lowered heavy lids over his little eyes, tipped back his head. "Proof?" He waited, eyes closed. Morpurgo found the performance calculated.

"Cast-iron? None. But supporting evidence, very strong."

"Hunch." The Minister opened his eyes to look at Morpurgo along his nose. "Don't discount them, have them myself. No good in court, though. Sir Hugh and I agree on that."

"Doesn't change anything, Minister. Someone's still hovering in the wings."

"Sir Hugh let you come here, didn't he?"

A light flick of the whip, as studied, Morpurgo thought, as the trick with the eyelids. The Minister was known as a bit of a bully. "Yes," he said. "He let me come."

"Hm." The Minister scowled at the flower arrangement. "Don't like it, Morpurgo. Sort of hunch that makes smoke, understand me? Black. Stinking. Very pervasive."

"Yes, Minister."

"Going to ask you something." The Minister crossed his legs, using the pause for effect. "Something you won't like. You're sure, quite sure, that this . . . bee in your bonnet . . . nothing personal, you understand, but quite, quite sure it couldn't, unconsciously perhaps, be politically motivated?"

13

"Minister?" Morpurgo instantly understood the significance of the question in spite of its attacking from the flank rather than the centre.

The Minister adopted a tone that Morpurgo found repellent. "Man to man, we aren't of the same – shall we say? – persuasion. Don't misunderstand me, Morpurgo, you're entitled to your political opinions and I'm entitled to mine. Remind you I was a member of the committee that recommended making the security services a broader church after the Philby nonsense. Room for all reasonable shades of opinion, moderate right to moderate left. Sometimes difficult to be politically impartial though, am I right? Wouldn't be human otherwise."

After what seemed to him to be an age, Morpurgo said, "I have political views, Minister, but not political prejudices. If I believe, as I do, that someone in Whitehall has a link with Moscow Centre, it's based on observation and judgement, not politics. If you doubt that, you should bloody well boot me out."

Completely unabashed, the Minister said cheerfully, "Never doubted it, dear chap. Had to be asked though." But he *had* doubted me, Morpurgo thought; probably still does.

"Stand by your hunch, that about it? Not afraid" – The Minister decided to laugh again: *hyuk-hyuk-hyuk* – "you'll be gently steered on to other work? Sideways promotion?"

Lose this one, lose the lot. "Stand by the evidence and my experience, Minister? I must, mustn't I? If you even hint at the possibility of a traitor in the highest echelons of government, you've already gone too far."

"Damned if you're wrong, damned if you're not."

"I think so." Especially, Morpurgo thought, when the government had a bare working majority under a weak-kneed prime minister who had already barely weathered two minor security scandals, and was only held together by rival strongmen. Morpurgo's Minister and the Foreign Secretary would each be party to a palace revolution if either could be sure that he and not his rival would head the new administration. The large and cultivated man who sat opposite was both ruthless and ambitious.

"All right." The Minister counterfeited candour. "Let's hear some more of your argument."

"I think you've already heard it from Sir Hugh, Minister."

"I want to hear it from you."

"You were kind enough to say we've been doing a good job. I

14

think so too. As near perfect a piece of long-term surveillance, once we were on to them, as I've ever seen. Disinformation for nine months, Stringer to his wife, the pair of them to Sattin and Sattin to Kagalov. Nine months. Almost literally never lost sight of them except when they were in bed. Then, quite suddenly, when the game is nearly over and the only remaining question is when to bring them in, everything stops. Everyone plays possum, but especially the Stringers."

The Minister looked impatient. "Sherlock Holmes's curious incident of the dog in the night-time? Don't quote that one. The dog did nothing and that was what was curious, am I right? But this is different, these are people, not dogs. People can't go on passing secrets, night and day. Sooner or later they reach a stage when the job's done, when there's nothing worthwhile left to pass."

"There was plenty left. Fresh stuff. Cooked up practically every week." Morpurgo knew his tone was aggressive, almost insolent. So what!

"All right." Morpurgo saw that the Minister's mind was already made up. "I know the maxim; never bring a spy in the moment you find him. Uncover him, use him to pass bogus information, but never bring him in until he's no more use. But there's the other side, isn't there? Moscow decides it's got all the information it wants, so it stops while it's still winning. Or it begins to realise that the material it's getting is phony. Or any one of a dozen good reasons."

"Agreed. But in this business you develop a sixth sense. So do others. Sattin's a professional. Sattin can do nothing and make it look wholly natural. But the Stringers are amateurs. Quite suddenly they start doing nothing in a way that would be suspicious to people with a lot less experience than ours."

"But if Sattin's a professional, he's going to think of himself, not the Stringers, am I right?" The Minister thought he was. "So Moscow tells Kagalov that's it. Kagalov tells Sattin at their next meeting – treff, I believe you call them – and Sattin tells the Stringers. That done, Sattin doesn't give a damn about the Stringers any more. Why on earth should he?"

"Well, he'd prefer them *not* to be caught, Minister. Particularly as long as he's still around. A good agent likes to do a clean job. I'm prepared to swear that none of them, Sattin, Kagalov or the Stringers, had the smallest reason to believe that the game was up until we started talking about whether to pull them. Then, nothing. Stop. No further contact. Someone warned them. Someone from our side."

"Then who?" The Minister's voice had hardened. So had the planes of his fleshy face. Morpurgo knew he had won the DSO in Normandy in '44, its bar after the slaughter at Arnhem. There was muscle, bone and a visceral toughness behind the urbane front.

"Who?" the Minister demanded again. "Have to name names. Who's the guilty man? Haven't got that, haven't got anything."

"That's why I need more time, a chance to get a bearing. And a chance to bag Kagalov red-handed."

The Minister made a meaningless but not unrevealing gesture, opening and closing the fingers of one hand before letting it fall to the arm of his chair. "Do you realise just how popular you could make yourself, you and your unsubstantiated ideas? Don't for a minute think you'd get a medal."

Morpurgo waited. "Sorry," the Minister said grudgingly. "Shouldn't have said that." He hoisted himself from his chair, motioning to Morpurgo to stay put, and promenaded seemingly aimlessly around the big table, one hand walking its fingers along the gleaming surface.

"However," he eventually continued, "the matter's resolved, like it or not. Prime Minister's personal decision, no proof, no traitor. You've given me nothing to make him change his mind."

Beginning to guess something, Morpurgo said, "I see."

"Do you? I wonder. I could just say the Foreign Secretary won, leave it at that. Kick you out, do as you're told and like it. But you wouldn't, would you?"

"No," Morpurgo said without emotion. "No, Minister, I wouldn't."

"Sure you won't have that drink?" The Minister's hand hovered over crystal decanters, each on its silver bottle stand, engraved silver labels chained about their necks like gorgets.

"Too early, thank you, Minister."

The Minister, Morpurgo thought, left the decanters reluctantly. He came back to his seat, reached out a hand almost but not quite to touch the flower arrangement in the fireplace, withdrew it to point at Morpurgo. "Theirs is the better story, do you see? The Secret Service. They've lost their agent, fieldman or whatever they call them. They want him back badly, something he knows but doesn't know he knows, you know the sort of blather they use. So they need someone to trade, and you can't deny it, Sattin is the only possibility. Don't know why I'm spelling all this out. You've heard it often enough by now. Point is, they convinced the PM."

Morpurgo's guess had been right. Not the least reason for the Minister's irritability was being defeated by the Foreign Secretary in a bout of Cabinet Committee infighting.

"Convinced him," the Minister said, "that clearing up a spy ring and getting back a good agent is a better deal than risking scandal over a non-existent mole."

"So I've got to bring them in." Nothing to lose now, Morpurgo thought. "I have a feeling you could have told me this at the beginning."

"What a prickly fellow you are! You've had your hearing. I was completely open-minded, prepared to go back to the PM, prepared to do battle again. Facts, man! Facts versus speculation! We *know* Moscow Centre's holding one of our people. We *know* they're willing to make an exchange. We *know* Sattin's the man for the swap, all facts, whereas . . ."

"That's my other point, Minister." Morpurgo had been saving it until he could see the whites of the Minister's eyes. "Things pretty well sewn up, just keeping them ticking over until we're ready to put up the shutters. Quite suddenly, they announce that they've picked up a British agent in East Germany and they're open for trade. The idea's obviously to get Sattin back, but who told them we were on to him? Who told them it was time for a deal? And why such a hurry? These swaps usually take months, sometimes years."

"Who told them?" The Minister fumbled momentarily. "Sattin, Kagalov, one or the other. Passed the word back, smoked out, liable to be collared at any moment. So Moscow does its own bit of bargain hunting, probably been feeding our chap junk for months, just like Sattin."

"And the reason for the hurry?" Morpurgo, running the risk of an imperial rocket, might as well have his money's worth.

"What reason?" The Minister's urbanity was beginning to develop hair cracks. "We don't know. Why should we? SIS says standard ploy, get your own man back before he forgets any useful information he might have."

17

"Or before the other side persuades useful information out of him."

"What information, man?" At any moment now the Minister would throw the whole of his weight at Morpurgo. "Don't waffle! Make your point!"

"The name of the fifth man."

The Minister was the kind of man to see persistence as defiance. "For God's sake! Look at what you're saying. That somewhere in Whitehall, or Westminster, at a very high level, there's a traitor. Let's not mince words, a traitor. Haven't the smallest proof, this is what you're saying – but if we leave things as they are, we might get some. Or might not. But if we don't, let's *not* leave things as they are. Let's bring 'em in, *not* to make a swap, but because Sattin knows the name of this non-existent traitor, and that's far more important than an exchange. Is that a fair summary?" The Minister had a reputation for fairness, based chiefly upon listening to other people's views before doing what he had already made up his mind to do.

Morpurgo stood up. "I don't know about fair, but obviously final. I'm wasting your time."

His point won by *force majeure*, the Minister was typically anxious to be conciliatory. "Don't take it too much to heart. We must all bend when the wind blows. Now, bring your spies in. I'll make sure credit's given where credit's due. And give my regards to that wife of yours. She's a clever girl, tell her I said so."

"Thank you, I will. I'll find my own way out, Minister."

"Oh, one more thing." Morpurgo halted. "This man Kagalov – What is he? Second Secretary? – pity you couldn't catch him in flagrante delicto, but there's no reason at all, none, why you shouldn't make life as difficult as possible for him. You've got the photographs, dates, times, places. Shove him around a bit, old boy, encourage the others. All bloody spies, when you come down to it."

"Yes, Minister, of course." Aware that he was being invited to rampage around in the Foreign Secretary's territory, Morpurgo took his leave.

When the Minister heard the street door close he poured himself a generous measure of the rather decent single malt whisky, and took his glass to the green scrambler phone.

"Hugh? Dicky. Switch over, old boy, will you?" He waited until they were reconnected on the scrambler circuit. "Ah, good.

Listen, he's just left. Good man, sticks to his guns, but he must learn not to make waves, no more of this mole nonsense . . . What? Oh, yes, stupid word, couldn't agree more. Anyway, keep him busy now, real spies instead of imaginary ones, imagine you'll be moving on it straight away . . . Good man. Hugh, listen, would you swear that he *never* lets his politics interfere with the job? I mean, he *is* a lefty, am I right? . . . Ah, yes, see what you mean, more a question of attitude than anything else . . . All right, old boy, keep me informed. And Hugh, let's not be *too* eager to dance to the SIS tune, know what I mean? . . . Oh, you leave the Foreign Secretary to me. He's no jurisdiction over domestic security, not even squatters' rights now we've knocked your chap Morpurgo's nonsense on the head. Good man! Great life if you don't weaken, what?''

* * *

The operation was swift and tidy. Stringer, though temporarily attached to the Admiralty's Underwater Weapons Research Establishment at Portland, had been in London for the previous twenty-four hours for a meeting and was arrested on his way to Waterloo Station. Mrs Stringer, a senior clerk in Classified Records at the Ministry of Defence, was taken from her place of work. Sattin, who for some reason had stayed in his modest flat in Notting Hill Gate since the weekend, was arrested in his own sitting room. Stringer was dispatched by car to Weymouth to be charged. His wife to Rochester Row police station. Sattin was driven to Tuck's, a Security Directorate house in north-west London.

Chief Superintendent Placket, telling himself that Morpurgo was a tight-mouthed customer and no mistake, was in charge of the Special Branch officers who made the arrests. Steve Archer, Morpurgo's deputy, represented Security Directorate. He and Morpurgo met in a temporarily borrowed office at Rochester Row.

"No trouble?" Morpurgo's question was a formality.

"None. Sattin's a pro all right, said damn all, still hasn't spoken. Stringer's shit-scared, diarrhoea, the trembles, almost in tears. He'll sing like a bird.''

"And his missus?"

Archer pulled a face; distaste. "Played the wide-eyed, silly-me role to begin with, but she's as tough as nails. Sacrifice her old

19

man like a shot, given half a chance, but he'll do fine by himself. There, Johnny, is a man in terror, couldn't be more frightened if he knew we were going to use rack and thumbscrews."

"So you'll work on him first, leave the woman to the running boys?"

Archer nodded. "Right. Let the Branch knock off the rough edges before we start confronting her with what we've got from her dearly beloved." He was looking at Morpurgo with open curiosity. "Why the sudden rush? Isn't Comrade Kagalov important any more?" He lit a fresh cigarette from the old with the casual manner of the heavy smoker, the actual moment of exchange blurred.

"Comrade Kagalov," Morpurgo said grimly, "doesn't know how lucky he's been, not yet. He'll guess, though, later on. It'll all be good for a laugh in Dzerzhinsky Square, the Brits botching their tradecraft and letting a KGB colonel dressed up as a Second Secretary slip through their fingers when they could have put egg on the ambassador's face."

"Of course," Archer said. "The question is, why?"

"The swap's more important than the mole. That's what the Prime Minister thinks, anyway."

Archer's face cleared. Morpurgo knew he was secretly relieved. Old boys' net, he thought. Nothing changes. If the choice is between a traitor of your own class and letting off the foe, you slip the foe his ticket back home.

Archer said, "Pretty thin, though, wasn't it? I mean the mole would have to have been so high up it's practically unthinkable. Pity about Kagalov, though. I'd have given a lot to see the bastard's face when the Branch grabbed his collar. But the damage, Johnny, if the rumour got around that Blunt and Leo Long weren't the last, that even if Hollis were innocent, there was still another one left! The fact that it wasn't true wouldn't make a scrap of difference. There are always people around who're glad of any old lie to smear the top echelons."

For top echelons, Morpurgo translated, read the Tories, the Establishment, the people who drop names but not aitches. More mildly than he felt he said, "Smearing's a two-way traffic. Anyway, we're still in with a chance."

Steve Archer was a good many things that Morpurgo found it hard to be over-enthusiastic about; good family, public school and Cambridge, ex-Guards like the Minister, a couple of clubs that were a personal reference in themselves. With that kind of background, unquestioning commitment to the political right could be taken for granted. Morpurgo himself was a product of state education, redbrick university and the Trades Union Congress. Steve's family was minor county; horsy, doggy and hunt balls. Morpurgo's father had been a schoolteacher, his mother the elder daughter of a family that had run a corner grocer's shop. But he had worked in harmony with Steve for a good many years and, as he had told the Minister, took care, or so he believed, to keep prejudice out of his professional judgements.

Within the limits of what Morpurgo would have described as his blinkers, Steve Archer was not slow of thought. "I wouldn't have called it much of a chance," he said now. "As I told you, Comrade Sattin's going to be a hard nut to crack. If there really had been some sort of traitor in the ranks, I very much doubt you would have got Comrade Sattin to reveal it."

"Worth a try."

Steve grinned humourlessly. "Worth a try? You haven't met him yet. Incidentally, you won't be expecting me to go to The Other Place now?" Something hard and knowing in his gaze? No, guilt pricking conscience.

"No. What I do want you to do is to tuck Stringer under your motherly wing. If he's in a talking mood your upper class brand of decency's just the thing to reassure him." They said things like that to each other, he and Steve, and only occasionally did one or other of them come up against the cutting edge.

"Okay, comrade." Steve pulled another face. "Weymouth. Not really my scene, Johnny, all cockles, crumpet and Mackeson's Milk Stout. Still, if you insist. At least I'll enjoy the drive, now the sun's shown up. Everything under wraps, yes?"

"The press? Damn right! Until we're ready to make charges, I can do without the headlines. In any case, I want to see how long it takes Kagalov to react."

"You never give up, do you?" Steve looked at Morpurgo with a mixture of respect and something else, something Morpurgo was unable to define. Sometimes he wondered if Steve Archer viewed him, privately, with more prejudice than he got in return.

"No," he said equably. "I never do, not if I can help it. Why should I? That's why we're not going public yet, headlines, questions in the House."

21

Steve said, "Joe Padley, MP! Muck-raker! Left-wing muck-raker, which is worse."

"Without raking a generous sample of right-wing muck," Morpurgo said, "I wouldn't know."

He rang his Director-General to report. Sir Hugh Wyndham, ex-ambassador to Poland and a lifelong buccaneer on the high seas of diplomacy, had come to Security Directorate with a hitherto undetected but active dislike of the Foreign Office and all its ways. Once installed in his new post, he had wasted little time in making it plain that Security Directorate had no intention of playing second fiddle to the Friends, or, for that matter, the Cousins over in Grosvenor Square. Known as the Knight of the Long Knives, the unofficial title bore reference to his skill in the perpetual infighting of the Whitehall mafia.

"Good," he said eventually. "A spy in the hand is worth two moles in the undergrowth. I take it Sattin's on his way to The Other Place."

"Tomorrow. He'll stay at Tuck's tonight, a question of convenience. I thought I'd pay him a brief social call, make him the usual offer."

"I've a feeling you'll cut no ice. If he could sleep all these years, he's hardly likely to fall at the first hurdle. That reminds me, the Minister . . ." He stopped abruptly. "I suppose we're on a safe line?"

"Of course. I was going to warn you, incidentally. The Minister toyed with the idea that I might be a mole myself, or at the very least, an agent of sympathy. I told him he should ask for my resignation."

The Knight groaned. "You do go out of your way, don't you? Anyway, I know. He's simply not used to the idea that the political left cares about the safety of the realm just as much as the Conservative Party."

"Sometimes," Morpurgo said, "I get the idea that you have the same problem."

The Knight ignored the remark. "I'll let the Minister know that everything went off smoothly. Won't do you any harm. Well, I suppose that's the end of Operation Bowman, just a question of tidying up." Someone having produced, in the early stages, the rather dreadful pun that Sattin had two Stringers to his bow, the surveillance exercise had been christened Operation Bowman.

22

"I suppose so," Morpurgo said. "Though I won't give up all hope of taking Kagalov until he's actually out of the country. Anything else? If not, I'll be on my way to Tuck's."

The Knight's tone changed. "Johnny! You haven't given up, have you? You still think you might squeeze a name out of Sattin. You've been officially warned off. Now stay off. I've the Directorate to think of. Do I make myself clear?"

"You do, Director-General." The Knight was a man of absolute integrity. So are they all, all honourable men, Morpurgo thought. Their only fault was to be unable to think what the received knowledge defined as unthinkable. So he would not, for the time being, tell the Knight that surveillance on Kagalov was being maintained, nor that he had no intention of giving up that easily.

"Good." The Knight was affable once more. "Letting Kagalov off the hook goes against the grain, mine, not just yours. But that's life, Johnny, not getting what common justice says is rightfully ours. It'll be painful enough for Kagalov to know he failed. Now, go and tuck Sattin up, if you must. Offer him the earth if you think he'll take it. But since he's going to be back in Moscow in short order if this exchange goes through, don't, for heaven's sake, give him the chance to tell his debriefers that we were prepared to believe we'd got a super-Philby sitting in one of the best seats in Whitehall."

Or the government front bench, Morpurgo thought sardonically, but in fact he didn't go quite that far himself.

His car came, forcing him to leave the claustrophobic office with its permanent smell of stale tobacco smoke and God knew what else. He was pleased to find the driver was Callow, the least communicative of the Directorate's drivers. He provided Morpurgo with the rare opportunity to do a little uninterrupted thinking.

They were a considerable way along the Edgware Road before he remembered Helga. There was no possibility of seeing her that evening, and the sooner she knew it, the better.

He spotted a call box almost at once. "Just pull up at the next corner, Peter, will you?"

"Sir." Callow never expressed surprise, or commented on what did not concern him.

"Shan't keep you long." Morpurgo shut himself in the box.

"Helga? Listen, Steve's had to go out of town. Back some time, but not tonight. He asked me to let you know."

"Steve? Asked you to let me know?" She seemed amused. "I suppose you sent him."

"No. I didn't. That's why I'm ringing, really."

In the way she had, she guessed instantly. "You're not coming. You must." Her voice was slurred, so very little and yet unmistakably.

"I can't. You must believe me, Helga. Business. Serious business."

"You must come, Johnny."

"I'll come as soon as I can, but it can't be tonight. Please understand."

"You promised."

Had he? He couldn't remember. It made no difference. "Look, I've got someone waiting for me outside. I must go. I'll call again, as soon as I'm able."

"You must come. If you don't, Johnny, if you don't . . ." She kept him waiting, for whatever reason. "If you don't," she said at last, "I shall ring and ring and ring. Everybody. Curzon Street. Sylvie. Everybody. I shall ring and ring and ring." Another pause, and she said, "You must believe me. You must seriously believe me." He had no idea whether she was mocking him by imitating him, or simply speaking whatever words came first to her mind. Oh God! he thought; blackmail, whether she deliberately intends it or not. She might ring Sylvie. She might ring anybody. He dare not take any chances.

"All right. I'll try. I can't say when. If there's any problem, I'll ring back."

"You will come, Johnny," she said firmly, and then, "Please," in a tone that surprised and even touched him with its unconcealed, almost childlike expression of longing.

Oh God! he thought again, getting back in the car, how did I ever get into this one? Two women, and trouble with both. He saw less and less of Sylvie, and thought it a matter for regret. And Helga, whom he had seen rather too often, he would now prefer to see less; much, much less.

It had begun at a time when Steve was away, doing some patient and extremely intricate untangling of the background of a supposedly Scandinavian-born but naturalised British doctor who had provided, or was at any rate suspected of providing, medical aid for an Iraqi terrorist group that had made a brief assassination visit to London. Steve had telephoned to ask if

24

Morpurgo and Sylvie would give Helga an evening on the town to mark a wedding anniversary. At the last moment Sylvie had been called away on professional business. At her suggestion, he had taken Helga out himself.

He had also taken her home. It had seemed to be nothing very special; two people brought together, still feeling the afterglow of wine and pleasure, each feeling – resenting, if the truth were known – the absence of their respective mates. Practically tucked up in bed together by their respective mates was the way Morpurgo had seen it at the time; Gather ye rosebuds, Time's wingèd chariot and so on.

Unfortunately, Helga, he discovered too late, was not prepared to see it in the same light. He hadn't known, at that time, of her unhappiness, of the gulf that now separated her from Steve, of the desperate feeling she experienced, now that their children had left home, of purposelessness, of not belonging. He had not been left unaware for long, and when he allowed her to discover that he had seen it as no more than the affair of a night, her determination to continue the relationship had, if anything, strengthened, though she knew as well as he that nothing could come of it.

Since there was nothing he could do about it at the present moment, he attempted the all but impossible task of persuading Callow into conversation.

"How's the family, Pete? Everybody flourishing?"

"Little one's got a touch of colic, makes sleeping a bit tricky, otherwise okay, sir."

"Remember the day before your wedding? You'd have ducked and run if you could."

Callow said soberly, "True enough, sir. Shows how wrong you can be."

"I think quite a few of us have last minute doubts. It's natural enough, you'd have to be pretty thick not to realise that it's a major change of state." *The* major change, he thought, apart from birth and death. Or ought one to count the slow death of a marriage as the fourth?

"Sir." Callow's way of saying yes, also his way of ending a conversation.

Morpurgo persisted. "But afterwards you knew you were on to a good thing, especially when the kids arrived." If he and Sylvie had had children, a lot of things might be different.

"Before the service was over, sir. Knew it was a good thing before we'd left the church." A speech, for Callow, and, astonishingly, he hadn't finished. "How's Mrs Morpurgo, sir? Don't seem to have seen her around for quite a while."

Nor me, Morpurgo thought, and wondered how many other people in the trade might have noticed the same thing. "Oh, she's fine. Her work keeps her pretty busy these days. Just hasn't happened to be about on the odd day when you've collected me from home."

"Sir." Callow left the honorific hanging between them while he seized the chance of overtaking a battered truck with a load that looked less than securely lashed. Back in line, he surprised Morpurgo again. "Saw one of Mrs Morpurgo's pictures the other day. At the dentist's. Magazine, it was. Only a check-up, never had a filling in my life."

We're all proud of something, Morpurgo thought. Callow's proud of his teeth. And his wife and kids. I ought to be proud of my wife.

"That picture." Callow still hadn't finished. 'Can't remember what magazine, but it was a beauty, that picture, a real beauty."

A beauty by a beauty. Sylvie Morpurgo was a beauty, everyone agreed on that. Only when it was a question of a picture, it wasn't Mrs Morpurgo, it was Sylvie Markham, same initials but a change of name. Sylvie Morpurgo was just a *nom de guerre*.

"Seemed sort of too good for a magazine, that picture." Callow was becoming positively voluble. "Not, well, not commercial, know what I mean, sir?"

Oh yes, Morpurgo told himself, it would be too good, if it were possible for a work of art to be too good. Sylvie never sold for the sake of selling, any more than she matched the quality of her work to the size of the commission that was paid. Even in the early days, when she was only just beginning to establish herself, she had turned down several opportunities her agent had worked hard to get. "I'm going to make it one day," she had said. "Maybe not to the top, but thereabouts. And when I do, there won't be anything to reproach myself with."

She had said it jokingly, and yet not jokingly. It was Sylvie's practice to joke gently about things that were important to her, as if laughing at herself might forestall other people; people like Morpurgo.

"What picture was it?" Why should he care? It had been taken at his expense; to concentrate on perfection in one thing was to deny it in another.

"An old lady, sir. The face of an old, old lady, all wrinkles and that. Nearly bald, she was, no teeth and that, but Mrs Morpurgo made her look beautiful. No." Callow's ability to surprise took another giant step forward. "She *was* beautiful, but it took Mrs Morpurgo to see it."

"She'd be pleased to hear you say that, Pete." That much was true. "I must remember to tell her." He wouldn't, though; wouldn't tell her. Or she wouldn't be there to be told.

"Rather you didn't, sir." Callow made it sound urgent, a kind of sacrilege. Good God! had Callow become another of those who thought Sylvie could do no wrong?

"Why ever not? She'd be delighted."

"No, sir." Callow was firm. "Compliments don't count unless the one that's paying them knows what they're talking about."

Morpurgo laughed. This was a Callow he had never met before.

"Oh, come on! The only thing that matters about a compliment is that it's sincere."

"That's as may be, sir," Callow said patiently. "But a sincere compliment from someone that doesn't know what they're talking about can be kind of back-handed, sometimes no compliment at all."

He would tell her, after all. They were separate, but not yet apart.

His little shocks all administered, Callow lapsed into a more normal silence. Morpurgo succeeded in returning his own attention to Joseph Sattin and his two subverted agents.

Sattin had slept for fifteen years. The mere thought of such dedication was awe-inspiring, the more so since Morpurgo himself was instinctively opposed to any act or state that diluted his own individuality. In particular, he was opposed to it in his job, arguing that the man who never stepped far enough back from a picture to see it in its surroundings, never saw it as a whole. Context, he had often argued, was as significant as content; they were the yin and the yang.

Sylvie disagreed. According to Sylvie, any creative act supplied its own context. Applying the theory to his own occupation, he found it nonsensical; good counter-intelligence demanded the widest possible, indeed a global, view. The quarry could most quickly be tracked and snared when one knew not only its habits but its habitat.

"Sir?"

Callow was glancing at him.

"Sorry, I was thinking."

"I said, do you want me to wait, sir? You're not staying the night?"

"No, and I don't expect to be all that long, either."

Morpurgo had not realised how close they were to their destination.

Tuck's house, in keeping with the bourgeois dreamworld of which it was a part, was mock-Tudor, the ground floor red brick with a lavish use of fishbone patterning, the upper rendered and painted white to set off nailed-on black-painted timbering, as unconvincing as a bespectacled Henry VIII at a fancy dress ball. It was the largest of the Directorate's houses, hence its name. The others, not counting the flat, were referred to as Robin's house, Will's house and, appropriately enough since it was in the charge of a daunting maiden lady who catered for what she described to the neighbours as overseas gentlemen on short home leave, Marian's. In the Directorate, inevitably, her paying guests, regardless of their humour, were always referred to as Merry Men. It was all a bit too precious for Morpurgo.

McMurdoe opened the door, stood aside to let Morpurgo pass into a hall as impersonal and spick as the entrance to a doctor's surgery. "It's Oates and Gilligan," he said, closing the door behind them, "with Pratt as back-up. How are you, Mr Morpurgo? We don't often have the pleasure." He was an East Coast Scot, somewhere not far from Aberdeen.

"I'm fine, Mac. Oates, is it? Good."

"Aye, he's a dependable laddy, is Oatsey." McMurdoe waved Morpurgo on ahead of him. Dropping his voice a little, he added, "But that Pratt, now, shouldn't say it, but he's a hard man to like."

"Can't expect angels in this kind of work, Mac. How's Mrs Mac? And how's the patient?"

"Mrs Mac is fine, just fine. The patient, well, middling." McMurdoe showed his visitor into a sitting room that was all chintz and gleaming oak, Mrs McMurdoe being both houseproud and a collector of minor pieces of antique furniture. "As well as can be expected in the circumstances. A cool customer, yon

28

laddy, Mr Morpurgo, a very cool customer. I'm thinking he'll give you a hard time."

Someone knocked at the door. Oates inserted his head through a minimal gap. "Afternoon, sir. Nice to have a bit of business. Things have been a bit quiet lately." Opening the door a good deal wider, he brought the rest of himself into the room. Oates was a chunky man, black hair close-cropped, face open and healthy-looking, with a strong chin and a questioning, almost anxious way of looking at people, as if the minutest lapse of attention might lose him the chance of understanding what was required of him. His moustache resembled Stalin's.

"Any trouble?"

Oates shook his head. "Like a little lamb to the slaughter." The simile might have sounded sinister but for the fact that Oates, a Londoner born and bred, seldom sounded his Ts though marking their absence with a respectful pause.

"Not so much as a squeak," he said. "Inspector Quayle says that when they go in to take him he opens the door of his flat, then just stands there while Super Burgess goes through the 'We are police officers and we have reason to believe' caper, stands there while they find him clothes to put on, follows them when they say go, stops when they say stop and all the time he doesn't so much as open his mouth to let out a peep. And that's the way he still is, Mr Morpurgo."

"Waiting for you," McMurdoe suggested. "Wouldn't be the first who'd only talk to the security laddies."

"That's right," Oates agreed. "Reckon the Branch are just coppers and coppers are rubbish."

Morpurgo followed Oates' broad shoulders down the corridor to the back of the house, where the windows looked out on a garden with trees and borders of flowering shrubs that made the ground floor all but invisible to the neighbours.

The room in which Sattin was held was small and bare, nothing but a chair, a bed, a light permanently on.

He must have heard them coming but gave no sign of awareness at all. He remained absolutely motionless, eyes closed, the rise and fall of his chest so slight as to be barely perceptible. Oates shrugged and grimaced to indicate that the prisoner had been more or less like this since his arrival. Morpurgo signalled that he wanted to be left alone, remaining standing, just inside the door, while Oates locked it behind him.

Sattin had been under total SV for more than nine months. During that time Morpurgo himself had frequently joined the surveillance team, yet now it was as if he had never seen the man before. Heavily built, of medium height, Sattin gave an impression of mass rather than weight; a large frame, well-covered but without surplus. He had big hands, big feet; the hands, in particular, very broad, the fingers short and stubby. Even in stillness, the feet somehow suggested purposiveness, steps taken determinedly, a stance that would be foursquare to wind and weather.

What Morpurgo could see of the face was sallow, almost sickly, the skin smooth and waxy, the hair, such as there was of it, a mousy brown with a slight hint of greyness at the temples. There was no movement, voluntary or otherwise, of the eyes beneath the lowered lids, but Morpurgo was quite certain that his captive was not asleep.

It was Morpurgo who finally found himself constrained to move. He took another step or two toward the bed, and in the same moment, as if he had been waiting for just such a move, Sattin opened his eyes, his head shifting sideways until they rested on Morpurgo. There was no change in his expression. Indeed, his face, broad, with a strong nose slightly flattened, the cheekbones prominent without suggesting gauntness, the chin thrusting, determined, betokened an ability to conceal whatever went on behind the wide forehead. Morpurgo stood there, openly studying Sattin, Sattin lay there, openly studying Morpurgo.

After a little while, Morpurgo took the chair and drew it to the centre of the room, so that it faced the bed and its occupant from a distance of some six feet. He said, "Good afternoon."

In one sense, the greeting was bizarre. In another it reflected Morpurgo's view that little was to be gained, at least initially, from any display of hostility or menace. In his occasional lectures at The Other Place he reminded his listeners that interrogation was a two-way matter, an exchange between one human being and another whose emotions were something to be, preferably, enlisted rather than aroused. If a prisoner were frightened, he must be assured. If he were angry, he must be soothed, if defiant, respected and disarmed. To begin with, anyway.

The other reason for politeness was that it served to keep an abnormal situation firmly within the parameters of normal behaviour, to foster the idea of a business meeting between people highly skilled in their respective jobs, but on opposite sides of the table. Between them, willingly or unwillingly, a bargain must be struck in which one of them would gain more than the other, but in such a way that the other might feel he had not been totally demolished, had not totally lost his self-respect.

That, too, was to begin with, and, of course, seldom applied to the dentists, who worked in a different way.

Morpurgo, prepared to wait, felt certain now that Sattin was an original; not just different but superior. The task of attempting to break him down would be long, arduous, but not, he felt, boring. He had speedy confirmation. Sattin took the initiative, saying calmly, without opening his eyes, "I will speak this once, simply to tell you that I shall not speak again."

Admirable, Morpurgo thought. He said, "We shall see. We have plenty of time."

He drew his chair somewhat nearer the bed, stretched out his legs to match the relaxed image presented by his captive. He tilted his head back, concentrating his thoughts. "Your name," he said, "is Joseph Sattin." He spelled out Joseph, letter by letter. "In your business literature and letter headings, that is. Also in your British passport. Your Canadian passport, on the other hand" – he lingered momentarily over the nationality – "describes you as Josef Sattin." Again he spelled out the name, matter-of-factly, as if the discrepancy were no more than a technicality.

Sattin stirred, but not in response. His right hand unfastened the top button of the shirt that had been provided in exchange for his own.

"Feeling hot?" Morpurgo expected no answer and was not disappointed. "A genuine British passport, no alterations. We traced the documentation, all perfectly proper. We must wait to see whether the Canadian authorities will be equally satisfied.

"You work as a translator. Sorry, I should have said 'worked'. We shall have to have a little chat about your clients. Your business clients. I'm sure it's all in your excellent records, but there may be things you could explain. Engineering, that's your special field, isn't it? Lots of opportunities there for a good linguist, and, of course, you are good, no question of that. English, German, Polish, Czech. Oh, nearly forgot; Russian. They tell me you've clients in most European countries, even Finland. But not the Soviet Union. I must admit I find that a little surprising. If

31

you can translate into Russian, you can surely translate from? Still, perhaps they don't like employing foreign nationals on that kind of work, charity beginning at home, that sort of thing."

In the following silence, Sattin drew in a long and audible breath. The muscles of his mouth quivered a little. He was clearly suppressing a yawn. Going to be a long haul, Morpurgo told himself. Get the preliminaries over fairly quickly, then the dentists can soften him up a little. He unzipped his document case and took out a large manilla envelope.

"Photographs," Morpurgo said chattily.

He lifted the flap of the envelope and drew out a thick set of prints, all blown up to wholeplate size. "Here's rather a good one, you on one of your trips to Highgate, the grounds of Kenwood House. I expect you remember. You seem to have found something interesting in a litter basket, can't imagine what it could be. Oh, and this one's in Kensington Gardens, something behind a loose stone in the fountain court. Perhaps we ought to tell the Parks Superintendent to get it fixed."

Sattin had closed his eyes again but Morpurgo, for no reason that he could explain, fancied that he really was listening now, paying attention. "Of course," he said, "they're not all just of you. Some of the ones with you and the other man really have come out rather well, even the ones taken at night. That one, at the Number 11 bus stop, for instance, marvellous, these light-enhancing cameras. The ones I like best, though, were taken in Oxford Circus Underground station. Rush hour, wasn't it? but our man did very well, all the same. A sort of series, really. You might almost say time-lapse photography. You walking toward the ticket machine, the twenty pence machine, can't get far for twenty pence these days, can you? You're carrying rather a nice little case. You put it down while you look for the right coins. Here we are, you've got the right money now, but while you're looking, along comes this other chap, forty pence machine, right next to yours. Funny thing, he's carrying a case, too, puts it down right next to yours while he gets his ticket. You're ahead of him, though, got your ticket by this time. So, you pick up your case and off you go, down the escalator, Bakerloo Line. Couldn't have been going home, Notting Hill isn't on the Bakerloo Line, not that it matters. But there's something that does. You picked up the wrong case, the other bloke's. When did you find out? You *must* have been surprised! Oh, and the other man, mustn't forget him. *He* never noticed, either, not at the time, but then, why should he? He's got yours, identical, one of the snags when you buy cheap, mass-produced goods. Except they weren't, were they? Good, well-made, real leather, first-class fastenings and locks. Neither of you any the worse off, so long as you weren't carrying anything important. That's something you can't tell, just from the pictures."

Morpurgo zipped up his own rather battered case, real leather all right, but somewhat the worse for wear. "Still, natural enough, I suppose, you decided you'd rather have your own case back. God knows how you knew how to get in touch with the other chap, but you managed it, didn't you? W H Smith's bookshop at Victoria Station, the big one, right in the middle of the con-course. You bought an evening paper, he bought a paperback, now, what was it? Oh yes, the Penguin Twentieth Century History. Not a Marxist interpretation, of course, but quite good, so they tell me. Anyway, same thing, I must say you seem to have brought it down to a fine art. Put down one case, pick up t'other, off you both go, not so much as a word. Wrong cases again. Except, of course, they were the *right* ones, nearly forgot that."

Morpurgo laughed. "Amusing, though. You'd enjoy the pictures. Take a look when you feel like it, plenty of time." He slid them back in the envelope, held it up between thumb and forefinger, let it drop. It hit the shiny floor with a flat slap, skidding a little way across the polished surface.

"The other bloke – did you ever wonder in all those times? – the other bloke's a Russian. A diplomat, there's something, you've got the same kind of case as a diplomat. His name's Boris. Boris Kirillin. He's a second secretary, commerce, at the Soviet Embassy, quite a useful contact, I should think. The really inter-esting thing, though, is that he has a double. Yuri Borisovich Kagalov, KGB colonel, room 147, third floor in the new building. Specialises in microchip technology, currently on attachment to Section D, First Directorate. He and this man Kirillin look so alike you couldn't tell them apart. In fact you might say identical."

Morpurgo slapped his case gently against his free hand. "Full cooperation. In return, an easy time, complete security, full freedom in due course. Country of your choice, within reason. A house. An income. Not extravagantly large, but probably bigger than mine. Protection for as long as necessary. Think about it."

He went to the door, knocked loudly. He heard a chair scrape as someone stood up in the room next door. The key rattled in each lock in turn. Morpurgo turned for a last look at Sattin. To his surprise the man was sitting up. His face had gone almost white. He was looking in Morpurgo's general direction, but not at him. His face showed the blotchy shininess of sweat that had not been there a moment before. Moving his body carefully, he swung his feet toward the floor on Morpurgo's side of the bed. Instinctively, though simultaneously suspicious, Morpurgo took a step toward him. Behind him, the door opened. He said, "Come in. But lock the door."

It was Oates. He took in the situation very rapidly, moving to back up Morpurgo, but they were both too late. Sattin's feet touched the floor, but there was no strength in his legs, so that his feet continued their slow progress across the shiny blueness of the waxed vinyl, leaving his body behind. He went down very solidly.

Oates pushed past Morpurgo to go down on his knees beside Sattin. He lifted an eyelid. "Out for the count. Don't like the look of that colour, sir."

"No," Morpurgo said almost reluctantly. "I thought at first he was going to try an old one."

Oates shook his head, then bent forward to put an ear to Sattin's chest. "Bit fast. Nothing to worry about, though, not by itself." He raised his voice. "Gilly? Gilly, give us a hand here, will you?"

Another chair scraped next door. Gilligan came in, looking anxious. Gilligan invariably looked anxious. When they had lifted Sattin back on the bed, his deadweight requiring an effort from all of them, Morpurgo said, "Get the local doc in to take a look at him." Security Directorate had arrangements with the area police surgeons for all its safe houses. "If he says it's all right for him to travel, I want him out to The Other Place tonight. I'm going to give Doc Vickers a ring and ask him to be waiting for you. He can give him another going over, and then do whatever's necessary. Okay?"

"Okay, Mr Morpurgo." Oates had been feeling Sattin's pulse. "Stay with him, Gilly, while me and Mr Morpurgo gets things fixed up." As he spoke, Sattin's eyes fluttered. He sighed, a tiny exhalation which Morpurgo found himself somehow resenting. It was unwelcome, a signal that said: I am human, weak, fallible, just like you. Morpurgo had no wish to be reminded of the fact.

Oates followed him out of the room, stopping to lock Gilligan in. "Don't think he's trying anything on, sir. Not with that colour. Nervous strain, could be something like that. Sometimes takes them suddenly." The door of the next room was open. Morpurgo caught a glimpse of Pratt, thin-faced, sinewy, impassive. There was something he didn't quite like about Pratt, but he had never had time to pin it down.

3

Cousins

Claas came round his desk, hand outstretched. "Pierre, good to see you. They should have let me know you were here. I'd have come down."

"Take 'em by surprise," Weber said. "Rule number one for a good boss." He took a look around the office before sitting. "Nothing changed. That's good, no signs of restlessness. It's bad, too, aversion to change. Let me think about it." He stood smiling at Claas. "Big stuff, huh?"

Claas nodded. "Doesn't come any bigger." He watched Weber settle in his favourite chair, the dark red leather one with the missing button. Weber, too, was big stuff, but not so big that he could remain totally indifferent to the nature of their business.

Weber said, "Not *too* big?"

"Only if we goof."

"We mustn't." Weber picked up a sheaf of telexed messages from Langley, scanning them for a general idea of their contents.

"We won't," Claas said.

"Like to give me that in writing?"

"Uh-uh." Claas shook his head vigorously. "You're the boss. I just take orders." He glowered at his shoes, resting on the glass top of the desk. They were new and a little tight. He had bought them in a summer sale at not much over half-price, but they had still cost more than he had ever paid for a pair of shoes before. He had always wanted a really good pair of English shoes. Only when he got them home did he discover they had been made in Portugal.

Weber and Claas were, as it happened, two third generation

36

German-Americans. Weber came from St Louis, Claas from Kansas City. They had come together to plan a business deal, a hazardous business deal. They would give it the care and attention that was given to a space shot. Weber was older than Claas, sandy-haired, his thin, lugubrious face belying the sense of humour that could make his face light up when he smiled. He nevertheless had an intense approach to life in general and his work in particular. He said, "Nothing in writing."

"I know it." Claas nodded, his square, flat face serious. Weber sometimes told him he was a hick, that Kansas City was a cowtown. They liked each other. "Okay," Claas continued. "I made those summaries as comprehensive as possible, but no more summaries, right? You want to ask me some questions?" He wiggled his left little toe. Was he developing a blister from the goddam shoes? "I don't claim to have the whole picture, Pierre."

"Heisenberg's uncertainty."

Claas looked blank. He was good at looking blank; it made people think he was stupid. "You change a situation just by becoming involved in it," Weber explained. "It works with sub-atomic particles, but I don't know about people." He adjusted his posture without appearing to make himself any more comfortable. "Okay, let's talk. I'm here to take over London station from you, okay?"

"But not now. Not for several months. You just came over to get the feel of things, that's how I've been putting it around."

"Well, that's right, I do want to get the feel. Then, afterwards, plans change, I slip out, something else, somewhere else."

"Check. Unless we blow it. If we blow it, you don't slip out. You get kicked out. I get kicked out. Everybody gets kicked out."

"I don't want to think about it," Weber said. "We have to think success, generate the right vibes, that's what. That's what my kid's always telling me."

"Yeah?" Claas looked very unimpressed. "How is he, the kid?"

"Obscene. Tell me about Delahay."

"He's the Prime minister."

"I know he's the Prime minister, for God's sake!"

"So let's hear it for you," Claas said. It was an old relationship, comfortable as the shoes Claas had hoped to buy but didn't. The

37

running gags helped them to adjust to the fact that the business they had in mind was politically explosive in the megaton range. "Okay, what can I add, Delahaywise? The original weak sister, likes to be loved, which is why he has a hundred enemies. And that's just in his own party."

"They can't ditch him, even though they'd like to."

"Not supposed to be that sort of party. Loyalty, rally round the flag, that kind of garbage."

"Yet if he stays, the Opposition will do the job for them, sooner rather than later. Which would mean a general election."

"And the Labourites would win. Sorry. Labour would win."

"Anti-nuke platform."

"You'd better believe it!" Claas was almost animated. "And not just the British independent deterrent, we could live with that. They'd . . ."

"The British deterrent," Weber observed, "is about as independent as British Ford, or the British movie industry."

"A Labour government," Claas said patiently, "would be against *any* deterrent. A Labour government is pledged to maintain US nuclear bases in this country the way Sitting Bull was pledged to maintain Custer and the Seventh Cavalry."

"I know it." Weber had become deadly serious. "New homes for the missile subs, bombers, Pershings, Cruises, not to mention all the unmentionables. There isn't another country in Europe that could provide the facilities, no, that would even give 'em house room. A change of government right now would be the worst thing to happen to the US since Pearl Harbor."

"We reckon six months to Pearl," Claas said. "That's being optimistic."

"We?"

"Us. London Station. Plus the Friends. Plus a lot of high-placed Brits who don't like the idea any more than we do."

"Half of them in Delahay's cabinet, isn't that so?"

"No names," Claas said. "Makes me nervous. But give them the chance and they'd run the country the way Uncle Sam would like to see it run."

Weber smiled faintly. "But to keep the anti-nukers out, we have to keep Delahay in."

Claas shrugged. "You want to play devil's advocate, it's okay with me, boss."

38

"Since it's my head on the block if we're wrong-footed, I'll play any damn role that helps to keep me in one piece."

We're going to try it, Claas suddenly realised. We're really going to try it. Adrenaline took off through his veins.

"Of course," Weber was murmuring, "if we could give Humpty a nudge."

"He has a majority of six in the House of Commons. Nudge too hard and he might bring his administration down with him."

"A teeny nudge. A teeny-weeny nudge, before he finds himself in a no-go situation where some of his own party abstain. Or even vote against him. Lose a confidence vote and he has to go to the country, yes?"

"And lose. That's for sure."

"But if we could play musical chairs."

"Home Secretary, Foreign Secretary. Though if it's left to the Friends . . ."

"All that matters to us is that the horse comes from the right stable." Weber sat looking at Claas expressionlessly. "The right kind of scandal could waft Humpty away, yes?"

Claas nodded. "His own party. Experts. White gloves in public, red hands behind the scenes. New times call for new men, the standard-issue crap."

"And you think you've found it. The scandal."

"Strictly speaking," Claas said, "I had a little help."

"From your Friends. You're sure it's safe? I mean, the British Secret Service working with the CIA, okay, nothing new there, but helping us topple a prime minister, boy! that's something else again! Still, okay. Tell me about this other guy."

"Morpurgo."

"Morpurgo. What's your idea of the average spook, Warren?"

"Brilliant thinker," Claas said promptly, "good analyst, nose of a ferret, hard worker, devoted family man, underpaid. Me."

"This Morpurgo, does that cover him?" Weber punished Claas by taking him seriously.

"Umm." Claas considered. "Underpaid, anyway. He's not a spook. He's a spook hunter." He thought a little more. "Smart. Too smart. What the British call too clever by half."

"Okay, so he's a smart-ass. That's a crime?"

"In this country, you're damn right. But I guess the most

interesting thing about Morpurgo is his politics. Yes, I guess it is at that."

"Left."

"Left of centre." Claas smiled a little. "Only here in this country the centre is way left of centre back home. Your average Republican back home would have a hard time seeing any difference between Morpurgo and a commie. And I have to say, your average Democrat, too."

"But he isn't."

"He isn't. Like I said, he's left of centre nationally. But in the political spectrum of the Labour Party, maybe even a little to the right".

"Is he a member? A card-carrying member of the Labour Party?"

Claas shook his head. "Used to be, way back. Let it lapse."

"But he was active to begin with, right? In college. And when he was working as a researcher for – what do they call their trades union federation? The TUC?"

"Yes, he was. And it has to be said for him, he was active against the extreme left, commies, Trotskyites, that sort of people. That's what interested Security Directorate, well, that and the aftermath of the Philby show. Security Directorate and the Secret Service had a directive, top level, to broaden the area of recruitment. I mean get away from the public school, Oxbridge, buddy-buddy situation, bring in people from the real world, state school system, middle class, less Princeton, more Ohio State, get me?"

"I still don't exactly have the impression that the British security services employ too many blue-collar, hard-hat people."

"You're damn right. But I guess you could say it was okay in Morpurgo's case. Maybe it was too okay. Top man in his section, you know that. And he has seniority."

"Ambitious?"

"Fancies himself in the top slot, Director-General. His knight has only three more years to go." Claas pulled a face. "Them and their goddam knights! Once you get above a certain level in this country, it's like the Round Table."

Weber smiled faintly. "It comes through loud and clear in your reports, not anti-British, just not too pro. Anyway, what do you have against knights? Does it hurt anyone?"

"The knights? Maybe not. The system, you bet. Working class, artisan class, lower middle, middle, upper, aristo; more levels than the Empire State Building, and every one with fine tuning."

"And he doesn't like it. Morpurgo."

"He's part of it, that's what he doesn't like, only he can't see it. He won't get the top slot. Reserved for outsiders, amateurs, chaps with the right background. They don't listen to the words, they listen to the accent. Morpurgo wouldn't get the job if his blood was as blue as my suit. He's tolerated, sort of showpiece, one of their token lefties. And he got where he is on merit. But the top slot's a political appointment. I mean the guy who gets it has to have the right political background, sure, but he also has to know how to play politics. And – yeah, I almost forgot – he has to be a knight. To hold his corner against the other knights."

Weber smiled more broadly. "I remember. The Silent Knight. The Dark and Stormy Knight. And the Knight of the Long Knives."

Claas smiled too, but it was a smile with a touch of contempt. "The Silent Knight, that's Sir Howard Fuller, coordinates security in the Cabinet Office, keeps the prime minister in the general picture. Holds the ring between Security Directorate and the SIS too. The Dark and Stormy Knight is Sir Jason Bowers."

"Bowers is head of SIS, a tough operator, did I get it right?"

Claas nodded. "The kind of guy that kicks sand in your face on the beach and then shows you his muscles."

"And the Knight of the Long Knives is Sir Hugh Wyndham, Morpurgo's boss?"

"Check. They get along pretty well together, like a guy with a German Shepherd, knows it bites, hopes it won't bite him." Claas began to chuckle. Weber waited patiently, most of his tension gone. Always the same, he thought; once you get down to nuts and bolts, it's just another job.

"Morpurgo's knight," Claas said, quelling his amusement, "calls the top echelon of civil servants, people like Fuller, the Incas; last advanced civilisation living out of contact with the rest of the world."

Weber smiled obligingly. "What makes Wyndham afraid Morpurgo might bite. Politics?"

"Politics, you bet. Morpurgo thinks he has everything well in check, politics and business don't mix, no prejudice. That's what he thinks."

"And that's the button we punch to make his wheels turn?"

"Not exactly. Well, let's say that once you've got him going, political prejudice is the booster. What starts him, the button we punch, is something more basic."

Weber stirred slightly. "This is where you jump from the beginning to the end."

Claas looked puzzled. "How's that again?"

"Standard vetting procedure; professional background, biographical data, then the dirt. You're going to jump to the dirt."

"So I don't work by the book," Claas said, unruffled. "All right, the dirt, and you know what it is. He screws his 2 i/c's wife. Or she screws him. Either way, the effect is the same."

"And she's German. Naturalised British, but German. That should make her one of us."

"Who are you kidding? Anyway, if you're German, how come they called you Pierre?" Perhaps for a temporary lifting of pressure, they had gone back to an old script, one they both knew by heart.

"St Louis was French," Weber said equably. "All the *echt* Krauts and the cows went to Kansas City. Why don't you tell me about this dame?"

"Helga. Helga Schlegel, born near Magdeburg, refugee from the Russians in '45, when she was only a kid. Found herself stuck in East Germany when they put it together in '49. Refugee again in '59, got to West Germany just ahead of the Wall. Met Steve Archer, Morpurgo's number two, in Berlin, when Archer was still in Secret Intelligence. Married, eleven years younger than Archer. Two kids, eighteen and twenty. Vetted twice in the Federal Republic, twice in the UK, squeaky clean."

"And Morpurgo screws her." Weber considered that fact for a brief spell, then veered. "Archer. He's the poacher turned gamekeeper."

"Right. Military intelligence, switched to SIS in '46, field agent up to '67. Blown in Czecho, lucky to get away, but no more use after that so they steered him into Security Directorate. Specialises in counter-intelligence, like Morpurgo. Except he doesn't."

Weber frowned. "Come again?"

"Like Morpurgo. Archer. Doesn't like Morpurgo. Not from where I stand, anyway."

"Open? I mean, does Morpurgo know?" Before Claas could answer, Weber said, "Hey, wait. First things first. Does *Archer* know?"

"About his wife? Not sure. Don't think so, but not sure, not yet." Claas considered. "Maybe we ought to do something about that. I mean check it out. He's not the kind of guy to go public on it."

"I saw. Old school tie, the kind of guy British security likes, Oxbridge, Brigade of Guards, the *right* clubs, yes?"

"You bet. Only let you in if you look good in the studbook, wouldn't let Morpurgo in." Claas was as impatient about top British clubs as he was of British knights. In all his time in London he had failed to find any magic in unsociable bars half full of men talking in whispers, echoing dining rooms where many of the diners ate alone, common rooms, lined with oil paintings of the long since dead, where large, confident men and small withdrawn men ostentatiously avoided one another or came together to create zones of impregnable exclusivity.

"Okay, so we've got dirt. Dirt first, that's the rule with me. And it's got to be paydirt. No dirt, no deal, nothing else matters."

"Boy," Claas said respectfully. "I've said it before, I'll say it again. I can see just why you made it to the top."

"I made it to the top, junior, by picking good deputies and leaving them to get on with it. That's a compliment."

"What do I have to do to repay?"

"You already did. You found a window. Now we have to see if it's open. If it is, we climb in."

"If it isn't, I think we can have it opened from the inside."

"The Friends."

"Check. You talked with Fish?"

"I did. And then with – which one is he? – the Dark and Stormy. They'll help all they can. They want Delahay fixed too."

Claas grinned. "Sure they do. They think this guy Merrilees, the Foreign Secretary, will be the one to replace him. That's as good as getting their own man into Number 10. They've a score to settle, remember."

"Do I ever? When the Philby thing exploded, it was Security Directorate who were given the job of going over SIS with a fine-tooth comb. None too gently, as I remember."

"You're damn right! The Friends have never forgotten, never forgiven, either. They have a lot to gain."

"And a lot to lose, which is better. Back to the dirt. What about Morpurgo's wife? Sylvie Markham, isn't she?"

Mildly surprised, Claas said, "Did I put that in?"

"Met her." Weber tried not to look smug. "That exhibition she had in New York, came to Washington afterwards, so Betty and I took it in, got ourselves invited to one of those swish receptions at the F Street Club. Quite a looker!"

"She'd know you if she saw you?"

Weber shook his head. "One of a couple of hundred faces she said hello to. And I'm not exactly the most memorable guy in Washington."

"Okay, so she's a looker. But Morpurgo's gotten tired of looking."

"Is that right?" Weber's look was sharp and shiny. "Anybody scoring with her?"

"Nope!" Weber noted the promptness of response.

"Tell me what you think of Archer."

Claas considered. "To look at, natural heavy. Not given to making speeches, but still waters running deeper than you might think. Stiff upper lip, very laid back. But it's a front. Narrow mind, short fuse, long memory, that's the real Archer."

"What did you do? Go over him with a measure?"

"I go over all of them with a measure."

"That's my boy. Right, now let's take a look at the crunch zone. What's new?"

"They brought Sattin in, today. And the two Brits. Security Directorate lost out to the Friends."

"As we knew they would. Any news on the swap?"

"No. Security Directorate lost the battle, but not the war, not yet."

"They'll lose the war too. I'm beginning to think we'll get Merrilees if we lever Humpty out."

"Security Directorate's minister still has more than a chance. Home secretaries carry a lot of clout. If we pull it off, Merrilees might go down with the ship."

"It's a thought. But the mole is discounted. Is that what we have to assume?"

"It's not what Morpurgo assumes. He thinks the mole is why

Moscow wants to make a quick swap. He thinks Sattin could know the name of the mole."

"Hm." Weber's sleepy look was back. "You're sure this is where Delahay is vulnerable?"

"Certain sure. So sure that it wouldn't really matter whether there's a mole or not, so long as we can make it look as though there was. So long as we can make it look like a cover-up." Claas nodded emphatically. "Sure. He's vulnerable."

"Kagalov?"

"Still here. So far."

Weber sat up straight, suddenly. "So there's no mole! Not if Kagalov's still here. How long since they picked up Sattin?"

Claas looked at his watch. "Four hours. Roughly four hours. Isn't much, Pierre. I can think of any number of reasons why a mole couldn't have got to Kagalov yet. If there *is* a mole. And if there is, I can think of at least one good reason why Kagalov might stay and take his lumps."

Weber's thin face lit up a little. "Damn right! The more important the mole, the better the reason for Kagalov to stay until he's kicked out. Good thinking!"

"Don't do any other kind. Nice to have you notice."

Weber ignored the provocation. "When did Morpurgo make his pitch?"

"This a.m."

"Do we know where Sattin is now?"

"Yup. Safe house they have in Stanmore on the London outskirts."

"That where they're going to keep him?"

"No. Their country hideyhole, sort of mini stately home they call The Other Place."

"And you know where that is, too?"

"Sure I do. The perfect agent."

"Just stay clean, that's all. Get your face smeared and we don't know you."

"That," Claas said, "is what I like about our service. Real supportive. You want to hear what I think we should do next?" He told Weber what he thought they should do next.

When he had finished, Weber sat back in his chair. "Oh boy!" he said softly. "Ooooh boy! What won't you do? I think you're catching the European disease. Deviousness. Going to end up spying up your own ass, junior." He looked at Claas

45

thoughtfully. "Would Archer play with us, do you think? I mean directly?"

"Best not. He's been signed up by the Friends and the Friends have a thing going with us. For my money that's the way we leave it. Anything changes, we can think again."

"So when do I get to meet Morpurgo?"

"As my eventual replacement? Let's say a couple of days. I have to meet him accidentally first, and these accidental meetings take a lot of arranging."

4
Archers

"Miss Robbins said you wanted to see me, sir." Sibley's eagerness was a source both of pleasure and anxiety to Morpurgo, reminding him that not everyone in Curzon Street had been wasted by the professional hazards of incredulity, cynicism and ingrowing, all-pervasive suspicion; reminding him also that there had been a time when he was as shiny-bright as Sibley. Sibley had come on to the strength of Security Directorate via Special Branch. That was a hazard in itself; Special Branch, although working in the closest cooperation with the Directorate, tended to regard any of their own who made what should have been a wholly natural if infrequent transition as being half creep, half traitor. Sibley, certainly, was neither.

Dark, fresh-faced – the Directorate would steal the cherries from his cheeks if nothing else, Morpurgo had prophesied – and, to use the word that had first come to Morpurgo's mind, comely, he was also enthusiastic, hard-working, patient and honest to a fault. The combination filled Morpurgo with gloomy premonitions of disaster.

He waved Sibley to a seat. "Well, your first spy hunt. How's it feel, now it's over?" A pretty stupid question!

"Great, sir." He might have known he could rely on the lad to play it straight. "A lot of hard work, long hours and that, but worth it. Will he talk, do you think?"

"I think we shall manage to persuade him." Morpurgo forgave himself the lie, or was it less a lie than a forlorn hope? Either way, he didn't want to dash the boy's expectations so soon after the climax. Sibley had been with the Branch inspector who arrested Mrs Stringer.

47

"In the meantime," he went on, "there's a certain amount of tidying up to do. Mostly paperwork."

Sibley pulled a face, exaggerating his reaction to a thankless task. Almost as quickly, though, he said the right thing. "Where do you want me to start, Mr Morpurgo?" God! Morpurgo thought, simultaneously impressed and amused, he's too good to be true.

"Knowing how much you enjoy working in Registry," he said, and left the sentence unfinished. Sibley did his paperwork well, but made no secret of the fact that he rated it low among Curzon Street's attractions. Central Registry and anything to do with it he placed at the bottom of the list.

For one thing, though it was scheduled to move to new premises, it was in the basement, where the light of day never penetrated. Then there was the security procedure. Anyone wishing to enter Registry, and few did, had to receive written authorisation from his immediate senior. He was then allowed to withdraw the files he wished to study, but not to take them away, though he was obliged to sign for them. He took them instead into one of a number of cubicles usually referred to as the rabbit hutches, and was locked in with nothing more elaborate in the way of furnishing than a chair and a built-in shelf with a reading light. His researches completed, he rang to be released and was required to walk away 'clean', the files, even if he had been responsible for their contents in the first place, remaining in Registry.

When Sibley had replaced his grimace with a grin, Morpurgo said, "I want you to go through all the encounter reports, right from scratch, and make a list, a graph, a chart, you'll have to decide for yourself what's best, of the dates and times of all the drops, pick-ups and treffs. A complete picture of the to-ings and fro-ings, cause and effect, get the idea?"

"Yes." Sibley was immediately interested. "I think some sort of diagram's going to be the best way. And different colours, there'll be some overlapping at times."

"Whatever you think best. Okay?"

"Yes, sir. How soon do you want it?"

Morpurgo realised that he didn't really know, didn't really know why he wanted the thing at all. "Soon as you can manage," he said vaguely. "But don't neglect the priorities, right?"

"Right, sir." Sibley was already out of his chair. "I'll get cracking right away, nothing too pressing at the moment."

"All right, but don't stay down there all night. A growing lad like you needs his sleep. Early to bed, etcetera."

"I'm all for it," Sibley said, grinning. "Bed, I mean. Sleep if there's nothing better on offer." He went out jauntily, leaving Morpurgo relieved at the discovery that the boy, for all his virtues, was fundamentally normal. He buzzed for his secretary and asked her to track down Steve Archer in Weymouth.

The call was prompt. Steve had just arrived back after a visit to Naval Intelligence. Morpurgo asked him how he was getting on with Stringer.

"Comrade Stringer's founder, president and leading member of the Steve Archer fan club, old boy, displays a rather nauseating wish to lick my boots. Isn't doing me any good with Inspector Dai Griffiths, though. Inspector Dai fancies himself as Grand Inquisitor, you'll remember, doesn't too much like the idea of Stringer's slavish devotion to someone who isn't in the Branch."

"Well I do. Got your copy of the SV summary with you?"

"To hand, old boy. To hand."

"Then see if you can persuade him to go over the dates with you. I mean his dates, not anyone else's. I don't want him to know about anyone else's."

"Can I jog his memory?"

"As much as you like, but don't mention any dates yourself."

"Okay, will do. How'd it go with Comrade Sattin?"

"It's going to be like trying to crack a coconut with your teeth."

"What's he have to say for himself."

"Nothing. Issued a pronunciamento, nine or ten words to the effect that he's saying nothing."

"Dentists leaned on him yet? Amazing how they can make a comrade change his mind." Anyone to the left of Genghis Khan was a comrade in Steve's book.

"I think they'd find it easier to change the Pope's mind on abortion. No, they haven't had him yet. He's off his feed, touch of shock, nervous reaction, something like that. Doc Vickers is going to check him over before we start the softening up. I rang Helga, by the way." Now why had he said that?

"Oh, thanks." Steve didn't sound very interested. "Everything as it should be, I take it. Give her a ring myself when I get a free moment."

"Everything as it should be," Morpurgo said, thinking how untrue that was.

49

"Good. Gets a bit moody sometimes, does that girl. A bit strung up, a German sort of thing. *Angst*, metaphysical indigestion, don't understand it myself. Anyway, thanks for ringing."

"My pleasure. Everything all right otherwise?"

"Sure. The admiral's a bit on his high horse, thinks we take a poor view of their security procedure, inclined to take it personally, but he'll come round. Anyway, I'm coming back up tomorrow a.m, flying visit to the Min. of Def. One or two things to check before I chat up Mrs Stringer. Anything else?"

"That's about it. Let me know when you've got the dope. Not urgent though."

Morpurgo replaced the phone and sat back to consider Steve Archer, running through snippets of their conversation like a film director checking the rushes. *Was* he right in thinking that Steve knew nothing about himself and Helga? A bit strung up, what did he mean by that? Come to that, why did he say it at all? Steve was of the male school that thought anything to do with its wives was strictly private, anything important, that was. He would classify anything concerning Helga's relationship with him top secret, not even EYES ONLY and certainly not EARS. So had he been casting, in the hope of a bite?

Just how observant was Steve of Helga these days? Not very, at a guess, but even so, it was hard to believe him unaware that Helga had become a secret drinker. *Angst*, for God's sake! Either Steve was lacking in perception, or, more probably, in the matter of intimate domestic problems, he was playing his cards very close to his chest. In which case, what else might he be aware of without revealing it?

Steve had first met Helga when she was one of millions of refugees drifting or driven around Europe like great herds of starving sheep that few were willing to feed or care for. Her family had died in Dresden on the night of 11th February 1945. She had seen them heaped, mutilated and lifeless, on one of the many great pyres that had been the only way to dispose of the thousands upon thousands killed by the Allied bombing.

Trapped by the speed of the Russian advance, she had been repeatedly raped although only a child. Eleven years later, she and three others succeeded in escaping to the West, where, after screening, she was recruited by the Gehlen organisation to work for West German intelligence as a cipher clerk. Not long afterwards, she met Steve. According to Steve they took a shine to each other – his own words – married, and returned to England when Steve's tour of duty expired and he left the army to join SIS, subsequently transferring to Security Directorate when his name and function became known to the KGB. It was Morpurgo's private belief that Helga had married Steve less for love – she was eleven years his junior – than for security and British citizenship.

They had two children, both more or less permanently away from home, though still in London. That left Helga in the classic situation of a mother with no one to mother, a wife with no one to love. What was so stupid about the whole thing was that Morpurgo, middle-aged, man-of-the-world Morpurgo, had walked blithely into that deadly trap.

It had not taken him too long to discover that she floated and muddled and slept her way through day after day with her alcohol level just short of outright intoxication. Gradually but inexorably, his visits had changed from being a source of pleasure to a duty from which Helga, like a demanding mother with an only son, was so far unwilling to release him.

No, he was being too hard. Helga was never less than attractive, and he, Morpurgo, still had a wish to help and comfort her. As a sexual liaison it was over. What remained was, at one and the same time, a sense of responsibility based on bad conscience, and a genuine and growing conviction that the best way to help Helga was to bring things to an end before irreparable harm was done to both of them in their family relationships.

He sighed, and was reminded of the small sigh with which the unconscious Sattin had proclaimed his humanity. He looked at his watch and swore; it was later, in every way, than he had thought. He rubbed his face a little wearily and told himself that he was too old to play the lover, the mastermind or the misunderstood husband. He put in a call to Sylvie; there was no reply.

*　　*　　*

Crossing the road, he entered the block by the rear entrance and went up to the sixth floor by the stairway rather than the lift. His private life was becoming too much like his professional life, see without being seen. Helga opened the door at the first touch of the bell. She was wearing a simple off-the-shoulder dress that enhanced her figure, which was slim, and her breasts, which were small and rounded. She was bare-foot, a little girl playing grown-ups.

51

She stood straight and still, her arms at her side. Her eyes had grown larger, but no, that was ridiculous; it was her face that had grown thinner – why had he not noticed that before? – and the lack of sun so far into the year had left her with a more than wintry pallor. He put a hand on each shoulder, taking care that the pressure should be minimal, and kissed her on each cheek, lightly, then, with an equal lightness, on the mouth. She remained motionless, submissive, a child who must accept certain kisses though they give no pleasure. He could smell wine on her breath, faintly fruity. She liked white wines, but never drank the good white wines of Germany. Morpurgo found that interesting. After a long moment, she said, "Come and sit."

The sitting room of the flat was in Helga's taste, light and bright, the colours all muted, unoccupied space as much a part of the general effect as furniture. It was striking and yet pallid, the achievement of someone who for whatever reason had avoided all strong or controversial statements, space, time and existence fixed at only a few places, as if any attempt to bind them more securely might frighten them away altogether.

She sat quite close, but without touching, to some extent facing him yet without looking directly at him. Her face was small, triangular, secretive. Her hair, corn-blonde, was the strongest statement in the room. She was near enough for him to chart, all over again, the tiny stress lines at the corners of her eyes and mouth. She had lived through more than a lifetime of chaos and anarchy before she was twenty. Its imprimatur, a testimony of survival, was indelible.

Her forehead was smooth; one might have said unnaturally so, in view of what she had endured. Emotion was a weakness of which advantage would be taken, so that a kind of swift evolution had taken it from her face and buried it in her thoughts, to be visible, if at all, only through her eyes. She had lived for so many years on uneasy terms with disaster, he thought, as to consider its absence no more than a period of grace during which she must prepare for its certain return.

Touched in spite of his tight guard upon himself, he reached forward to gather her hands. They lay limply in his, like some small, dead creature. She said, "Well, Johnny, what are we going to do?"

"I don't know."

"Was it just a game?"

"I don't think so. Perhaps a diversion. But not a game."

She nodded. "I believe you. So it's you we must do something for, don't you agree?"

"I'm not sure I understand." Behind her he was vaguely aware of the narrow, vertical slice of Kensington Gardens visible above the balcony of the flat through a gap between two tall neighbouring blocks. Walkers, distant dots, moved in twos and threes under the green arches of the plane trees; beyond them, sliced thinner still, the distant wink and glitter of the Serpentine.

"For me it was no game." She said it without resentment. "That makes it my fault, perhaps. I must make myself easier to read." Gently, she tugged her hands free. "I think I will have a drink." At the door she turned. "And you?"

"I've had very little to eat today," he began, but she had not waited for his answer. "Yes," he called after her. "Yes, I'd like one." He heard her open and close the door of the refrigerator. Returning, she placed an already part-drunk bottle of wine and two glasses on the low table in front of him. "You pour."

He picked up the bottle. The wine was warm. She had only pretended that it was in the fridge. Her hand hovered, ready to pick up the glass the moment he stopped pouring. She intercepted his glance. "I drink a little, yes? What else is there to do?"

"How are the children?" Martin was eighteen, an art student at Birkbeck. Ursula was in her last year at the London School of Economics. They lived their own lives, Ursula in a Bloomsbury house shared, in some extraordinary communal arrangement, with six or seven other girls; Martin in a one-room bedsitter in Lambeth.

"They're very well. They come home from time to time." He knew it. They were – literally – making conversation.

She said, "How is Sylvie?"

"Sylvie? Sylvie's fine too."

"So everything is fine?"

"Looks like it, doesn't it?"

"Doesn't it?" She was looking at her hands in her lap. On a table in a far corner of the room was a photograph of Steve. He looked stuffy, Morpurgo thought; even pompous, which wasn't quite fair.

She followed his gaze. "I shan't tell him. But I'm not letting you go, not completely."

"You don't love me, Helga, not really."

"You don't know what I feel. No one knows. But I was thinking of me, not you. Steve in a forgiving mood is something I don't want. Even if I could be sure he would forgive."

"What if he finds out?"

"If he cares, he has found out already. He prefers not to find out."

Even after so many years, she had difficulties with tenses. Did she mean that Steve had found out but said nothing? Or that he had not found out as yet? Steve was one of those who bent and squeezed contradictory events until they matched his preconceptions, like someone who, buying shoes of the wrong size, was stubbornly determined to wear them. Except that with shoes, one was perfectly aware of the source of discomfort. "So what do we do?" he asked.

For the first time she turned to face him directly. "Nothing you don't wish. Is that fair?"

"Very. But not clear. What sort of things?"

"I don't know. You must decide. Or perhaps Sylvie."

The mention of Sylvie made him uneasy. This whole business was beginning to make him uneasy.

"Sylvie," he said. "Well, that's my affair. I'm afraid I don't know what this is all about, Helga."

"No, you don't, do you? If you want to know, you must find out for yourself. For me it is better than boredom."

"And better than wine?"

"Wine is better than boredom."

"What can I do to make you less bored?"

"Talk to me. What can you tell me? Steve tells me nothing."

"About what?"

She shrugged, exaggeratedly. "Anything. Your work, since it keeps you so busy."

"Steve doesn't tell you about his work because he's not supposed to. You know that." Yet it was not strictly true. Security Directorate, like any similar organisation, knew that it was expecting too much to think that the passing of sensitive information from husband to wife was preventable. The best that could be expected was to regulate it.

He remembered a famous memorandum written by the Knight's immediate predecessor. Circulated as a classified document, it had been headed: INTIMATE DOMESTIC SECURITY. It attempted to lay down the extent to which married

54

personnel were permitted to discuss their work with their partners without infringing the relevant sections of the Official Secrets Act. Its author, unlike the Knight of the Long Knives, had been a confirmed bachelor.

It is always difficult to parody anything that appears to parody itself, but someone – for all its professional expertise, the Directorate chose not to discover who – nevertheless succeeded. The product was circulated under the title SECURE DOMESTIC INTIMACY. In two pages of bawdy wit, the most memorable paragraph discussing official procedure in the event of a state secret being inadvertently revealed at the uncontrollable climax of orgasm, it destroyed with ridicule the document it mocked, and with it, so Directorate mythology had it, the reputation of the Director-General. Certainly he retired within twelve months, almost two years before the due date.

Steve had probably told Helga the story. But why the sudden interest in his work?

Unprompted, she gave him an answer of sorts. "Oh," she said, following her thoughts, "Steve tells me a little, enough to stop me becoming too curious. But it can't all be secret. To know so little means I have a husband who keeps secret a large part of his life."

"You're pretty good at that yourself," he said. Sylvie had held few things that mattered from him, at any rate, until recently. But Helga kept a great many of her thoughts in deep recesses of her mind, bringing them out, as a jeweller produces choice items from his safe, in ones and twos for his consideration.

Helga nodded, her little non-smile peeping and then vanishing again. "Secrets breed secrets. It is how Steve and I are becoming estranged. He keeps back one secret thing so I also. Then two, three, four, and almost we have stopped speaking to each other."

He could visualise it, Steve standing pat on the house rules. And yet the Directorate, after that one absurd effort to go against the rules of marriage, had accepted that there would always be pillow talk, had accepted, properly, that it must put its trust, as with everything else, in the common sense and innate loyalty of its employees.

With a stab of anguish, he found himself recalling the days, those many long, good days, when he used to tell Sylvie a little of whatever was currently occupying him; the days, in short, when they still shared that telepathic mutual understanding and

55

concern that supersedes and surpasses the unripe fruit of love. But his job had begun to work on their relationship like slow poison. Hers came into being as a natural antidote. Eventually, they crossed a watershed.

A man patiently tracked down after a terrorist bombing had slipped away, due to poor surveillance. Morpurgo came home full of anger, disappointment and self-pity. Sylvie had just preceded him after a day-long session with a woman executive from a New York agency that had proposed a commission with money and prestige. The woman, on her first trip to Europe, had been pathologically convinced that everything was a disguised rip-off. Sylvie, finally exasperated, had called the whole thing off. She and Morpurgo came together like the two halves of a fusion bomb, but he cherished the idea that it was he who had provided the detonator.

When everything subsided, they were knee-deep in previously suppressed recriminations, all the more maddening to Morpurgo because Sylvie had somehow managed to remain herself, cool, calm, self-contained, while he, in restrospect, had behaved abominably. It was the beginning of a change in their relationship that had led eventually, on Morpurgo's side, to Helga and a case of dalliance gone sour. On Sylvie's side? Well, that was something else he didn't know about.

So he must, he told himself, be fair to Steve. "There's quite a lot he isn't allowed to tell you, Helga, and neither am I. But there's no harm in your knowing that Steve's down on the coast looking after the civilian end of a spy ring operation you'll read about in a few days' time." Recruited nationals were referred to as civilians in Directorate jargon, an unofficial recognition of the fact that trained agents like Sattin and Kagalov were a kind of adjunct to the armed forces of their country of allegiance.

"Is it important?" She had withdrawn again, not looking at him, not looking at anything external. She held her glass in her hands, revolving it endlessly without seeming to be aware of it.

"Important enough. I mean, we don't uncover a spy ring every day of the week. It's not just Steve you won't be seeing so much of."

That drew her attention. "I see. That's convenient, isn't it, Johnny? Easier than saying you don't want to see me at all. I expect that's why you tell me."

"I didn't say that." Yet it was true, he supposed.

Her eyes clouded. "Spies! Nothing changes, does it, Johnny? I've never really escaped." She dipped a finger in the dregs of her wine, then licked it, like a small child. "Oh yes, I am comfortable, such a good word. A good house in a good country, waking up each day to find the world, this little English world, still the same snug place. Snug place, smug place, so smug, so many people who are happy to take things without looking too closely, without lifting the lid to look underneath. But what is happening underneath? Spies! Rats! How long before they come into the open? Before they decide to stay in the open? You have your camps too, Johnny, all you English have your camps, but they are camps for the mind. This way for blacks, that way for the skinheads, this way for the trade unionists, that way for the bosses, this way to be a slave, that way for the gas chambers."

"Helga!" Morpurgo was alarmed. "You mustn't think like that. It's not true and you know it. There's still freedom."

"And you and Steve, your job is to protect it?"

"Yes." Morpurgo said it firmly because he believed, on the whole, that it was true.

"Then you are losing, yes? Because it gets less and less. More and more people, more and more laws, to protect less and less freedom."

"We're not perfect, but we do our best. We try to make sure that no one puts safety and freedom in danger. That no one gets an unfair advantage, no one is strong enough to put the state in danger."

"Oh, yes," she said with a passion. "The state mustn't be put in danger. But what about the people? You protect the state from the people, but do you protect the people from the state?"

He reached out to touch her hand gently. "It balances out, Helga. It balances out. You must remember that in this country the people *are* the state." He knew as he said it that it was not true. Trying to improve on it, he said, "What we have isn't ideal, but it's better than we'd get from any other kind of government. So we must always try to keep a step ahead."

"Which is why you have caught these spies. What are they? Are they Russians?"

"One is. The other two are British."

"And you will put them in prison?"

"The Stringers, yes. We may swap Sattin. Use him as a kind

of currency, to buy back someone who's been caught by their side."

"So your spy equals their spy?"

"More or less."

"Then if you think enough of your spy to want him back, and they think the same, what is the difference?"

He felt a surge of irritation, less to do with her than himself. The point she was making stopped well short of reality, but it was also reaching in a direction in which he had no wish to go because he sensed that it might bring him to thoughts that would undermine his position, threaten his carefully constructed rationale for the work he did. With a disproportionate impatience, he said, "You're talking about things you don't understand, Helga. It's all a lot more complex than you think."

Just what one said to persistently questioning children.

She nodded emphatically. "Of course. Everything is always more complex than we think, isn't that true? Including me. Including you." Her head came down to her chest so that he could see only its crown. In a muffled voice, she said, "Including Steve and Sylvie."

Oh damn it to hell! he thought. Why did she keep bringing in Sylvie? It was an irony of his situation that only when he had become entangled with Helga did he discover that she admired Sylvie very much. As for Sylvie, she had once said, "If I photographed Helga, it would be against a background of shadows, and it would really be the shadows that were important." At the time he had thought he understood.

"I must be going."

Helga looked up. "Yes. You must go. So many things to do."

He found himself thinking that dealing with other people ought to get easier as one grew older, more experienced. But it didn't. Was it because one looked for and often found more, without always increasing one's ability to understand? Or because past disillusionment made one reluctant to try so hard? Or because the more one knew, the more one realised that there would always be more than one could ever know?

He said awkwardly, "I expect Steve will ring when he can."

"Yes, I expect so." She stood. "Aren't you going to kiss me?"

It was that final proof that things had changed. To ask. To have to ask. He bent his head to kiss her, and it would have been easy to go on from there, just as they had gone on before. But now, surely? they must go back; back to their relationship at the time it had all begun, and perhaps farther than that.

The kiss lasted for some little time but was unchanging, the same at the end as at the beginning. She had rested her hands lightly on his shoulders. He had placed his, chastely, a little below her shoulders. Just before they stopped, she withdrew the pressure of her lips. There was moisture on his cheeks, transferred from hers.

She stepped back. "There. Now you are free to go to your spies. Free for all the spies. What if one of them should spy on you? For Sylvie. For Steve. What would we tell them? It was only fun, only a game. Something to drive away the boredom. Goodbye, Johnny."

When he arrived home there was no sign of Sylvie, nor any sign of her having been and gone. What did he expect? A note telling him dinner was in the oven? A PS saying: 'Don't wait up'?

5

Patrons and Partners

Security Directorate had always been in Curzon Street, from the days, after the war to end wars, when it began to widen its original responsibilities for tracking down the Kaiser's spies. In those early days, Security Directorate had occupied a straggling collection of small houses of the kind that might, nowadays, in that part of Mayfair, be leased by a medium-sized advertising agency or a minor property company with a resounding name. Though it still has a scattering of premises in various parts of London, including the entire sixteenth floor of the Euston Tower at the northern end of the Tottenham Court Road, its headquarters remain in Curzon Street, right at the Berkeley Square end and well within earshot of the legendary nightingale.

Pedestrians cutting through toward Piccadilly from the southwest corner of the square come instantly upon it as they turn the corner of Fitzmaurice Place, heading for Bolton Street. They are unlikely to be impressed. The building is architecturally undistinguished, vaguely suggesting a hotel. If it were a hotel, it would be a curious one. The entrance would be at the Park Lane end, impressive enough in size but sealed off by huge reinforced doors big enough to swallow up a fair-sized bus. The ground floor windows, placed in pairs as with the floor above, have, unlike them, been bricked up with large stone-faced blocks matching those with which the ground and first floors were built. And along almost the full length of the building, some ten feet above the pavement, is what might be mistaken as a canopy to protect guests from the rain as they alight from cars or taxis. Canopy it is not; it is a deflector screen, protecting the upper stories from the blast effects of any car-bomb that might be left by the casual citizen as a token of dissatisfaction. The entire length of the street outside the building is under scrutiny from closed circuit television cameras. At the rear of the building, in Clarges Mews, is a private carpark, separated from the road by a red and white boom which is raised and lowered under the supervision of uniformed policemen, who also man reception.

So far as Morpurgo was concerned, the Curzon Street building had little or no charm, which made it much like most other places of work; but then, charm was not one of the amenities of Security Directorate. Its other major centre, the Euston Tower, even denies its sixteenth floor occupants their rightful view across the city to the Surrey hills, some twenty or more miles away, by keeping the windows permanently screened.

Morpurgo's room was on the fourth floor. From its windows he could look down across the street to the sliding roof of the Mirabelle. Once upon a time he had promised Sylvie dinner at the Mirabelle, where the gourmet elite or, otherwise, filthy rich seldom included members of the security services. The Mirabelle's prices had effortlessly managed to keep ahead of Morpurgo's good intentions until their changing relationship allowed both parties the discretion of forgetting the promise. Since then, Morpurgo suspected, Sylvie's newfound friends and clients might well have lunched her at the Mirabelle. It was something about which he had no intention of inquiring.

He opened the door of his room to find Steve Archer waiting for him, waiting for him through three or four cigarettes, to judge by the quantity of smoke. He fanned the air to express token apology, all the while watching Morpurgo as if they had never met before. Morpurgo, unlocking his desk and simultaneously trying to read a note Miss Robbins had left him, said, "Early bird, aren't you? It isn't nine o'clock yet."

"Early to bed," Steve said, lighting another cigarette, "and early to rise. Not much to do in Weymouth, let me tell you."

Morpurgo was surprised. "You didn't come back until this morning?"

"That's right." Steve was talking to the glowing tip of his cigarette, for some reason or other unwilling, as yet, to look directly at Morpurgo.

"You must have started appallingly early." Morpurgo was on his guard. What was it Helga had said the previous night? What if they should be spied on for Sylvie, for Steve? It was odd in Steve, to say the least, to stay the night in Weymouth, then get up in the early hours to drive well over a hundred miles to London, when he could have slept in his own bed by coming home the night before.

"Enjoyed the drive, as a matter of fact. Practically nothing on the roads until I got this side of Basingstoke." It was true that he enjoyed driving. He had a modified Jag that could outrun any police patrol car.

"Speaking for myself," Morpurgo said, "I'd sooner be by the sea in this weather."

"Swap," Steve said easily.

"I wish I could."

"Want me to take over?" Steve's look was mocking. In a quiet, over-reasonable voice, he added, "I wouldn't want anyone to get the idea that my idea of satisfaction for the rest of my time here is just to be a good 2 i/c, Johnny."

Morpurgo was startled, partly because he had come to believe just that, partly because something told him that raising the matter was only in part the cause of Steve's present mood. Had he really driven up this morning? Or had he been in London the previous night? It would be easy enough to check. A moment later he found himself shaken at the idea, even if it were no more than half serious, of checking on his own deputy.

And Steve had not finished. "Nor," he said, "do I always enjoy doing the minor league stuff, Stringers, not Sattins, that sort of thing."

"I'm sorry," Morpurgo said. "I really am. Though I'd like to think we both do work of equal importance."

Steve nodded ironically. "Teamwork. Well, yes, there has to be that. And, of course, you're the boss. I mean it, you have the right."

"And the responsibility." Morpurgo's unease was growing. Was this really only concerned with the job? Or was it simply the one-seventh visible above murky waters? "Anyway" – he launched himself on an effort to get the conversation back on more familiar lines – "no one has the chance of doing anything with Sattin for the time being. I haven't heard from Doc Vickers yet about the chap's sickness."

"Sickness?" Steve, too, seemed prepared to change tack. "Is it even that? Comrade Stringer's sick, too, but only from fright."

"Whatever it is, Steve, it's not fright. Sattin won't frighten easily, if at all."

"Wait until he comes up against Placket's special."

"Placket's special? What's that?" Special Branch would get their turn at interrogation and Detective Chief Superintendent Placket did not figure in Morpurgo's thoughts as a man unwilling to lean hard on any obdurately untalkative subject.

"Only got to know by accident myself, matter of fact. Seems he tried it on that Irish bomber, the one who pretended to be half-witted, not that they all aren't." Steve was a long way from being the only one in the Directorate with racialist views. "Came in with three of the others to hold Paddy down, then slid a soldering iron between his buttocks and asked him how he'd like to have it shoved up his arse and switched on. *Did* switch it on, I gather, just long enough for it to get warm and make his point. Paddy suddenly became a lot less half-witted, started to spill. Do you think Comrade Sattin would be any better?"

Morpurgo didn't know what to say. The rules were clear enough; no overt violence. But when did a threat cease to be a threat and become an act of violence? Before you switched on, or after? He was not soft himself in his attitude to the kind of people they sometimes brought in, people, for instance, who saw nothing wrong in packing high explosive and a mixture of scrap metal and broken glass into a suitcase and leaving it where the victims were more likely to be innocent than not. But how far did you go before you became like them? Where did you draw the line between what was permissible and what was not? He had a secret dread that, one day, they would be faced with a choice; those forms of torture that civilised society found abhorrent, or the deaths of scores, hundreds, perhaps millions in an age with weapons that could make scrap iron and explosive look like the antics of jesters with popguns and inflated bladders.

"When you heard, what did you say?"

"I said the next time I heard of anyone trying anything like that, he would be out faster than the speed of sound." Steve said it lightly, even the hint of a smile on his lips.

And the effect of that, Morpurgo told himself, would be that they would make damn sure, next time, that he didn't hear.

"Why didn't you tell me?"

"I'm your deputy, not your assistant. If I told you everything you'd soon reach the state of doing nothing. I dare say you feel the same about me." Steve grinned. "Teamwork, Johnny, right?"

The telephone rang. Steve answered it, held it out to Morpurgo. "Vickers."

Taking the phone, Morpurgo felt a sudden premonition of bad news. Though it was easy to explain away in terms of the charged atmosphere in which he and Steve had had their discussion, it was with a kind of reluctance that he answered, and in consequence spoke more roughly than he had intended. "Yes, doc?"

"Morning, sahib." Doc Vickers was ex-army, regular army, and therefore, during his long and not particularly distinguished career, colonial army; one of the many who, before the Nazi war blew away the empire almost as an afterthought, had been sent from one hellhole to another, until he finally found a cushy billet with Security Directorate. "Got out of bed on the wrong side, have we? All grouch and grumble?"

"Sorry," Morpurgo said. "Didn't mean to bite your head off."

"Better men than you, sahib," Vickers said cheerfully, "háve tried and choked to death. Anyway, greetings. After which, may as well get to the point, tidings not to your liking."

"Few tidings are, these days. Still, let's have yours. You're not going to tell me he's dead, I hope."

"Not that, old son, not that. Isn't just belly-ache either."

"Well, come on then, let's have it."

"Nothing specific yet, but I've put him on the sick list, no extra duties, pending further investigation. Thought you'd want·to know."

"Is that all you can say? Can't put a name to it, give me an idea how long before he's back to normal?"

"Rather not, Johnny, rather not. Thinking of getting a second opinion, matter of fact. In the meantime, no pressure, particularly no dentists. Doctor's orders. Sorry."

Downright evasive, Morpurgo thought, yet within his rights. Vickers knew more or less exactly the kind of pressures someone like Sattin might find himself under. He had the right, between sessions, so to speak, to examine the prisoner, to make sure things did not go beyond the permissible bounds. But only in exceptional circumstances could he call off the interrogators before their task was finished. It would have to be very exceptional circumstances that allowed him to call them off even before they'd started.

"You'll have to tell me more than that. The amount of time we have is probably going to be limited. I don't want to see it wasted."

"Course not, sahib. But in this case I have the right to keep you at bay until we know what's what. Sorry."

"So you keep saying." Shifting his position, Morpurgo happened to look in Steve's direction. What he saw was *schadenfreude*, a grim and not fully concealed satisfaction that trouble had found what Steve, Morpurgo saw in that fleeting glance, considered to be a deserving victim.

He returned to Vickers. "Is it serious?"

"Can't tell, not yet. Don't want to cramp your style, old son, but it may be a bit beyond a poor old sod of an ex-army doctor whose experience doesn't go much farther than gut-ache, phony back trouble and a wide acquaintance with the various forms of VD."

"All right. When will you be able to tell me what it's all about?" Morpurgo stole a quick look at Steve, but he was in the process of lighting another of his interminable chain of cigarettes, his face unrevealing.

"Tomorrow, maybe? Wouldn't want to mislead you by rushing things."

Morpurgo sighed. "All right. Tomorrow. Morning? I hope so."

"Have to see, sahib. Going to call old Tiddleywinky, come and do his famous imitation of a specialist, share wad and char round the campfire, give his opinion before he's drunk too much firewater. Why don't you join us, stay to lunch, sink a couple of jars together? Idea appeal?"

"I can't promise. Do your best, Doc, will you? Every second counts."

"Not just a touch of the squits, I gather." Steve prompted.

"Damn right. And Doc's not exactly in a hurry to give it a name."

"Unlikely to be all that serious. Moscow wouldn't have activated him if his health was suspect."

"That's true. Oh God! Moscow may not be so keen on a swap if they hear we're offering damaged goods."

"So what? You're the one who's been moaning about handing him over."

Morpurgo's face cleared. "It might persuade the Friends to call things off."

"No chance. They'd want to see him, arrange for an independent medical examination. Half a dozen! They'd probably go as far as hinting that we'd deliberately made him ill, just to hang on to him." Steve's face showed nothing beyond normal interest but Morpurgo sensed again a pleasure in adding to the anxieties of the man who was his section head.

"Oh well," he said. "At least we've got the Stringers to work on. *You* have, should say. Which reminds me. Did you have time to do anything about the timing of the drops and pick-ups?"

Steve stood up. "I must go. I've a date with Forbes, in Naval Intelligence. They're in a bit of a tiz over the way Mrs Stringer, nasty little bitch that she is, managed to find a hole in their security and use it all that time without being spotted. Incidentally, what about charges? She keeps asking about that, almost as if she thinks she can just put on her coat and walk out if we haven't charged her within forty-eight hours."

"Tomorrow. Private hearing, no bail, remand for seven days for the police to continue their enquiries."

"I know the drill," Steve said pointedly. "I'll deal with Comrade Stringer as well as his dearly beloved, though it's pretty clear the only thing he has to rejoice about at the moment is that he's in Weymouth and she's in London. Oh, the drops! Sorry, I forgot. I did make a start, but we didn't get very far. Probably have to wait another day or so. Anything in particular?"

"Just a general correlation. Sibley's dealing with the London end and it just helps if we have Stringer's side of the story."

Not all that interested, Steve said, "I'm off. I got the impression that there was some variation in timing, if that's the sort of thing you mean. Sattin never told Stringer exactly when he was going to make a pick-up, naturally, but Stringer has the impression that it was never very long after the drop. I'll get back to him on it as soon as I can."

The door opened to admit the Knight in his usual state of bustle. "Ah," he said, "the conspirators." He looked at Steve. "I've seen you once already this morning. You told me how busy you were, important meetings with MILINT or whatever it was. That was half an hour ago. Take care I don't start disbelieving you."

"Off now," Steve said, smiling, and went.

The Knight rubbed his hands together briskly. "What's up, Johnny? Lost a pound and found sixpence?"

"It's time that sort of thing was decimalised," Morpurgo said.

The Knight was in one of his puckish moods. "You mean it's time fogeys like me were pensioned off. Well, soon enough. I'm off to see the Minister. I think it would be a good idea for you to come too." Far from looking ready for retirement, he was at his jauntiest, Morpurgo thought, rosy face bright, silvery quiff giving an impression of crackling with electricity, blue eyes at one and the same time alert and innocent.

"Why must I come with you to see the Minister?"

"Because I say so, Johnny. That good enough for you?" The Knight was carrying his black bowler and the umbrella, rolled to pencil thinness, that went everywhere with him, regardless of weather and season. "And because the Minister said so too, if you must know."

"I think there's something you should know first." Morpurgo retailed the essence of his call from Doc Vickers.

The Knight listened, frowning. "Tomorrow," he said when he had heard the whole story. "Well, that's not long to wait, certainly nothing to make a fuss over."

"I didn't make a fuss. I could have, but I didn't. And the Minister asked you to bring me along so he could keep an eye on me, or be seen to. Is that it?"

Exasperated, the Knight snapped, "Yes. In a sense, yes. I also had it in mind to demonstrate that you had my full confidence, but I had hoped not to have to spell it out. And now, if you're ready . . ." He rammed his bowler on his head, the angle aggressive rather than jaunty, and marched out, umbrella at the trail.

Notwithstanding the sharpness of the last words, Morpurgo saw that he was forgiven. The Knight was not a man to nurse grievances. Giving Morpurgo a firm but gentle prod, he said, "What a bloody awful man you are. You've managed to invest what should have been a fairly routine exercise with all the elements of a witch hunt. Not to mention the complications that could result from the fellow's ailment, whatever it turns out to be."

"Oh, probably nothing very much," Morpurgo said with more conviction than he felt. "Strain, stress, some minor infection he managed to pick up when he was under pressure."

The Knight must have been having his own thoughts. "Yes," he said, after sitting in silence for several minutes while their driver filtered out into Piccadilly and headed east for Whitehall, "if it had been anything serious, we should certainly have had some indication from the encounter reports."

"What a world," Morpurgo said. "We want him well enough to do him some heavy mischief. Like nursing a sick man until he's well enough to go to the gallows on his own two feet."

The Knight had two basic rules about the less civilised part of the business; don't identify, don't sympathise. "Fellow knew what he was doing when he first came over here. We don't hang or shoot them any more, but if they're caught, they must take the consequences. Anyway, hang it, he's lucky. If he's ill we'll make him well. If he's cooperative, we shan't lean on him too hard. And cooperative or not, he'll be back in Moscow a damn sight sooner than he's any right to expect."

"Which is something you won't expect me to tell him, not until we've squeezed him dry."

The Knight studied him suspiciously. I know what you're wondering, Morpurgo told himself; whether I've given up on the mole. You want to demonstrate to the Minister that you can bring me to heel, that your judgement was sound when you promoted me over Steve. And, most of all, that, although I vote Labour, I'm one of the chaps at heart.

Aloud, he said, "And come to that, I don't even know whether we'll tell him what's wrong with him. Since we shan't have much time to work on him, anything that increases the mental pressure will work in our favour."

They were in Whitehall. The light summer breeze made the flags on the government buildings swirl languidly. A squadron of pigeons came low out of the sun to make a scrambled landing where someone had abandoned a half-eaten pastry on the pavement. As the car drew up outside the Home Office, Morpurgo was watching a middle-aged woman in a blue cape and an extraordinarily broad-brimmed straw hat walking slowly round the Cenotaph in the middle of the wide road. After a careful glance to right and left, she produced a small bunch of flowers from inside her cape and placed them where the Queen's tribute had been placed the previous November. Another careful glance and she was across to the far side of the road, walking quickly away toward Parliament Square. Morpurgo, following the Knight from the car to the ministry steps, wondered what story lay behind the unnecessarily surreptitious act.

The Knight bounced up the steps to the lobby, nodded at the

attendant, stalked about with short, quick steps while the Minister's private secretary was summoned to do the honours, then left him, breathing heavily, several paces behind as they all trouped upstairs to the Minister's room on the first floor front. The Minister got to his feet to greet them, and Morpurgo noted that while he talked first to the Knight and shook him by the hand, it was to Morpurgo that his eyes had gone as they entered the huge and sombrely impressive room.

"Now, Hugh," the Minister said, pointing out a large chair to the Knight and a small one to Morpurgo, "what's the form? Everything in apple-pie order so far, am I right?"

"Johnny." The Knight, their brief tiff set aside, gracefully invited Morpurgo to do the talking. Afterwards, all Morpurgo could remember was the spacious room with its mahogany panelling, silk flock wall-covering, splendid carpet and rugs, the painted portraits of famous incumbents; every last detail of a room in which historic decisions had been taken in the days of empire to which it was now a memorial and little more.

"I see," the Minister said when he'd finished. "So what we're waiting for now is a medical report, am I correct?"

"Yes, Minister." Morpurgo decided to be a model department head.

"And that will be tomorrow?"

"Tomorrow morning I'm going there, Minister. Doctor Vickers should be phoning me this afternoon or evening."

"And in the meantime?" The Minister liked to be thought of as a man of few words. Morpurgo suspected it might well be because he was a man of few ideas.

"In the meantime, nothing, Minister. Just rest."

"If this were Moscow," the Minister said in a loud, almost aggrieved voice, "we'd make treatment depend upon full cooperation. All right, Hugh, don't worry. I'm not offering it as policy." His little eyes wandered from one to the other of them. His large baby-face unnaturally free of the signs of wear and tear, the Minister, Morpurgo thought, was not unduly troubled by conscience.

There was a knock at the door, light, confident. "Come!" the Minister barked, part of the image; accustomed to command, no time-wasting, straight to the point. The Minister's middle-aged secretary, commanded, came in with a nicely furnished tray; coffee and biscuits, Wedgwood naturally.

"Will you be mother, Miss Grosvenor?" Morpurgo stifled a wish to laugh. Miss Grosvenor, unruffled by the implication of moral laxity, was efficiently mother, retiring afterwards while Morpurgo juggled with a cup of coffee and biscuit he didn't really want.

The Minister stirred his coffee vigorously, face unruffled save for a constriction of the eyebrows. "Point is," he suddenly burst out, "what's to be done about this swap? Can't keep him too long, can't let him go too soon. The PM agrees."

He was worried, Morpurgo guessed, at the prospect of another tussle with Merrilees, the Foreign Secretary, but only because he could not be certain of the outcome. If he were sure of the Prime Minister's backing, he wouldn't be in the least averse to using Sattin's indisposition as a way of avenging his earlier defeat. The fact that some poor bloody British fieldman was getting a going over from the KGB in the meantime was the Friends' affair, not his. And you, my lad, Morpurgo warned himself, would get just as short shrift if you stepped out of line.

"We're obliged to be careful, Minister," the Knight said. "We don't want Sattin to know too much, or he'll use his condition as a bargaining counter."

"You're forgetting something, Director-General," Morpurgo said. "He's not talking. No talking, no bargaining."

The Minister frowned heavily. "Bad thing to start off thinking you're going to lose, Morpurgo. Very bad psychology. Positive approach, that's the ticket, tell yourself you'll win and you will."

"Even if he talks," Morpurgo said, "he'll not give us much, Minister. He's a pro."

"Well," the Minister demanded, "what are you, man? A bloody amateur?"

"Oh, we've ways and means, Minister." The Knight saw a need to soothe. "He'll soon get tired of holding his tongue."

"Course, course," the Minister said hastily. "Leave it to you chaps to handle that sort of thing." His face hardened, his truculent chin thrust out a little farther. "No pussyfooting. Nobody's going to write a letter to *The Times* if the goods take a bit of hard wear, so long as it doesn't show later. Got good facilities out there, have you?"

"Everything that's needed." Spotting the trap too late, the Knight tried to get away with brevity, but the Minister was winding himself up for one of his perennial grievances.

"Course. Course," he said, brushing aside what had become irrelevant. "Comes to something you know, Hugh, when a Minister of the Crown has to sanction deliberate evasion. How am I to know you're not running some sort of luxury camp out there? Living it up with fast women or whatever they call 'em these days."

"They call them wives and daughters, often as not." The Knight was unwilling to be trapped by the Minister's resentment that The Other Place, while partially under his aegis, must remain, geographically speaking, *terra incognita*.

"Yes, well, that's as may be." The Minister did his best to suppress disgruntlement. "Now, what's the timetable? Discussed it with the Attorney General's office yet? That's the difference between us and Ivan, am I right? Due process. Aha, that reminds me, so much for your mole, eh, Morpurgo? Less of a mole than a wild goose, what?" The Minister's broad shoulders went up-down-up-down: *hyuk-hyuk-hyuk*.

"Minister?" Morpurgo ignored the Knight's attempt to signal a warning.

"Kagalov." For some time the Minister had been trying to find some aspect of their business that could give him unadulterated satisfaction. "No overnight bunk? No moonlight flit? Well, reason's pretty obvious, isn't it?"

"He doesn't know what's happened yet." Agree, the Knight's tone of voice told Morpurgo; for God's sake agree. "And if he doesn't, no one's told him."

Ever the genial bully, the Minister beamed at Morpurgo, waiting for him to back down before rubbing his nose in the dirt.

"Not necessarily." From the corners of his eyes, Morpurgo saw the Knight's roll heavenwards in despair. He was unpleasantly aware of the risk he was running. Very quietly, he said, "I'm prepared to swear that no one outside those directly concerned knew at the time or knows now what happened yesterday. If Kagalov had skipped, it would have been the clearest possible proof that one of those directly concerned had told him." He gave the Minister an opportunity of retreating to safer ground.

The Minister scowled at Morpurgo, his small mouth shaping a rebuke. Just as the Knight seemed about to intervene, the Minister's face changed. "You mean," he said grudgingly, "that if Kagalov had done a bunk, it would be as good as saying that

71

there was a mole. And a mole works better underground than in daylight."

"On the other hand," the Knight said, talking to his Minister but looking at Morpurgo, "if there were no mole, precisely the same thing would happen. Kagalov would still be here."

"Agreed," Morpurgo said. "So we can't take the matter as settled one way or the other."

"We can." The Minister was suddenly steely. "And we shall. No proof, no mole. I am *not* prepared to sanction the continued expression of suspicion on grounds that are absolutely baseless. Do I make myself clear, Mr Morpurgo?"

"Perfectly, Minister. May I say something? Something different?"

The Minister nodded, nursing suspcion.

"It would be very helpful if we could keep Kagalov in the dark for as long as possible." Something began to take shape in Morpurgo's mind. He had a slightly clearer idea now of why he had set Sibley ferreting through Registry, why he had asked Steve to check drop dates with Stringer. "If we dispense with the idea of a mole, then so far as Kagalov is concerned, the ring remains unbroken. And if he thinks that, then there's a chance, just a chance that he might keep the next treff." The Knight shifted doubtfully.

"We don't know that, Johnny. He might do nothing at all, waiting for some kind of message from Sattin. You can't be totally sure that you cut off communication between him and Kagalov completely. So many tricks, the curtain half-drawn, just so, the message in a matchbox, our old friend the drawing pin."

Morpurgo was suddenly confident, for no good reason, that the analysis of the movements of the three members of the ring would reveal some kind of pattern. "Maybe. The point is, he *might* attempt another treff if we can keep this whole thing under wraps."

"And if he did?" It was the Minister who asked the question.

"If he did, I think we might bluff him into an exchange of bags, just once more. Pictures are one thing. Bringing him in would be another." *How* will you bluff him? part of Morpurgo wanted to know, and the other part said: Wait and see, something will turn up.

In the silence that followed, the sound of the Whitehall traffic was unnaturally loud. Cutting through it, the four notes of the quarter boomed into the room from Westminster tower, followed a second or so later by the much gentler chime of the bells in the Horse Guards clocktower.

"He'd know," the Knight said musingly. "That's the snag, isn't it? All his treffs have been with Sattin. He'd know at once if it were anyone else."

"Don't think so. I've not only seen the film of the treffs, I've watched two of them. Places agreed long before. The changes run systematically, a fixed pattern. Make your ID from a long way off, because you know what you're looking for, and where. Then move as inconspicuously as possible to that place. That's the point, inconspicuously, which means paying no attention to anyone else, just doing what you're supposed to be doing and nothing more. He never so much as glanced at Sattin, behaved as if it were a complete stranger, the way *you'd* behave, because he knew it was Sattin. I think he could be fooled for as long as mattered, long enough to be filmed and then picked up."

The Minister looked at the Knight. "Hugh?"

The Knight nodded tentatively. "Could be. Could be, at that. Worth a try, yes." Will he, Morpurgo wondered? Without knowing what kind of game he's in, will he play the ace?

He did. He said, "Have to keep everyone in the dark. Especially the Foreign Secretary. He won't turn up the opportunity of hauling Mr Ambassador Voloshin over the coals, but if he knows about it in advance he might start weighing up the pros and cons and then lose his nerve."

It did the trick, almost visibly. Through the Minister's mind, like a magic lantern show, ran pictures of the Foreign Secretary being upstaged and finally outshone by the Home Secretary. It was one of those visions that elicit an instant decision.

"Yes." The Minister's chin came up like an artillery piece to the angle of aggression. "Why not? Hit the bastards where it hurts, am I right?"

The Knight, favouring Morpurgo with an impassive stare, said, "I think so, Minister. I think you're absolutely right."

"Then what," the Minister demanded, "are we waiting for?"

"Only the matter of Sattin," the Knight said hurriedly, as if anxious not to waste any more of his master's time. "Once we've got the thumbs up from the quacks we shall start to squeeze him. Nothing too physical, of course, but it might produce some squeals from the Friends in due course."

"Forget it, old boy." The Minister waved a genial hand. "They do things their way, we do them ours."

And their way, Morpurgo told himself, is more or less like ours.

The Minister's secretary opened the door a little way and looked in, disapproving of the empty cups, the used plates, the general slummy state of men in disorder. "You're due to meet the Christian Women in five minutes, Minister. They're just being shown into the small committee room."

"Coming. Coming." Eupepsia renewed, the great man showed condescension, ushering his visitors to the door. "Now, unless you'd like to come along and meet a delegation of Christian Women Against Pornography – my PPS irreverently refers to them as CWAP – I'll bid you good day. Saved yourself in the nick of time, Morpurgo. Had half a mind to put you in the Tower a while back."

*　　*　　*

When – and only when – they had emerged into Whitehall, Morpurgo said, "He'd still like to, really. Make him feel safer. Put me in the Tower," he explained. "He's one of Us, just as you are. I'm one of Them."

"Class." The Knight was disapproving. "You make too much of it, Johnny, too much altogether. Personally, I don't believe in it, all in the mind."

"That", Morpurgo said, "is like saying you don't believe in a round world. Say it as often as you like, it's still not flat." He looked around for their car and driver.

"One-way trip," the Knight said. "Told him we'd walk back. Thought it would do us good, me anyway. Thought we wouldn't be in too much of a hurry, either, let things simmer a while. Come on. I need the exercise." Without waiting for Morpurgo's assent, he set off at a brisk pace. Morpurgo caught up, adjusting his stride to the Knight's fussier step.

"Pulled a couple of fast ones, didn't you?" the Knight said. "Managed to keep your wretched mole in play, then top it with the idea of making a pass at Kagalov."

"You could have shot me down."

"Could have, probably should have. Played your cards well, though."

"I wasn't playing at all. I just thought we ought to keep the possibility in mind."

74

The Knight made a vicious jab at the pavement with his umbrella. "Heads you won, tails we lost, you and your not necessarilies."

"Oh, but it's demonstrably true. Either there's no mole or he's lying low."

The Knight was clearly taken with the idea. "Don't think you've a cat in hell's chance of fooling him, especially in a treff. Stringer fixed his drops with those newspaper small ads. Sattin arranged his treffs at a fixed time after the drops, and in a fixed series of places. Kagalov obviously watched for the ads too. All right, you could place a similar ad, no guarantee that Kagalov would keep another tryst. Even if he did, he'd spot your substitute a mile off."

"Possible. Still, nothing ventured. Boult's the man I had in mind. Same general height and build. Not much of a facial resemblance to Sattin, I grant you, though make-up might help. According to past performance, Victoria Station should be the next location. So there's Kagalov, doing a bit of mingling somewhere over the far side, in the small refreshment bar, say, or maybe the archway to the Underground. What's he looking for at that distance? Someone of Sattin's height, someone in Sattin's clothes, and a bag that matches his own. That's all. Once he's spotted that, he moves in, makes the swap, beats it, all in the space of thirty seconds or so."

They had come to a halt outside the entrance to the Privy Council office. The Knight stood with his feet apart, apparently trying to screw his umbrella into the pavement. "Lot of ifs. A devil of a lot of ifs." He looked up. "All right. Worth a try. Give you a decent lunch if you pull it off. You do the same for me if you don't."

"You're on." The Knight's idea of a decent lunch would cost Morpurgo more than he liked to think of, if his gamble failed. But the Knight knew nothing of the other little gamble Morpurgo had in mind. If *that* came off, it would be worth more than any lunch.

The Knight was off again, marching across the Horse Guards entrance under the very noses of the sentries' horses. "I must be mad," he said. "As if we haven't enough trouble on our hands already. Are you thinking of going out to The Other Place today?"

"Not necessarily today. I'll make up my mind when I hear from Doc Vickers."

"Grass," the Knight said, "has as little chance of growing under your feet as it has in the middle of Piccadilly. Now, I know your patter, Johnny. You want to understand Sattin's thought processes, tune in on his wavelength, see things through his eyes, so that you can spot the flaws in his ideological armour."

"You say it all so well."

"All right. But when you start going around thinking Sattin's thoughts aloud, asking yourself aloud the kind of questions that Sattin must have asked himself, so that you can decide what kind of answers he arrived at, people begin to wonder whose side you're on."

"I'll watch it," Morpurgo said. "It wouldn't exactly help my career if the Minister thought I was a crypto-commie."

"Your career?" The Knight took Morpurgo's arm confidingly, drawing him forward in an imperfectly synchronised and thus erratic progress. "Yes, let's talk about your career. How do you see your future?"

"A day at a time, sometimes less."

"Very funny. We all get by a day at a time. But the future, my dear sir, is something we're entitled to enjoy on a grander scale. The future, my dear sir, is where we're allowed to do our long-distance running."

"Ah, yes, running. Well, I see my future as running the Security Directorate." Morpurgo favoured his Director-General with a brief, glittering smile.

"Non-starter. You know it. It's a politician's job. Now, if you'd said Deputy Director-General."

"You know I won't get that either."

"Not unless you learn to bend to the political winds, Johnny. Most of them are zephyrs, really. They only blow Force Ten from the Opposition."

"Or when they're called Joe Padley." Padley's running parliamentary vendetta against all security services made him an anathema to the security knights and their senior staff.

The Knight refused the bait. "You're trying to annoy me. Come to the club. A little masterly inaction would be appropriate at this stage. We'll put in a call to Vickers, tell him where you can be found when he has something to tell. Coffee and a chat. Then a drink or two and luncheon, you always enjoy their cold leg of lamb. What do you say?"

"Thank you, Director-General, but I'd rather not."

The Knight shook his head ruefully. "Still won't accept that there are times when the smart thing to do is nothing. Well, I'm not fooled, Johnny. I know exactly what's on your mind. The non-existent mole. Kagalov's still here because it's altogether cleverer *not* to bolt. Next thing, you'll be saying that the mole *has* warned Kagalov, but not to bolt, to stay."

Morpurgo smiled. "Could be." They were outside the Whitehall Theatre, their backdrop a titillating display of full colour nudity.

"Sometimes," the Knight said exasperatedly, "I do find myself wondering whether your lefty leanings don't encourage you to stir things up a little."

It was a joke; Morpurgo knew it was a joke. To show that he knew, he smiled again. "Fight against it. But tell me this. If my party was in power and there were signs of a mole, would you be so set on letting things drop? And what do you think the Minister would say in opposition? Would he tell me I really must stop making waves?" Morpurgo produced a fair imitation of the Minister's plummy voice. "Do your duty, Morpurgo, and be damned to the consequences. These people must be rooted out. The public must see them for what they are."

The Knight reddened. "You do me wrong, Johnny. Never mind the Minister. You do *me* wrong."

"I know," Morpurgo said simply. "I apologise."

For a moment the Knight looked startled. Then he smiled, shaking his head despairingly. "You bloody horrible man! But thank you. You have my support. All I ask for in return is yours. I beg of you, Johnny, do see things in perspective." He lowered his voice. "No use blinking at the fact, we're dependent on the whim of the politicians, left, right, whatever. You walk a narrow line, old boy, half civil servant, half palace guard. Ours is a delicate art. To perform it is to spend much of the time on the dark side of the moon. The risk, if we upset the politicians, is to be abandoned there. Unpersons, ham-strung by the Official Secrets Act. Bound, gagged and left to rot.

"You may think you've heard it all before. Maybe, but this time it matters. Don't think, because the Minister appeared to give you his official seal of approval, that he's decided to trust you. Not a bit. He's going to watch you more closely than ever, one mistake and down you go. So to give you time to think things over, I'm going to do you a favour. You've been working too hard, too long. Go home, relax, take Sylvie out for the evening. You're a lucky dog to have her. I'll deal with Vickers, you're not to telephone him. If his news is good, I may pass it on to you. Or I may not. Now, off you go to Sylvie."

"I share her with a camera," Morpurgo said, but the Knight wasn't interested in that.

"Keep this in mind," he said as a last rider to his homily. "Because the Minister does. The government only needs one unsavoury piece of publicity, one scandal, and it could be out of office. Keep it *well* in mind, because the Minister does, and between his losing his job and your losing yours, he won't hesitate a second."

He tapped the head of his umbrella gently against Morpurgo's chest. "Off you go. Render unto Sylvie that which belongs to Sylvie, but to the politicians enough to keep them off your back." He struck the pavement sharply with the umbrella's ferrule and marched away toward Admiralty Arch.

Morpurgo watched him go. He doesn't believe in class, he thought. He doesn't need to. He's Us. When anything happens to one of Us, unless it's something really bad, like overexposing your feelings or being caught in the act of buggery, the rest of Us Rally Round. They can't help it. It's in their genes. *Brilliant chap, really gifted, but just a touch erratic, needs the occasional helping hand to stop him going astray.* Or perhaps *Fellow's made a clean breast of it, best let bygones be bygones.*

He remembered the arrogance of Blunt, courtesy of E M Forster: *Had to make a choice between loyalty to the country and loyalty to my friends; glad to say I chose my friends.* Burgess, Philby, Maclean; those were his friends! Us!

But if, Morpurgo thought, staring at the traffic, people, London, and seeing right through them, if it turned out to be one of Them . . . ! *Well, good God! Grammar school and redbrick, what do you expect? And these are the oiks who think they know how to run the country!*

He stepped off the pavement into the suddenly unleashed traffic from the Strand and was almost run down by a Rolls.

6

Sylvie

"John! Hey, John Morpurgo!"

Morpurgo looked back. Coming up fast behind him, his short legs and stocky figure making his progress look hard work, Warren Claas showed his teeth in a very white grin that reminded Morpurgo of a concert grand. As he hurried along, Claas was making wide, sweeping gestures of restraint. Morpurgo slowed, by no means sure that Claas would have been on any list of people he might have chosen to come across in the park.

Claas was wearing a suit of lightweight material, impeccably tailored, of a lustrous blue. It made him look alien. Slowing as he caught up, but not, Morpurgo observed, out of breath, he said, "*Ciao!* Playing hooky?"

"You could say that."

"Just did. Well, this is a good place to play it." Claas opened his arms in a wide embrace. "You want to know something? This is my favourite piece of London real estate." They were in St James's Park.

"You could pick a worse," Morpurgo admitted. They shared a floating double act, Claas and Morpurgo. The outside observer might well conclude that they were not only colleagues but the best of friends, capable, on occasions, of something fairly entertaining in the way of patter.

The facts were otherwise. Beneath the apparently amiable flow of banter lay reefs, some of them jagged. Claas, for the previous five years head of the London station of Central Intelligence, and therefore responsible for some seventy men and women directly employed, frequently professed admiration for the skill and efficiency of the British security services, but there was a tendency to lay particular stress on past achievements.

Or so Morpurgo thought, while secretly admitting to himself that the poor man's attitude to a rich patron has always run the risk of turning from gratitude to envy and denigration.

Morpurgo felt it the more because the CIA had access to a great deal of British source material, while the British, in comparison, lived on crumbs from the American table. Point out to him, which the Knight frequently did, that secret funds from Langley enabled Security Directorate, like the SIS, to extend its operations into areas that Whitehall was unwilling to fund; he still felt privately that the better organisation was working for the poorer, and for peanuts at that.

"Going somewhere?" Claas had fallen into step. They reached the bridge over the lake and walked to the middle. Just beyond them, a small boy hurled chunks of bread erratically toward a small armada of ducks and geese.

Claas leaned against the rail, the sun bouncing undulating patterns of light from the water on to his broad undistinguished face. He gave an impression of being at peace with the world, his dark lenses big enough to have hidden any intention short of a full scale declaration of war.

"So", he said after a while, "what do you know?"

"That my Redeemer liveth. That so many beans make five. And what I like. Oh, yes, I know what I like."

"But nothing about art, right?" Claas watched an old man feeding the pigeons. "The big question, John old man, is, do you like what you know?"

Oh yes, Morpurgo thought, he's after something. "Sometimes, but not often."

"Well let me tell you something. I certainly liked what I read in the digest this a.m. Looks to me like you did a great job."

Morpurgo's suspicion increased. Claas, for all he could have been the son of the husband and wife in *American Gothic*, was a double graduate of one of the Ivy League universities, he couldn't remember which. The fact that he indulged in the American habit of syntax assassination was no reason for writing off his intelligence. He said, "Thanks. We aim to please."

"You aim. But you sometimes miss, right?"

"What exactly did you read?"

"Sattin, I read about a guy called Sattin."

"Did we miss something?"

"Kagalov," Claas said. "You missed Kagalov."

After five years, Morpurgo told himself, Claas was showing signs of over-exposure to the British way of life, particularly in the use of understatement. If there were one out of the many KGB highfliers Claas and his bosses back in Langley would be pleased to receive trussed up like a Thanksgiving turkey, it was Yuri Borisovich Kagalov.

"You may remember," Claas said, turning his back on Whitehall, "we were rather counting on Kagalov. Strictly between you and me, John, which of your three knights screwed it?"

Perversely, things Morpurgo was only too willing to say himself were altogether less acceptable when they came from Claas. "No one screwed it." He began to walk. Claas accompanied him, whistling under his breath. They turned on to the grass, picking their way between sandwich-eating office staff from Victoria Street and semi-nude sunbathers.

"And anyway," Morpurgo added, "the knights didn't come into it."

"Is there anything I don't know? We heard this little rumour that Moscow had set out its stall."

The trouble was, Morpurgo thought, that you never knew just how much Claas did know. The sheer volume of information that poured into Langley from every quarter of the world made it virtually certain that Langley knew of the SIS's East German dilemma, although the Friends were secretive about their failures. But quantity was not quality, and in intelligence work it was quality that mattered.

"What do you mean, set out its stall?"

"Made it generally known, noised it abroad, that it's open for trade. That Sattin's been guaranteed a return ticket." Claas kicked aside a piece of fallen branch with one of his nicely polished shoes.

"Standard procedure," Morpurgo said. "They're all promised return tickets, you know that."

"Is that why you overlooked Kagalov? Is he part of the deal?"

"I don't make deals with them, Warren. I only catch them."

"Sure you do, but you know what's going on. Or is that something between the knights? Not for the rank and file?"

"I know some of what's going on, just like you. If it's going on

81

across the river, in Century House, I know less. Sometimes, and that's the way the Friends like it, I know nothing."

"You think we've got a direct line. Well, so we have, but it gets the wrong number from time to time." A yellow rubber ball scuttered across Claas's feet, closely pursued by a dog with more bounce than breeding. The dog grabbed the ball, stood on its brakes and brought it back to Claas, tail wagging frantically. Claas scooped up the ball, looked for the dog's owner, a stylishly dressed girl swinging a leash. He pantomimed a pitcher's wind-up and projected the ball in her direction.

Morpurgo was never averse to picking up a little off-the-record information on the Friends. "How about telling me what you heard?"

Claas wagged a hand judiciously. "They're out to make a trade, and a trade they'll make even if it sends you guys in Curzon Street back to square one."

The dog and the ball were back, the ball's yellow surface shiny with saliva. This time Claas ignored it, looking at Morpurgo fixedly.

"But that's not all you heard."

Claas decided to kick the ball away. "You think there might be something else?"

Morpurgo smiled, wishing to please.

"Okay," Claas said, "you want me to level. Listen, I will. But I don't give, not this time. I trade. I'm probably not going to be here much longer – oh, I almost forgot, my replacement's visiting with me right now. You and he should get together soon – so when I go back it will do me no harm at all to take some beads for the Injuns."

"So trade."

"Moscow Centre wants Sattin back. They know you have to process him first. But Moscow wants him badly, and they have something the knights and all want in return. Something they just happened to have picked up at the exact moment – lucky, huh? – one of the Friends' friends, doing a Sattin over there in the GDR."

He paused. Morpurgo, knowing he was after some kind of confirmation, said nothing. It came to Morpurgo that Claas was not, as he had thought, an American with mingled feelings of admiration and impatience for the British cousins. Claas was a man who was very willing to consider the British cousins as a liability, as a bunch of people who would get kind words and comfort just so long as they served an American purpose, and not a moment longer.

Claas said, quietly, "But that leaves Kagalov. Why'd you let him go, John?"

Morpurgo began walking again. "Do you mean me personally?"

"I'm talking," Claas said very softly, "about all those fine English gentlemen – knights, lords, who cares? – who are so expert at looking after each other before they look after anyone else."

Morpurgo stopped dead. "What are you trying to tell me?"

Claas flashed his frigid smile. "What I'm trying to tell you, John, is something like this. Moscow loses Sattin. They're not supposed to know that, but they do. So they pick off one of the Friends' field men. They're not supposed to know of his existence, but they do. Yet Moscow still isn't happy, and why? Because they have pieces still in play, better pieces than Sattin. They have Kagalov, sure. But what if Kagalov isn't the highest?"

So there was Claas spelling out what Morpurgo himself was already convinced of, although, coming from Claas, it sounded uglier. He said, "So what's in it for you?"

Morpurgo began to walk toward Queen Anne's Gate.

"What's in it for me? Well, I told you, beads for the Injuns. Meaning confirmation. Better yet, a name, something to help us help you put an armlock on the knights." Claas took off his outsize sun-glasses, flicked a silk handkerchief from his breast pocket and polished the lenses carefully. "The word," he said, "the word, John, is 'mole'." He inspected the lenses, holding them up to the light. "I guess we're stuck with that word for good and all."

Morpurgo checked the time. "Want to walk with me as far as the Yard? I have a date." He could always find a reason for going inside.

They had reached the edge of the park. On Birdcage Walk the important people were setting off for their important lunches, the proportion of chauffeur-driven cars noticeably on the increase. Morpurgo found himself assailed by depression. He wondered whether what he did, what Security Directorate and SIS did, was worth it? Was the country, were the people, worth it? His uncertainty about the answer added to his depression. We were worth it once, he answered himself, but are we worth it now?

Kagalov had had a tour of duty in the States before coming to London. During his time a Soviet intelligence network had been uncovered. The trouble was that the uncovering had led no farther. Someone had alerted the field agents and though a leakage of highly sensitive military information had been stopped, only small fry came into the net. Langley had been certain that Kagalov had masterminded things, but they had turned up no real proof. Shortly afterwards, Kagalov had returned to Moscow. The Director of Central Intelligence, in so many words, had let it be known that the reward for catching Kagalov by the balls, home or away, would be something very special.

"I'd like to talk some more," Claas said as Morpurgo prepared to cross the road. "And soon at that. How are you fixed?"

"Pretty busy. Kagalov we can't fix up. Sattin we can."

"Sure," Claas said. "But I want you to meet Weber, my replacement later this summer. How about giving you a call?"

Morpurgo looked left and right, checking the traffic. "I'll do my best. But if you want to do business, you're going to have to come up with a better product."

"Maybe you should take a closer look at the one we have already," Claas said crisply. "*Ciao!*"

With a wave, Morpurgo committed himself to the traffic. Claas stood looking after him, a small smile on his lips.

*   *   *

"Henry Liddle's secretary. Can I help you?"

"Is he there?"

"Who's calling him, please?"

"Tell him it's Uncle John."

"I'll see if he's in. Just a moment, please."

Morpurgo waited while Liddle's secretary, having given her boss an escape route should he decide not to be in, went to find out if he was. Almost at once she put him through. Liddle's voice, loud, confident and breezily classless, honked in his ear. "Uncle John! How's the world? Long time no see."

"Can you get away?"

"Is it worth it?"

"You must be the one to judge."

"Okay, I'll trust you. Usual place?"

"Usual place. Give me thirty minutes."

"Don't be late. I'm busy." Liddle broke the connection. Arrogant bastard! Morpurgo thought, but with Security Directorate bedfellows were apt to be proficient rather than pleasing.

A little under half an hour later, he paid off his cab at the corner of Ludgate Circus and Farringdon Street and walked the few yards to a snack bar that was all bare plastic surfaces and minimum comfort. There were two black girls behind the counter and in front of it four black men, two of them Rastafarians with dread-locks. No one took any notice of Morpurgo.

Perched on a stool at the innermost end of the counter, looking as much at home in the general surroundings as a plastic gnome in a garden full of Henry Moores, Henry Liddle was not a man to miss the chance of establishing a psychological advantage.

"Call this half an hour? I've been here practically half an hour, cully."

"Buy yourself a watch."

Liddle's voice, in contrast with the high, musical tones of the blacks, grated. "What'll you have?"

"The usual." It occurred to Morpurgo that his reply was a good reason for changing the venue for any future meetings.

Liddle had no need to raise his voice. "Service, sweetheart." All the blacks looked round. Liddle raised the palm of one large hand. "Peace, brothers." The men laughed loudly. One of them, his tightly wound locks hanging below the brim of a giant peaked cap, said, "You here on suffrance, man, so we goin' make you suffer." All the men laughed again, but one of the girls left to serve them.

Liddle laughed loudest of all, but under his breath he said, "Black shit!"

The girl arrived. "You take no notice, they just throwin' their weight about."

"Sure they are, but they don't have much weight to throw. Two coffees, black, two raspberry doughnuts."

"No raspberry left. Cream or plain."

Liddle reached out to take one of her hands. "Two doughnut-flavoured doughnuts. Say you've got two doughnut-flavoured doughnuts."

She smiled. "See what I can do."

"You do that, sweetheart." Henry Liddle turned his full attention on Morpurgo. He was tall, broad-shouldered, dressed

85

expensively but untidily in tweeds and a silk shirt and tie. He had a flushed and craggy face providing anchorage for a nose that would have made Wellington's look retroussé.

"So far today I've had a threat of action for libel, a thinly disguised attempt to bribe me, and a public relations creep who thinks I was hard on his client. Next time I shall step on his client like a turd. If I told everything I know about his client the syphilitic sod would have to flee the country. If I told everything I know, half the bloody country would have to flee the country."

The girl returned with his order. "God bless you, child," he said. "Turn up the music a shade, will you? My friend's a trifle deaf."

She turned up the music deafeningly, one note, often repeated, making something on the counter buzz like a trapped hornet. "Good girl," Liddle said, watching her undulating bottom as she walked away. "I'd gladly give her a poke if she asked me, and that's more than I'd say for most of 'em."

He stuffed his mouth with doughnut, following it with a noisy gulp of near-boiling coffee. "Thinks I like acid rock. Maybe I would if I wasn't tone deaf, or maybe I wouldn't be able to tell the difference. On that stool of yours, old boy, have sat some of the most influential backsides in London."

"I know your habits," Morpurgo said. "Now shut up, and I'll give you something to put in the bank."

"Ah," Liddle said through half a doughnut. "A leak, is it? I get enough leaks to sink your average supertanker six times a week."

"Not just a leak. A deliberate breach of security." Now he was committed.

"Trust me, Uncle John," Liddle invited. "I'll see you get a favourable press when you come up at the Bailey." His hard, calculating eyes were narrowed with interest.

"Commit a word of this to paper," Morpurgo said evenly, "and I'll make problems for you that will put you out of business."

"There you are," Liddle said. "Mutual trust. You know I can pick up the blower and ask for a favour from half the Establishment? Including all the Cabinet? I know some very important people. Okay, spill."

"We've just busted a spy ring."

"Today?"

"Yesterday."

"Yesterday is history."

"While you were having your expense account lunch."

"I thought you liked to do these things at unsocial hours?"

"Like didn't come into it."

"Ah." Liddle looked up, interested at last. "Opposition?"

"You could call it that."

"I probably will."

"I think we neglected to look behind the arras."

Liddle tilted his coffee cup, extracting the dregs to a musical accompaniment. "Would this, by any chance, have anything to do with one Yuri Borisovich Kagalov, sometimes marketed under the name of Kirillin?"

"Perhaps you'd like to finish the story yourself."

"There are times, Uncle John, when my sources have been altogether bloody better than yours."

"You've got a bigger slush fund."

Liddle signalled the girl who had served them, miming a repeat order. "Want to come on the payroll?"

"You understand the terms? You bank it until we go public. And it's unattributable. Totally. Even by implication."

"Hold on a tick." The girl had brought the repeat order. Liddle poked his doughnut viciously. Jam oozed from it like congealing blood. "This is raspberry. The bitch was holding out on me." He looked at Morpurgo sideways, like an evil-tempered parrot. "Holding out on me can be bad medicine, very bad medicine. Never been to one of my rural beanfeasts, have you? I could introduce you to some very useful people."

"Not much mileage in saying, 'This is Uncle John Morpurgo. He's very big in security.'" Liddle's *fêtes-champêtres*, like his social register, were legendary. "Anyway, we were talking about Kagalov."

"Order of the boot?"

"No. That's the point." Morpurgo looked at Liddle very directly. "I won't ask how you know so much about him."

"Wouldn't tell you if you did. You should be glad. It's your warranty." He drew jammy arcs across his plate with an indefatigable forefinger. "What do you mean, that's the point? Has brother Yuri been running a little business on the side?"

Morpurgo gave him a concise and edited account of the story to date. Or almost to date. He could see Liddle's memory sucking the facts down like a whirlpool.

"That's it?" Liddle said at the end.

"That's it."

"No, it's not. Yuri's still here. Because if he bolts when he's not supposed to know of any reason for bolting, he's as good as saying someone tipped him the wink. Someone more important to Moscow than brother Yuri. In other words, a . . ."

"Mole," Morpurgo said. "That bloody word!"

"Bloody? Got everything! Including four letters. Great in seventy-two point bold or bigger. Are you going to leave that doughnut, uncle? In that case . . ." His attention supposedly fixed on transferring the doughnut from Morpurgo's plate to his own, Liddle said, "And *that's* it."

"Exclusive."

"But embargoed. Don't like embargoes, uncle, never did." He ate some of Morpurgo's doughnut, then began to peck up sugary crumbs with his finger, his great nose hovering hawklike over the plate. "How shall I know when it's been lifted?"

"You'll know." Now he had done what he had set out to do, Morpurgo was feeling strangely tired. Even stranger, he had a growing wish to see Sylvie, pale but incorruptible Sylvie.

"I've got to go."

His voice much harder, Liddle said, "Why don't we meet at my place, tonight, earlyish? A drop to drink, a bite to eat and another canter through the piece. Say around eight? It would please me, uncle. I'd definitely be pleased."

Morpurgo had been studying the sunlit street through the big windows plastered with stickers for hamburgers, freshly cut sandwiches, *Luncheon vouchers welcome*. Now he grinned nastily. "Don't come that tone with your Uncle John, Henry. I know you've got a hidden tape machine in that retreat of yours. And I know ways of making life very tedious for people who try tricks. You'll get your story, but not until I pass the word."

"Consider yourself disinvited, cully," Liddle said, unabashed. "No harm in trying."

"In my case, yes." Morpurgo slid off his stool. "Don't try to be smart, just do what comes naturally." The music system blared out heavy metal. The blacks murmured and laughed and murmured again. Morpurgo nodded. "Cheers, Henry. Do me a favour. Give me five minutes. I have to be careful who I'm seen with."

"For you, Uncle John" – Henry Liddle was already on his third doughnut – "anything." He watched Morpurgo turn out of the entrance, then added softly, "Up to a point."

*　　　*　　　*

Morpurgo's house was a tall, thin townhouse in one of the less fashionable areas of Kensington. It stood in a row of tall, thin houses in a street that led nowhere and was consequently always clogged with parked cars. The only obvious way in which his house differed from its neighbours was its street door, a gleaming scarlet on which brass fittings stood out as splendidly as the buttons on a guardsman's tunic. The scarlet had been Sylvie's choice. Sylvie had painted the door. Sylvie had done most of the decorating in the house, a fact unbelievable to those who saw only her elegant public persona. Morpurgo believed he had not done it himself because Sylvie liked decorating. Or had, then.

Sylvie was not, and never had been, the kind of woman to sit around buffing her nails and wondering what to wear next. She had been an enthusiastic shopper among the innumerable afternoon and evening classes that made the metropolis a vast bazaar of the practical, the entertaining and the recondite.

She had plundered freely to begin with; Restoration playwrights, Athens in the Peloponnesian Wars, baroque architecture, music of the French Renaissance; two or three together until it was only a question of time before she would simultaneously be studying case grammar, Sufism and the Liverpool poets.

But then she had discovered photography.

He had bought her a camera for her birthday; not cheap, not expensive. Being Sylvie, she was not content to point and press the button. After attending beginners' classes and being told by an instructor hopeful of having an affair with her that she had an exceptional talent, she abandoned almost everything, including that particular instructor, in order to discover how far she could go.

She was still travelling, ten years on.

Slipping his key into the lock of the scarlet door, Morpurgo opened it upon unnecessary reminders of just how far she had gone, examples of the work of Sylvie Markham, all of people or places or people in places. Little by little over the years, she had abandoned every subject but these; no travel brochure gloss, no smart magazine glamour; only life, those who lived it and the places in which they lived.

And no colour; perhaps the most striking thing about her eye and her talent. In one of her rare personal interviews – she had generated her own publicity in recent years, though she tried hard to avoid it – she had said, "I think truth is black and white. If you can't show it in black and white, it's very rarely the truth."

He had wondered for some little time now whether she had already guessed or deduced that there was – had been – another woman, but the very vulgarity of the cliché made it un-Sylvielike. And also, more recently, when, between his business and hers, they had not so much made contact with each other as passed and repassed at close but still separate and unbridgeable quarters, as people might approach and then recede on opposite sides of a glass partition, he had found himself wondering whether Sylvie, too, might have found a lover.

Again, in his judgement, the answer must be no. Sylvie had only one love, to which she had come late and therefore with passion. Or was his judgement merely the slave of his will?

He went to wash big city grime from his person, then opened the refrigerator to see if there were the makings of a meal. There were, though not the kind of meal he would enjoy. He poured himself a drink, took it to the piano, lodged it safely and lifted the lid. He played with plausibility rather than talent, which was perhaps, also, the way he lived his life. He scampered off a series of ascending chords. The telephone began to ring. He answered it with hope, but it was his knight.

"Ah, you are there. Good man. Going out, I hope. Tell Sylvie to wear something that'll knock them in the eye, good for your morale. Now, business before pleasure. Vickers rang. In a nutshell, friend Sattin's got something a bit more nuisancial than a pain in the tummy."

"Do we have a name for it?"

"No. Not yet. Leastways, Doc didn't see fit to tell me. Specialist wants tests before he's willing to go into details."

"Serious?"

"Doc was very cagey, even when I tried leaning on him, that's why I'm glad you're going out there, see for yourself. Wanted to catch you tonight, because we've a get-together with the Friends, ten sharp at Century House. General review of the situation, should get away not much later than eleven."

"Pound to a penny they won't believe us about Sattin. They'll think we're trying to stall them."

"So we won't tell them," the Knight said serenely. "Not until you've heard everything from the horse's mouth. Well, there you are, Johnny, don't let it spoil your evening. Not that it should, with Sylvie for company. Give her my love."

Morpurgo, thoughtful, eventually found himself back at the piano. He struck a one-handed chord, then closed the lid. In due course the ensuing silence was disturbed by the rattle of a key in the street door. Sylvie came in. She closed the door and turned to look at him. "Hello. What's happened?"

He was still looking at her. Sylvie was . . . well, Sylvie. She was wearing jacket, skirt and shirt in complimentary shades of tan, with a silk scarf of a brilliant orange. She looked cool, crisp, efficient, but that was Sylvie; crisp, efficient, cool.

"Should something have happened?"

She smiled. She had honey-coloured hair, the pale, dense honey that sets hard in the pot. Her complexion was pale, too, but healthily pale, the skin as silken as her scarf. "You're early, that's what I meant."

"Why am I home at all, is that what you really meant?"

She poured herself a sherry, very dry, the colour of her hair. The floor beneath them shook to a muted rumble. The Underground ran deep below. Mole, he thought. Normally he never noticed it.

She took her drink and sat facing him. "No, not why are you home at all? But why now? It's a normal sort of question."

He was going to say: Since when have things been normal with us? He said, "A natural break. Between one thing and the next. Where's all your gear? Don't you carry it around any more?"

"When I'm working. Between one thing and the next, I leave it at the other place."

For a moment he was startled, The Other Place very much on his mind. She was smiling at him again, this time, he thought, ruefully. "You don't remember? No, you don't remember."

He did now, of course, some sort of premises she'd rented in the vicinity of Baker Street, a sort of studio-cum-office. He had let it slip his mind, perhaps because he had not particularly wished to remember. In ten years, Sylvie had changed from dependent wife to Establishment success story. They had a joint bank account but she never used it, hadn't used it for a long time, on the insistence of her accountant. Yes, Sylvie had an accountant. And an agent. And a part-time secretary who did audio-typing and took care of her correspondence. Sylvie Morpurgo had become Sylvie Markham; those of her things that had been monogrammed were still usable, but not her husband.

"Yes, I do remember. Of course. Is that where you've come from?" How the hell did *he*, Morpurgo, come to have an Establishment wife?

She nodded. "You've an open invitation, did you forget that?"

"No. Of course not." But he had, or had refused to remember. She had a separate home, that was what it amounted to, since he had gathered that the studio had some kind of cooking and eating facilities. When her growing quantity of equipment began to turn the top floor of the house into a kind of upholstered workshop, he had been vaguely aware of her professional problems. Even so, the news that she was splitting herself in two had come as a jolt.

It was, of course, Sylvie Markham who had moved out. He had told himself as much and said, in effect: So what? Sylvie Markham, as he saw it, was someone who, uninvited, had created a *ménage à trois*. When she moved out, things should have gone back to normal, but they had not. What had been left behind was a new Sylvie Morpurgo, not the one he had married, not, seemingly, one to whom he could adapt.

"So when," Sylvie said, "had you thought of paying a visit?"

"Soon," he said vaguely. "Things are a bit hectic at present."

"Yes. Me too." She looked at him through a drifting haze of cigarette smoke. She smoked elegantly, the opposite of Steve Archer. "But this is a break? A lull? Is your lull likely to last until Monday?"

"Why Monday?" With things as they were, he couldn't even be sure of tomorrow.

"House-warming party at my new place. I *have* told you, Johnny. Several times. Will you come? Please."

"House-warming, in a darkroom?" He had meant to say it lightly. It came out leaden and graceless.

"Say you'll come."

"I'll try. I can't be more definite. I wish I could. Would you like to go out to eat somewhere this evening?"

He surprised himself, the words less intentional than unexpectedly exposed.

He had surprised Sylvie, too, her cigarette halted halfway to her mouth. "Whatever gave you that idea?"

"Does there have to be a reason?"

"Wait a minute." She went to the telephone, tapped out a number.

He could hear the faint *brrr-brrr* of the ringing tone. Her left hand, the free hand, was plucking at the seam of her skirt, the first time in a long time that he had seen her composure the least in disarray. The ringing tone stopped. A distant, scratchy voice said something monosyllabic. Sylvie straightened, her fingers stopping their plucking. "Is Mr Porteous there, please? Sylvie Markham." A silence, then more scratchings.

"I see." She sounded disinterested, as if she were making the enquiry on someone's behalf. "And he won't be back?" *Scritch*, said the little voice. "Is there anywhere I can reach him?" *Scritch-scritch-scritch*. "I see. Thank you very much. Goodbye."

Sylvie walked over to the window. The street, what could be seen of it over the roof of a parked car, was submerged in a flat, indirect shadow of palest blue. High above it, golden light made cubist structures of rooftops. Sylvie touched her temples with her fingertips. "I'm sorry, Johnny. I can't."

"No," he said, as if that was what he had been waiting to hear all along. "It's all right. Some other time." He picked up his drink.

"I wanted to. I have an engagement. I tried to cancel it."

"It's all right. Really, it's quite all right."

She said, "It's a business engagement. I'm free tomorrow night. Any night except Monday, the party."

"Tomorrow wouldn't be possible." He told her about Sattin and the mole.

At the end she said, "I find it very hard to believe, Johnny."

"Of course. So does everyone else. They always have. And of course, they don't share my politics."

"You think it's a question of politics. Right wing, naturally."

"What else?"

She looked at him for a long time, then at her watch. "Johnny, I'm sorry. I've just time to shower and change, then I must leave. If I could have done anything at all to get out of it . . ."

"I said, it's all right." They were like two astronauts adrift in space, the gap between them slowly widening, any movement, the smallest gesture, only taking them farther apart.

Having signalled her intention of leaving, Sylvie, womanlike, stayed. "You want it to be true, Johnny, don't you?"

"That's absurd."

"You do. Part of you does. Headline stuff. All right, they're privileged and they're powerful. It doesn't make them traitors."

She hesitated, as if waiting for a reply, then went upstairs. When she came down, he saw someone superb, Sylvie Markham, someone of stature, someone of achievement, and all in a way with which John Morpurgo had no link, to which John Morpurgo made no contribution, of which John Morpurgo, by accident or design, had little or no understanding. Sylvie was Establishment? Had she also become Us?

As she passed, she bent and kissed him lightly on his cheek. "I'm still here, Johnny. I hope you'll come back soon."

In the silence that always seemed total after Sylvie had gone, he said to himself: Of course it's true. It must be true. But did he mean the mole or Sylvie?

7

Friends and Foes

Weber looked up as Claas came in. "Hi! Boss gets in before staff, ploy number one. What kept you?"

"*Ciao!*" Claas said. "I have this sleep problem, can't give it up."

"Did you make your meet?" Weber took a seat.

"Uh-huh. St James's Park, just like they said. Oh, we strolled. We talked. We watched the ducks being fed. All as sweet and sugary as momma's apple-pie. I told him a tale and he told me one. I made it look like I didn't too much care for him or the British. He made like he loved me too."

Weber turned his chair round a little, so that he could see Claas more easily. "*Do* you like him? I'm not so sure that you do."

"I like his wife," Claas said inconsequentially.

"We're not dealing with his wife."

"More's the pity. He's good at his job. I have to say he's good at his job. It's his attitude that bugs me. Everything to the right of him has to be a capitalist conspiracy."

"Don't knock it," Weber said, "when you've got it going for you. You have got it going for you?"

"No sweat. He acted like he wouldn't buy it, but he sold it to himself. Now we have to make sure it's what he thinks it is."

"When do we get to meet?"

"This afternoon," Claas said. "That's what I plan. Soon, anyway."

Weber had begun to leaf through a file from Claas's desk. "I see there's this meeting between Security Directorate and the Friends this morning. Routine?"

"No, not that one. We do have Lassalle go over to Century

House every morning, routine checking of signals, but it's not that one. That one the knights cooked up."

"I see Fish will be there."

"He'll be there. We'll get the report soon after."

"This other guy, Epworth. Who's he?"

"I asked Fish. He said something like, oh, like he's a DDR specialist. Directly concerned with this guy the Friends have mislaid in the DDR, something like that. Anyway, not too important, I guess."

"Hm." Weber wasn't entirely satisfied, but he let it go for the time being. "Do we know where that guy's being held? The one the East Germans picked up?"

"We don't. The Friends are on full boost trying to find out."

"Not Normanstrasse, then?"

Claas shook his head. "Karlshorst, they think."

"Karlshorst!" Weber pulled a face. "KGB got him, that's bad news. What was that lag?"

"Between what?"

"Between the Friends spotting the correlation and the SD turning up Sattin. Oh, and between the beginning of the SD operation and the *Hauptverwaltung* job."

"From memory, about nine months on the first, maybe four for the second. Want me to check?"

"Later. How did it all go again?"

Claas concentrated. It made him look stolid, unimaginative. "This guy they lost was handling a feed of stuff from that East German weapons research centre at Rostock. All going routinely well until an analyst at Century House spotted a correlation between the work the EGs were doing on counter-measures against the Narwhal torpedo – that's the British heavy, Stingray's the fast one – noticed that their electronic counter-measures tallied pretty well exactly with the technology the British are designing into the Narwhal homing facility."

"So the EGs knew all about Narwhal technology. So someone was keeping them informed."

"Right. And it didn't take Security Directorate long to find them."

"The Stringers. All pretty tidy, wouldn't you say?"

"You just lost me."

"Tidy that the British pull a man Moscow Centre wants back in a hurry, and simultaneously, in East Germany, the *Hauptverwaltung* pull just the man for a good swap."

"Oh." Claas's face cleared. "You're forgetting something, Pierre. Nine months is what you're forgetting. Nothing simultaneous about it."

"You're right. So this field agent of the Friends could have been on ice, kept happy with disinformation for six months? Maybe more?"

"Before they brought him in? Sure, about that."

"Not much of a gap."

"The Friends thought what you're thinking. But unless you buy the idea that Moscow Centre blew their own agent . . ."

"That'll be the day!"

"Okay, so you have to go along with the idea that it was luck."

Weber nodded. "I guess that's how it was. Do we have anything on Sattin that didn't come from the British?"

"Snippets," Claas said cautiously. "This is one hell of a delicate area, Pierre."

"I know it. But do we?"

"What are you, some kind of thought reader?"

"Did you think I didn't know you're scavenging?"

"Because Security Directorate didn't. They got Sattin himself, so what was the point in scavenging, that was the way they figured it. But I don't have much to tell you yet."

Weber was frowning again, his mournful face even more lugubrious. "There's something missing, Warren. Don't ask me what. But something. Some piece of information that would fill in a lot of gaps, something the British haven't come across yet. Or if they have, they don't think it's important."

"Don't tell me. You want it."

Weber was contemplating some thought he wasn't yet ready to share. "Want it?" he echoed absently. "You bet your sweet life I do!"

*   *   *

Morpurgo's mood was irritable as he unlocked his desk, listening to a series of messages that Miss Robbins was reading out. They covered a list of new positive vettings that had to be allocated as soon as possible; a planned sweep, later the following week, of selected people from the Suspects Index; a quiet word of warning to the managing director of a business that sold a range of high speed electric motors in Hungary and was thinking of hiring . . .

That was as far as he got. Steve Archer came in, when Morpurgo had thought he was already back on the coast. He said as much.

"Change of plans," Steve said. "Anyway, one last trip there, charge Comrade Stringer, then we can tuck him away, let him reflect on his sins for a bit." He took a seat. "I gather you're due at Century House."

"Coordination meeting, keep everyone in the picture. Except that, as usual, there'll be at least three different pictures we hope to persuade each other to be kept in."

"Three?" Steve seemed to have no good reason for taking up Morpurgo's time, unless he was trying to keep himself in the picture too.

"All the knights," Morpurgo told him. "Fuller's going to be. there. Keep the PM and the Cabinet sub-committee in the picture."

Steve lit another cigarette. "Sounds more like private viewing day at the Royal Academy. Interesting, though."

"Interesting? Why? You know what that sort of thing's like, everyone taking hours to make points they could have made at the beginning, Fuller making notes for a summary he'll probably have in his pocket when he arrives."

"And what's the point you're going to make?"

"Time," Morpurgo said tersely. "That's my point, we need more time. Especially with Sattin ill."

"No further news?"

"Not yet. I'm off to The Other Place as soon as I can get away from Century House. No change of heart in Mrs Stringer yet?"

"None. Fortunately, her old man's a proper little vocal artiste."

Steve looked at Morpurgo with a faint smile, as if to say: How long are we going to go on playing this game? Why don't you tell me what you'd really like to know?

The trouble was, Morpurgo wasn't sure what he would really like to know. "I presume the running boys have him at present?" The Special Branch did most of the legwork and routine interrogation.

Steve nodded. "Dai, the Golden Boy, all that smooth-tongued Welsh charm, laced with a dash of calculated stupidity. 'Now then, boy *bach*, let's go back a bit, don't want me to get it wrong, do you?'" Steve had a talent for mimicry. "''Are you sure . . .' Comrade Stringer's getting very cross now. 'These plans you 'andled on the twentieth, is it? Are you sure they were . . .'

'Circuit diagrams,' Comrade Stringer's bleating. 'And it wasn't the twentieth, it was the nineteenth.' 'Oh,' says Dai, 'righto, glad you put me right on that one, boy. Right, so these circuit diagrams you 'andled on the eighteenth, would they be . . .' By the time he's finished, Comrade Stringer's getting very cross, wants Dai to get him pen and paper so he can write it all down before this bonehead Taff can muck it up again."

Morpurgo duly laughed. Sometimes, rumour had it, Steve produced a takeoff of Morpurgo himself, full of outraged references to Us, Them and the sickening superiority of the ruling classes.

"Those dates, the ones you asked me to check on. They don't all tally. Always a drop within a few days of the Stringer female following through on Comrade Stringer's tips. Always a treff within a few days of Comrade Sattin collecting from the drop. But not always a treff following a drop. Are you with me?"

"No."

"Put it another way. When Sattin had goods for shipment, the treff always followed fairly quickly, as we know. But some treffs, I haven't unravelled all this yet, some treffs took place when there'd been no drop, got it?"

"I'd really like to see it written down, the entire sequence in order."

"That's what sequence means," Steve said, preparing to leave. "You'll have to give me a bit more time. Incidentally, we're charging them this afternoon, Chief Superintendent Placket at the London end, Percival down there. What about Sattin?"

"Not before we have a full medical report."

"Why don't you sock it to him?" Steve asked the question as if, instead of full interrogation, no holds barred, he were suggesting a rest cure. "Okay, he's ill. That means his resistance is lower than normal. One good push, now, before any more quacks get in on the act, and he might cave in. Worth a try, Johnny."

Morpurgo hadn't got the easy ruthlessness of people like Steve, who found it perfectly simple to class representatives of extreme political opposition as a sort of inferior life form. They didn't exactly say, 'They're not like you and me, old boy, they haven't got feelings', but that seemed to be the general philosophy.

"No," he said. "Might work, might not, either because it makes him worse or because the Friends start screaming that damaged goods could queer the trade agreement."

Steve clearly thought otherwise. "That's about it, then. See you." He went out, whistling under his breath.

Sibley must have been hovering outside. "Got a minute, sir?"

Who, Morpurgo asked himself, could ever refuse Sibley a minute?

"Pretty well finished, sir," Sibley said. "What I wanted to know is how much time I've got. There's a couple of other things I'm supposed to be getting on with, routine, but still, got to be done."

"Where've you got to?" Morpurgo saw that he would be leaving for Century House with little to show for his hour in the office. "All the dates and times, or is that being optimistic?" Something Steve had just said came back to nag him, but it was like someone scolding from an upstairs room; you were unable to hear the words, you only recognised the tone of the voice.

"Pretty well, sir. It's just a question of organisation now, cause and effect, you might say."

"When do you think you can finish it? I'm off to Century House, then down to The Other Place."

Sibley grinned. "All go, isn't it, sir? I might manage to finish it by this evening, depends. Rather say tomorrow, if that's all right." He hesitated uncertainly. "Mr Archer seeing Stringer again, Mr Morpurgo? If he could do a bit of cross-checking, might help me to sort things out a bit."

Of course! Morpurgo thought he must be going senile. Sibley must have bumped up against the same thing as Steve. Treffs when there'd been no drops. In other words, Sattin and Kagalov meeting to exchange information when there was no information to exchange.

"Mr Archer may still be here. See if you can catch him. He's been verifying dates with Stringer, just what you need, okay? Now, I'm off over the river."

"Okay, sir, will do." Sibley hastened to open the door for Morpurgo. "Funny thing, sir," he went on, falling over his words slightly, as if this were something he had only just decided to say and knew he would have to be sharp about it. "There's a dud encounter report among all that stuff. Funny the weeders haven't spotted it."

"Oh?" Morpurgo, preparing to leave, was only listening with half his mind.

100

"Nothing really, just surprised me a bit. Sergeant Gallup, not like him to make a mistake."

"You're telling me that George Gallup thought he saw Sattin and it wasn't. I find that a bit hard to believe."

"Yes, sir." Sibley dogged Morpurgo down the corridor. "He did, though. The Two Brewers, just off the Euston Road. Should I point it out to the weeders?" The weeders worked in Central Registry, thinning down documentation as it grew bulky, repetitive or outdated. With over three million names on its files, Security Directorate's records were a growth industry.

Morpurgo was more attentive now, but only a little. "Interesting to see what could have fooled Gallup. Tell Registry I want it pulled. I'll sign the chit as soon as I'm back."

"Will do, sir." Sibley went back, happy, having cleared up everything on his conscience. Lucky lad, Morpurgo thought, summoning the lift.

*   *   *

Century House is a raw-looking monolith, twenty storeys of glass and concrete with not one redeeming feature. Close to the Lambeth North Underground station, just south of the Thames and Westminster in one of the poorest and least lovely boroughs of London, it is readily accessible from both the known and secret centres of government but cheaper to run in terms of real estate. Almost any London taxi driver, asked for Century House, is likely to say, "Secret Service? Right you are, guv."

Security Directorate and the Secret Intelligence Service might be said, in a sense, to work hand in glove. If so, the glove was frequently too large, too small, or liable to be for the right hand when the left was the one in need.

And in the case of the SIS it had never been forgotten that the culminating and least bearable consequence of the business that started with Burgess and Maclean and ended – 'Perhaps', Security Directorate was known to mutter – with Philby had been that it was Security Directorate that was authorised to investigate the SIS with a fine-tooth comb and set its house in order. It would be at least a generation before the corrosive bitterness that this humiliation had caused was finally forgotten.

Escorted to a conference room on the fifteenth floor, Morpurgo found himself alone with two senior Friends. One he had met on a number of occasions before, but still knew little about;

the SIS did not encourage inter-service intimacy. This known Friend was a man called Fish, London coordinator of European intelligence activities. The other was Epworth, function unknown.

Fish, dark and squat, smoked long, thin, brown cigarettes that looked like cheroots and weren't. He was full of suppressed energy, with quick movements, sudden jerks of the head and darting of the eyes. He had a talent for building up long, ashy tips on his cigarettes and then, in the act of transferring them to an ashtray, dropping them.

Epworth was a puzzle, his most remarkable feature his unremarkability. Tall, thin and stooped, his thin, fair hair had already retreated sufficiently far from his forehead as to make him look bald from the front. His face was young and old at one and the same time, his manner self-deprecatory. Morpurgo supposed he must be important to attend this meeting, but a *What's My Line* panel, invited to guess his profession, would have homed in on such things as chess playing, stamp collecting – butterflies *much* too active – or the compiling of crossword puzzles for some intellectual weekly.

"Hello," Fish said without much enthusiasm. "The Knights are in camera. We lesser mortals must await their pleasure. Coffee? Help yourself. The biscuits are quasi-edible." Epworth smiled diffidently at Morpurgo, pushing a plate of chocolate biscuits across the table.

Morpurgo took one of the biscuits, discovering too late that the summer sun, streaming in across the dreary South London landscape, had softened the chocolate. It adhered clingingly to his fingers. "I assume we're here just to compare notes at this stage. I'm trying to get some idea of how long the meeting's likely to last."

"Hard to say," Fish told him, "especially when the lords and masters may not appear on time."

"Mmmm." Morpurgo was to learn that this noncommittal sound was the way Epworth prefaced a good many of his remarks. "Two's company, three's none," Epworth finished. He smiled at Morpurgo, a smile that seemed to say: I know. Silly remark.

"Probably right," Fish said. "Any two of them can bitch about the third, but all three together, cramps their style."

Epworth's remark, Morpurgo realised, had not been silly at all. "How goes your little affair?" Fish asked the question casually.

"Oh, chugging along." Morpurgo was, if anything, more casual than Fish. "Mainly routine so far."

"Mmmm," Epworth said again, "has the interrogation started yet?"

"Possibly. Possibly not. I shall know by this afternoon."

"We all hope we're going to be able to sort this one out without any corns being trodden on," Fish said, adding mendaciously, "We appreciate your difficulties."

"Good of you to say so." Morpurgo was beginning to feel like an ecumenical delegate, radically different in dogma but obliged, as his Christian duty, to be meek and charitable.

Before the strain grew too great, the knights arrived.

In the company of Sir Jason and Sir Howard, Morpurgo's knight looked the most innocent, the least likely to be able to hold his own. Sir Jason Bowers, the Dark and Stormy Knight, was larger than life, his jet black hair glossy and abundant, his broad, high-cheeked face shot with the dangerous purple of hot temper and high living. Like Morpurgo's Minister, he was a natural bully, but with less finesse.

Sir Howard Fuller, the Silent Knight, pallid and impenetrable, wielded high power as Cabinet security coordinator. In three decades of changing male fashions he had found himself three times in the avant garde for no better reason that every new suit he ordered was exactly like the one before.

Sir Jason, typically, took charge. "All right, no time to waste, let's get on with it. Simple question, can we split the cake down the middle, no bickering over the crumbs?" He looked at Fish. "Humphrey?"

Humphrey! Morpurgo thought; Humphrey Fish, yes, well!

Fish, dropping more ash, said, "I don't see why not. They're interested in our goods, and of course, they're willing to release theirs. Schnitzler's made contact in Berlin. He's talking in terms of three weeks. That includes getting our goods to Germany for checking and verification before the exchange." Schnitzler was an East German lawyer who had arranged a number of earlier exchanges and was acceptable to both sides.

Sir Howard said, "Berlin?" He wore his hair short, and emitted a faint aroma of bay rum and rectitude.

"Or wherever," Fish amended.

"Which might be?" Sir Howard asked, setting a punishing pace of two questions in four words.

"Helmstedt. Wartha-Herleshausen. A place to be agreed."

"Does it matter, Howard?" Sir Jason opened his innings, with a cheerful display of scorn. "I don't give a damn, so long as we make this exchange with the minimum of delay." Going to use battle tank tactics, Morpurgo realised; plough through the opposition, reverse on his own troops if he has to.

Sir Howard gave no ground. "It matters for the record, Jason. If the PM were to ask the same question, I would prefer not to have to come to you for the answer."

Unabashed, Sir Jason said, "Make a note, Humphrey. Sir Howard is to be kept fully informed."

Epworth, gently, said, "Mmmm, don't think we got an answer to the question."

All three knights looked at him. Sir Jason said, "What *was* the question?"

"Can we agree on the timing?"

Morpurgo was beginning to revise his opinion of Epworth. He might look like a minor public school Latin master, but he had a facility for brevity and directness.

Morpurgo's knight, too, had recognised that fact. "Cakes and crumbs, false analogy," he said briskly. "We're talking, as Mr . . . ?" "Epworth," Epworth said apologetically. ". . . as Mr Epworth has just reminded us, about division of responsibility."

Morpurgo watched Sir Howard react to the last three words like a metal detector to buried danger. Responsibility, or, rather, stubborn and protracted resistance to the very idea of its division, was what any civil servant, particularly a very senior civil servant like Sir Howard, had been reared to as the hippo to the swamp.

"With respect, Sir Hugh," he said, and the formality of the title crackled like thin ice, "the responsibility, the overall responsibility, does not rest with the security services, but with the Prime Minister."

"Absolutely right, Howard." Sir Jason's colour had darkened. "But let's not split hairs. If the responsibility's not divided, it's certainly delegated, some to you, some to Hugh and some to me. The PM would be the first to want to know the reason why, if we didn't do our jobs properly. Now," – His barely restrained aggression loomed over them like a latter-day King Kong – "my responsibility is to free a faithful and valued servant of Her Majesty's government from the hands of her enemies with maximum speed and minimum risk to national security . . ."

"And ours, Jason" – Morpurgo's knight flashed the steel that had earned him his nickname – "is to exploit a Soviet agent to the maximum benefit of state security." He turned his attentions on Sir Howard. "Surely, Howard, you can persuade the Cabinet Secretary to sell that to the PM?"

"Cabinet Secretary doesn't come into it." The Silent Knight became almost voluble. "I am perfectly able to obtain the Prime Minister's approval myself." Unaware that he, too, had been pricked by Sir Hugh's blade, this time in the guise of a suggestion that the Cabinet Secretary had greater influence than his own, he sat back with the air of a man who had resolved matters beyond any possibility of dispute.

"Mmmm." Epworth was again signalling. "Do you think, Sir Jason, that we might discuss actual dates?"

The Dark and Stormy, vaguely aware that he might have been outmanoeuvred, made a fresh assault. "Yes, old boy, dates. All right, we grant you first bite at the cherry, but do you think you could manage it just a wee bit faster than the KGB? Or have they got the edge on you?"

"I'm sure they haven't, sir." Fish slipped in smoothly, Mister Soft to his master's Mister Hard. "I'm sure that Security Directorate has tricks up its sleeve that Moscow Centre would pay good money for."

Morpurgo's knight, all rosy innocence, chuckled. "Can't say I altogether care for the way you put things, Mr – er. Not much we'd stop short of, but trading with Moscow Centre's one of 'em."

Dismayed and delighted, Morpurgo tried not to look at anyone while the ambient temperature plummeted toward zero, all of them reminded of how Philby and his little clique had fled to Moscow to collect rewards in cash and kind. Stepping in quickly, he said, "What we don't get from Sattin inside the month won't be worth having."

It did the trick. "A month!" Fish, suddenly as jerky as a marionette, turned toward Sir Howard. "Moscow Centre's signalling in clear. As soon as possible, or no exchange."

"There's a limit to what you can get from a field agent anyway, Sir Howard." Epworth had dropped his warning *mmmm*. "They work to a cut-out, an intermediary, who tells them what they need to know, nothing more."

"Ah." Sir Howard was back on familiar ground. "The need to know."

"Here's – mmmm – an agent," Epworth said, "who's been in this country for a long time. He may have done one or two home runs, but only to be serviced. What he knows won't really be worth the trouble of extracting." They all looked at Sir Hugh.

"Two problems," Sir Hugh said. "One, the Joint Intelligence Agreement. You want to exchange Sattin. The Cousins have already made a formal application for a share of the goods."

Morpurgo had seen Warren Claas only the previous day. No mention had been made of sharing Sattin. Was his knight trying to pull a fast one?

If so, Sir Jason had swallowed the bait. "Now look," he blustered, "I'm damned if I'm going to leave one of my people at risk for one second longer than is strictly necessary, just because Warren Claas wants his pound of flesh."

As Morpurgo's knight must have known, the Silent Knight needed no prompting. "I feel obliged to point out," Sir Howard said, "that failure to honour an agreement freely entered into with the United States would be viewed with great concern by the Prime Minister."

"So you see," Morpurgo's knight said brightly, "*we* have a claim on the man, CIA has a claim and you, my dear Jason, likewise. All before we come to the second problem. Sattin is a sick man."

His remark had the anticipated effect. Sir Jason interrupted peremptorily. "Sick? What do you mean, sick?" We weren't going to tell, Morpurgo remembered.

The three SIS men listened to the explanation in silence, Fish and Sir Jason barely able to conceal their distrust.

"Our man," Sir Hugh concluded, "is bringing in a specialist. As soon as we know any more, you'll be advised."

Sir Howard had come to a decision. "I propose," he said, "that we adjourn on the understanding that Security Directorate reports back as soon as possible on the state of Sattin's health, and that this meeting be reconvened the moment it becomes possible to prepare a timetable covering the various interests of those concerned, or after seven days, whichever is the sooner."

Having produced what he perceived as a suitably amorphous and consequently acceptable proposition, he placed on it his ultimate imprimatur. "I think I may say that a proposal of this nature would be acceptable to the Prime Minister."

Not long afterwards Epworth, instead of summoning a guard, escorted Morpurgo to the main entrance of Century House himself. At the point of their final separation, Epworth said, "Mmmm." Morpurgo was instantly on guard.

"No question of this illness being a ploy?"

"None at all. We'll have the specialist's report very shortly."

"Strange," Epworth murmured, and then actually giggled, a disarmingly ingenuous sound. "I mean, that he should be taken ill practically as soon as you bring him in. Still, best of luck, anyway." He nodded affably, leaving Morpurgo wondering just where luck was supposed to come into it.

8
Other Places

As he approached the lodge, Cawtrey came out to meet him. The other guard – it would be Gower – stayed inside. They had been advised of his visit and estimated time of arrival. They knew his car and registration number. They would have identified Morpurgo himself with the aid of the binoculars. He was still required to stop.

He rolled down his window. Cawtrey, taking the proffered keys, checked the interior of the car and the boot. "Morning, Mr Morpurgo. Bit of summer at last, sir, not before time neither." Cawtrey took Morpurgo's ID pass into the lodge and fed it into the contraption that checked its continued validity, simultaneously recording his visit and time of arrival. "Okay, Mr Morpurgo, you're expected." Cawtrey slipped the catch on the steel gate and swung it open. Morpurgo drove through. Arriving in the wide gravelled forecourt at the side of the house, he noted that Doc Vickers' car was already there.

The view from the terrace was enchanting, embracing, across wide lawns, almost the whole of a small but exquisite valley. Most of it was grassland, with a small stream running along the bottom, but the facing crest was wooded. The land to the side and rear told a different story; a series of huts and portable cabins that, arriving on a temporary basis – The Other Place, as well as housing Special Unit, was also a training centre – demonstrated the unwritten but universal law that all temporary arrangements tend to become permanent, especially when made by the State. The permanently temporary arrangements at The Other Place were commonly known as Soapbox City.

Turning away, Morpurgo passed under the high Georgian

portico. The house consisted of a main building with two low, symmetrical wings in the Palladian style. Entering, he was faced with a hall of run-down elegance, a fine stairway, dividing to left and right. There was also a Kent fireplace and some rather nice plaster panelling, looking distinctly the worse for wear because the Department of the Environment, nominally responsible for the house's upkeep, was enforcing one of its interminable series of economy drives.

"Nice to see you again, Mr Morpurgo." Matty Wilson pushed the register across the desk for his signature, endorsing it afterwards with her own initials. "Dr Vickers is in the Bin. I think he's with the patient."

Morpurgo headed for the west wing, pressed the button that operated a bell in the day-staff office, and waited under the impartial stare of closed circuit television. Almost immediately, the intercom said, "Come on in, Mr Morpurgo," and a buzzer announced the release of the lock.

Oates had a cigarette drooping below his dark, luxurious Stalin moustache. "Morning, Mr Morpurgo. Come to see Doc Vickers, have you? He's in Number 2."

Morpurgo lingered briefly. "Everything okay? Keeping you busy?" He was wondering whether Vickers had told Oates anything new about Sattin.

"Mustn't grumble," Oates said as if reciting a rule. "Patient's nice and quiet so far, sir." Although a dentist, there was something gentle about him, the kind of man who would be cruel only to be kind. His moustache always presented itself to Morpurgo as part of an enigma, as if Oates were only playing at being Senior Medical Attendant while masterminding some shadowy and more sinister operation elsewhere. Which of course, Morpurgo thought now, he was. Senior Medical Attendant, like the word 'patient', was one of Security Directorate's more euphemistically titled functions.

An electric kettle was just coming to the boil. Standard issue cups and saucers, large and clumsy, with bright blue rims, had been set out. In an open tin cheap biscuits filled the room with a sickly-sweet odour of vanilla.

Accompanying Morpurgo for a short distance down the corridor, Oates bellowed, "Gilly! Gilly! Kettle's boiling, mate. How about making the bloody tea?" Gilligan appeared, stringy, anxious.

"Some bloody char wallah *you* are," Oates told him with mock severity. "*Come* on, dozy! Wakey-wakey! Chop-chop!"

Morpurgo walked on. Number 2 was in the heart of the Bin, no outside windows, only indirect lighting from the night guard's tiny closet. He tried the door, found it unlocked, which was against regulations, and went in. Doc Vickers, his great height a fresh surprise every time one saw him, looked round from his position by the bed. Andy Vickers was six feet, seven inches in his stockinged feet. He made a gesture of silence, came toward the door. Morpurgo stood back to let him through. People in general tended to stand back and let Vickers through. He steered Morpurgo into the night guard's office. The one-way glass of the windows looked out on Number 1 and Number 2. It had a pattern, part decorative, part functional, of vertical silver stripes. They gave the impression of a stainless steel prison. Through the window on to Number 2, Morpurgo could see the bed. It held a hunched-up figure.

Vickers increased his fearsome size by hoisting himself up on the built-in table below the window, from which he towered tremendously. "Bloody bogeys have come," he announced to the world in general. "Carrion crow, spots trouble a mile off. Well, not going to push my patient around."

"What's up? Is he worse or something?"

"Worse? Than what? No better, if that's what you mean. How bad is something you'll just bloody well have to wait for." Before leaving the army, Andy Vickers had been offered the medical equivalent of desk jobs at such military bastions as Aldershot, Warminster and Catterick. "Too much bullshit, sahib. Too many bloody colonels on too many high bloody horses."

He had finally accepted the post of MO in a hush-hush outfit, his own boss. Not too much work, most of it routine, but just occasionally something a bit more interesting, a fracture or two, the occasional sickness that had to be nursed in privacy, a foreign-accented gent to be given a careful once-over.

And, of course, a decent little bar. Andy Vickers was unmarried, as much from choice as the shortage of six feet, seven inch women. He liked shooting, fishing, an occasional round of golf, but none of it was properly arranged unless it could be thought over, better still, talked over, in a decent little bar with one or two decent chaps who knew a variety of esoteric but interesting things, travelled to and from an unusual number of outlandish dumps, were obliged to chance their arm in a tight spot now and then and, above all, could, especially after a few noggins, be entertaining without blabbing their bloody heads off.

Today he had Morpurgo, who had come to see about yet another foreign gent sent into the country for a rest cure. He beamed down on Morpurgo from his commanding height. "Already told you, wasting your time today."

"What do you mean?" Morpurgo demanded, "already told me."

Vickers gazed on him first in puzzlement and then dismay. "Oh lordy-lord, clean forgot to ring. Miss Otis regrets she's unable to lunch today."

"I can't talk to him? You said he was no worse."

"Can't talk to him?" The idea clearly struck Doc Vickers as highly comical. "Oh yes! Yes indeed! Didn't think to tell me that when you shot him down here day before yestere'en, did you? Not a word, not one solitary dickybird, didn't think to warn me about that, did you? My job to look him over, that was your gist, sahib. So that's what I do. The tovarich hasn't said anything so far, mind, just sits there looking at me looking at him, not so much as a nod or a wink, don't know exactly what you want, my friend, but whatever it is, you're bloody well going to have to work for it.

"Wasn't until I was underway that I tumbled. Think about it! Like examining a deaf mute. Only I'd get more from a deaf mute in five minutes than I'd get from your boy in a lifetime. Say ninety-nine! Nothing. Say *ah!* Nothing. No bloody thing, see what I'm getting at? Where does it hurt then? Nowhere, least-ways, that's what I'd have to think if I rely on this merchant. All right, don't always get a patient's cooperation. Knocked out. In a coma. Shut himself up in his attic and thrown away the key. But *nothing*. He's there, oh yes indeed, he's *there* all right, but not at home, thank you. Won't give out. Won't say boo. Won't say nutt'n.

"Seriously, sahib, bloody tricky! Like being back at Barts, finals, sweating over some bloody-minded volunteer patient, certain it's either mild indigestion or terminal cancer of the bowel but not sure which, old Praise-Be-To-God Thixton sitting there sneering openly and looking at his bloody watch every five seconds."

"Did you come up with anything? You must have, or you wouldn't have called in the specialist."

"Couldn't find much wrong in the obvious places. Probably put off by non-cooperation, like being honorary MO to a Trappist Monastery. And then, *aha!*" He snapped his fingers with the sound of an oak shedding a branch, then tapped several times against his broken-veined nose. "Routine check, glands and lymph system, duffer couldn't have missed it. Nodes in neck hard as bullets. Followed my fingers around, one or two things I didn't care for, and couldn't ask the tovarich a single bloody question. Feel fagged out most of the time? Temperature jump about a bit now and then, touch of fever? Get the sweats in the night? Oh yes, and booze! Knocked it off? *Had* he knocked it off?"

Baffled, Morpurgo said, "If he went into a pub, which wasn't often, he drank soft drinks."

Vickers nodded as if pleased. "Could have told *you* that, once I got the old grey stuff working properly. Sink a shot of the hard stuff, nasty pains in various places, quick as a flash."

"So?"

Vickers gazed benevolently down on Morpurgo. "Old faker like me, not supposed to be able to tell Hodgkin's disease from housemaid's knee, got to put up a decent front when I call in an expert."

"Is that what it is?" Morpurgo asked, still uncertain. "Hodgkin's disease?"

"That's what I think. That's what old Tiddleywinks thinks. Now we do tests, sahib." He leaned forward persuasively. "Now you've come, stop to lunch, I hope?"

"Doubt it, doc, there's a deskful of paperwork waiting for me back there. Now, be serious, what's Hodgkin's disease? Is it serious?"

"Not the sort of thing you'd want to see on your family doc's certificate when he tells you you'd better stay off work a while."

"How long?" Morpurgo was beginning to feel worried. "Time's precious. I want to talk to him."

"Talk! Didn't you hear me? Hasn't said one bloody word since he arrived."

"I said talk *to* him. Say a few things that might bring his voice back. Doc, I need him. I'm under pressure. If I tell my Director-General we've got to wait until you quacks make up your minds,

112

he'll go through the roof." Not to mention, Morpurgo thought, all the Friends, Cousins and everyone else. "Damn it, we haven't even shoved him in front of a magistrate yet."

"Here he is. Here he stays. Bring your magistrate here. Won't be the first time you've had to."

That was true, but hardly the point. Within three days, Sattin had become politically important. Waiting to roll was machinery to which he was as essential as lubricating oil. He said, "Can we have him while you're doing your tests, shared time? There's more dependent on this than you realise."

"Nope. Have to find someone else to play with."

Morpurgo lost his temper. "Christ, doc! This isn't a bloody football match, send on a substitute!" Later, thinking back, Morpurgo decided that this must have been the beginning of everything, the idea sculling around in his brain ever since his last meeting with Sibley. But at this moment, claustrophobically enclosed with Vickers, he continued with what was in the forefront of his mind. "I can override you. You know it. He's in full possession of his faculties. He's been leading a normal life for the past nine months or more. Damn it, he can even talk. It's just that he chooses not to."

Vickers looked down at him sadly. "Listen, sahib. We *think* he's got Hodgkin's. We don't know, not for sure. It's in your interest to know, as well as ours. Tell you something else, didn't pop up overnight, been around a long time." He propelled Morpurgo gently out into the corridor. "Tell you another thing. Someone in his state is open to bacterial infection, could kill him. No immunologically effective response, makes him a sitting duck for anything that's going. If you want your boy to be of any use to you at all, my advice, Johnny, is to leave him alone until we see what we can do for him."

Morpurgo felt like a man in a car crash; one moment sailing blithely along, the next, disaster. "Can he be cured?"

"Look, Johnny, don't pretend I know all the answers. Had to go away and look it up when I found those little lumps. Cured? Depends what you mean. Halted, possibly, cured, simply can't say without the tests. Radiology. Careful examination of tissues, ditto bone marrow, all takes time. *No* way to hurry it, *none*. Absolutely *none*," and with each negative he patted Morpurgo heavily on the shoulder. "Come and have a snort," he said hopefully. "Snort and a chinwag."

Suddenly the country had lost its charm for Morpurgo. The country was doubt and disease. Rejecting it, his mind was preoccupied with the search for anything that might compensate for this present disaster.

"No," he said. "I'd like to see him anyway, if it's all the same to you."

"See him?" Doc Vickers looked at him doubtfully. "Could say no, right? What can you get from seeing him?"

"Probably nothing. But I'd still like to."

"Harbouring any pathogens? No tame strep, no naughty virus?" Vickers was still in half a mind to deny access to the man for whom the word patient had ceased to be a euphemism and become a fact.

Vickers spun Morpurgo round with one great hand. "Coming in with you, Johnny, so don't start prodding." He unlocked the door and they both went in. Morpurgo nudged Vickers, nodding at the door. With a guilty look on his face, Vickers locked it behind him. "Never remember," he admitted. "Still, this bloke's not going anywhere."

Sattin lay on his side, legs straight, head pressed into the pillow. His eyes were closed, but as Morpurgo and Vickers reached the bedside, they opened. For a second their gazes locked. Morpurgo had a strong feeling that Sattin was trying to read his thoughts, that he was questing for something he hoped or feared to find. Then the gaze shifted to Vickers, and from Vickers to no one.

Morpurgo said, "Still not talking?" There was not so much as a flicker of an eyelid in response.

"Seems you're not in very good shape," Morpurgo said. "Well, we'll sort you out, the proper medical treatment. After that, we'll see." He was saying things with no real thought behind them, mechanical remarks that enabled him to go on looking, assessing, almost measuring; printing as much detail on his mind as his eyes could record. "Yes," he said after what must have seemed a particularly long silence, "we'll do whatever's necessary. We're not inhuman. We have standards."

This time Sattin's head turned. Their eyes met once more and there was something in Sattin's gaze that Morpurgo found difficult to meet. He drew a deep, deep breath as if, up to that point, he had been living only upon what was already in his lungs, a diver, superoxygenated to prolong submersion. In Sattin's depths

114

he read an awareness that was as plain as if he had spoken, but if there had actually been words, Morpurgo knew that he would not have understood them. Sattin's eyes closed. He turned himself away with no more noise than the rustle of the bedclothes.

Morpurgo, too, turned away. Vickers locked the door behind them. "Well," he said with no trace of satisfaction, "now you know." He set off down the corridor.

"Catch you in a tick," Morpurgo said. "Call to make." He turned into the little pharmacy and asked PBX for London.

He was in luck, catching Sibley on the point of going out to lunch. He explained what he wanted. Sibley understood instantly. "Make a start on it now, sir. What time will you be back?"

"Two, thereabouts. Before you start, do something about lunch. The job will wait that long."

"Don't worry about me, sir. Proper old camel, I am, go for days on my hump."

"You may have to," Morpurgo smiled, grateful for the chance. "So go and top it up, there's a good lad." He rang off and went to look for Doc.

Vickers had disappeared. Oh well, Morpurgo thought, peering into his office, get on my way, stop at a pub for a beer and a sandwich. There were two books, open and face down on the desk. He picked up the nearer one, its title *Lymphomas*.

He glanced at the page at which it was open, part of an introductory chapter. Words with only hazy meaning came successively to his attention . . . *neoplastic disorder . . . primarily in the cell-mediated arm of the immune system . . . risk of enhancement from infection . . . interference with normal control systems.*

He grasped, belatedly, the fact that it concerned Sattin's illness. What on earth was a neoplastic disorder? He went on, skimming . . . *superclavicular or mid-cervical nodes . . . spread by blood vessels and lymphatics . . . spread not random.*

Once again, just words. Then one of them leaped out at him, plain, understandable . . . *terminal.* Hearing footsteps returning down the long corridor, he raced on . . . *terminal form may be characterised by general malaise, sweating, fatigue, loss of appetite, wasting and irregular pyrexia . . . depressed renal function.*

Yes, but what? Lymphoma, Hodgkin's disease? But what *was* lymphoma? His fingers shuffled the pages impatiently.

Finally . . . *abnormal tissue growth . . . tumour . . . cancerous . . .*

Cancerous.

He had just sufficient time to lay the book down more or less as he had found it. "Ah, there you are. Thought I must have locked you in with the tovarich by mistake. Now, what about that noggin?"

No, he heard himself saying, got to be off, pressure of work, things to be done, blah-blah-blah.

*   *   *

"John," Claas said, "this is Pierre Weber. Pierre, John Morpurgo."

"Glad to know you, John." Weber's voice was soft, warm, suggesting a sensitivity that Morpurgo never found in Warren Claas. His face gave Morpurgo an impression of sadness and weary resignation, instantly dispelled by his attractive, almost shy smile.

"Pierre's the guy I was telling you about," Claas said. "No direct responsibilities yet, just a look and learn situation." He flung himself into his chair and put his feet on the desk, displaying inches of hairy calf above dark blue socks with a pattern of crimson stars. "You went to see Sattin, right? What can you tell us today?"

"Nothing new." Sooner or later, Claas would have to know, but not yet.

"And Kagalov?" Claas asked. "Do you have anything for us in that area? For instance, do you . . ."

"Let's suppose he does." Weber's eyes were almost closed, his head back as if he were on the verge of dozing off. His voice was quiet, almost diffident, but Claas stopped abruptly. Morpurgo began to consider Weber in a different light.

"And let's suppose," Weber went on in his mild tone, "he doesn't want to tell us." He opened his eyes, looking toward Morpurgo. He could have been secretly amused or secretly impatient. "Why should he? There's a whole lot we're not telling him."

"Okay," Claas said after a momentary pause. "So we've been in a huddle with the Friends. No, let's get it right this time, they went into a huddle with us."

"You mean they asked for a meeting?" Fish, Morpurgo decided, Humphrey Fish; though he didn't know why.

"The reason," Claas said, "was supposed to be to talk us out of any claim we have on Sattin. I mean, that's what they said."

116

"But it wasn't."

"It wasn't. Sure, they'd like us to waive our rights, but they just happened to let it drop that you have other reasons for wanting to hold on to Sattin. Like, for instance, he's taken a vow of silence."

"He isn't the first to do that," Morpurgo said.

"No. And he won't be the last. Think you'll persuade him to change his mind?"

Fishing expedition? Morpurgo wondered. Or did they know the rest? Did they know about lymphomas? Or that it might be terminal? Imminent and inevitable death could be a powerful ally to a man trying to resist strong persuasion to talk.

"Listen, John," Weber said in his quiet, reasonable voice. "We're not trying to shaft you on this one. If we were, we wouldn't be so direct. We didn't go to the Friends, they came to us. And here we are now, telling you all about it."

"Did they tell you anything else?"

"That he might be sick," Claas said guardedly.

"He's sick."

"How sick? What with?" Claas was not a man to ask elliptical questions.

"Let's say he's got more than a head cold."

"Will he recover?" It didn't surprise Morpurgo that it was Weber who asked the key question.

"No reason to suppose otherwise." Not yet.

Claas came in again with his sledgehammer. "Will there be anything left to trade with?"

"Not our concern, is it?"

"Does he know?" Weber's eyes had closed again, but his mind was clearly very open.

It was a hell of a good question, Morpurgo saw, and one which he had not, so far, asked himself. "He knows he's sick." But how sick?

"It has to be fairly recent, doesn't it? Weber's mental processes were something Morpurgo was prepared to give time to. "I mean they're not going to use a sick man on a job like this, a long-term job. Not if they knew he was sick to begin with."

"No."

"When will you know?" Claas asked. "Know what the guy's got?"

Morpurgo shrugged. "A question of tests."

"If Moscow Centre gets to know," Weber said very carefully, "it might change a lot of things. There *and* here." What Weber meant, principally, was: *Would* Moscow Centre get to know? Because if they did, someone would have to have told them.

Weber said gently, "I'd like you to know we understand. Don't forget we've had them, moles. Guys at the top, too. Some of them we gave the bum's rush, some of them quit."

"Let me tell you one thing." Morpurgo said. "There'll be no cover-up where I'm concerned."

There was a brief silence. Then Weber uncoiled himself, smiling his pothook smile that went down at one end, up at the other. He held out a hand. "Good of you to come. I want you to know we appreciate it. I'll look forward to working with you." His hand was dry and cool, with just the right amount of pressure.

"Call on us," Claas said. "For whatever."

Morpurgo released Weber's hand. The scene was becoming emotional. He had no intention of working for the CIA. He looked for hidden hostility in Claas's gaze, without finding it. So what?

Claas took Morpurgo down, talking only about the weather. When he came back he shut the door with slow, exaggerated care. "Well?"

"Looks good."

Claas nodded. "If we're never far from Morpurgo, we'll never be far from the action."

"But you don't like him."

"Not too much."

"Love-hate?"

"Too strong. Call it like-dislike. Sort of okay-well-maybe."

Weber looked up. "Screwing him on Kagalov would be the trick all right."

Claas nodded. "What I told you," but he sounded uneasy.

"What's up?" Weber gave Claas his full attention.

"We have to watch our step," Claas said. "For my money, Moscow would get a hell of a lot more mileage out of a substantiated accusation that we spy on our allies than a whole raft of other things."

"Sure we spy on them," Weber said comfortably. "Just as they spy on us. Anyway, relax. We know it. Langley's not solid bone, it just gives that impression."

"What if it came out?"

"I said relax! Poppa's *pleased*! Hey, you're certainly right about the Friends. His face when we said we'd been talking with them!"

"You'll see that every time you mention one to the other. Especially the Friends."

"So if Morpurgo fell in the poop, they wouldn't come running to help."

"Too busy looking for more poop for him to fall in. They got a big charge out of forcing him to grab Sattin before he was ready. He has two strikes against him; one, he's Security Directorate, two, he's Morpurgo and a self-proclaimed pinko."

"How's the outside job going?"

"Snippets," Claas said cautiously. "Look, this whole area is delicate."

"You're using a British national. Do you think I've lost my touch?"

Claas was relieved. "It's just that telling could have embarrassed you if you didn't want to know. Especially as we turned up something that Morpurgo's people missed."

"Like?"

"Like Sattin had these occasional bouts of fever. Never lasted more than a day or so, but he woud stay in bed until they were over."

"Doctor?"

"Uh-uh. Not even an aspirin or whatever, just carried on until things were too much for him, then a day in bed. Just a day, then he was okay again."

"Periodicity?"

"No idea, not yet anyway." Claas keyed his secretary. "Cindy-Lou, how about some coffee and cookies?" He returned his attention to Weber. "I may as well tell you, we got a lucky break on this. Our guy happened to get acquainted with the man in the flat opposite Sattin's. Security Directorate had questioned him, of course, well, Special Branch anyway, but he only told them what they asked for. Our guy got something he didn't ask for, something this feller didn't think was important himself."

"The fevers?"

"The fevers. Saw the milk hadn't been picked up this one time, Sattin's, that is. Knew he was home, got to wondering, called in to see if he was all right."

"And Sattin told him about fevers."

"That's it."

Weber closed his eyes. "Interesting. Any suggestions?"

"No. Not yet."

"Security Directorate have any?"

"Don't know," Claas said, wooden-faced. "Haven't got around to asking them yet."

'That's my boy." Weber began to chuckle. Claas's wooden look splintered. They were both laughing when Cindy-Lou, a matronly woman with blue hair, came in with coffee and cookies. "You boys!" she said, laughing a little herself. "I just *know* it's something dirty."

*   *   *

Sibley, waiting for Morpurgo when he returned, was pleased with himself.

"Okay." Morpurgo settled himself. "Let's hear what you've got."

"The works," Sibley said.

Morpurgo sat up straight. "You actually found him, the ringer?"

Sibley's face fell before he realised that Morpurgo was joking. "No," he said. "But I don't think it would take too long."

He motioned Sibley to a seat.

"The pub, the Two Brewers, where the false ID was made, that was where I decided to start. Then I remembered it was Sergeant Gallup who made the miss. Before I went to the pub I rang the Yard to see if I could catch him. And I did, lucky really, he was just going out."

"What could he give you that wasn't in his report?"

"Ah, yes, but that's it, sir. There was something he hadn't put in his report. The thing is, he *knew* it was a false ID. He rang through from the pub to Sergeant Ramble on Bowman SV control. Ramble told George he couldn't have seen Sattin because Sattin was at home in bed."

"In bed? What time was all this?"

"Oh, sorry, sir, should have said. Lunchtime."

"And Sattin was in bed?"

"That's right, sir. As I was saying, Sergeant Gallup knew it wasn't Sattin, soon as he phoned his report in. Ramble told him so. Sergeant Gallup told me he'd had it booked anyway, just to be on the safe side."

"So it was a good likeness."

"Spitting image, that's what Sarge Gallup says, gave him quite a shock. And he gave me something else to go on. This double of Sattin's, seems he was in company. Another man, drinking friend, he reckons. Remembers him very well, calls him a sporty gent, check jacket, suede boots, regimental sort of tie. George Gallup got his name."

"Sattin's double's name?"

Sibley took a quick look at his notebook. "Trigg, sir. Eustace Roland Trigg." Sibley beamed at Morpurgo as if he had just pulled Trigg himself out of a hat.

Morpurgo was impressed. "Good work all round. Pity Gallup didn't get the other chap's name too."

"Not really, sir, not the way things turned out."

Morpurgo found himself smiling. Sibley's pleasure was infectious. "All right. You've been a clever boy, so let's have it."

"Yes, sir. Well, Sergeant Gallup gave me such a good description, I reckoned I ought to be able to pick this guy out practically in the dark."

"The Two Brewers! Good God!" Morpurgo was beginning to get Sibley's drift. "You're going to tell me you actually saw . . ."

"The double? No, sir. Wish I had. Next best thing, though. The sporty gent was there."

"Is there more?" A fantasy that had begun to emerge during Morpurgo's visit to The Other Place, standing at Sattin's bedside, was, incredibly, taking on flesh.

"Yes, sir. Sporty gent's name is Joliffe. Works in a big office block, just round the corner from the Brewers. Assistant office manager." Sibley sat back proudly, a man who had not only discovered a living dodo but trapped it and brought it home.

"All right." Morpurgo made no attempt to disguise his pleasure. Sibley deserved that much. "How did you do it?"

"Easy, sir." It was another of the incomparable Sibley's virtues that he made no attempt to magnify any difficulties he had overcome. "Just tagged along when he left, sir. Went into his work place, I followed straight behind. Receptionist said, 'Afternoon, Mr Joliffe', just like that. So I just pretended I wanted directions. Then I rang the firm, asked the switchboard to tell me Mr Joliffe's initials and title, 'cause I had this business matter I wanted to write him about." He held out his notebook. "All in here, sir."

121

"Ian," Morpurgo said, "if you're not careful, we shall have to promote you."

"Now for the bad news, sir."

"Tell me you've just shot the Director-General. I'll think of extenuating circumstances."

"The other job, sir, checking the encounter reports. Do my best to finish it tomorrow, sir. One or two points to check with Mr Archer first."

"Tomorrow, next day. I have the utmost confidence in you."

"Yes, sir. Will that be all, sir?"

"For God's sake," Morpurgo begged, "don't start using expressions like that, or I shall soon be calling you Jeeves." Before Sibley could leave, Morpurgo remembered something. "As a matter of interest, how far *have* you got with the SV reports?"

"Pulled everything out, sir. Check a couple of things with Mr Archer, like I said, then it's just a question of getting it all on one sheet."

"Were there other times when Sattin spent a day in bed?"

"More than one, yes, sir. Can't remember how many. I was looking at drops and treffs, didn't bother too much about anything else."

"Would it be too much trouble to ask you to plot those too, the days he spent in bed?"

Sibley looked relieved. "Easy. Thought you were going to ask me more, breakdown of routine, that sort of thing."

"You shouldn't have said that."

"Sir?"

"Breakdown of routines. Would it be a lot to ask for?"

"It's all right, sir. Only joking. No problem."

"Ashamed," Morpurgo said, "that's what I am. Instead of Jeeves, I reckon I'll call you The Admirable Sibley, not that it isn't an insult to compare you to a couple of bloody butlers."

9
Eustace Roland

Joliffe was ticking off a filing clerk when Mr Travis rang.

"Joliffe," Mr Travis said, "come up. A little matter you may be able to assist with."

"Right away, Mr Travis." Joliffe pushed back his chair. "Off you trot then, Doreen. And, don't forget, pink for a little boy, *and* in chronological order." He headed Traviswards, ignoring the lifts in order to mount by the echoing, little-used stairway, two steps at a time.

Outside Travis's office on the directors' floor, he smoothed down his hair and jacket, adjusted the knot of his regimental tie, and waited for the old ticker to settle down, before knocking.

"Morning, Joliffe." Mr Travis was grey, self-important, with a nose for non-existent conspiracy. "Joliffe, this is Mr Morpurgo from Scotland Yard."

"Morning, sir," Joliffe said, and was surprised when Morpurgo left his seat to shake him by the hand.

"Good of you to spare your time," Morpurgo said.

Flustered, Joliffe returned the handshake overvigorously. "Not a bit, sir. Never met anyone from the Yard, don't mind me saying so. Makes you wonder if you've been nabbed for something or other, certainly hope not, ha!"

Morpurgo was unzipping a briefcase. "A little enquiry, that's all."

"Ha!" Joliffe grabbed joyfully at the cliché. "Helping the police with their enquiries, right?" Catching a look from Travis that was less than approving, he gabbled on. "Do my best, always do, course, can't ask for more, can you? Where was I on the night

123

of the twenty-fourth, something like that? Ha! Ha-ha! Sorry, you were saying?"

Morpurgo had produced a number of photographs, large, glossy. "Mind taking a look at these?"

Joliffe, his curiosity aroused, took them toward the window, less for the better light than to make things more trying for Travis. As he looked at the first print, his eyebrows rose. After the second, he said, "Well, I'll be . . . !" and then, "*Good* lord!" He shuffled through the remainder.

"Recognise someone?" Morpurgo glanced at Travis. "A matter of identification, Mr Travis. I didn't want to lose any effect by saying so in advance."

Travis, sourly, said, "Quite! Quite! Don't mind me. Carry on."

"Recognise someone?" Joliffe echoed. "Certainly do! Trigger, old Trigger! Once seen, never forgotten, what we used to say. Ha! Ha-ha! I should say so!"

"Trigger," Morpurgo repeated. "We're talking about the same man, of course? Broad, rather squat, not much hair? The other man isn't important." Not much he isn't, he thought wryly, since the other man was Kagalov.

Belatedly, a thought occurred to Joliffe. "Taken secretly, were they? Telephoto lens and all that? Well, well, well! Real deep 'un, that's what we used to say, real deep 'un, old Trigger."

Morpurgo took back the photographs. "Let me make this quite clear, the point of this enquiry is to eliminate your friend. Identify and eliminate him." He motioned Joliffe to a chair. Joliffe took it, carefully avoiding Travis's increasingly acidulous gaze. He had never sat down in Travis's office before. Old Travis, feeling a bit out of it, he thought. Too bad! Ha! Ha-ha!

"Now," Morpurgo said. "Is it all right if I ask a few questions, Mr Travis?"

Travis made an expansive gesture which was distinctly at variance with his mouth and eyes. "Please. You have your duty to perform."

Pompous ass! Morpurgo thought, turning back to Joliffe. "Now, let's start at the beginning. You call him Trigger. What's his full name?"

"Name's Trigg. Eustace Roland Trigg. Did his national service with my mob, back in the fifties. Queer sort of bloke, I can tell you."

"Trigg, Eustace Roland." Morpurgo smiled. "Trigger, of course. Quite sure this is him?"

"Absolutely pos. Funny old world it is, isn't it? Only a couple of months or so since – bumped into him, first time since I came back to Civvy Street. Recognised him straight away. Same now, those piccies. Once seen, never forgotten. Ha! Got himself mixed up in something, has he? No, sorry, asked you that before. Confidential and all that, right?"

Looking at Joliffe's amiable face, weak and complaisant, Morpurgo shook his head, smiling. "Not really. It's the other one we're interested in. Connections."

Joliffe nodded knowingly. "Connections. Won't ask any more questions, mum's the word, right?"

"And your last meeting was accidental?" Morpurgo wondered how long it would be before it occurred to Joliffe to wonder how his accidental meeting with Trigg had become official knowledge.

"Absolutely!"

"Ah." Morpurgo nodded wisely. "*That's* how you came into the picture." It explained nothing but it would do. "And you had a drink together, talked about old times?"

"About the size of it," Joliffe agreed.

"Lives in London?" This was the crunch.

"Trigger!" Joliffe's reaction was instantaneous. "Not Trigger! Not old Trigger, oh no! Why, the *amazing* thing is that he comes here at all. Cleethorpes, that's where Trigger lives, man and boy as they say. Ha! Ha-ha! London? Let me tell you, old man, London's not a *patch* on Cleethorpes!" Belatedly aware that he had just, to Travis's evident disapproval, called this authoritative-looking copper 'old man', Joliffe hastened to retail the story of how Trigg became part of the regimental legend.

"Cleethorpes." Travis could no longer tolerate his spectator role. "Somewhere on the east coast, I rather fancy. Adjacent to Hull. Or do I mean Grimsby?"

"Yorkshire, Lincolnshire, never quite sure." Trigger's was a joke with universality, applicable to any back-of-beyond, Sticksville dump in the two hemispheres.

"Rather fancy they call it Humberside these days," Morpurgo said vaguely. "What does he do in the way of work?"

"Work?" Joliffe went blank, as if Trigg and the concept of work were incompatible. Then he brightened, giving a little chortle. "You're not going to believe this."

"Try me."

"Rock!" Joliffe looked triumphant. "From his own lips. Old Trigger's in rock."

"Are we" – Travis made a second attempt to enter the conversation – "talking of rock and roll?"

"I'm in rock, Mr Joliffe." Joliffe, carried away, ignored Travis. "Rock! In Cleethorpes! Completely bowled me over. Then" – Joliffe made quick dismissive movements of his hand – "gone. Cheerio! Nice to see you! Not a bit of it! Just gone, not even time to ask whether he sings or plays the guitar."

Morpurgo, too, was making movements of departure. "I'm very grateful, Mr Travis, for your valuable time. And to Mr Joliffe for some very useful information. Incidentally, I'd be obliged if you would keep this whole business to yourselves."

"I think you may rely on us to be discreet," Travis said with a meaningful look at Joliffe.

"Likewise," Joliffe said. "Still think a lot about the old mob, wouldn't like old Trigger to think I'd been telling tales out of school."

Morpurgo left, photographs under his arm. Taken over a period of months, they were all excellent likenesses, not of Eustace Roland Trigg but Joseph Sattin.

*　　*　　*

"Cleethorpes!" The Knight looked as astounded as if Morpurgo had just performed the one-handed clap of Zen. "Are you out of your mind, Johnny? The craziest thing I ever heard!"

"My weekend. What I do with it is my affair."

"What do you want? Just a yes?"

"Not even that. Or you could give me a chit for a chopper."

The Knight took a deep breath. "Where's the bloody chit? Don't tell me you haven't got it with you."

Morpurgo produced it.

The Knight scribbled his signature. "Get out. You're mad. We're all mad."

"Diminished responsibility?" Morpurgo tucked away his transport requisition. "Qualification for the job, isn't it?"

*　　*　　*

The helicopter flight was enjoyable. They flew low, around two thousand feet. Even the towns, from the air, had their new, raw edges cauterised and moderated by soft sunlight and the invisible veil of exhalations from green and growing things. Perhaps, Morpurgo thought, two thousand feet above reality, Sylvie and me, if we moved to the country . . .?"

His pilot, middle-aged, taciturn for most of the trip, broke silence as they reached the Lincoln Wolds, dropping, steep-sided, to the coastal plain. "Flight deck of the unsinkable aircraft carrier." He jabbed a downward finger. "Keep your eyes peeled, skip. You'll see ghosts."

Morpurgo saw what he meant. As they racketed north and east, the archaeological remains of flying fields that, during the war, had sent their Halifaxes, Lancasters and Fortresses in ever growing numbers to pound Nazi Germany, became so numerous that, at one stage, Morpurgo could see four at once among the fields and hedgerows of the fertile farmlands. And not all were dead; their flight path took them successively close to Phantoms and Tornadoes, parked at the ready against the nuclear red alert.

Finally, with the great estuary of the Humber a silver trumpet flaring into the North Sea between the coastal lowlands of North and South Humberside, the sizeable conurbation of Grimsby and Cleethorpes, came into sight. So, too, did their destination. "North Thoresby," the pilot shouted. "Another ghost field. Watch out for Blenheims and Wellingtons." He put down so lightly that Morpurgo was unable to detect the actual moment of contact. The rented car booked by Sibley was waiting.

"Any idea how long you'll be, skip?"

"Hours. Weeks. Forever." Morpurgo grinned. For a short time he was free of the necessity to dance to the tunes of other pipers. "The fact is, I don't know. What's the arrangement?"

"Going over to RAF Binbrook. Only a few miles away. Something to eat, couple of beers if I'm lucky, get this old egg-beater checked and refuelled." He gave Morpurgo a neatly typed strip of paper. "Give me a ring when you're about to leave the town. I'll be here as soon as you are. Another passenger, is that right?"

"If I come back by myself," Morpurgo told him, "the mission's a washout."

The address Sibley had turned up for him was not far from the seafront, a long, straight road with interwar houses and

127

bungalows neat behind their neat gardens on both sides. The house itself was somewhat larger than most, a solid, self-important structure of red brick, heavily enclosed by shrubbery. To add to its somewhat oppressive assurance, old-fashioned roller blinds of faded green were drawn across the downstairs windows as protection, Morpurgo supposed, from the fierce sunlight of this land of far horizons and huge skies.

Before he could ring, the door opened to reveal a woman of perhaps sixty years. She was clad in black, at least three decades out of fashion, with the faint sheen that comes from repeated brushing.

She was small, slight and feverish, face pinched, nose twitchy with nervous excitement. As a final touch of strangeness, she wore black lace gloves with long sleeves that vanished up the too short arms of her costume jacket.

"By, you've left it late, you have," she whispered, northern accent stretching the vowel of 'late'. "You'd best go straight there." Her breath smelled strongly of cheap sherry.

"Is Mr Trigg at home?"

"I told you. They've gone. You've got a car, I see. You'll do it in five minutes, easy. Do you know where it is?"

Morpurgo shook his head.

"Well I'll tell you then, but you'd best hurry, don't want to be late. She's the one who's late." She tittered. "The late Mrs Trigg, like. By! It's not bad, that isn't, is it?"

Revelation came to Morpurgo. "Oh, look," he said, "I'm not family."

"Course you're not." She giggled again; it was definitely the sherry. "Don't have to tell me that, sticks out a mile. From down south, are you, London way? You don't want to worry, there'll be only a handful there."

"Perhaps," Morpurgo suggested, still not sure precisely who it was that had died, "it would be better if I came back later."

"Nay!" She dismissed the idea instantly. "You've come, so you'll go, he'll expect it. Anyroad, no telling what he'll be up to now he's off the leash. Now, listen while I tell you." She gave him directions, insisting that he repeated them twice before she ˇvas satisfied.

"Got it," she said mockingly. "By! They must be quick where you come from. You'll not get far here, though, if you go around asking for *pabs*. *Pabs* you may have in London but round here they're *pubs*," detonating the blunt last vowel with all the explosive power of derision and brown sherry.

Morpurgo said, "Thank you very much."

"Thank you very match." She screeched with pleasure. "A match is for footballers. A match is for smokers. A good match is what he could make but won't, things being what they are and always have been. Now then, off you go, left, right, left, you had a good job and you left. Don't just stand there gawping, get a move on."

Driving off, Morpurgo's inclination was to abandon his efforts as the forlorn hope they had been from the start. Reaching the seafront with its long, gardened promenades, something in the quality of the light, the gold of the exposed sands, the blue of the enormous sky made him change his mind. He went up a hill that gave him a six- or seven-mile view across the estuary mouth to the long, low point of Spurn with its lighthouse, made the last of the series of turns he had been given, and came, as predicted, almost at once upon a pub called the Fisherman's Arms. Nosing down a narrow street at its side, he emerged on the dusty open space of a demolition site.

He was clearly in the oldest part of the town; narrow streets and alleyways, back-to-back houses with tiny gardens in which, variously, were lines of drying laundry, a small boat on trestles and a crudely-made weathervane in the form of a man endlessly cranking a propellor at the urging of the breeze.

Parked on the wasteland was an enormous and old-fashioned hearse that challenged the glitter of the day, in it a simple coffin with a few sprays of summer flowers. Two others cars, black and shiny as a squaddy's toe-caps, waited nearby. Their drivers, together with four men in black, ill-fitting suits, stood smoking and talking in artificially hushed voices. One of them indicated that he could leave his car behind theirs. He went uncertainly toward the house. The helpful driver, in the flat, brash tones of the region, service without servility, called, "Just step inside, lad, they'll not bite you." Morpurgo stepped in.

After the summer glare, it was like entering a cave. To his right was a larger room; an oblong bay window, a table covered with a faded red cloth bordered with hanging bobbles, a scatter of unmatched deal chairs, built-in cupboards that had been painted a muddy brown in some dim past, and a horsehair sofa that had seen better days long gone. There were also a number of people, dressed in dark clothes, the close gloom permeated with a notable smell of mothballs. Their conversation, far from animated, stopped altogether at his appearance. A stout, middle-aged woman in an extravagantly flowered dress and an unbecoming hat of black straw came to meet him.

"It's all right, luv, no need to fret, we've a minute or two left. Port or sherry?"

"Neither," he said, "thank you very much," waiting for his eyes to adjust to the dusky light squeezing under yet another drawn blind.

"Nay," said a voice unaccustomed to being disagreed with. "Tek summat, lad, just to show willing." Morpurgo could make out a massively built man who sat with a black bowler hat on his knees and a glass in his hand. "Uncle Norman," he said, "that's me, lad. Younger brother. Seventeen year younger, never meant to come into the world, me, see what I mean? Come on, lad. Never mind bloody port, 'ave a sup of this." He pulled a flat half-bottle of Haig from his hip pocket and slopped a generous quantity into a glass.

Two, perched side by side on the sofa like a pair of crows on a telephone line, he guessed were man and wife. They were also clearly disapproving of Uncle Norman, the woman's sharp features frozen in a permanent sniff of repudiation. She wore her black like a suit of armour and it was she who exuded the sad odour of naphthalene. Her husband was round and shiny, his egg of a head little more than a lambent crescent in the restricted light from the window.

The remaining mourner, in the darkest corner, occupied a spoke-backed chair like a monarch his throne. With a thrill of shock, Morpurgo thought: Sattin! Joseph Sattin! It was, of course, Eustace Roland Trigg. The first impression was marmoreal, not so much a question of mass as immutability. He too had a black bowler, dangled beween splayed, heroic thighs like a giant cod-piece. He was looking fixedly at Morpurgo, his face impassive, unreadable.

"Yon," Uncle Norman was saying, "is my sister Emmie and her espoused, Robbo, come all the way from Doncaster to pay their respects, not having been in communication for the last seventeen years to my certain knowledge. And over in't corner, as I dare say you know, is our Roly, who no doubt is about to tell us who *you* are."

"Never set eyes on him in my life," Trigg said, and Morpurgo experienced another frisson; even his voice was not unlike that of Sattin. "But he's come," Trigg went on as if passing sentence, "so he's welcome."

"And who *might* you be, young man?" Uncle Norman enquired. "Friend of a friend, is it summat like that? Or did you 'ave something going with the old lady?" His shoulders beginning to heave, he produced a sound like a creaking gate.

"Stop it, our Norman," Emmie snapped. "You get worse as you grow older."

"Nay, that I don't," Uncle Norman contradicted with relish. "Like old port, me, crusty but mellow, isn't that so, Robbo?"

"Don't ask me," Emmie's husband said in a depressed and exhausted voice. "I'm not paid to have opinions."

The stout and flowery lady was back at Morpurgo's side. "You'll sign the book?" She poked a ballpoint pen at Morpurgo. He wrote his name. Uncle Norman, breathing potent dispensations of Scotch, peered over his shoulder.

"Morcombe," he announced. "Mr John Morcombe, of London."

The stout lady pressed the book to her full and overflowing breast. "There," she said. "The last. House going, business going, me and the old man going, but not before her, since it was a promise. Ethel," she said, "you've done for the rest of my family and you must promise to do for me." She dabbed at her eye-corners with a fist the size of a welterweight's glove. "She knew we were the last of the old school, do you see, Mr Morcombe? Family business, decent but nothing fancy. That's what she said she wanted and that's what we've given her. Right, lady and gentlemen, let's be having you," and they all shuffled toward the bright day and the imminent ceremonies of death.

"Two cars!" Uncle Norman pointed out disapprovingly. "I've told him, our Roly, we could all of us've managed in one. Come on, lad, you and me'll sit with Roly." Trigg, last to leave, came out into the sunlight as if on to a stage. Morpurgo could tell at once he was not a man to be rushed. Yet rush him is what I've got to do, he thought, and for the hundredth time found his confidence dribbling away like sand.

131

Even in daylight, the likeness between Trigg and Sattin was remarkable, the one notable difference that Trigg clearly enjoyed a rude and earthy wellbeing, a blocky self-confidence making it plain that he considered himself as good as any man, if not better.

Trigg stumped toward Emmie and her spouse. "You and her," he said to the turnip-headed Robbo, "can ride in the second car. Me and Uncle Norman'll go in the first" – his basilisk gaze switched to Morpurgo – "along with Mr Morcombe here, seeing he's a stranger."

Emmie decided to take offence. "Get on with you then," she scolded Robbo. "If we're to be treated different, at least we don't have to hang about."

"By!" Uncle Norman confided to Morpurgo, "There's nowt like a burying to bring the family together," and he wheezed his way into the old car with its strong smell of old leather and wax polish. "Come on, our Roly," he shouted at Trigg, "don't 'old things up and don't forget your billycock hat." He took off his own and used it to fan his red and overheated face.

Morpurgo had pulled out one of the jump seats, guessing correctly that Trigg and Uncle Norman between them would take up every available inch of the back seat. Trigg settled himself facing Morpurgo, pulled a fat silver watch from a waistcoat pocket and raised his voice. "Right then, Charlie, don't let's hang about."

Trigg perched his bowler on one knee and turned an unwinking stare on Morpurgo as the *cortège* crunched slowly over the rubble. "Now then, sunshine, sent by the insurance, were you?" He had, Morpurgo saw, the northener's habit of stripping his words of all emotion other than a kind of underlying and barely concealed derision.

Before Morpurgo could answer, Uncle Norman threw him a lifebelt. "Oh," he said, "so that's it, is it? Well, no offence, young man, but I take leave to doubt whether we'll get half as much back as we paid in, 'er having more than exceeded 'er allotted span as you might say."

"Well," Morpurgo began, but Trigg cut him short. "Now, Uncle Norman, chap's here, isn't he? That's good enough for me, so it should be good enough for you."

"Aye," Uncle Norman said after a little consideration, "'appen you're right, our Roly, 'appen you're right." He produced the half-bottle of Scotch from one pocket, a glass from the other. "Now then, who's going to be first?"

Again Trigg demolished the foundations of conversation. "Give some to this feller. He's got some catching up to do."

"He has that." Uncle Norman promptly poured Morpurgo not so much a shot as a cannonade.

"Sup up," Trigg said. "Show us how they deal with their liquor in London." His eyes were sardonic.

He knows, Morpurgo decided, knows I'm not insurance, not a relative, not a friend, so what's *his* game? Left with no option, he drank his whisky faster than he had drunk anything in a long time.

"Not bad," Uncle Norman conceded. "Shall you have another, do you think?"

"Not bad?" Trigg scoffed. "Letting your standards slip, that's what you're doing, Uncle Norman. Not bad? Why, I saw him swallow!"

Uncle Norman was magnanimous in defeat. "What about you then, our Roly? Can you do with one to keep your spirits up?"

Trigg shook his head in a way that reminded Morpurgo almost eerily of Sattin. "Time for that after. Time for all manner of things after."

Trigg's remark clearly excited Uncle Norman's curiosity. "What shall you do, then? Have you made plans?"

"Plans?" Trigg spoke the word as if he had never heard it before. "What plans might they be, Uncle Norman?"

"Don't ask me, lad." Uncle Norman literally put his tongue in his cheek and winked at Morpurgo. "Get wed, 'appen?"

"Get *wed*?" Trigg's scorn would have routed a lesser man than Uncle Norman. "Don't talk daft! Out of the frying pan into the fire that'd be, and no mistake."

Buttoning his coat against the risk of catching cold from the hot sunlight, Trigg turned to Morpurgo. "You'll sit with the family." Not long after, following the coffin of the late Mrs Trigg into the crematorium, he found the instruction a little more comprehensible. Apart from the family, the only others there were two pale-faced, spinsterish women with sharp red noses and a shared liking for incompatible items of clothing.

The service was brisk, even cheerful, Uncle Norman proving to have a rich and unrestrained baritone that made short work

133

of two hymns and the twenty-third psalm. When the curate, a starved-looking young man with a bleating voice and nervous hands, enunciated, "Man that is born of woman hath but a short time to live, and is full of misery," Uncle Norman, in a carrying rumble, said, "Got you dead to rights there, Roly."

Afterwards, Trigg clapped his fleshy hands vigorously, as if to free them from all that dust and ashes. "Now then, Uncle Norman, you can ride with Emmie and Robbo this time. Me and sunshine here'll take the other, seeing as we have a bit of business to transact."

"Nay," Uncle Norman protested. "Not with Robbo and our Emmie. I'd sooner ride alongside the deceased," but he got in beside the driver and they rolled away to Uncle Norman's booming, "Step on it, lad, if you fancy a drop before you take this bathtub back to t'garage." Morpurgo and Trigg were left to each other.

Trigg was clearly in no hurry. He pulled a battered leather cigar case from an inside pocket, took out a half-corona, studied it, sniffed it, crinkled it against his ear and decided that it would pass muster. He lit it, expelling a leisurely quantity of smoke. Throughout the performance, his eyes never left Morpurgo.

At last, he took Morpurgo by the elbow and steered him toward the remaining car. "Hop in, lad. Worst bit's over. Now we can make ourselves comfortable." His blunt vowels hammered home his self-confidence with the force of a riveter's hammer. To the driver, he said, "Did you put that bag of mine in, Charlie?"

"I did that, Mr Trigg. Reckon you must be emigrating or something, but it's none of my business."

"That's right, lad." Trigg settled back comfortably. "It isn't. Your business is to take us to the Cons Club as fast as is decent." He turned to Morpurgo. "Now, sunshine, it's time you and me had a little chat."

*   *   *

Claas and Weber met, as arranged, in the crowded saloon bar of a fashionable pub just off Knightsbridge. The clientele was, on the whole, patrician; chiefly girls with the high, clear voices of Chelsea and Kensington and modishly dressed young men with easy manners and a tendency to laugh a good deal. Claas had managed to take possession of a tiny table hemmed in by the clamour of people whose general delight in life was matched by their own joyous self-approval.

"Did he deliver?" Weber asked.

"Yes and no," Claas said. "Meaning the usual mixture of fact and garbage."

Weber drank a little of his lager. Nodding at Claas's pint mug, he said, "I can't take that British stuff. Too heavy."

Claas held it up, admiring its tawny clarity. "Trouble with you is being born in St Louis. This is the real thing, Pierre, malt, hops, no chemicals. Let's start with the screwiest thing first. During the time he was in that apartment, Sattin used a local washomat, launderette, what you will."

"So?" Weber winced as an enthusiastic young man behind took a half-step back and collided with him while relating a story that had something to do with cars and required a positive frenzy of illustrative actions.

"Mostly sheets. Normal laundry once every week or so. Sheets, every other day."

Weber frowned. "I don't get it. Cleanliness obsession or something? I knew a guy who used to wash his hands, then wash the soap."

"Maybe he felt his sheets got soiled faster than his clothes."

"In a big city? You've got to be kidding."

"Maybe. I just thought I'd give it to you a little at a time. Turns out this thing was cyclical. It worked up over a period of weeks."

"Cyclical? I still don't get it. Sounds kooky, though."

Claas smiled. "I didn't get it either. Then I remembered what we heard yesterday. Remember? The magic word? Lymphoma?"

Weber looked little the wiser. "My cousin Sue's a doctor. She married a guy called Souza. They live in Sioux City. You want me to give her a call?"

"I had a chat with Langley. You know what those guys say, what they don't know between them isn't knowledge. Medical section filled in on a few things about lymphoma." About to continue, he stopped. "You made that up."

"What?" Weber looked startled.

"Your cousin. Sue Souza, Sioux City. Go ahead. Tell me she sews shirts for soldiers, or is it seashells on the salt sea shore?"

Weber said, "Made it up? I certainly did not. You say that in front of witnesses and I'll sue. Okay, let's hear the expert."

"Night sweats. One of the symptoms. The more advanced the disease, the heavier and more regular the sweating. Once it starts, it goes on. Unless."

"Don't rile me," Weber said. "Just give."

"Okay. From time to time he spent a whole day in bed. Afterwards, for a while, he would stop taking the sheets to the laundry so often."

Weber's face was becoming steadily sadder, his forehead wrinkled like a beagle's. "What does this boy of yours do? Crawl all over the neighbourhood with a false nose and a magnifying glass? Give the Brits cause to suspect and Langley is going to have your balls for marbles."

"You have the sweetest way of putting things. Okay, let me spell it out for you. You remember about the neighbour? Right, well, here's where Sattin broke one of the rules. No matter how good they are, they always break a rule, sooner or later. He told this guy about the virus thing. He could have left it at that, but he didn't. He embroidered it, said he had these feverish sweats, woke up in the night drenched, that sort of stuff."

"And it was the lymphoma."

"It was the lymphoma."

Weber took another blow from a sharp elbow, but this time it was a dazzling young creature in a far-out jumpsuit. "Did I hurt you? How awful! Terribly sorry!"

Weber smiled ingratiatingly. "My fault, maybe."

Claas said ironically, "Equal rightser, huh? Want to hear the rest of the story?"

"If she does it again," Weber said, "I'll punch her on the nose."

"Did I tell about the itching?"

Weber groaned. "What are you trying to do? Give me the treatment?"

Claas leaned close across the table. "He had night sweats. He had bouts of itching. Coughing, lots of sputum. And there were other things. Like every so often he looked so exhausted, he could hardly get around. But all cyclical, get me? Which is *not* what you'd expect, unless."

Weber, turning his lager round and round between his fingers, stopped. "Treatment. How about that, he had some kind of treatment."

"Well," Claas said, "*not* just a pretty face! Right! He had treatment. The only thing that makes sense, that's what Langley says. But it seems the cycles were irregular. The periods not fixed. Get me?"

"I'm impressed. Is that what you want me to say? Or is there a correlation somewhere? With something you haven't told me yet?"

"There's a correlation. And incidentally, *I'm* impressed. Maybe I'll go on working for you a while longer."

"How about this?" Weber said. "There's a correlation between those periods and another set of periods."

"Right. And I can prove it."

"Periods," Weber said softly. "Well, we don't have too much data on Sattin and what we have is all courtesy of Her Majesty's Curzon Street snoopers. But the only thing in those summaries on Sattin that could be called cyclical is the pattern of drops and treffs."

Claas laughed. "Okay, the bases are loaded. Now hit the big one."

"The guy had to get himself straightened out each time there was an exchange."

"Strike one."

Weber considered. "No, I goofed on that one. *How* did he get himself straight? Treatment. He had to have treatment. Okay, let's try this. He timed whatever it was he had to take so that it tied in with the Stringers. Kagalov couldn't operate at all until Sattin had something to pass on from the Stringers."

"Strike two."

"Okay, but don't crowd me, smart-ass!" After a while Weber shook his head, baffled. "Now, if we happened to know . . ." He pulled up abruptly. His face changed. He said, "Hey!" and then, *"He-e-e-y!"*

Claas said, "You got it. How about that?"

"Damn right, how about that? Oh man!" Still shaking his head over the implications, Weber went to buy them another round.

*   *   *

The Grimsby Conservative Club bore a certain family resemblance to Trigg's house; red-brick solidity, architecturally dogmatic. "Fish," Trigg proclaimed obscurely as they got out of the car. He pushed a pound note at his driver. "Go round the back and have one while you're waiting, Charlie. Tell 'em I sent you."

He turned back to Morpurgo. "This." A jerk of his head at the building. "Fish. Don't tell me you've come to Grimsby and don't know what I mean." He propelled Morpurgo through the entrance. "This town was built on fish. Show me a big house that's over fifty years old and I know it was built on fish." He tossed his hat at a peg. It hung, clearly the consequence of much practice. The interior of the club, which Morpurgo now realised had once been a private house, was grandiose and sombre, comfort on a brown and Brobdingnagian scale.

Trigg took them into a room with a bar. They were the only ones there. "And what," he demanded, "should you like to drink?"

"Beer?"

"Aye," Trigg said with his first sign of approval, "it's thirsty work is a funeral. Pint of best, love, and the usual for me." He progressed to a corner table. "Sit down, lad. You're making the place untidy. Now, let's have another look at that card of yours."

Morpurgo handed over his identity pass. Trigg pored over it at length, his breathing slow, judicial, "How do I know this thing's what it says it is? Or you what you say you are, sunshine?"

"You could make a telephone call. To be honest, I'd rather you didn't."

"If you being honest," Trigg told him, "is to do with me not doing things, you'll be behind bars in no time at all. I'm not what you'd call a biddable chap." He returned Morpurgo's pass. Morpurgo's beer and Trigg's Guinness were set before them. Trigg poured down Guinness as if he were the crematorium stoker suffering from dehydration.

"And that's it?" he asked for the fourth or fifth time. "I stand in for this feller Sattin while a couple of cases are swapped. You pick up the other feller and I'm free to go?"

"That's it."

Trigg considered, simultaneously finishing off his Guinness and signalling for another. "Can't say I like it," he said finally.

Morpurgo's heart sank. It had, after all, been a crazy idea.

Before he could say anything, there was a sudden disturbance outside, someone with a giant's voice saying, "Gave it him straight, I did. I were a force in this business, I said, when you were nowt but milk and mucky nappies. Your father were a nincompoop, I said, and your mother were a fool to wed him, and you've got the worst of both. Try your tricks on me, I said, and I'll put you out of business before you know which day it is."

The speaker finished this monologue as he came into the room, and it was instantly clear to Morpurgo what type of man the club had been established for. He was as large, red and raw as a side of beef, and with as much grace. He wore a good suit with contempt, walked with a swagger in spite of a limp and a rubber-ferruled stick, and brought with him a sense of crude power that was almost physical. He was accompanied by a grey man; grey of suit, grey of hair and manner; lawyer, accountant, bank manager, Morpurgo guessed.

He stopped just inside the doorway, surveying the room as a monarch his kingdom. His eye fell on Trigg. "Now then, you daft bugger!" he shouted. "How you getting on? All right?"

Scarcely raising his voice, Trigg said, "Sod off, Eddy. I'm busy."

Not one whit offended, the other turned on his heels. "All right, all right!" he bellowed cheerfully. "Know when we're not wanted, don't we, Ernie?" Ernie murmured something inaudible. The big man paused for a parting shot, addressing Morpurgo directly, "Best watch out, lad. Half a chance and he'll have your arm off at the elbow." Greatly pleased with himself, he departed, his voice booming from the farther reaches of the club like a thunderstorm among the mountains.

Trigg looked after him, unoffended. "Fish," he said again. "Made his pile, sold out; ships, stores, the lot. Next thing, the whole industry's on its back, never recovered. This town was built on fish, thrived on fish, damn near died on fish. They don't make 'em like him any more." He looked inscrutably at Morpurgo. "Here's to us. Who's like us? Damn few!" After that demonstration of power, Morpurgo was beginning to realise that, in Eustace Roland Trigg, he might have a bear by the short hairs.

Trigg reverted to the matter in hand. "Why should I? That's what I'd like to know, sunshine. What have you got to say to that?"

It took Morpurgo a moment or two to make the right connections. It would take more than a moment or two to give an answer that would convince this granitic sceptic who could quell elemental forces without raising his voice.

"I imagine you're not exactly pro-communist. Unless you keep it a secret from the club secretary."

Trigg chuckled indulgently. "Nay, lad, that horse won't run. I'm only here for the beer, as they say. I take my politics as I find them, politicians too, not much time for either."

He stared at Morpurgo with open curiosity. "Is that why you do it? Patriotism? Saving the country from Moscow? Or is it just a job?"

"It all depends . . ."

". . . what you mean by patriotism," Trigg finished with relish. "You're all the same, you clever chaps, whittle away at meanings until there's nought left to answer. Come on, lad, you'll have to do better than that."

Morpurgo's quandary was that he hadn't considered his own motivation for a very long time. Back at the beginning, it had been a kind of shabby glamour, a young man with a sharp mind and a black and white picture of life taking pleasure in pitting his wits against received definitions of the public enemy. 'Bliss was it in that dawn to be alive, But to be young was very heaven!' Since then, everything had become increasingly blurred, the enemy less a face than a shadow.

"I suppose," he said, "it's because, on the whole, I prefer our way to theirs."

"Eh," Trigg said mockingly, "you sound none too certain."

Morpurgo shrugged. "No. That and the fact that I don't like to be outsmarted."

"Now then," Trigg said with approval, "that's a bit more like it, that is! Tell me about *him*, Sattin. Do you know what goes on in *his* skull?"

"He's tough. He'd break before he bent, but he'd take some breaking."

"Like me," Trigg said, taking Morpurgo's thought and putting it into speech. "But then, you know all about me, don't you?" He stood up. "Come on. I've something to show you."

Car and driver were waiting for them. "Now then, Charlie," Trigg said, getting in, "you're to take us on a little trip round the town, so let's get on with it."

"Mystery tour, is it?" Charlie asked without deference. "Or are you going to tell me?"

"Down the end of the front first, you cheeky bugger," Trigg responded with gusto, "then we'll see. But stop in the market

140

place first. I'm fair clemmed," all of which was double-dutch to Morpurgo.

The car took them back to Cleethorpes, turning off from the main shopping street into a vast, open marketplace, empty but for a scatter of parked cars and two local buses. "Two haddock and chips," Trigg said, thrusting money at Charlie. "Salt and vinegar, and make sure they're fresh fried. Tell 'em it's for me."

A few minutes later, Charlie returned with two steaming-hot packages with a pungent smell of vinegar. Trigg passed one of them to Morpurgo. "The Almighty made fingers before forks, even down there in London." He opened his own parcel to reveal golden, batter-coated fish in a nest of chipped potatoes. Morpurgo discovered that he was ravenously hungry as the car pulled away once more, this time only a short distance before their road debouched on the seafront.

The tide was out. A vast expanse, scribbled and daubed with brown, wave-patterned sand and pockets of trapped water, stretched halfway to the horizon. Beyond it, a strip of dusky green, lay the deepwater channel, two cargo ships and a large tanker keeping each other company until the rising tide enabled them to dock. The sun struck down whitely on a wide, seemingly endless promenade, the iron geometry of pier and pavilion stretching ineffectually toward a remote, indifferent sea.

The beach below the promenade was forlorn, notwithstanding the brilliance and warmth of the day. Here and there, family groups had dug into the sand, making small laagers of deckchairs. Here and there, children excavated moated castles of sand, awaiting a sea that would never reach to fill them. Morpurgo found it all faintly depressing.

"Aye," Trigg said, following his gaze. "Grimsby for fish, Cleethorpes for trippers, and both gone forever. In the old times, back in the thirties, they'd come for a day by the sea with a quid or two in their pockets. Fish and chips, a pint or two of ale, a plate of cockles, all go back happy as Larry. Now it's Majorca for a fortnight and come back grumbling because they can't make tea like mother. All right, Charlie, this'll do."

They had stopped alongside a colonnaded row of shops; souvenirs, shellfish, bric-a-brac and slot machines. Directly opposite was one gaudy with the crude colours of hard candy. Rock! Morpurgo realised. Trigg was in rock!

It was stacked in layers, foot-long cylinders, pink, orange and

141

yellow, interspersed with the striped pincushion shapes of out-size humbugs. They left the car. Greeting the middle-aged woman behind the counter with, "Now then, Elsie, love, how're you getting on, all right?" Trigg picked up a single stick of rock and thrust it at Morpurgo. "There you are, lad. Cleethorpes all through, one end to t'other."

He pushed Morpurgo before him, round the side of the counter and through a small door at the back. Morpurgo found himself assailed by hot smells of peppermint, synthetic fruit and sugar. The room they had entered was not large, its space further reduced by a great, metal-topped table and, at the far end, large metal vats, source of the overpowering odours. Two men worked at the table, each with long and sticky cables of pulled candy. One was building up fat pink bars to form an E. The other had already constructed a C in cross-section, its axis reaching almost from one end of the table to the other.

"There you are, sunshine," Trigg said. "There's a national secret, how to get MOSCOW running clean through a stick of rock. They'll build up those names, do you see? They'll fit 'em together, then they'll roll and pull, roll and pull, until it's the right thickness, then they'll cut it up and wrap it ready to sell. That's how I started, how my dad started, and his dad before him."

"Not forgetting the late Mrs Trigg," one of the men said. "Just like 'er to say we shouldn't go to the funeral. Business first, pleasure after, that was your mam, Mr Trigg." He said it with respect.

"Aye," Trigg said. "Well, you had the work and I had the pleasure, Dick. She's gone, we'll do things our way from now on and they'll never be the same again."

He removed his jacket, washed his hands, towelled them vigorously, and took charge of a huge sugary dropping Dick had just brought to the table. He thudded this warm, sticky mass on the point of a huge steel hook suspended from the roof and pulled. The lump extended. He pulled again. It extended farther. He gave it a twist one way, a twist the other, unhooked it, pummelled it, hooked and tugged again, fought it across the table top like an all-in wrestler and in due course achieved a white worm six feet long and several inches across. "Now then, lad," he said to Morpurgo, "all you've got to do is get them letters in."

"Eh, Mr Trigg," Dick said admiringly, "you're still t'best in t'business, bar none."

"And that's the last time I'll do it," Trigg said, washing his hands and breathing heavily after his exertions, "though I've done it, on and off, since you were nought but a bit of Saturday night nonsense."

He turned to Morpurgo. "Now, do you think yon lad we've been talking about could do a thing like that?"

"No," Morpurgo said, then, seeing Sattin's face in Trigg's, "but he'd learn."

"Would he then?" For some reason, Trigg seemed pleased at the answer. "Come on! We don't want to hang about here all day." He turned to his two employees. "All right, you dozy buggers, don't go to sleep on the job or I'll be after you when I get back." The admonition clearly delighted them.

Back in the car and retracing the route along the almost empty promenade, Morpurgo asked, "It's a family business?"

"I'm the last, now the old lady's gone. Things," Trigg said with certainty, "are going to change a lot from now on."

"Mrs Trigg," Charlie said without invitation, "would have been right delighted to see you come 'otfoot down here from the crematorium. By! Right little bundle of energy, she was!"

Trigg turned to Morpurgo. "What about *his* mother, then? What do you know about her, I wonder?"

He saw Morpurgo's involuntary glance at Charlie, leaned forward to slide the window shut. "Come on, lad, what else do you know about him? Read his mind, can you? Or do you have ways of making him talk?"

About to ignore the question as another example of Trigg's pawky humour, Morpurgo was brought up sharply when Trigg said, "Do you? It'd be important to me, would that."

"We don't go in for torture, if that's what you mean,"

For some reason, the answer turned Trigg inward. "Pull up here, Charlie," he shouted, and the car stopped, not far from the pier entrance, facing the all but invisible sea. Trigg's head sank between his broad shoulders, his mind occupied. After a while it lifted, and Trigg gazed fixedly at the low silhouette of Spurn Point, seven miles across the estuary. "Goes out nigh on a mile, does that tide." He lapsed into another silence.

Eventually he came to life. "Seaside rock-puller against a

translator, educated feller, no doubt, and smart as paint if he's managed to dodge you this long. By! I wonder you bothered to come."

"I'm sure you're a man of parts."

"Happen I am, happen I'm not."

Lost, Morpurgo thought, a small man faced with a big problem and not the slightest reason to take it on. He thought of the Knight, of Steve Archer with his ready *schadenfreude*, of the Friends and their superior ways, and of how they would receive this story when, as it must, it reached them. Siberia would be preferable to that as a punishment. It came to him that according to the smug Morpurgo of pre-Trigg days, this coastal backwater with its population of cheerful anarchists, was Siberia.

"Now then," Trigg said, suddenly brisk, "Shall you be going back today? I dare say we'll manage to get you wherever you've a fancy to go."

"Hired car," Charlie said, sliding his window back to show that it had offered no barrier. "One of Hockey's, recognised it straight off."

"In that case, you can forget it, lad," Trigg told Morpurgo. "Unless you were thinking of driving it all the way to London, which is something I wouldn't recommend with a car from Hockey's, we can take you straight to the station and Charlie'll see to the car."

Morpurgo was in a quandary, reluctant to admit to the helicopter in front of Charlie.

Trigg resolved the dilemma. "Charlie, me and this gentleman's going to take a short turn along the front, back in a minute." With no more ado, Trigg unloaded himself. "Now, what's to do? Lost your return ticket or something?"

Morpurgo told him. "By!" Trigg said, using what was clearly a local shorthand oath, "One of *them*? Just for me? No wonder you wanted to keep it quiet, taxpayers' money and all! Come on then. There's a phone box. Make your call, lad, then Charlie'll take us to the aerodrome. Don't you fret, he won't talk. Safe as houses, is Charlie."

Morpurgo got through to his pilot without difficulty. "One or two of you, skip?"

"One." Tactfully, the pilot said nothing.

Returning to Trigg, who was once again staring eastward as if willing the sea to return, Morpurgo stuck out his hand. "Thanks for everything. I do understand. If your driver would take me, I'd be grateful."

Ignoring the hand, Trigg said, "About how long will you take to get where you're going?"

"Couple of hours."

"Eh, that beats the train," Trigg said, impressed. "And does it take you right to London?"

"Battersea. Right on the river."

Trigg bawled, "Have I asked you if you've got my bag in that car, Charlie?"

"If you've asked me once, you've asked me six times," Charlie told him, "and every time, the answer's been t'same, yes."

"Come on then, lad." Trigg steered Morpurgo to the car. "Best be off if we're to get you to Thoresby."

"Oh, look," Morpurgo said, "no need to see me off." He held out his hand again. Ignoring it, Trigg pushed him into the car, giving him his driest look yet. As a Londoner, it said, I'd expect you to be dafter than most, but not *that* daft.

"What do you mean, see you off? I'm coming with you, sunshine."

* * *

The Knight had just begun to separate a box of nemesia, ready for bedding, when Mary called him in. Their roots would begin to die back if he left them for long. But now he had a greater cause for distress. He detested having to conduct Security Directorate business in his own home. Its relative remoteness in the downlands of West Sussex saw him all too often spending his weekday nights in the Director-General's town flat, or, at the best, getting home more or less in time to go to bed and rise at crack of dawn the following morning.

Steve had refused a drink, an indication that his visit meant trouble.

The Knight, unhappy, said, "I can't believe it."

"It's true. I wish it weren't." Steve, as one had come to expect of him, kept his feelings firmly under control. When Johnny was angry, no one was left in any doubt. But then, Steve's background was of the kind in which any open display of emotion was rather bad form.

"You're quite sure?"

"Quite." Steve lit another cigarette. He was putting them

145

out half-smoked, the Knight noted, a betrayal of inner stress after all.

"How long? Damn it, Steve, I very much dislike asking this kind of question, but you do see that I have no choice?"

"Maybe four months. I can't be sure, it could have been well under way before I noticed anything."

"And it's still going on?"

"As recently as last Tuesday." The day Sattin had been brought in, the Knight realised, checking back.

The Knight stirred uneasily. "You're absolutely right to tell me, of course. It can't have been easy." But I wish to God you hadn't, he thought. No, damn it! that was unfair. Apart from the delicately personal side of it, it was very definitely a security matter.

"You've said nothing?"

"To Helga? Not yet."

"But you will."

"Can't be avoided." Steve looked up. "Can it?"

The Knight side-stepped the question. "I could break him, of course. Is that what you want?"

Steve didn't answer immediately. That's what he wants, the Knight decided. "You'd take over, Steve, it goes without saying."

"Thank you." After another pause, Steve said, grudgingly, "It would be a loss. I know that."

"For the Directorate? Yes. In more ways than one. The incidental damage." Roger Hollis, one of his predecessors, the Knight was thinking, had run the Directorate well enough while conducting a long-term affair with his secretary. No one at the time had detected any falling off in efficiency. But that was with a secretary, not the wife of his second-in-command. And of course, there had been the allegation, much later, that Hollis had been working for Moscow Centre all along. An enquiry had produced no substantiation, but no exoneration either. It would not have been the first time that Moscow Centre had used a clandestine affair to exert pressure.

Aloud, he said, "I mean the damage to the Directorate. It would be bound to become known. The SIS. The ministries. The press."

"Yes." Steve had an air – no, nothing so obvious as an air – an aura? – of implacability. He means, the Knight observed to himself, to have his pound of flesh. Steve said, "Of course,

146

there's the other thing, too, the press man. I don't see how it could possibly be overlooked."

"Liddle. You're quite sure?"

Steve nodded, a single quick, emphatic movement. "Quite sure. Last time, Wednesday afternoon. I can supply dates, times, places." He caught the Knight's gaze and held it.

The Knight knew why; dates, times, places; that was what you got from full-scale SV. So there was a question to be asked, how had Steve acquired so much detailed information about the activities of his section head? Certainly not by using Directorate facilities. Steve's steady gaze was an invitation; ask me how I know these things, and I'll tell you.

No, the Knight thought, I'd rather not know, not yet. The accusation is sufficient. If it's true and if Johnny's confronted, he will confess.

Steve said, quietly enough, "Give him enough rope to hang himself," but the Knight's experience detected vindictiveness. *It's his wife*, he reminded himself. He would be superhuman if he bore no animus at all.

Steve said, "If possible, I wouldn't want it to come to a head before we've wound up the Sattin business. He's too deeply involved to be pulled out now. Unless he does something to endanger it, of course."

Little do you know! the Knight thought wrily. No one else knew at this stage where Johnny had gone, or for what reason.

"We just carry on as if nothing has happened?"

"Until the exchange is out of the way."

"And then?"

"I'll handle Helga myself. The whole business of Helga and Johnny." Steve said it evenly, a man offering to tidy up some small, overlooked trifle.

"Steve," the Knight began seriously, "you won't do anything . . ."

Steve smiled thinly. "Foolish? No. *I* value *my* career."

The Knight saw it plainly now. To tackle Morpurgo about his contacts with Liddle would be sufficient so far as the Directorate was concerned. Between the official charge that he had broken security regulations by giving secret information to a newspaperman, and Steve's charge, pressed privately and almost certainly with the gloves off, that Morpurgo had seduced his wife, Johnny would have nowhere to go but out. The Knight felt a pang of regret. He would lose an able man and an experiment would have failed. His twinge was short-lived. To make Johnny section head had, after all, been a mistake. And the loss of someone everybody from the Minister downwards knew to be a lefty, practically a working-class lefty, would save him a good deal of future anxiety.

"All right. But I'd like to have chapter and verse."

"Don't worry, Director-General. You'll get it."

The Knight went back to his summer border, but instead of continuing his planting out, propped himself on the handle of his fork in the manner of a shooting-stick.

Eventually, he reached a conclusion. Steve was ex-SIS, still had contacts, the man Fish, for example. It was no secret that SIS had always looked on Morpurgo with private suspicion, the more so after his promotion over Steve's head. SIS would be glad to see him go, happier still at Steve's promotion. The Knight owed it to Morpurgo to check that he was not being railroaded out of the Directorate, but the evidence would be indisputable, since it would be supplied on the basis of SV carried out by SIS. Steve wouldn't have acted on suspicion alone. Steve was a gentleman; cuckolded maybe, but still a gentleman.

Sighing, the Knight went to connect the hose. He would water the bedding plants in to make sure that the delay had done them no harm.

*   *   *

Even the rattling tumult of engine and rotors took nothing away from Trigg's pleasure. "By!" he shouted at Morpurgo over the din, "It beats all, does this." Hunched forward, he gazed avidly at every detail of the world that passed below, as if he himself had created it, found it to his satisfaction and was now enjoying the seventh day.

It all seemed to be too good to be true, Morpurgo thought.

But if he had managed it so far, why not the rest of the way? It required a kind of cheek, but that was where he scored over most of the people in his line of business. They, with their superior backgrounds, their superior philosophies and their superior language, spoke from time to time of dash, panache. Well, Morpurgo was talking of cheek. Dash, he told himself complacently, was cheek with a private education. Cheek was dash with a working-class accent.

In due course, one of his infrequent observations, the pilot said, "London," and sure enough it was slowly emerging from the heat-haze ahead of them.

Morpurgo bellowed at Trigg, over the din, "As soon as we're down, I'll do something about fixing you up with a hotel. Somewhere small and quiet, I think, somewhere where you'll be out of the way until we can set things up." He had yet to tell Trigg that the setting up depended on a great many things not yet established, including the possibility that Kagalov, by this time or in the near future, would have learned that Sattin was no longer in a position to keep treffs.

"Hotel?" Trigg repeated. "I don't need a hotel, lad. I've already got one."

It was Morpurgo's turn to frown. "Got one? What do you mean?"

Trigg looked at him with the air of a man who has just found that his travelling companion, though harmless, is mentally deficient. "I told you. I'd have been off today whether you'd shown up or not. Uncle Norman knew that. Our Emmie knew that. Everybody up there knew that, lad."

Whatever his feelings over the final loss of that formidable lady, the late Mrs Trigg, he had long planned to mark his release, he had already explained, by taking himself off to wherever he felt like going and for as long as he should feel like staying. "If it hadn't been you, lad," he had told Morpurgo, "it would have been something else, women always excluded. I'm not a ladies' man," he had added unnecessarily, "nor specially a man's man neither. What I am, I don't mind letting on, is a chap who manages quite nicely, thank you very much, with his own company."

He prodded Morpurgo's knee with a powerful finger. "When I go to London, which, whatever Captain Joliffe might have told you, is often enough, on business, I always stay in the same place. Strand Palace Hotel, lad. Folk from Cleethorpes have a special relationship with the Strand Palace Hotel. It would surprise me if the Strand Palace Hotel didn't go bust if folk from Cleethorpes stopped going there."

The trouble was, Morpurgo thought, it was almost impossible, other than by sheer reason, to tell when this man was serious and when not. And on reflection, he was inclined to put little faith in reason.

"Anyroad," Trigg was bellowing above the racket of their progress, "there it is, take it or leave it. Booked myself in the moment I saw the old lady wasn't going to get her own way for once."

He prodded Morpurgo again. "To be honest with you, lad, it wasn't this little scheme of yours that was the attraction. It was two hours in this contraption, against a stopping train and change at Retford into the bargain. Still," – He squeezed Morpurgo's arm quite painfully – "I'm not one to break a promise, nor give less than full value for favours done. I'll see you through, never you fret, so long as it doesn't hold me up more than a day or two."

Morpurgo stared at him aghast. Trigg misunderstood. "All right, all right! Up to four. But after that, I've my own affairs to attend to, no telling what I'm bound to do now that I'm off the leash, so to speak."

At that point his attention was distracted. The pilot had been conducting a laconic exchange with air traffic control at West Drayton. Now, with their ship only a few hundred feet above the Thames as it wound like a silvery serpent through the car-crawling, brick and concrete maquis of central London, he eased forward the collective and reduced power. Their descent, still following the river, was steep. Trigg, unaffected, crouched forward, relishing every second of this final manoeuvre.

As they climbed out, Morpurgo saw that Callow was there with the car. He could think of no one less likely than Callow to talk about the arrival of a stranger by helicopter. He would trust Callow to keep the secret of the Second Coming.

"Where to, sir?" Callow asked.

It was Trigg who said, "Strand Palace Hotel, lad, and don't spare the horses."

10
Politics and Parties

The Knight had taken Trigg's insistence on staying at the Strand Palace very lightly. "Good heavens, Johnny, you can't kidnap the man, and then incarcerate him like a common criminal. After all, who is he? No one at all until you use him. And still no one at all unless your scheme succeeds." The tone of his voice had made it clear that he expected little or nothing to come of it.

So there was Trigg, whose plans went no further than "a few shows, a few pints and a bit of thinking", lolling in the lap of bourgeois luxury at the Strand Palace while Morpurgo was obliged to bide his time.

He disliked Sundays on principle, though he would have been hard put to it to name the principle. He found this Sunday somehow harder to bear for Sylvie's absence. Whatever jaunt she was away on, he knew nothing of it, though honesty compelled him to admit that he might have been told and forgotten. It was another matter of principle – he tended to be strong on principle – not to be too curious about Sylvie's personal activities, though the only person who drove him to that kind of honesty was Sylvie herself. If he was aware of any ambivalence in his attitude toward Sylvie, well, he was ambivalent about that too.

It was a kind of fidgetty desperation that led him eventually to call Doc Vickers.

"Greetings, tuan." It was apparently Doc's Malaysian period. "What does the tuan wish?"

"News. Good news. Got any?"

"'Good tidings of great joy I bring,'" Doc carolled and then, crushing Morpurgo's instinctive surge of hope, "Sorry, nothing

151

to uplift your heart, quite the opposite. What's the weather like up there?"

"Hot. Stuffy. Smelly."

"Then come, my lord, mount thy steed and join the old doc for a steak and a stengah, what say?"

And because he had nothing better to do and because of his frustrated love for the country and because it was where Sattin was, he went.

To his surprise he found Vickers in his office. "Paperwork, old son. Can't work for Whitehall without having to do paperwork." Vickers pushed away whatever it was that Whitehall required him to deal with. "Not to mention," he said casually, "a bit of swotting up on cancer of the lymph nodes. Didn't like to spell it out before. Come on, kind of thing that needs a noggin or two to wash it down." Vickers took him away to the bar. "Twixt me and thee, old son," he went on as they crossed the lawn toward Soapbox City, "get a bit slack in this line of business. Old Tiddlywinky isn't exactly the standard bearer of the medical vanguard, but I don't mind admitting that he nattered on about macrophages and contractility until I didn't know my anus from my ulna. Just had to sit there like a loony, saying yes, sir, no, sir, until I could scuttle off and do a bit of cramming."

Once installed in the bar he clinked glasses with Morpurgo. "*Slainte-mhath!* Lang may your lum reek." He smacked his lips appreciatively. "Suppose you'd think the old doc pretty callous if he said it was a nice change to have something new to work on. Not heart, lungs, reflexes, mental state and the odd bruise and fracture."

"Whatever turns you on."

"Might as well face it, old son," Vickers said. "Your boy has no future." Even sitting down he was able to tower above Morpurgo, as if trying to dominate him into the acceptance of the unacceptable.

In Morpurgo's mind, various schemes began to unravel like snagged fabric; a hole, unexpected yet expanding by the second, in his plans for the future. "Are you telling me he's dying?"

"Thought you'd want to know. Wish I could give you an answer. Trouble is, not as easy as that."

He took his refilled glass from the steward. "Let me ask *you* something for a change. How sure are you that the tovarich hasn't been having treatment?"

"Positive. Not in the last nine months, anyway."

"Couldn't, for example, have gone into some big block, all kinds of tenants, one of 'em a quack? All you know is he went in the main entrance, came back the same way?"

"He couldn't. We've been that close. All the time."

"Thing is," Doc said apologetically, "I haven't got the specialist mind. Generalist, that's me, anything for the quiet life." He drank a little Scotch, held the glass up to the light for no good reason. "Old Tiddlywinky gives his judgements" – he puffed himself up comically and made his voice plummy – "like this, tablets hot from the mount. He thinks the malignancy's followed a classical course from which" – he was still mocking Tildesley – "it is possible to predict, with some accuracy, the point of termination."

He resumed his normal voice. "Whereas one Vickers, poor benighted army sawbones, has the cheek, the downright, unmitigated gall, to think there might have been a period, maybe fairly recent, during which it might have been checked. Temporarily checked. Artificially checked. Had a word with the radiologist, little chat with the histologist, didn't confirm, didn't shoot me down either." Bringing his meshed fingers to the point of his considerable chin, he studied Morpurgo solemnly.

"Treatment. You're still on about treatment?"

Vickers nodded ponderously. Morpurgo found himself feeling a little angry, not against Vickers, against fate, but he knew what he knew. "Forget it." He forced a laugh. "Look, I'm not disputing your professional competence" – "The tuan is kind," Vickers interposed ironically – "but it's out of the question. No treatment, certainly not since we were on to him. If there ever was it would have to have been long before. Successful treatment at that, at least, they must have thought so."

Doc's heavy eyebrows rose comically. "Care to tell me why?"

"Sattin's no fool. He must have known what it was all about. And he must have told Moscow Centre. More likely they told him. Well, you can take it from me that they wouldn't motivate a sleeper with an active illness. Active *and* eventually fatal. Not just a question of ethics, you simply don't begin an important job with a tool that's going to pack up before you're through with it."

"See that," Vickers said reluctantly. "Still."

"Still," Morpurgo agreed. "Raises some problems. What makes you think he's going to die?"

Vickers pushed his glass around a little on the polished table. "Wants to," he said finally, and looked up to stare at Morpurgo challengingly.

"*Wants* to?" And yet, Morpurgo thought, he did not find the idea totally surprising.

Vickers turned his head to stare out of the window. The rambler roses on the other side of the glass were heavy with buds. And with greenfly. "Let me put it this way, Johnny. There comes a point – any practising doctor knows this – when, in some kinds of illness, you can throw away the book. When someone who's still alive ought to be dead, when you can say, 'Damned if I know what's keeping him.'" His face showed an exaggerated astonishment, as if he were acting out the feeling. "I'm not talking about our popular press cabbage stereotype, tuan, kept going until someone switches off the juice. Conscious and lucid, makes no difference. Book says they should have gone. You say they should have gone. *They* say, 'Bugger the book and bugger you! Go when I'm ready!'"

"And that's Sattin?"

"Sort of. Me and old Tiddleywinky, we did agree on this. Once Hodgkin's gets past a certain stage, it's an iffy business. You're not surprised if they linger, you're not surprised if they go. Get me?"

"He's reached that stage?"

"Think so. More or less." He leaned forward, very serious at last. "Condition's far gone, Johnny. Past the point of no return. The question is, is the patient?"

"Do you think he knows?"

"Knows he's ill, yes. Knows just how ill?" Vickers shrugged.

"Cool customer."

"The coolest. Use him to chill your Martini."

"Yours is a rotten job, Doc," Morpurgo said. "How do you square your Hippocratic oath with your conscience?"

Doc Vickers picked up his glass. "How do you square yours with anything?"

*   *   *

Sibley had a black eye, a beauty, also a superficial but nasty-looking contusion on his right cheek. "You fell off your bike," Morpurgo said without sympathy.

"Don't you start, sir." Sibley was grinning. "My mum hasn't

154

let me alone since I got home. Anyway, you've got it wrong. My bike fell on me."

"Like the man," Morpurgo said, his Monday morning feeling lifting a little with the appearance of Sibley, "who accidentally hit the copper's truncheon with his head. What do you want, anyway?"

Sibley unfolded a large sheet of paper. On it were ruled vertical and horizontal lines. Here and there in the series of rectangles so formed were bars of colour; red, green, blue. The whole thing was annotated in Sibley's neat printing. "Finished," he said with a certain pride. "Including Mr Archer's bits, too. Very helpful they were, sir."

"I hope you're going to explain this to me."

"All explained, sir, if you read the notes. Still." Sibley came round to Morpurgo's side of the desk, to use his forefinger as a pointer. "I've put the dates along the top and the hours down this side. If you look at this bit, you'll see the blue stops all of a sudden. That's Sattin's pick-ups, after Stringer made the drop. You remember, that's when we thought they must have tumbled to us."

Or been warned off, Morpurgo thought, but kept it to himself.

"The green," Sibley went on, "is treffs *after* drops, you can see how they tie in with the blue. And, of course, they stop too, same time as the drops."

"Now." The eager way he said it brought an involuntary smile to Morpurgo's lips. "This is the interesting bit, sir." There was also respect in Sibley's voice, Morpurgo realised, the respect of a man told to look at some unremarkable part of the sky and finding, sure enough, a previously unknown comet. Sibley's finger was stabbing at the red areas on his chart. "These are treffs, too. But with a difference. No drops. See what I mean, sir? Take this one. Then go back a bit. Stringer made a drop on April 23rd. Sattin collected, April 24th. Sattin and Kagalov treffed April 27th, bags exchanged. But look at this, another treff, May 1st. Bags exchanged."

"Cash," Morpurgo said. "We knew about that. Checks with Stringer's pick-up from a Sattin drop – see, here it is on your chart – and it checks with Stringer's payments into his secret account as well."

"Okay." Sibley was not to be put off. "That's true enough, sir. Checked it myself. But what about this, and this, and this?" His forefinger went thump-thump on the tabletop. "All exchanges between Sattin and Kagalov, but no Stringer-Sattin exchange and no connection with bank payments. Not only that, look at the pattern." He twitched the paper over. There was another chart on the reverse. "See, sir? Just over four clear weeks each between these three, but four months to the next, and another four to the last. It's got to mean something, sir!"

So it had, Morpurgo agreed, but he had a faint sense of disappointment. He had not been expecting revelations, yet, now there were none, it was an anticlimax.

"Know what I think, Mr Morpurgo? I reckon those were reverse treffs, instructions and stuff to Sattin from Moscow Centre. Stands to reason there had to be something like that, we know Sattin and Kagalov never spoke, not direct, not by telephone, not by post or anything. Well, that's how it was done."

Morpurgo pulled himself together. What *had* he been expecting, damn it? And what was wrong with Sibley's theory anyway? Communication between sleeper and Moscow Centre, once the sleeper had been activated, was one of the areas of interest, so far as KGB procedure was concerned.

"Ian, you've done a really good job, and I'll see that the Director-General knows. Go on like this and I'll be looking over my shoulder whenever you're . . ." He stopped himself. "Damn! I meant I'll have to look to my laurels."

Sibley laughed. "It's all right, sir. I knew what you meant. Where do we go from here, sir?"

The tone of Sibley's voice gave Morpurgo warning that he was in danger of slipping. "Where do we go from here? We go for Kagalov, of course. What else?"

Once again, Sibley prodded his chart. "There you are, sir. That's when it would be, eight days' time, fits the pattern just right. I mean we could have had weeks to wait. And it'll be Smith's at Victoria all right. That's where all these reverse treffs were, no small ads, no treff sign, no anything. Want me to start the ball rolling with the running boys, sir?"

"The running boys?" Morpurgo displayed mock disapproval. "It's not long since you were one yourself, young Sibley. Don't let anyone in Special Branch hear you talking like that. Anyway, hold your horses. I'd better have a word with the Director-General and Chief Superintendent Placket first."

He got no farther. The Knight was on the intercom. "Johnny,

I've been thinking. In view of what Doc Vickers told you, I think we'd better square ourselves with the Minister before the dentists get too enthusiastic."

Sibley tactfully withdrew. "You know what the politicians are like," the Knight was saying. "Moral problems are things they like talking about. Dealing with them is a thing they like to leave to other people."

"I'm not absolutely sure I know what you're talking about, Director-General."

"Cruel to be kind," the Knight said, unconsciously aligning himself with Oates. "Look at it this way. We have Moscow's spy, they have ours. Ours, so the Friends tell me, is in basically good shape, stand a bit of rough stuff, pull round in no time at all with proper attention when we get him back. Theirs, well, we know what Vickers said. Sooner we get him off our hands, the better. At the same time, we have our rights, and the main one is to extract whatever information we can before we let the fellow go. Incidentally, it nicely gets us off the hook with the Friends, they want the exchange much more than equal time, and they'll persuade the Cousins likewise."

When, Morpurgo wondered, was he going to get to the point?

"Now," the Knight continued, "we have to make the Minister happy. He'll fudge all right, they all do. What he wants from us is a good plausible excuse for fudging. So, as I said, cruel to be kind, but keep it under wraps. We don't want anybody thinking there's no difference between us and the Kremlin, use of drugs for non-medical purposes."

Morpurgo's mind unexpectedly presented him with the image of Sattin's face; calm, determined, contemptuous. Christ! he thought, there won't be all that difference.

"After all," the Knight finished, "which would Sattin himself prefer? Keep him going, on condition? Or just ignore him until he talks?"

Morpurgo was still looking at his remembrance of Sattin. It made him see that the Knight's question was utterly specious, and for that reason as pleasing to the Minister. "Wouldn't be too sure," he said, and was ashamed of himself for mumbling.

It hardly mattered. The Knight was not listening. "I think that's the essence of your argument, Johnny, just wanted to check. Must run. Minister's off in an hour or so, to make a speech in the Socialist Republic of South Yorkshire."

Morpurgo's phone rang while he was still wincing at the corny political joke. Steve, he thought, for no reason at all other than bad conscience, and prepared himself to be affable. Though not too affable, as that might arouse Steve's suspicions. Dear God! he thought, we're all secret agents born! But it was not Steve. It was Sylvie.

"Hello," she said. "I'm back. I hope you don't mind me calling you at the office."

"Delighted. I don't often have the pleasure. Did you have a good trip?"

"Very. Fancy you remembering. Did you manage all right?"

"Perfectly all right." What was it he had supposedly remembered? He couldn't ask now.

"Have you remembered the other thing?" Sylvie asked. Her voice, as always, was cool, unrevealing, yet he could fancy her smiling.

"Which other thing in particular?" He wasn't going to get out of this one.

"Ah, you don't." She was definitely smiling now.

"Sylvie, please, don't talk in riddles. I'm well supplied."

"Sorry. I should have thought. My flat-warming, remember?"

No, he hadn't, but yes, he did now. A party of some sort in her new premises.

"Yes, I had forgotten. I'm sorry."

"But you're coming? You said you'd come."

"I'd like to."

"Then come."

"I'm a bit pressed."

"If I said I'd like you to come?" She sensed victory in his silence. "Please come, Johnny. Seven to nine, it's hardly a major commitment. You'd meet some interesting people."

"You know how I get on with your kind of people. Bull in a china shop."

"Say you'll come. Please."

"All right. I'll come."

*　　*　　*

Sylvie's new place was just off Baker Street. He had somehow had the idea that it was in a run-down area, some short-lease building that would fairly soon be pulled down to make room for yet another office block. In fact, the street was very respectably

158

residential, a general air of discreet wellbeing. There were four bell-pushes, each neatly tagged with a name. The top one said *Sylvie Markham*, this semi-stranger who had enticed away his wife. About to ring the bell, he noticed that the door was not fully closed, pushed it and was inside.

Morpurgo went up. He wouldn't know anyone. They wouldn't know him, might ask him who he was. And what should he say? John Morpurgo? Sylvie's husband? Why not Mr Sylvie Markham? For Christ's sake, he told himself, sort yourself out! It's not Sylvie who's bothering you. It's Sattin.

Reaching the top floor, his preconception of the kind of place Sylvie had acquired was already substantially demolished. He realised that he had no idea what Sylvie earned, that, in fact, he had accepted her success in some hazy, relatively disinterested way without particularly associating it with money. The financial aspect presented itself to him forcefully now. The door of Sylvie's place was open. Even a first glimpse of the interior told him that it had a degree of luxury.

Standing in the doorway was a tall, lean, hungry-faced man like an advertisement for Dormeuil. Glass in hand, he was talking with soft-voiced intimacy to a girl with the unearthly, and, to Morpurgo, slightly repellent looks and air of a top model. Sylvie didn't do fashion, didn't do anything at all in the consumer field. He had no idea who they might be or why they should be here.

Beyond them in the thickly carpeted corridor were several not dissimilar groups with one thing in common, the loud, uninhibited conversational tone of success. The last traces of his false image of Spartan makeshift were dispelled. This was no dispiritingly comfortless attic but an apartment, an apartment of style at that.

True, what he had first thought to be a living room held a striking modern desk of steel and glass and a scatter of chairs, which, he supposed, made it an office or reception room. True, the walls were dense with geometrically arranged blow-ups of Sylvie's pictures, many of which he had never seen before. And true, he had passed, at the farther end of the little corridor, a door with a small sign that said: *Dark room. No entrance when light is on.*

But there was also a kitchen, and a small, elegant bedroom – single bed, his mind recorded – where numbers of people had left summer coats and a number of others were talking to one another with ears pricked for the first indication of better conversation elsewhere.

He looked for Sylvie, and found her, wearing a trouser suit he had never seen before. She had her back to Morpurgo. He made his way toward her as directly as the thronged room would permit.

Just as he reached her, she turned, looking past him toward the door. Morpurgo turned to see who it was that had drawn her attention, and found himself stiffening instinctively. In the same moment she saw him. "Johnny," she called. "You've come. How nice." Moving toward each other, they met in the centre of the room, he, she, and the man who had just arrived. She slipped an arm through Morpurgo's. "Meet Janos Petröfi. Jan, this is my husband.

Petröfi was a small man, neat, even dapper. He wore a good dark suit, but his tie was a little too wide, a little too bold and he had it secured with a conspicuously costly gold pin. When he smiled, he displayed two gold-capped incisors, exactly symmetrical at either side of his upper teeth. He also smelled quite strongly of aftershave, if it was aftershave.

He held out a small, fleshy hand with a good ring on each of the three centre fingers. "Mr Markham. A great pleasure."

Morpurgo touched the proffered hand briefly, nodding a curt greeting. He said, "Excuse me. Sylvie, can I have a word with you?"

"Of course." If she was at all surprised, she kept the fact concealed. "As soon as Jan has told me something I hope I'm going to be pleased to hear."

Petröfi took her hand solemnly, raised it toward his lips, bent his head and kissed her palm. He folded her fingers over the palm and continued to hold her hand. "Mr Markham, you have a very talented wife. You are a very fortunate man."

Sylvie used her prisoned hand to give Petröfi a little shake. "Tell me. You're doing it on purpose, Jan. Yes or no?"

Petröfi smiled more widely. "That you should doubt! Yes. Of course. *Why* do you doubt? Yes." His English was excellent, only a trace of accent, but Morpurgo knew his nationality, along with everything else about him. Central Registry at Curzon Street had a plump file on Janos Petröfi.

"Marvellous!" Sylvie said. "You just don't know how thrilled I am. I didn't dare think." She turned to Morpurgo, her eyes

160

shining. "Oh, do be pleased for me, Johnny. The Hungarian Ministry of Labour's given me the most marvellous commission. Carte blanche to photograph Hungarian workers in their jobs, all the jobs, any jobs, it's up to me to decide what I want. They'll just provide the back-up."

"And the money, dear Sylvie," Petröfi said. "My government is capitalist in such matters. It thinks, what do you say? that the labourer is worthy of her hire."

Sylvie laughed. "Jan, you know perfectly well that I'd do it practically for nothing. We'll come and talk to you again in a minute." Still holding Morpurgo's arm, she drew him gently away, Petröfi still smiling and bowing elegantly from the hips. "We must dine," he called after them. "A celebration, I insist."

"Where can we go?" Morpurgo did his best to keep anger out of his voice, but Sylvie knew him too well.

"Oh dear," she said. "Perhaps we'd better go in here," and she drew him into the dark room. Closing the door behind them, she pressed a switch. Morpurgo was disconcerted when it filled the room with a deep and sinister ruby light. "Puts a warning light on outside," Sylvie explained. "I don't suppose you want anyone barging in."

"Who *are* all these people?"

"Clients. Potential clients. Friends and friends of friends. You came determined not to enjoy it, didn't you?" Sylvie sounded resigned and a little sad.

"No," he said untruthfully. "Anyway, it's beside the point." Looking at her, even in this oppressive light, he could see all over again that she was beautiful in a quiet, unspectacular way, a way that made the model girl, indeed, most of the women there, look contrived, even bizarre. But she had crossed a border, leaving him behind.

Suddenly, he wanted very much to reestablish the relationship they had once had, a relationship based on love, on friendship – not always the same thing – on mutual respect and understanding. But first there was something to be cleared up. "Your friend Petröfi, how did you meet him?"

"Ah." She nodded wisely. "Of course. Oh dear."

"Yes," he said. "Oh dear. You know he's the London correspondent of *Magyir Hirlap*. And that *Magyir Hirlap* is the Hungarian *Pravda*, the state daily newspaper."

"Yes, I do know that. He also does work for some of the other Eastern European countries."

"Ceteka, the Czech news agency. *Trybuna Ludu*, the Polish . . ."

"The relationship is strictly professional."

"Oh, I'm sure." Morpurgo backed off a little, not wanting to be unreasonable. "But do you know what else he is? One of Moscow's wheeler-dealers in the West, listening for sensitive information, acting as go-between for all sorts of little deals. How did you meet him? And when?" He was trying hard to sound reasonable, but the damned crimson light was beginning to get on his nerves.

"I was introduced to him by Gordon Sukeley at the Press Club." Sukeley was the eminently respectable political editor of the eminently respectable *The Daily Post*. "When? I'm not sure. There'd be something in my engagement diary. I think about nine months ago. Would you like me to check?"

"No. It doesn't matter. It's just that . . ."

" . . . that it won't do for the wife of a man who's professionally hostile to people like Janos? Is that what you have in mind?"

"Did you invite him here?"

"Of course."

"Did he know I was coming?"

She laughed, genuine amusement. "I didn't know myself, not until I saw you. Listen, Johnny, I got Stella" – Stella was Sylvie's agent – "to make enquiries about doing a photo tour in Eastern Europe. Janos heard, got in touch with her, that's after we'd met at the Press Club. Strictly business. I'm the first Western photographer to get this kind of commission, they like to use their own people. I don't need to go looking for work, Johnny. It comes looking for me. So I invited him to my house-warming."

"This isn't your house. Your house is where we live."

"That's *our* house," she said gently. "This isn't a house at all. House-warming, that's just an expression." She unlaced her hands, fluttered her fingers at her sides as if uncertain about something. "I'll give it up if it really upsets you."

"What?"

"This. All this." She gestured to indicate their surroundings.

It left him temporarily wordless. He supposed that in this baleful light he must look as strange to her as she to him, except that she didn't look strange, looked . . . Sylvie. Just Sylvie.

He said, "I'm sorry. I've a lot on my mind. My job's important, too."

"You're wondering if this commission has any connection with your work. I don't discuss your work, Johnny. Not with Janos, not with anybody."

"Petröfi knows who I am, take it from me."

Someone knocked at the door. A loud voice, slightly tipsy, said, "Sylvie? Are you there? Come out. We miss you."

Morpurgo said, "When this is over, perhaps we could . . ."

There was another, louder knocking and another, louder voice, amid laughter, said, "Sylvie, come out. Someone's spreading the disgraceful story that you've got your husband in there."

Turning his head, Morpurgo shouted, "Piss off, will you?" A silence ensued.

Shaking her head a little, Sylvie said, "It isn't them, Johnny. It's you. They're all nice enough people, truthfully."

"So you tell me. What time will you be free?"

"Eight-thirty. Whether it's over or not, eight-thirty. If you were going to suggest that we went out somewhere."

"That's what I was going to suggest."

She nodded, smiling once more. "Welcome back." She kissed him very lightly on the cheek. "I'll have to go. It is *my* party." She switched the crimson light off, the white light on. Neither of them looked directly at each other, as if the new light were too revealing. She slipped out to a loud ironic cheer. Morpurgo let her vanish before he followed. The crowd seemed to go with her. Left behind, as if waiting for him, was Helga.

She knows! he thought. Sylvie knows!

Helga said, "Hello, Johnny. Steve couldn't come. I expect you know. I haven't had time to tell Sylvie."

She looked waifish, her eyes even larger than he remembered. She looked tired, too; more than tired, invisible strings tuned almost to the point of snapping. "I didn't know you were going to be here. I'm glad, though. Johnny, we've got to talk."

"Not here. Not now. Look, come through. I'll get you a drink." She would certainly get one for herself if he didn't.

Sylvie, in a far corner, appeared to be talking about colour temperature. *Appeared*, Morpurgo found himself thinking, why do I see everyone as *appearing* to do something. Does my kind of work prevent me from taking *anything* at its face value? Yes, said his alter ego; even your wife.

He got a drink for Helga, and went back. "I'm going to slip off. Sylvie won't mind and it's better for you." He looked round for Petröfi. "See that chap over there, little, dapper man?"

She looked, nodded. "Rings on his fingers."

"And bells on his toes. Steer clear of him. His name's Petröfi, Hungarian, KGB poodle."

"All right." She said it mechanically, agreeing simply because he insisted. Somewhere in the room, a telephone began to ring, shrill, somehow ugly in all the talk and laughter. A man's voice, trying to penetrate the general racket, said, "John Morpurgo? Anyone here called Morpurgo?"

"Here." Morpurgo made his way toward the voice, aware that some of those present were looking at him curiously. He thought: Mr Sylvie Markham. "Morpurgo." He stuffed a finger in the other ear to cut down the din.

"Sibley here, sir. I think you'd better come in."

"What's happened?" No more than a couple of yards away, Janos Petröfi, supposedly listening to some highly comical tale told by a girl in a purple jump suit, had his squirrel-bright gaze fixed on Morpurgo.

"Best not say anything on this line, sir, not too sure myself. The D-G's on his way from his club and night staff's in an uproar."

"I'll be there as fast as I can. Tell the D-G, if he gets there before me."

"Will do, sir. I think it's something big." Sibley cut himself off, or had the sampler come down on him, better safe than sorry?

He looked for Sylvie and could see neither her nor Helga. He went downstairs on the run.

*   *   *

He had seen Curzon Street looking less busy during normal working hours. As soon as he came through the street entrance he was told that the Knight was in Room 37, the small conference room. Going up in the lift with him were Miss Protheroe, Collins of Special Branch liaison and Kennedy of Political Research. Collins said, "Anybody know what it's all about?" Nobody did. Kennedy accompanied Morpurgo to Room 37.

The Knight, wearing dinner jacket and black tie, was at the

head of the oval table. Pryor, head of Communications, Venables, Political Adviser, and Steve Archer sat in a tight group around him. Sibley had a seat next to the communications trolley, just behind the Knight. The Knight beckoned Morpurgo to a vacant seat at his side. Kennedy joined Venables. Mrs Inche, of Reprographics, came in without knocking and laid a thick stack of A4 paper before the Knight; something important enough for a good many copies to be made.

Without raising his voice, the Knight said, "No formal briefing. Just read one of these and then we'll discuss." Someone gave Morpurgo one of the freshly replicated documents. He began to read. Almost immediately, he said, "Good God!"

It was a high-speed teleprinter tear-off, referenced and timed by GCHQ, Cheltenham, reproducing a TASS release from Moscow, 9p.m their time. Verbatim, unedited, it was a characteristic sample of CCP Newspeak in all its tendentious, melodramatic glory.

The Ministry of Foreign Affairs and the Ministry of State Security of the USSR have authorised TASS to make the following statement:

On Tuesday last, the British secret political police arrested a British national, Joseph Sattin, self-employed as a technical and commercial translator, on the charge of being a spy employed by the Committee of State Security of the USSR. This false accusation is categorically and totally denied by the Ministry of Foreign Affairs on behalf of the Ministry of State Security, the denial being issued in person by Comrade Leonid Karamzin, Head of the International Information Department of the Central Committee of the Communist Party of the Soviet Union. In his statement to TASS, Comrade Karamzin said, 'The accusation and arrest, news of which has so far been kept from the British people, are a deliberate and slanderous attempt by the British Government to worsen relations between the peoples of Great Britain and the USSR.

'Nor is this the sum total of this deliberate and malicious attempt to instil British workers with an unnatural hatred of the Soviet Union. The British secret police are currently torturing the innocent Joseph Sattin in a savage and inhuman attempt to force from him a so-called confession. The innocent Sattin is known to be a seriously sick man. As part of a brutal and cynical effort to break his will, the British secret police, the infamous Special Branch, are deliberately withholding drugs and treatment that would mitigate if not cure Sattin's illness.'

The citizens of the Soviet Union, and its many friends throughout the world, will know that Comrade Karamzin's true statements will be denied in London. On behalf of the Soviet Union and the many nations that share its concern for the rights and humane treatment of the oppressed classes of the capitalist West, Comrade Karamzin asks the following question: 'Why, in a country given to making hypocritical comparisons between its own legal system and those of the socialist democracies, has Joseph Sattin not been produced before a properly constituted court of law and publicly charged with his alleged crime?

'The world will supply its own answer, that the British authorities know better than to parade Sattin when any public appearance will provide the clearest evidence of the fact that he has been brutally used. They cannot hide the fact that he is a victim of the British secret police in their incessant attempts to slander the peace-loving people of the Soviet Union.'

Staggered, Morpurgo read through a second time. As he finished, George Pryor's senior assistant came in with a sheaf of teleprinter tear-offs. "Pouring in from all over the world," he said, "so are the FFIs." Fullest further information, Morpurgo thought; well, yes, they would be!

"Before we go any further," the Knight said, "I want to get two things straight. The first is that we remain calm, no heated arguments or accusations. We'll get enough of that from other people before this is over. And secondly, we say nothing, nothing to anyone at all, until this has been thought through, discussed and a proper response agreed with all concerned. The charge is political, the response must be political. We are not politicians, only public servants."

Somewhat political public servants, Morpurgo amended in his own mind, and then, amending the amendment; somewhat political, somewhat private public servants. He said, "I don't think any of us are going to disagree with that, Director-General, but holding off the Friends isn't going to be easy, if only because it means holding off the Foreign Office."

"And the longer," Steve Archer said, "we wait before making some kind of statement, the worse it's going to look."

Tim Kennedy laughed hollowly. "It doesn't exactly look good now." Pryor's assistant came in with another sheaf of paper, placing it silently before his boss. The telephone trolley produced a long, insistent trill.

"Which one's ringing?" the Knight demanded crossly. "Damn it, I thought I'd made it clear, no calls."

Sibley had located the offending phone. "Sir Jason, sir."

The Knight sighed, signalled to Sibley to switch the incoming call to the speaker.

"Hugh? Hugh? What the devil's going on?" The Dark and Stormy's voice, amplified, produced winces around the table. "We've got calls pouring in from half the world, they're trying to track down the Foreign Secretary, all the FO desks are having to call in staff. What in God's name have your lot been up to?"

"My lot?" The Knight frosted over instantly. "They don't get up to things, Jason. They get down to them. I recommend yours to do likewise." Morpurgo pulled a face. All that was needed now was a stand-up fight between the two knights.

"By the way, Jason" – the Knight permitted himself a faint smile – "where are you speaking from?" The smile spread to those at the table. They, too, could hear extraneous sound effects.

"My club. Just happened to be passing the tape machine, as luck would have it."

"Is this line secure?" The Knight used his silkiest tones.

Sir Jason knew it was not. So did the Knight. "I think we should continue this conversation another time, Jason. Good night to you." The Knight signalled to Sibley to break contact. "There," he said. "A sample, that's why I put it on the speaker. Now, let's see if we can thin out the wood sufficiently to see the trees. Leaving aside their usual intemperate language, it's nicely carpentered, all on a good solid basis of fact."

"Not on the business of having him charged," Steve told them. "All over in five minutes, remanded for seven days for the police to continue their enquiries." He seemed careful to avoid catching Morpurgo's eyes.

"Thought we'd better get it out of the way, Johnny," the Knight said casually – Too casually? – "You were tangled up in that little business that took you north." He returned his attention to the others. "He's sick, yes. Nothing secret about it, or won't be."

"Not now," Morpurgo said softly.

The Knight ignored him. "His illness has been thoroughly investigated. We shall be in a position to publish the findings, call in expert evidence if need be. And he'll get the appropriate treatment, naturally."

Pryor said, "Seriously ill, what does that mean? Will he die?"

"Sooner or later," the Knight said, "like the rest of us. As I said, we shall be in a position to publish a full medical report." He glanced towards Morpurgo, then at Steve Archer. Morpurgo found himself slightly puzzled; was there something he didn't know about? He shoved the question aside. There was another, bigger one to be asked, the question first and foremost in his own mind. He hoped he would not be the one to have to ask it.

He was not. Kennedy, sitting in thoughtful silence for some little time, said apologetically, "Just one thing I don't quite get, Director-General. How do they know?" Morpurgo saw that it was the question everyone had been waiting for.

Before it could be answered, Sibley said hesitantly, "And does *he*?" His face reddened a little. He had interrupted a discussion among men much his seniors.

The Knight, like Steve, was somehow managing to avoid looking directly at Morpurgo. "I noticed Head of Registry's still here," he said with seemingly inexplicable irrelevance. "Track him down, will you, Sibley? Give him the gist of events with my compliments, then say I told you he's only to stay any longer if he considers his night staff are incompetent. Don't want him turning into a workaholic."

Sibley left. The Knight repeated, "How do they know?" He was looking at Kennedy. "Or do you mean, who told them?"

Like Sibley, Kennedy reddened, fishing his pipe from his pocket and fumbling for his pouch. "Well, yes, I suppose I do, Director-General. Isn't it what everyone's going to ask?"

"The press, certainly." It was the first word from Steve Archer for a considerable time, and now he was looking directly at Morpurgo.

Before the conversation could continue, Sibley was back. "Sorry, sir." Sibley was flushed and breathing hard. "This just came up. Message from Inspector Baites, Special Branch, Heath Row. Kagalov's just arrived at Number 2 terminal, only hand luggage, hell of a hurry, Aeroflot flight to Moscow held for him."

He laid the message before the Knight, who looked at it without touching it. "Yes," he said. "Well, we do rather appear to have more questions than answers." Sibley left to complete his interrupted errand.

"I think we have our answer to the main one," the Knight said. "Kagalov didn't develop a suddenly irresistible attack of home sickness. We'd be fairly safe in saying he masterminded this one." He glanced at Morpurgo. "Lost your treff after all, Johnny."

Morpurgo said nothing. Won't wash, he was telling himself. Easy enough to dodge a leading question by saying everything was masterminded by Kagalov, but where did Kagalov get his information from? Who told him that Sattin had been scooped up? Who told him that Sattin was seriously ill, or that the word was about to be passed for the dentists to begin the softening-up process?

There was an answer to all of it, but it was a word rather than a name. The Knight, for all his skilled handling of an exceedingly delicate situation, knew the word all right – the four-letter word, Morpurgo commented wrily to himself – but he was not yet prepared to use it.

Steve tried to take the heat off. "The media will play hob with us."

"Never mind the media," Kennedy said. "What about Joe Padley?" There was a universal groan.

"Crucify us," Pryor said morosely, "right or wrong."

"Another of his endless demands for a Commons Select Committee," Steve said. "Chap ought to be locked up."

Kennedy made a noise of agreement. "Get him a good press in all the lefty papers."

One by one they realised that the Knight was sitting in an icy silence of condemnation. "May I point out," he said frigidly, as he regained their attention, "that I am not in the habit of conceding defeat in advance, particularly when we happen to be in the right." The rebuke had its effect. Sibley, returning for the second time, sensed the atmosphere without knowing what had caused it. A telephone began to ring.

Sibley took it. "Mr Claas for Mr Morpurgo," he said.

Morpurgo looked enquiringly at the Knight, who stiffly gestured assent. Morpurgo said, "Switch to broadcast, Ian. This is another one we might as well all hear."

"Boy, have you got trouble!" Claas said.

"Did you ring me to tell me that?"

"I take it the story's untrue."

"It's from Moscow."

"Okay, okay!" Claas said. "But you people will be making a statement?"

"Someone will. Can we discuss this another time?"

"Sure thing! Just wanted you to know whose side we're on. *Ciao!*"

"*Ciao!*"

"Whose side *are* they on?" the Knight asked stuffily. "And what's wrong with goodbye?"

"Doesn't begin with CIA." Morpurgo thought that wasn't bad for the spur of the moment, but let it go.

The Knight had come to a decision. "I don't think there's much more to be gained from just sitting here. Johnny, you and Steve stay for a moment. Everyone else can go, but stay by your phones and brief anyone who calls in." There was a small exodus.

"We're trying to track down the Minister," the Knight told Morpurgo. "I just hope we find him before the Foreign Secretary gets into the act."

"Perhaps," Morpurgo said, pushing his luck, "they haven't got telephones yet in the Socialist Republic of South Yorkshire."

*   *   *

"What do you think?" Claas asked.

Weber said, "It all adds up. I said there was some vital piece of information missing, remember? Now we know what it was."

"I think so too. It's a hell of a plan. How do we play it?"

They were in Claas's office. Claas and Weber had just had a satellite chat with Langley.

"Gives Morpurgo all four aces." Claas, his feet up on the desk, was wearing one of his older pairs of shoes. The blister on his little toe, the result of his Portuguese-made English shoes, was still painful. "That's what he'll think, anyway."

Weber nodded reflectively. "Mole. With that timing, he's going to be hard to argue against."

"But if he knew what we know." Claas left his remark unfinished; it was still more or less unfinished in his head.

"The question of treatment?"

"Uh-huh. Someone might hit on it."

"But by then it could be too late."

"Could be." One of Claas's telephones rang. "Yeah?" He listened for a while. "When?" he asked finally, and then, "So what kept you?" The phone squawked protestingly. "Okay," Claas told it grudgingly. "I'll see you guys are issued with tom-toms next time," but he was smiling as he rang off. "Kagalov is up, up and away. At least we got that right."

170

Weber looked pained. "I sure do hate seeing that sonofabitch slip out."

"Forget it. He wasn't going to be around much longer anyway. The big question, now, is, who do we back?"

"With what we know? We go along with the Friends."

"No Morpurgo? No mole? You just agreed; all four aces."

"With what we already have, four aces is too many. A rigged deck."

"How do you work that out?" Claas was puzzled. "With Mr Prime Minister Delahay poised on the brink of a terminal scandal, molewise?"

"I know. And Morpurgo, given half a chance, poised to push him."

"Because Moscow Centre couldn't have gotten their timing right without someone high up in British security to tell them about Sattin. One, he's been caught. Two, he's a very sick man."

"The official buzz being that the mastermind was Kagalov."

"Which can't be right, because that would mean Kagalov – Moscow Centre – knew all along Sattin was sick."

"Yet nine months' SV didn't turn up one scrap of evidence to support the theory. In fact the SV says Sattin didn't even know himself it was serious, let alone Kagalov."

"All because SV didn't turn up any treatment."

"So no trap."

"Just Morpurgo's mole," Claas agreed. "Unless we're right and they're wrong."

"Maybe we're right," Weber said. "Or maybe this is the biggest load of horseshit two smart-ass Langley hotshots shovelled together since Alan Dulles and the boys in the back room told JFK the Bay of Pigs area was perfect guerrilla country."

"Somebody has to be shafted," Claas said, discarding his pen and list. "Who's it going to be?"

"Us maybe." They sat in a long, long silence.

"They'll make a statement."

Weber said thoughtfully. "But not in a hurry. I mean, not right this minute. No, wait, they have to say something pretty soon at that. So they make a statement saying they're going to make a statement. I'm being serious, goddammit!"

"I'm seriously listening. Yup, I'll buy that. Something along the lines of not being obliged to respond instantly every time Moscow tells another lie. And then – uh – yeah, and then say

171

that this particular lie will be definitively demolished in due course."

"Definitively?"

"Definitively. Chapter and verse. Tomorrow."

Weber had already ranged on. "Listen, Warren, you want to know how I'm beginning to see this Moscow Centre gambit?" Weber was gazing at some beautiful scenery in the landscape of his mind, Moses getting his first glimpse of the Promised Land. "Suppose Security Directorate operated like Moscow. No, not Moscow exactly. Lefortova." Lefortova, as well as being the KGB's Moscow remand prison, was the interrogation centre for 'specials'. "I mean – okay, I know they don't – suppose Security Directorate operated ruthlessly on the multidimensional principle?"

"By now they'd have zeroed in on Sattin's illness," Claas said promptly. "Withholding treatment, pressing where it hurts." The KGB's multidimensionality theory postulated that there were innumerable zones of human vulnerability beside such obvious things as fear and greed; that even a saint had his pressure points. The trick was to find and use them.

"Right, that's what the Sovs would have done. It's what they'll assume the British have done, too. So, after – how long since Sattin was brought in? – after seven days, away goes TASS with the torture charge. 'Okay', they say, knowing it'll be denied, 'so seeing's believing. If he's okay, stand him up where we can all see.'"

Claas was nodding. "Sick man to start with. Six days of intensive interrogation, leaning on his illness. They think he's going to look like something from *The Curse of the Mummy*. They think there's no way Security Directorate can put him on show."

"Not bad thinking for a cowtown dropout," Weber said. "And Kagalov's only involved to the extent of tipping off Moscow Centre that the party's over, after which he sticks around a few days to foster the mole theory. So what's the payoff?"

"Every do-gooder, every bleeding heart, every Amnesty freak in the world is going to be hollering, 'Torture!' Then Sattin dies, Moscow can guarantee that simply by spinning out the phony exchange negotiations. Tortured to death in the hands of the Brits, in the Land of Hope and whatever else it is they used to have."

Weber wagged his head gently. "Not thinking it through,

junior. The trouble is, we always kid ourselves we're smarter than the opposition. It ain't necessarily so. I mean, what's *going* to happen? not what's meant to."

"I just said. The Brits put to shame in every country there is, even the five and dime ones. Make as many statements as they like, produce as much independent evidence as they like, the mud sticks."

"You've forgotten something. Security Directorate doesn't operate like Ivan. Since they found out he was ill they haven't laid a finger on him except to check his pulse. No mummy's curse, right?"

"Hell, you're right at that. Sattin hasn't a notion of what's been going on TASSwise. *And* he's not talking, no fraternising with the enemy. So Security Directorate can stick him up for all the world to see, and all the world will see is a man with a sickness that doesn't show too much, also a man who is not going to say one single word, not even if he has a chance to."

"You got it." Weber tilted his head pensively. "And Prime Minister Humpty's still safe on his wall, push-proof for another exciting instalment. When was he charged?"

"Sattin?" Claas suddenly saw the point of the question. "Last Friday. Remanded for one week, means they have to produce him again this coming Friday."

"That's it then." Weber spoke with crisp certainty. "That's what the official British response will be. A bunch of lies, and to prove it, a public appearance in court on Friday." He nibbled his lower lip. "Doesn't leave us too much time. Still, just enough at that."

*   *   *

"That lad Sibley, he's bright." The Knight sounded thoughtful.

"I agree." Morpurgo waited.

"Penny's only just dropped," the Knight said. "Does *he* know? Meaning Sattin." Morpurgo remembered Sibley asking that question.

"Know what?" Steve Archer broke a long silence.

"Know just how ill he is."

"You don't catch Hodgkin's disease overnight," Steve said. "Especially in an advanced stage. Of course he knows. Just as Moscow Centre must know."

"I don't think," the Knight said, "that's necessarily what Sibley meant. We can ask him, of course, but I think he meant, does Sattin know that all this was due to happen? Had they promised him this was how they'd get him back?"

"That would mean they knew he would be caught," Morpurgo pointed out. "And it would mean that they knew at least nine months ago. There's been no contact since." Even at this stage, the Knight was looking for anything that would enable him to ignore the obvious explanation. He pressed his point. "You're practically saying that they knew when they activated him. You'll be telling us next that they set the whole thing up."

The Knight wavered, "That *would* be hard to believe, I grant you. There was nothing faked about the Bowman operation. And they'll know now that we must have been on to them for some time."

"So they'll discount at least some of the disinformation," Steve said. "Which will give them a chance of working out which was the real stuff."

The Knight was reluctant. "Hardly likely to pick him to run an important operation if they already knew his health might not be up to it."

"He might not have told them," Steve suggested. "It'd be too much to suggest he didn't already know himself." He lit one cigarette from another.

Morpurgo realised that Steve must have brought himself right up to date on the medical history. He also realised he had very little idea of what Steve had been doing for the last couple of days.

"Yes, well it looks as if we must fall back on Kagalov after all," the Knight said. "He certainly masterminded the Bowman operation efficiently enough. And even when we put an end to it, he played you beautifully, Johnny. He knew what he had to do and he did it, nervelessly. Now he's gone, but only now, timing perfect to the last."

But it wasn't so, Morpurgo told himself. Yes, Kagalov had played his part, and played it well, but only because someone else, someone at the very heart of the matter, had kept up a steady flow of information. Not to Kagalov direct; SV would have been on to it at once. No, the unknown informer had communicated with someone else, either at the embassy – you couldn't run SV on that many people – or direct to Moscow Centre, thence to the embassy and Kagalov.

He saw Steve watching him through a veil of cigarette smoke. Steve's eyes were narrowed, but not against the smoke. And though the Knight had no smoke to contend with, he too was watching Morpurgo with a kind of narrow-eyed concentration.

They know, Morpurgo thought. They know bloody well. But they aren't going to concede it to me. Before he could say what was on his mind, the Minister was on the telephone, using the radiophone in his official car to link him with a secure line. This time the Knight kept the call to himself, no amplification, no speaker.

The conversation was brief. At its conclusion, the Knight summarised. "An official statement from Number 10, on the Minister's assurance that the whole thing is a fabrication. Categorical denial, and a further statement to the House by the PM at question time tomorrow." He glanced swiftly at Steve, though not so quickly that Morpurgo failed to notice. "Ad hoc meeting of the Cabinet security committee, ten o'clock tomorrow morning. You're to be in attendance, Johnny."

Morpurgo was surprised. Cabinet committees were big stuff indeed, potentially more so than Cabinet itself. He said, "Any homework to do?" almost adding: Like making a list of suspects. He had just made a further connection in his mind. Pressure, that was what this whole thing was about; open blackmail. Give us back Sattin, fast, and the whole thing will blow away like dust in the wind. But why the hurry for Sattin? Answer – easy – because Sattin, under pressure, could reveal something that pointed directly to the mole.

He said, "I suppose we'd better take the dentists off Sattin."

Steve said, "Done, old boy, first thing."

The Knight said, "Sorry, should have told you, Johnny. Too many things happening at once."

So, already, they were considering the possibility of having to meet Moscow's challenge by producing Sattin in open court. "Don't forget," Morpurgo said, "Sattin hasn't spoken yet. Put him up in public and he might recover his tongue. Or his lawyer might." He turned to the Knight. "He's been charged. He has a right to be represented now. If we don't do something about it, you'll have the Soviet embassy broadcasting that too."

Steve was shaking his head. "No. The embassy story is that he's nothing to do with them. So they won't press for a lawyer or anything else."

"Just his release."

"Not that, either. You know better than that, Johnny. These exchanges are always made on the basis that nobody knows anything about them officially. If you don't admit to spying, you're not going to negotiate any spy's release officially."

"You've forgotten, Johnny." The Knight was looking at his watch. "Schnitzler's working for them, usual channels, East Berlin."

"And they've named their contact over here," Steve said. Morpurgo had a strange feeling that the discussion had turned into a kind of theatrical performance, previously rehearsed, with a script he hadn't seen.

"Who's the contact?"

"An old friend," the Knight said, beginning to push his chair back. "Janos Petröfi." He got up, making a finicky adjustment to his bow tie. "And now I'm going where I should have gone about ninety minutes ago. The Garden. My daughter will have given me up for lost." He looked down at Morpurgo. "*The Force of Destiny*. If I'm lucky I might be there in time to hear Melitone's sermon. And I haven't taken leave of my senses. I happen to know that Mr Ambassador Voloshin's there tonight. He knows who I am. I shall take care that he sees me." No mention had been made of this intention during the Knight's conversation with the Minister. Once again, Morpurgo had the sensation of matters being settled in his absence, but he could hardly object if the Knight went to the opera.

"What would you like us to do? Stay here? Mind the shop?"

"Oh no." The Knight looked surprised. "The holding statement will have gone out. Nothing left to do until tomorrow. Don't be late. We'll go to Number 10 together. Nothing else? No, well, in that case, I bid you goodnight."

Steve, lighting yet another cigarette, watched Morpurgo through the smoke. "I'll hold the fort, if you like. Didn't Sylvie have some kind of do on tonight?"

"Yes." At least Morpurgo would have a good story to tell Sylvie in his defence. "I'll just ring and find out what's happening." He did. There was no one there. Nor was Sylvie at home.

Morpurgo came to a decision. "I'll take you up on that offer. I'll call in to tell you where I am, when I know myself."

But instead of leaving the building at once, he went down to

Central Registry. Rogers was night duty officer. "Anything I can do for you, Mr Morpurgo?" Rogers must have been bursting with curiosity, but in true Security Directorate style said nothing about it.

"Just want to check the index, one small point, then I'm away." Morpurgo, as a section head, had the right to interrogate the computer himself.

"Which areas?" Rogers asked, waiting to enter the information.

"P. And maybe some crosschecking in M."

Rogers operated the electromagnetic lock. "There you go, Mr Morpurgo. Let me know if there's anything else you need."

Morpurgo nodded his thanks. Not bothering to sit, he keyed in the P index and set it to run at half-speed until it was approaching PE. He punched in a half-second scan. PETRÖFI came up after about thirty seconds. He keyed in the documentation, running fairly fast, since what he was after, if it was there, would have been relatively recent.

At least, he hoped it would.

It was almost the last entry; a cross-referenced code under the CURRENT KNOWN CONTACTS sub-section. He keyed in a hold for the reference, shifted to MO, and repeated the earlier procedure. There was nothing under MORPURGO. He was greatly relieved, not because there were no other Morpurgos on record, nor because he had been wondering whether he might have been on record himself. Then, just as he was about to drop the self-locking console cover, he thought of the obvious. He keyed in MA and set the computer to hunt once more.

There were two MARKHAMs. The second one was Sylvie. The entry was cryptic, a reference to a current dossier. It had a distinctive cipher cluster; one indicating that the dossier was to be released to no one except on the personal authority of the Director-General. It also had a cross-reference to Petröfi, not the Petröfi reference he had just inspected; a new one, very recent. Inspection required the same top-level authority. He suspected he would be denied the authorisation if he asked for it. He knew he could not ask for it, not even about his own wife. Particularly not about his own wife.

11

Answers

"OUR SPY ON RACK!" SAYS MOSCOW yelled the *Sun*, leaving very little room on the front page for the story. SOVS STAGE SPY SCARE claimed the *Mirror*. NO SURRENDER TO BLACKMAIL, the *Daily Telegraph* warned, while the *Guardian*, with some shrewdness, had KREMLIN SPY CHARGE: DIS-INFORMATION PLOY? Only the *Times* played it straight: BRITISH NATIONAL NAMED IN SPY CHARGE, sub-headed SERIOUS ALLEGATIONS BY MOSCOW.

He heard the BBC's political correspondent say that the Prime Minister was expected to make a statement in the House of Commons at three-thirty. Capital Radio had tracked down Sattin's flat in Notting Hill Gate, while Radio London interviewed a nervous and somewhat bewildered sales director who had used Sattin to translate an instruction manual for a new vacuum cleaner.

All quoted the statement that Her Majesty's Government was not in the habit of responding instantly to false accusations from Moscow. The Prime Minister would make a considered reply in the House that afternoon.

As he prepared to leave, the telephone rang.

"Uncle John? Good morning, Uncle John. Where the hell were you last night?"

"Good morning, Henry." If there was anything worse than having to talk to Henry Liddle at present, it was having to talk to Liddle in a temper.

"I tried nine times to get you last night, Uncle John."

"Sorry. A bit busy last night."

178

"Too busy to spare a thought for your favourite nephew?"

"I still am, Henry."

"You should be careful, Uncle John. You mustn't be too busy for your own good."

"Well, you know all about it now. And the piece of information I gave you is still valid."

"I hope I don't know all about it. Silly of me, I know, but I don't like being fucked about over my exclusives." Liddle's venom emerged like pus from a burst abscess. Let's get one thing straight. I don't owe you. You owe me."

"Henry, this is going to be a rough day."

"You're damn right! I could have screwed you more ways than a Soho whore, don't you forget it. What did you give me in return? Sweet fuck-all, when all it needed was one lousy telephone call. You used me, Morpurgo. You gave me something to look after, because you thought it might come in useful later. Then, when you found you didn't need me, you left me on the back burner. Know what my boss said to me last night? 'What's up, Henry, all your contacts crossing their names off your expense account?'"

"Do you mind, Henry? I've got to go."

"The biggest story of the year, and I come out with a piece that could have been written by a trainee with a list of ministry mouthpieces and a talent for fiction."

"I'll give you one tip. The PM's holding a special meeting at ten this morning."

"Take a look at my fucking piece this morning. I knew that last night. And it isn't at ten, it's at nine.

"If that's what you think, you don't need anything from me." Morpurgo put the phone down, consoled to some extent by the fact that the great Henry Liddle could get his times wrong. At Curzon Street, he found a message awaiting him; make his own way to Number 10, the Knight would meet him there.

He put in a call to the Strand Palace, got no reply from Trigg's room, had him paged without result, and left the whole thing until later. If Trigg had seen a morning paper, he might well have guessed by now that the case had altered. Feeling faintly regretful about that, he took himself off to Downing Street.

It was not his first visit to Number 10; security checks were regularly made; but his first as a potential participant in the activity of government. If he were called, that was. He thought it

179

much more likely that he would kick his heels in some anteroom. He was admitted from the Horse Guards entrance and escorted along the path bisecting the garden shared with the Chancellor of the Exchequer's home at Number 11.

The duty plainclothes inspector from the Yard took him briefly away for a cup of coffee. He was returned just in time to see the Prime Minister descending the golden-yellow carpeted stairway from his private quarters. Among those waiting at the foot of the stairs was his knight, who looked uncharacteristically subdued. Everyone there was a great deal more important than John Morpurgo.

Apart from the Knight, there was also the Dark and Stormy, with Pringle, his Foreign Office liaison man, both in close attendance upon Merrilees, the Foreign Secretary. Sir Howard Fuller, the Cabinet Office security coordinator, was in the company of Sir Abel Simmons, the Cabinet Secretary, inevitably known as the Able Seaman.

Following the Prime Minister, Morpurgo saw that they were heading for the Cabinet Room. He held back, expecting to be told where he should wait, but the Knight, turning to look for him, beckoned him on.

"Quite a throng outside," Delahay was saying in his mild, faintly bookish way. "Crush barriers to hold the media at bay. Interesting to see which of you leave by the front door and which through the Old Treasury Building." It was a typical Delahay remark. Publicity seekers invariably left by the famous front door. They shuffled after him through the green baize-covered door, equally famous, but unseen by the public, that led into the Cabinet Room.

Morpurgo found the Cabinet Room much smaller than he had expected. He was feeling very much the lower lifeform; minnow among sharks or, in the case of one or two of them, outsize jellyfish. Skite, Delahay's PPS, showed him to his seat. There was no mistake, there was his name, elegantly hand-printed.

He was at the pillar end of the room, with the Knight on his left and, to his right, Sir Howard Fuller and the Able Seaman, occupying the small table customarily used by the Cabinet Secretary. The Prime Minister had seated himself in his usual position, at the centre of the truncated oval table which allowed him to see everyone present without leaning forward, and facing out through the garden windows toward the Horse Guards. The remainder of those present filled the gaps between Delahay and the Knight.

The Prime Minister put on the gold-rimmed halfmoon glasses beloved of the political cartoonists, peering over them to check that everyone was settled. Morpurgo would have expected a silence at this point, but it was somehow deeper than was natural, as if everyone there were waiting with bated breath.

The Prime Minister had nothing that inspired. He had been a stopgap choice, neither of the two factions of which the Foreign Secretary, Merrilees, and Morpurgo's Minister were the respective leaders having been able to command sufficient support to project their man irresistibly into office. Delahay was the third best his party could put forward; seagreen Incorruptible, a solid but uninspiring speaker, a creator of consent through boredom, with a mind that craved popularity but was too rigid to make the necessary compromises. In a celebrated hatchet job, the Leader of the Opposition had said that if genius was the infinite capacity for taking pains, how were they to class the Prime Minister? who had an infinite capacity for causing them.

"Well, gentlemen," he said in his soft, perpetually uncertain-sounding voice, "we have a spy in our toils. The Soviet Union accuses us of torturing him. Are we?"

"No, Prime Minister. We are not." The Knight sounded less confident than defiant.

"But he's sick?"

"He's sick, Prime Minister."

"Dying?" Delahay asked the question in the mildly interested tone of someone checking job references.

"You've received the medical report," the Knight said, "as has everyone else." Morpurgo frowned. Vickers had promised a written report, but, so far as he knew, it had not yet arrived. Or was this something else the Knight had asked Steve to handle.

"Indeed," Delahay said mildly. "What I want now, Sir Hugh, is a second opinion."

The Knight said. "I haven't seen the man yet, but my section head, John Morpurgo has. I understand that it was your wish to have him at this meeting."

Delahay peered at Morpurgo over his glasses. "Mr Morpurgo?"

This can't be true, Morpurgo told himself; John Morpurgo, nobody in particular, sitting in the Cabinet Room at Number 10, being asked to give his opinion to some of the most powerful men in the country.

"He's sick. And he looks sick. He . . ."

Sir Jason Bowers, after a brief, whispered conversation with the Foreign Secretary, said abruptly, "How? In what way?"

Morpurgo found himself temporarily at a loss. How could one explain that Sattin's sickness was, in a sense, a sickness of the soul?

Merrilees, the Foreign Secretary, a small, birdlike man with a habit of darting his eyes about as if to catch people in acts they were not authorised to perform, asked, "How can you *see* Hodgkin's disease?" Morpurgo was suddenly sure that he and the Dark and Stormy were in collaboration.

Morpurgo, beginning to be flustered, said, "It's not the disease itself that's visible. It's the dying." But he knew that wasn't right, either; it was the will to die.

Delahay interposed. "If we were to go down there, what should we see?"

It was a simple question, yet it went straight to the heart of the business. Morpurgo said, "A man in his fifties, Prime Minister, most of his hair gone, big frame but not fat. A false impression of ponderousness." He hesitated, then continued. "A quality of ordinariness, but that isn't really true either. Wheels within wheels, depth below depth."

He became embarrassed, yet what he was saying was correct. "Sallow skin, a bit dark under the eyes, hint of strain, not much, to be honest. I suspect he's a bit below his normal weight, but that's not very noticeable, either."

When he stopped, no one spoke, though they were all looking at him. His Minister had his head tilted judiciously to one side, as if listening for some distant sound. Catching Morpurgo's eye, he let his own wander away.

Delahay, still peering above the frames of his glasses, said, "Graphic, Mr Morpurgo, but not the description of a sick man, had that occurred to you?"

Morpurgo's Minister said, "With your permission, Prime Minister," then turned toward Morpurgo. "If that wife of yours took his picture, would anybody looking at it know he was sick? Never mind dying." The PM murmured, "Of course! *That* Morpurgo!"

182

With Sylvie, Morpurgo thought, yes, because Sylvie photographs the soul. It was impossible for him to say a thing like that. Snappishly impatient, Merrilees said, "Never mind pictures. Stand him at the bar in the Number One court at Bow Street. Would he look any worse than most people?"

"No." Morpurgo was about to qualify his remark, but Merrilees, like a good trial lawyer, gave him no opportunity.

"This is what we're talking about, isn't it? Can we stand him up long enough for people to see that he's in one piece? Hasn't had his fingernails pulled off, been beaten up. Well, can we?" Once again, Morpurgo was puzzled by the unwonted quietness of his own knight, who, beyond endlessly rotating a new and perfectly sharpened pencil – each of them had one, the product of sub-Incan administration – had barely spoken other than to thrust Morpurgo himself into the limelight.

"Mr Morpurgo?" The Prime Minister was leaning forward once more, ignoring the supposed design objective of the table in order to give himself a better view of Morpurgo.

"Yes, Prime Minister." The words were forced out of him almost against his volition. As if trying to lasso them before they escaped entirely, he found himself adding, "If he gets no worse. But you can't guarantee what he'll say."

Morpurgo's Minister, possibly provoked by the extent to which Merrilees had so far imposed his personality on the meeting, said, "Doesn't have to say anything much, wouldn't be given the chance. Answer to his name, nothing very dangerous about that. Anyway, don't forget, he doesn't know what's going on. No radio, no papers – am I right?" He shot the question at the Knight, who nodded. "So far as he's concerned, safe as houses."

Morpurgo looked meaningfully at the Knight, but got no response. The Prime Minister said, "Mr Morpurgo, you have doubts."

Well, had he? Sattin had no access to outside news. Whatever his suspicions of his own state of health, he could hardly suppose it had become an international issue. He shook his head. "No, Prime Minister. It's nothing."

It was the Cabinet Secretary who spoke next. "In that case, Prime Minister, what we're discussing now is the appearance in court of the man Sattin, before the public and the press."

"That and something else, Secretary. The substance of the statement I make to the House this afternoon."

"Of course, Prime Minister. But progress in the one matter is progress in the other." The Able Seaman's first remark, Morpurgo saw now, had been an informal motion, a proposal that, more formally worded, could be put to a vote, placed on record.

"TASS," Merrilees said. "If you have the press, do you have TASS?"

"Interesting point." The Prime Minister quite clearly saw it as such. "They issued the challenge, so they must be publicly refuted. Or, because they issued the challenge, they must be publicly slighted."

"Can we leave that kind of thing for the moment, Prime Minister?" The Minister sounded aggrieved, true to his reputation as a man who put first things first, or at any rate, after himself. "The statement's what matters. Don't forget Padley."

For the first time since the commencement of this curiously amateurish discussion – Morpurgo recalled that more than one minister, in his memoirs, had talked about the sense of unreality engendered by the realisation that one was, oneself, actually sitting round a table with other people like oneself, talking about things that could actually affect the state of the world – a sense of reality seemed to pervade the proceedings. There was one thing on which all of them could agree, a loathing of the loud-voiced, irreverent and 'traitorous' Member of Parliament for Leeds South-West, Joe Padley.

"Yes, well," the Prime Minister said, "the statement. What have we got so far? Secretary?"

Sir Abel Simmons, who so far, Morpurgo would have been prepared to swear, had not made a single note, said, "First, Prime Minister, an attack on the Soviet Union for its never-ending barrage of slanderous propaganda. Second, a counter-charge against Moscow for subverting British nationals. Third, the facts about the charge and remand. Fourth, that the Soviet ambassador has been informed of Her Majesty's Government's displeasure. Fifth," – Morpurgo was trying to restrain his eyebrows from joining his hairline – "a summary of medical evidence as to Sattin's state of health. Sixth, a categorical denial of the use of torture and seven," – The Able Seaman paused – "I presume, Prime Minister, some statement to the effect that Sattin's appearance in court will be open to the media and the general public."

The Prime Minister nodded. "Let me see a draft before one

o'clock, Secretary. Does anyone wish to say anything at this stage?"

"Padley," the Minister and the Foreign Secretary said almost simultaneously. The Minister commandeered the subject. "He'll repeat his demand for a Select Committee, we may take that for granted."

And unless he's slipping, Morpurgo commented to himself, one other thing is certain, he'll want to know how Moscow got its information.

The Prime Minister had interrupted the Minister. "Questions are inevitable, not just Padley's. I shall have a word with the Chief Whip to make sure that he's ready with some kind of throttler. Mr Speaker won't need to be told the whole thing is highly sensitive and Chief Whip must make sure we've got a suitable series of questions lined up. We can rely on the Opposition front bench to keep Padley's nonsense to a minimum, they'll want to get their own views on record."

This time, Merrilees was ready before the Minister. "I think we can pull the rug from under Padley, Prime Minister, if you answer his other question before he has the opportunity to ask it. I suggest an eighth point for the Cabinet Secretary to draft."

The mole, Morpurgo told himself; it has to be the mole.

"A brief account of Kagalov's part in the business," the Foreign Secretary continued, "with a heavy stress on the extremely sensitive security aspect, should dispose of any attempt to suggest that some sinister person lurking behind the scenes has been leaking vital information to Moscow. A mole! The thought of that ridiculous word being bandied around in the press again is more than one can bear."

Unless Morpurgo's imagination was responding to the pervasive air of fantasy, the Knight had almost totally withdrawn from what was taking place. The pencil in his hands had ceased to turn, he sat as if turned to stone. And well he might! He and Morpurgo had had their disputes over leaks and their sources, but the Knight knew a deliberate cover-up when he came across one.

But there was still the Prime Minister. He, surely, as the man who must stand up in a few hours' time and make a statement that would be the subject of headline treatment all over the world, should say nothing of which he could not be absolutely

185

certain. Yet he was very slow to question the point so deceitfully presented.

He nodded. "Yes, good point. You've taken it, Secretary? Excellent! Then all that remains for me to do is to remind those of you who are in attendance, rather than permanent members of this committee, of your responsibilities." He smiled his vague, amiable smile. "Quite unnecessarily, I'm sure, but best be formal. All matters discussed or decided in Cabinet Committee are by their very nature private, confidential and in the highest category of security."

His smile seemed to linger particularly upon Morpurgo. "Very well, sense of the meeting – as summarised by the Cabinet Secretary. Responsibility for the points summarised; collective, permanent members of the committee that is." He rose. "Good morning to you, gentlemen, and thank you for your contributions."

Morpurgo held back, while the others filed out after the Prime Minister. One or two of them, the Minister in particular, gave him a perfunctory nod, but that was all. His own knight had gone on ahead. Morpurgo was left alone on the holy ground. One of the Garden Girls, face vaguely familiar, came in and began collecting the pencils and scratch pads, giving Morpurgo a little, impersonal smile as she passed. He took a last look around this famous temple in which power was the god, expediency the religion, and left.

They dodged it, his mind was repeating insistently, deliberately dodged the whole question of leaked information. A mole was preferable to a scandal when your majority in the Commons was down to six. He found himself back in the hallway just in time to see the Prime Minister disappearing upstairs. The others had split into two small groups, his Minister in one, the Foreign Secretary at the centre of the other.

His mind suddenly reshuffled images stored since the time of his arrival, when he had seen the PM coming downstairs toward the waiting group of politicians and civil servants. Or thought he had. But he had been mistaken. What he had actually seen was a group of people who, for the most part, had just come downstairs, followed by the Prime Minister.

That thought led to another. Neither the Cabinet Secretary nor Fuller had made notes during the brief, somehow artificial meeting, yet Sir Abel Simmons had been able to list – no, to recite – a series of points that would serve as the skeleton of the PM's afternoon statement in the House. His new perspective told him that it was because they had already been discussed upstairs. Henry Liddle's information had been better than Morpurgo's. The real meeting had begun at nine, not ten, which was why the Knight, knowing, had changed the arrangement that they should go to Number 10 together.

Long before he reached his car, he could see the Knight waiting for him. At the sound of Morpurgo's quick footsteps crunching toward him over the gravel, he turned. "Sent my driver off. Thought I'd wait for you. The air's fresher." Morpurgo knew he was making a comparison with Number 10, where the pollution was subtler.

As they entered the Mall, heading towards the Palace, the Knight said, "Now, perhaps, you can see why people like you never get my slot."

"Insufficiently servile?" It was cruel, and Morpurgo knew it.

The Knight chose to accept it without comment. "No matter how you run it, security is a political thing. Against one kind of political belief, in favour of another."

"Are we talking about policy or expediency? Or isn't there any difference?"

"You make it hard for yourself, Johnny."

"I don't make it. It *is* hard."

"Think I sold out?" the Knight said quietly. "Is that it?"

"Didn't you?"

"No. You weren't there at the time."

"You mean I was present at the second meeting but not at the first?"

The Knight laughed, a quick mirthless bark. "Yes, well, you're capable of using your brain on occasions. I know that. I only wish you'd use it more." He relapsed into a silence that remained unbroken all the way to Curzon Street. The Knight said, "Come into my place. We might as well have this out."

Established behind his desk, he said, "All right, let's have your side first."

Morpurgo shrugged. "My side? They'd sooner have a mole than risk a general election. That's my side."

"It's not only your side, Johnny. It's your politics."

"I don't follow."

"You'd welcome a mole. It would cater to your prejudices."

187

"And they prefer to believe there isn't one, because it caters to theirs."

"Pretend?" The Knight appeared to find something wrily entertaining in the word. "If that's what they're doing, they've a funny way of showing it."

"They've lots of funny ways. I could sense that. I suppose the basic points of the statement had already been hammered out upstairs?"

"That and one or two other things."

"Padley? I'm sure he wasn't overlooked."

"He's one of yours, isn't he? Left-wing, anti-Establishment, anti-American." He held up a hand, checking Morpurgo's attempt to interrupt. "I mean that's the way they see it."

"Then why invite me at all?"

"They wanted to use you," the Knight told him. "Our Minister, Merrilees, Sir Jason and the two Cabinet knights, they wanted you there for a purpose."

"The only man who's actually seen Sattin, is that it?"

The Knight was shaking his head. "Didn't you sense that the second meeting had one purpose, and one alone, to commit the PM to a particular line of action?"

"I think," Morpurgo said, deflated, "you'd better explain."

"First, they want a new Prime Minister. Incidentally, 'they' includes Jason Bowers and the whole top echelon of the Friends."

"Setting him up, is that it? Persuading him to make a statement they can wash their hands of if things go wrong?"

"The Ides of March. They smell a scandal. When it comes" – Bitterness crept into the Knight's voice – "they'll persuade themselves it's their duty to put party before personal loyalties. Delahay will go, just as Douglas-Home went in '64, Heath in '75. Then they'll elect a new leader. Merrilees and the Minister both think they're in with a chance."

"And the mole?"

"The mole." The Knight let the word drop leadenly. "One of the things the PM decided at the first meeting, ably assisted by Merrilees – so ably that the Minister had to go along – was that the security services should go through the motions of a mole hunt. To pre-empt Padley, to be able to say, if anything comes up, that no stone was left unturned."

"Another phony security sweep. Kick it around from file to file, secret committee to secret committee, until it dies of old age.

I'm sorry, Director-General, but not so long as I have anything to do with it."

"That," the Knight said in a voice purged of feeling, "is just the trouble, I'm afraid. You won't have anything to do with it."

Morpurgo's anger vanished. In its place came a sense of disaster. "For the record," he said, "I'd have been pretty slow not to realise that you and Steve have come together against me over the last few days. It could only be one thing."

"Perhaps you'd like to tell me what it is?"

"I imagine Steve must have found out about me and Helga. I imagine he must have told you."

The Knight nodded.

"It's all over, not that that justifies anything." That's it, Morpurgo thought; affair over, career over.

"It isn't what I had in mind," the Knight said almost reluctantly. "When I said you wouldn't be having anything to do with the mole hunt, I could have added, 'And neither shall I'."

Morpurgo found himself at a loss.

"There will be an enquiry." There was something curious about the way in which the Knight looked at Morpurgo. "A very thorough enquiry. It has been authorised by the Prime Minister, it will report to the Prime Minister, and it will spare no one. It will not be carried out by us, nor by the Special Branch. It will be carried out by the Friends."

Morpurgo stared, unable to believe. The Secret Intelligence Service, its upper levels still smarting under the recollection of Security Directorate's brutal post-Philby investigations, had turned the tables with – Yes! Morpurgo thought savagely – with a vengeance.

"Of course," he said, "you'll resign?"

"I did. My resignation was refused."

"Did they give you any reason for throwing you to the SIS?"

"The Friends are the one body of people that couldn't be harbouring a mole. They've had all their information at second-hand and some of the most crucial, Sattin's illness in particular, the fact that it was really serious, they knew nothing at all about until after the TASS release last night."

It occurred to Morpurgo that the Knight suddenly seemed much more willing to accept the idea of a mole, but he was too preoccupied to pursue the thought. He now had a clear and painful understanding of the second half of the morning charade at Number 10. He had gone there, he thought bitterly, like Charlie Brown's Snoopy: This is the great spy-hunter sitting in the Cabinet Room with the men who run the country. Balls! He had been hoaxed; correctly and coldly identified as the man most likely to blow the whistle on suspected treason, and consequently, with all the skill of the world's most experienced ruling class, set up for the kill. He knew now why Delahay had made his 'unnecessary' point about the absolute nature of Cabinet Committee security.

"Would you like *me* to resign?"

"Johnny," the Knight said wearily, "the Friends have got the investigation, nothing will change that. So let them get on with it, while you get on with your present business."

"It stays with us?" Morpurgo was surprised.

"With you," the Knight corrected with a certain emphasis. "The exchange is still on. They don't want Sattin going back to tell Moscow Centre the two British security services are at each other's throats."

Back in his office, licking wounds that, for all their painfulness, had as yet barely begun to hurt, Morpurgo found himself speculating on the Knight's reasons for suddenly accepting the possibility of a mole, almost everyone's reasons for leaving him, John Morpurgo, in charge of Sattin, and, finally, at some length, about Steve Archer, ex-Friend and poacher turned gamekeeper.

*　　　*　　　*

Weber was already in, sitting in Claas's chair with his feet on Claas's desk. "How'd it go?"

Claas took the chair Weber normally used. "I don't like this heavy symbolism. I know who's in charge, but I feel better about it when I'm sitting over there looking at you sitting over here."

Weber said, "How'd it go?"

"It went just fine. You don't let the grass grow under your feet, do you?"

"I'm not paid to. Neither are you. Langley wants the heat turned up. I talked through the satellite for the best part of an hour last night. They're beginning to get anxious."

"Only now? They should have thought before. Well, tell them to relax. Things are warming up. The Friends are in among Security Directorate, full powers, that's by the way. The main thing is that Delahay is going to put his head on the block this p.m. There's a queue to sharpen the axe."

"That much," Weber said, "I already know. We have an invitation to the show. Tell me more."

"So what do you want me to tell you? Fish cooperates, but he keeps his cards pretty close to his chest, just gives me an occasional peek."

"You think they're two-timing us as well as Security Directorate?"

"No." Claas said it with a degree of uncertainty. "They just don't mean to be caught doing under-the-counter deals with Uncle Sam. They'll do them, get me? but they aim not to be caught. Well, the mastermind is a guy called Epworth. Fish says he would make Machiavelli look like some small town ward heeler."

"The question is," Weber said, "will Sattin show?"

"The word," Claas told him, "is, no."

"But by then, Humpty will have committed himself?"

"By then, Humpty will be perched on a wall one mile high, so many guys in line to push there may be a domino effect."

"All the Queen's horses and all the Queen's men?"

"Can do nothing. Zilch! They come up with a new party leader, maybe the Foreign Secretary, maybe the Home Secretary . . . He has the support of his parliamentary party . . ."

"He can form a government. And he has about three years to build up support in the country."

"You got it," Claas said. "And if the polls show him he's pushed his party back into a really convincing lead, he'll go to the country sooner. Then he's back with the best part of another five years to play with, and a good, solid working majority in the Commons."

Weber looked rueful. "Where did we go wrong? Four years even if you're stuck with a loser, on the job training for the first two, then the third and fourth running for next time. Where in hell did we get it wrong?"

"Plus a good two months before a new administration takes over from the old," Claas said. "You forgot that. Here they do the lot in three weeks and a losing administration is on the street within twenty-four hours. Anyway, boss, this is how it's going to work, so settle back and enjoy the show. Tell Langley to tell the brass to relax. The guys over here are doing just fine."

"Did you get it in writing?"

"In *writing*? What?"

"A guarantee that it's all going to work. Like, for instance, how are they going to make sure Sattin can't be put on display? Or that Delahay or somebody who's still rooting for Delahay won't think of an out, even if Sattin doesn't show? Like how do we know this guy Epworth won't pitch a spitball? So, did you get it in writing?"

Claas came close to showing emotion. "You're trying to tell me you called in the heavies."

Weber flipped a paperclip at him. "You're a pretty smart boy. Kansas City doesn't deserve you."

"Okay, Frenchie," Claas said, "you talked through the satellite. Who to?"

"Barzelian."

"Brazelian! I thought we were just trying to replace Delahay, not take over the country."

"Well," Weber said comfortably, "let's just say I'm a belt and suspenders man."

*   *   *

The Lobby of the House displayed the controlled chaos typical of a special occasion, crowded with 'strangers'; officials, journalists, visitors and guests, many of them distinguished. The Speaker had taken his seat almost thirty minutes previously, after which the House had dealt with minor business before the commencement of question time. The only questions of major interest being those that would certainly follow the Prime Minister's statement, the galleries were only now beginning to fill up.

Morpurgo arrived with only a little time to spare. He had made several more attempts to talk to Trigg, none of them successful. On the other hand, he had caught Sylvie. She had thought she knew why he was ringing. "Don't worry, Johnny, I understand."

"I'm sorry. I didn't have time to explain why I had to go."

"I'm sure. Incidentally, what did you say to Helga? She told me she'd seen you, then burst into tears."

Careful, Morpurgo, he had told himself. We're in no-man's land.

"I hardly spoke to her, beyond getting her a drink."

"Yes, well that's something I fancy she could have done

without. Did you know that she and Steve aren't exactly enjoying connubial bliss these days?"

"It doesn't surprise me." Everything he said would be noted as evidence, to be used against him later.

"And she has a drink problem. I'm surprised you didn't notice that."

"Look, I was only with her for a minute or two, Sylvie."

"The reason I know so much is that I took her to supper after the party."

"I didn't forget our date, it was simply . . ."

"I do understand, Johnny. In any case, it was probably a good thing. Helga badly needed someone to talk to, and I just happened to be available."

"She thinks a lot of you."

"So I gathered," Sylvie said drily. "It may encourage you to know that what she said about Steve made me review my opinion of you."

For a moment he had thought that that was the crunch, everything so far a cool, low-key preamble, typical of Sylvie's style, to being confronted with his affair with Helga. But no, miracles still happened.

"If I say I never really liked Steve, it's neither told-you-so nor wisdom after the event. If what it takes is a combination of male chauvinism, selfishness and an appalling lack of sensitivity, then Steve's in the right job and you're in the wrong one."

The generosity made him ashamed. "Before we go any further, will you have dinner with me?"

No one, he thought, could hear Sylvie laugh and dislike her. "It's all right, I'm not singing for my supper. And the answer is yes. If I had an appointment with HM I'd still say yes."

"Will you be home first?"

"I shall make a point of it."

He had almost rung off, which would have been infinitely desirable. "Oh, I nearly forgot. Your friend, Petröfi. Drop him, Sylvie. I couldn't be more serious. He's *persona* very much *non grata* and it'll do you no good at all to be seen with him."

Let no one tell him, he thought now, that all you got over a telephone was sound; the temperature had dropped toward zero and he had instantly felt it.

To be fair to her, she had tried to be fair to him. "Johnny, we discussed this last night. Don't bring it up again, please." Last night, before he had gone down to Registry and discovered they had a file on Sylvie Markham. He couldn't possibly tell her that.

He did his best. "Sylvie, I know it's a business relationship. I know the business is important to you. I know it must look as if I'm interfering . . ."

"You *are* interfering, Johnny. And you're asking me to refuse the most important commission I've ever had, just because it doesn't look good for someone in your position to be married to someone in mine."

"Sylvie! Please! Just listen . . ."

*　　*　　*

Standing, elbowed and jostled, in the Lobby, trying to find the Knight, Morpurgo could sum it up by saying he was not dining with Sylvie Markham tonight.

"There you are." The Knight bustled up. It was rare for the Knight of the Long Knives to look other than relaxed. This was one of the exceptions. "As busy as Budget Day," he said, looking on the throng with disfavour. Following him toward the gallery steps, Morpurgo was discomforted to hear an unwelcome voice say, "Afternoon, Uncle John. Quite a little gathering." Henry Liddle, sporting a red rose in his buttonhole, bore down on them. His questing nose tilted briefly toward the Knight. "Not often I grace this place, but this is one story I'm not relying on anyone else for."

"I dare say you'll find it disappointing," said the Knight frostily.

"Never can tell, Sir Hugh, never can tell." Liddle's reply was mechanical, his gaze ranging restlessly over the Lobby before coming back to Morpurgo. "I'm pretty good at finding things that've been overlooked by everyone else." He grinned wolfishly. "A snapper-up of unconsidered trifles, as Walpole put it. And from time to time, the odd considered one as well."

"Autolycus," the Knight murmured. "Walpole was serendipity."

The man was yet to be born who could make Henry Liddle feel abashed. "Much of a muchness, Sir Hugh. Also above the heads of my readers. Assuming that my readers have heads. No, all that matters is the story. Especially if it's one the panjandrums would sooner keep locked in the closet." Nodding with strictly rationed affability, he headed toward the entrance to the press gallery.

"Gutter scavenger," the Knight said contemptuously. "Like to know what's on his mind, all the same. Better go up. The Minister's already gone in. The PM will make an entrance any time now." Morpurgo, as he accompanied the Knight, saw Liddle briefly halted by Janos Petröfi before they went on together.

It would have been hard to imagine the House fuller. Apart from the tightly packed benches, their green leather almost invisible, the Members' side galleries were thickly populated by those unable even to find sitting space on the steps. The visitors' galleries were crowded and still filling. It all reminded Morpurgo of a theatre with a smash hit, standing room only show.

The Minister was already in his place on the government front bench. At his side, whether by accident or design, sat Merrilees. To the left of the Minister, an absurdly small place reserved by an Order Paper had been left for the Prime Minister, who, notwithstanding his lack of theatricality, liked, on occasions of this kind, to make an entrance.

A moment later he appeared from behind the Speaker's Chair; a slight, unimpressive figure with a scholar's stoop and the mild, blinking gaze of surprise of someone, so his comportment seemed to suggest, who, absent-mindedly choosing the wrong door, has arrived on the stage instead of in the auditorium. At the sight of him, the volume of sound rose sharply, those on the government benches showing public support regardless of private reservations, the opposition benches cheering ironically. The crowded galleries buzzed with comment and speculation.

The Prime Minister inclined his head ritually to the Speaker. Conscious of movement to his left, Morpurgo turned to see Sir Howard Fuller, the Silent Knight, sink down next to the Knight, although, presumably, he could have taken one of the seats reserved for civil servants to the right of the Speaker. He nodded at Morpurgo, his expression utterly unrevealing.

A hush fell. The junior minister who had been droning an inaudible answer to an unintelligible question sat down. A moment later, the Speaker was calling Delahay. The hush intensified. No Order Paper fluttered. Resting one hand lightly on the table, the Prime Minister formally requested the permission of the House to make a statement.

"Can't refuse," the Knight muttered. Someone behind them said, "Ssshh!"

"Mr Speaker, sir." Delahay, Morpurgo thought, looked more

like a minor noncomformist preacher than Her Majesty's First Minister, but his voice was not of the timbre to win converts.

"The House will be aware," he continued, "that last night the government of the Soviet Union issued a statement purporting to relate to certain events and activities in the United Kingdom. I say the Soviet Union, Mr Speaker, since the news organisation which released the statement is, as is well known, the wholly controlled creature of the Kremlin."

The Prime Minister turned his gaze pointedly toward the press gallery, where the TASS man sat only a few places away from the unmistakable Henry Liddle.

"This House, Mr Speaker," Delahay continued in his donnish drawl, "is fully aware that the United Kingdom, in common with all other countries in the free world, is subject to an unending barrage of slanderous, libellous and untruthful comment from the Soviet Union and its many puppet organisations. Her Majesty's Government, whatever the party in power, has a well-established practice of treating this kind of propaganda with the contempt it deserves."

This time the hear-hears came from both sides of the House, although Morpurgo noted that Joe Padley, that scourge of the security services and bane both of the Conservative Party and the right wing of his own, sat expressionless, arms folded.

"However," the Prime Minister said, "there are occasionally exceptions to this rule. They arise in cases when the incessant flow of scurrility which we accept as normal from the Soviet Union concentrates upon the propagation of particularly vicious and shameless lies."

"Who would have thought," the Knight quoted ironically, "the old man to have had so much blood in him?"

"Last night, Mr Speaker, was just such an occasion, and the House, I am sure, will expect me to respond accordingly."

Have his blood if he doesn't, Morpurgo thought.

"I propose to relate, therefore," – "Get on with it, man!" growled the Silent Knight with a ferocity that was an eye-opener to Morpurgo – "the true facts of the matter so maliciously distorted in the TASS statement. They concern another form of activity energetically and invariably practised by the Soviet Union in all countries in which civilised custom and the accepted rules of diplomacy allow it to have and maintain an embassy.

"We are fortunate, Mr Speaker, in having security services

which, in both skill and dedication, are second to none. They operate a devoted and ceaseless vigil to counter the espionage and other subversive activities of the Soviet Union throughout Her Majesty's realm.

"Early last week, officers of the Special Branch, acting on the instructions of Her Majesty's Government had, in conjunction with the country's internal security services, arrested all the members of a Soviet spy ring engaged in an attempt to obtain information on this country's counter-measures against the Soviet submarine threat."

Now the silence in the House was absolute. The bewigged Speaker, an elbow on the arm of his chair, a hand supporting his chin, might have been carved and painted wood.

"The leader of this ring, of which the other two members, I regret to say, were members of Her Majesty's Civil Service, is a naturalised Briton, Joseph Sattin. Trained and controlled by the Soviet KGB, he worked under the direction of a member of the diplomatic staff of the Soviet embassy, a Second Secretary, Commerce, freely accredited by Her Majesty's Government under the name of Yuri Borisovich Kagalov, but now known to be Boris Kirillin, a colonel in the KGB and an expert in electronic counter-measures.

"Here I must briefly digress in order to inform you, Mr Speaker, that Kirillin has now left this country, and also to tell you that the Soviet ambassador was summoned to the Foreign Office by my right honourable friend, Her Majesty's Minister of State for Foreign and Commonwealth Affairs, this morning, to have made plain to him, in the strongest possible terms, Her Majesty's Government's deep displeasure that a member of the diplomatic staff of a foreign country should engage in activities of this kind. At the same time, my right honourable friend made clear to him the anger and contempt felt, not only by Her Majesty's Government but also the people of this country, for those responsible for the tissue of provocative lies represented by the TASS announcement."

This time there was no mistaking the approval of the majority of the House, though Morpurgo's Minister and the Prime Minister's right honourable friend, the Foreign Secretary, appeared to be too exhausted to manage more than a single faint hear-hear!

The Prime Minister took the opportunity to remove his right

hand from the table and replace it with his left. So far, he had delivered himself of his exquisite periods with all the emotion of a Chinese peasant on being informed that a foreign devil had been attached and robbed by a gang of transvestite juveniles in the Portobello Road.

"I now come to certain basic facts," he said. "It is true that the Soviet agent, Joseph Sattin, is a seriously ill man. He has, and has had since long before his arrest, a form of cancer known as Hodgkin's disease. I am informed by medical experts that this disease is now approaching an irreversible state leading in the course of time to death. I leave this House to draw its own conclusions as to what kind of organisation, in what kind of country, would compel a dying man to continue illicit operations in its service while denying him recourse to medical treatment."

A good point, Morpurgo conceded, even if untrue, since it was clear that Moscow could not have been aware of Sattin's condition.

"In contrast to this inhuman attitude," Delahay was saying, "this man, granted asylum in the United Kingdom, only to abuse it, has received concentrated medical attention from the moment the general state of his health was realised to be poor."

His own backbenchers, at this stage, loudly expressed their approval of Sattin's treatment, not, as Morpurgo knew, because of their burning wish to succour an enemy agent, but rather because it presented their party as humane and charitable even to its foes.

"I now come to the contemptible charge," Delahay continued, "that this agent of a foreign power, who has betrayed the country that gave him refuge, is being tortured in an attempt to extract information."

This time the silence of the House was so intense that the sound of traffic outside the precincts became a low, steady rumble in spite of the sound-proofing.

The Prime Minister might look like a Methodist preacher, but even so, and in spite of his less than commanding presence, he had come to dominate his audience.

His declaration of certainty that the House would treat the Soviet allegations with scorn brought an almost fierce response from his own backbenchers and not a few of the opposition. Among the cheer-leaders, Morpurgo noted, was the Minister, sitting squatly and with thrust-jawed pugnacity, like the last man in, with ten to make and the match to win.

"I am taking this opportunity," Delahay said with a certain cold passion, "to deny those allegations" – hear-*hear*! "with all the power at my command." This time almost all Members bayed their approval, though, once again, Joe Padley sat motionless and unmoved.

The Knight followed Morpurgo's gaze. "Pound to a penny he's first on his feet," he muttered, but his words were almost lost in the crescendo of approval that greeted the Prime Minister's reference to the established use of torture in the Soviet Union. Moving toward his peroration, he trotted out the mandatory references to the rule of law in a free country.

"Joseph Sattin," he continued, "has already been charged before a magistrate in a private hearing. The law permits it, and it is no more than prudent when the security of the realm is at risk. Sattin was remanded for seven days, again according to established practice. I feel obliged to point out, Mr Speaker, sir, that in the Soviet Union, where the law is frequently used as an instrument of oppression, prisoners charged with political offences may be held for up to nine months legally, and illegally, but with official sanction, for as much as two years.

"In our own country, the law requires that the prisoner be produced at the end of the seven days in order that the magistrate may decide whether there is a continuing case for detention. Sattin will consequently be due for review this coming Friday. This time, however, in open and absolute refutation of Soviet charges, he will appear in open court and, to the extent that the size of the court permits, the general public and members of the international press will be free to attend."

Without further ado, the Prime Minister took his seat. Both Morpurgo's Minister and the Foreign Secretary leaned to murmur in his ear and all about him his backbenchers waved their blue and white Order Papers and chorused their approval. Other members were instantly on their feet, hoping to catch the Speaker's eye. Prominent among them was the formidable Joe Padley.

The Leader of the Opposition had the advantage of precedence and the normal agreement with the Clerks. His performance was predictable. He approved of everything the Prime Minister had said, but exceeded him in sanctimony also managing to convey, though not in so many words, that when his party returned to power it would have better relations than the present government with the Soviet Union, but also catch more Soviet spies. He was followed by the Liberal Social Democrat leaders and one right-wing backbencher, but by this time Joe Padley had become increasingly vocal in his attempts to catch the eye of the Speaker.

"Can't shut him up for ever," the Knight said. "He's been hammering away at security for so long, even his enemies will feel he's been badly treated if he isn't called."

The Speaker called two more backbenchers, but by now there was genuine tension in the House, not only on the benches but in the galleries. The press, too, had stopped recording these lesser speakers; they were waiting for Padley. Finally he was called.

A tall, burly man, thick-necked, bullet-headed, with a voice that had its own built-in loud hailer, Padley was disliked by most Members, regardless of party, but they would reluctantly concede that he was unstinting in his championing of the poor and underprivileged, and in his attacks on what he considered to be the growing restrictions on national liberty.

"Mr Speaker, sir," he boomed. "The greater the efforts of the British security services and political police to preserve our traditional freedom, the less freedom we seem to have, since the security services are apparently unfettered in deciding what they're going to defend and who they're going to defend it from. In the circumstances, Mr Speaker, sir . . ."

He got no farther, a tumult of Members chanting, "Speech! Speech!" while others shouted, "Question! Question! Ask the question!"

The Speaker finally brought them under control. "The Honourable Member really must abide by the rules of the House. He knows perfectly well that he may ask a question arising from what has just passed, but he may not make a speech."

"Course he knows," the Knight growled. "Got to get his knocks in first."

Padley, a member for over twenty years, knew the rules backwards. Having made a declaration of what he opposed, he began again as if he had never spoken. "Arising from what the Prime Minister has just told the House, Mr Speaker, will he now tell us whether he considers it desirable and democratic for the people of this country to be protected by organisations that lay themselves open to charges of brutality by conducting their activities in secret, who have no public accountability, and are consequently their own authority in deciding what they should and should not do?''

The government benches had become increasingly noisy as Padley developed his heavily loaded question. Taking advantage of their angry opposition, the Prime Minister spent a few moments in whispered consultation with his colleagues. "Trying to dodge the supplementary," the Knight commented. "Can't just say yes or no, damned if he does, damned if he doesn't."

The Prime Minister rose. "The Honourable Member's question, which some Honourable Members may feel they have heard asked and answered on more than one previous occasion," – he paused for laughter, chiefly from his own party – "merits further comment, since it gives me an opportunity, to which I am sure the whole House will expect me to respond, of paying a heartfelt debt of gratitude to the security services. It is to their ceaseless vigil that the country owes the apprehension of a dangerous enemy agent. Nor, in view of the Honourable gentleman's remarks" – he ignored Padley's repeated attempts to regain the floor – "will they fail to note the direction in which they should look for examples of people who are their own authority in deciding who and what, in this country and elsewhere, is to be defended from whom."

"Neat enough footwork," the Knight conceded, but Padley was once more on his feet, bellowing above the approbatory roar from the Prime Minister's supporters.

"Mr Speaker, sir. Supplementary question, Mr Speaker."

"Mr Padley," the Speaker said with a tinge of reluctance.

"Mr Speaker, sir, you will have noted that the Right Honourable gentleman opposite did not trouble to answer my question as asked. Since it may be that he does not know the answer, will he now agree that this House appoint a Select Committee to enquire into the functioning and accountability of the secret security services."

This time the Prime Minister's response was instant. He rose, said, "No, sir," and sat down again.

The redoubtable Padley, as most Members clearly expected, was still not finished. "Mr Speaker," he roared above the hubbub, "I beg to move the adjournment of the House on a definite matter of urgent public importance, namely the need for a Select Committee of this House to enquire . . ." The remainder of his words were drowned in a torrent of jeers, catcalls and cries of, "Sit down! Sit down!"

The Speaker finally stood, to quieten the House. When he had obtained silence, he said, "The Honourable Member of Leeds South-West is as aware as I am that he cannot move an adjournment in these circumstances."

Barely had he finished than Padley was up again, Ajax defying the lightning. "On a point of order, Mr Speaker. On a point of order." The tumult returned, particularly as Padley refused to sit down. Eventually the Speaker, once again rising himself, and then threatening to withdraw, which would have brought all proceedings to a halt, restored order and took the House back to the normal business of the day. Now that the fun was over, many Members, and most of the spectators in the galleries, began to drift away. So did the Knight and Morpurgo, accompanied by Sir Howard Fuller.

"Man's a public nuisance," Fuller said crossly, his normally bland features pink with annoyance.

"Oh, I don't know," Morpurgo said from an irresponsible wish to provoke. "We have a pretty free hand. Public masters, sometimes, rather than public servants."

"This is a democracy," Fuller said, further annoyed. "We don't tell people what to do. We expect them to do it without being told." Not content with this revealing utterance, he focused his irritation on Morpurgo. "Which, in your case, I should have thought, would be to make sure that that fellow's fit enough, looks fit enough, anyway, to silence the criticism once and for all when he stands at the bar on Friday." About to leave, he turned back for a parting shot. "I really think that you, Morpurgo, should know better than to stand up for agents of sympathy like Padley."

"Johnny, Johnny!" The Knight shook his head despairingly. "Why do you persist in going out of your way to make enemies?"

"When there's no shortage of volunteers? If it's all right for Fuller to parade his prejudices, why not me? He's supposed to be neutral. I'm not. Make sure the fellow's fit enough to stand at the bar," – he mimicked Fuller – "just like that!"

"Has to be done," the Knight said curtly. "Has to be done," and he abandoned Morpurgo in the busy Lobby.

12

Questions

When he emerged into the late afternoon sunshine, someone was waiting for him. "Mr Morpurgo. Remember me, Epworth? Mmmm, like to talk to you if that's all right."

"Of course." A good many people seemed to want to talk to him this afternoon, but it was little to do with popularity. "Share a cab with me?" Morpurgo spotted one and signalled.

"I take no pleasure in this," Epworth said diffidently.

Morpurgo understood instantly. The Friends were wasting no time. He realised that he had paid insufficient attention to Epworth at Century House. It was partly the man's apologetic voice and manner, as if he were constantly excusing his existence.

They twirled around Parliament Square in a tangle of traffic. From the window he had a good view of the Churchill memorial bronze, the figure stubborn. A newspaper bill said: SPY LIES – LATEST. Epworth saw it too. He said, "I wonder if it's that easy. Are they lies?" They turned into Whitehall. As they passed the entrance to Downing Street, Morpurgo saw that there was a sizeable crowd, drawn, he supposed, by that vague but strong public sense which, for no precisely definable reason, responds to hidden crisis.

"Are they lies?" he repeated. "Well, can't pretend we're holding Sattin for his health, can we?"

"Mmmm. *Did* someone tell Moscow, one wonders?"

"Kagalov didn't blow his own ring. And he certainly knew nothing about Sattin's situation after we brought him in. So there must be someone else."

"Of course, it could be you. Absurd, really. But I have to start somewhere." Epworth giggled, smiling disarmingly.

"You do know I'm the one who first suspected a mole?" They were entering Trafalgar Square. Something had disturbed the pigeons. They soared, circled, swooped, a wind with wings. Cat, Morpurgo thought idiotically. Cat among the pigeons.

"I know you were. Of course, theoretically, it would make good cover." The point the Knight had made.

"Up to a point. Beyond that, a hindrance. Even dangerous."

"Agreed," Epworth said reasonably. "But we're all in the risk business, all potential betrayers, wouldn't you say?"

"If you really suspected me, would you be talking to me like this?"

Epworth smiled his sleepy smile. "More cover? Neither of us is trustworthy. To the other, I mean." He hunched himself forward as if to communicate something of special importance. "I've been instructed not to get in your way too much before Sattin goes to court. It means I shall have to ask questions behind your back. That's why I wanted to see you. I thought I ought to explain."

"Good of you."

Epworth ignored any sarcasm. "We owe it to you to eliminate you as quickly as possible. You'll get to know, of course. From your friends."

"And my enemies." They were bowling along nicely now, passing through clubland, where a couple of words from people like the Minister, Merrilees, Fuller, over a Scotch or a very dry martini, could make or break. For once he found himself looking at things through Claas's eyes; the national power-house overloaded, its efficiency impaired, by the endless linkage of knights, lords and uncrowned kings, deference institutionalised.

"Mmmm," Epworth said. "Look at it this way. We're at opposite ends of the same side. A certain delicacy isn't out of the question. How long has your wife known Petröfi?"

It jarred Morpurgo out of any gratitude he might have been tempted to feel. "My wife is under surveillance?"

"Not your wife. Petröfi. Do you discuss your work at all? I mean, with your wife?"

"My wife" – Morpurgo found it difficult to respond unemotionally to this probing – this necessary probing, his professional self admitted – of his private life – "and I have been a little" – he searched for and found an unemotional adjective – "estranged lately."

204

"Sorry." Epworth cleared his throat. "You didn't answer the question."

So Epworth was going to be apologetic but tenacious, wagging his tail as he sank his teeth in. "To a limited extent. I expect you heard about the memorandum on intimate domestic security?"

"Yes. Amusing. How limited?"

Lean and slippered you may be, Morpurgo noted; pantaloon you are not. "No breach of security if that's what you mean. And nothing until after it happened."

"I'm not sure I understand. The arrest of Sattin and the Stringers, for example. You didn't discuss it with her until it was all over?"

The biter bit, hoist with his own petar, all the clichés, Morpurgo thought. "Look, I don't remember exactly what I told her. What I *can* say is that I acted correctly. Professionally. I always do."

"Mmmm. I'm sure. You won't mind if I ask her? Discreetly. No harrying."

"Can't stop you, can I?"

"You can't, I'm afraid. But goodwill helps, don't you think in this sort of thing? Oils the wheels?"

"I like to think so."

Morpurgo waited for Epworth to continue with whatever it was he was going to say, but Epworth said nothing. The taxi pulled up. "Here you are, gents," the driver said. "Spooks' corner."

Morpurgo got out, expecting Epworth to follow, which he did, but only as far as the pavement. He asked the cabby to wait, and walked beside Morpurgo as far as the entrance. "I'll do my best to keep out of your hair. But I'll be around quite a bit, you do understand? Friends, acquaintances and so on. Of course, you're not the only one. There's a pretty wide field."

"And my wife? Is she going to be bothered much?"

Epworth gestured ambiguously.

"Okay," Morpurgo made himself say. "Though I can't help feeling that if you really suspected me, you wouldn't have gone through all this rigmarole."

"I almost forgot," Epworth said. "They tell me you're interested in music. A good pianist, too."

Morpurgo nodded, cautious. Epworth smiled his small, shy

smile. "So am I, not very good on the piano, though. We must have a chat sometime."

*   *   *

He was waiting for Sylvie when she came home. "We're likely to have people poking about the place a bit, over the next few days." Or weeks.

"Ah."

"Did you know? Has it started already?"

"Not to my knowledge." Sylvie lit a cigarette. "But then, it wouldn't be, would it?"

"I don't mean secretly. I mean openly."

She studied him through the smoke. "The obvious question's been asked?"

"What question?"

"How did Moscow know?"

Straight to the *terra deserta*, the area of conjecture that the Friends had been authorised to explore. "The question has to be answered."

"And you've been ordered to investigate your wife."

"Not me."

"Someone delegated by you. Is that delicacy of feeling?"

"We're all under suspicion. Including me."

"I *see*." This time, he saw, she really did.

"Have you . . ." he began, and then began again. "If you've any little secrets, they'll probably turn them up."

"Have I been sleeping with anyone, that sort of thing?"

He took the plunge. "Have you?"

"Have you?"

He saw his job, his whole working life, in a new and disgusting perspective. "Of course not." Oh God!

"Good. Neither have I. When will it all start, the gents with the pincers and thumbscrews?"

"You'll know when you know."

She watched a slender double helix of smoke dwindle toward the ceiling. "Is it because of Janos?" Her grey, steady eyes returned to him. "I expect you think it wasn't my talent that got me that commission. I expect you think I ought to turn it down."

"No." Even to himself he sounded unconvincing.

"Good. Because I won't." It came to him, almost unexpectedly, that she had worked it out, slipping past all his minefields and

206

barbed wire to filch from him the fact that it was he – not her, not Petröfi – who was the subject of interest; and not to his own people, to the Friends.

"When they want to talk to you," he said, "tell them whatever you can, don't try to hide anything. That way, you'll have nothing to worry about."

"Have you?"

"Sins of omission, maybe."

Did she believe him? He was unable to tell. She studied him for some little time before speaking. "It's all a bit of a mess, isn't it?"

He knew at once that she meant their personal life, but gave nothing away. "We'll get things under control in a few days. Incidentally, I'm going to have to go out again." It had just occurred to him that Helga must be warned of what was to come.

"I didn't mean your mess," Sylvie said quietly. "I meant ours."

"Is this the right time?"

"Of course not. It never is. Could they stop my trip?"

"They've no reason."

"They'd find one." She drew on her cigarette, exhaled endlessly. "I don't want things – us – to fall apart by default, Johnny, just because we never found time to discuss them. All right, you're mixed up in bigger things, peace, war, the end of civilisation as we know it, blah-blah. But it doesn't make the little things any less important, the little things people – we – live by. We all have to go on trying to deal with them, even if the world comes to an end tomorrow."

She crushed her cigarette. "Say what you like afterwards, but don't interrupt. I've found something I'm good at, Johnny. Something where I get out what I put in, *my* vision, *my* ability." Small, practical hands clasped, head bowed, all he could see was the soft, glowing crown of her hair.

"Yours isn't that kind of job. My camera can only lie if I want it to lie, which is when I want to capture a different kind of truth. But you – I'm not criticising, just commenting – you live in a world where truth is always something to be hidden, where nothing's what it seems because you don't want it to be."

She surprised him by looking up to smile. "One of my favourite stories, two men on a journey, by car, by train. One of them looks

207

out of the window and says, 'Look at those sheep. They've just been shorn.' And the other man says, 'Yes, they do seem to have been. At least, from this side.'" She was still smiling, but her eyes, he saw, signalled a kind of resigned despair.

"If only," she said, "you could accept that there's another world beside the one you work in. If only you could learn to believe that, with most people, the side you can't see is just the same as the one you can. If you could – and if my camera can do it, why can't you? – we might be able to come to one or two decisions. About our future. Such as whether we have one."

Lamely, he said, "Yes. But first I've got to find out whether I've got a future, whether I'd be an asset to you, or a burden." He made the disturbing discovery that he could find nothing more to say.

Sylvie said, quite briskly, "Right, now we know where we are. I think I'll take myself out. There's a film I want to see, probably make me howl, but there, one should suffer for other people's art as well as one's own."

He made an indecisive movement. She misinterpreted. "Don't say you'll come with me, Johnny. You don't like gloomy foreign films, and I don't like unnecessary acts of charity." She went upstairs.

He let himself out of the house and walked quickly away. He found himself wondering how much truth there was in what Sylvie had said about the effects of his work upon his private life. Did any attempt to counter the dark side of human existence carry its own in-built contagion? He thought of some of his own kind he knew, Chief Superintendent Placket, for example, and said to himself: Yes, the contagion is real, and has been transmitted. He thought of others and countered: No, the risk is real but can be kept at bay. He thought of Sibley, young, enthusiastic, agreeable. Which way would Sibley go? Another question, the first question, returned: Which way had John Morpurgo gone? And if to the bad, was the disease curable, or had it, like that of Joseph Sattin, established a hold that nothing could end but death?

By the time he became once more fully aware of his surroundings, he had crossed the park and was more than halfway toward Steve Archer's – Helga's – flat, recognising an exquisite irony; he and Sylvie were on opposite sides of a widening gulf, yet he had a duty to her, and so, to protect Sylvie, he must protect Helga.

The Security Directorate called a certain five-storey building in Ebury Bridge Road – its function, to cater for another growth industry, telephone tapping – Tinkerbell. Sophisticatedly computerised, it was capable of selectively monitoring fifteen hundred calls simultaneously. Tinkerbell, he had little doubt, would have his own home telephone tagged by now, but Helga's, when she came to the Friends' attention, was Steve Archer's number too. There would be some inter-service infighting over sanction to tap. It would, for a while longer, be safe to call Helga from a public call box.

*　　*　　*

"If you're not on your own, it's an obscene call."

"I'm alone. Where are you?" Her inevitable question.

"First things first. Listen. This is the last time I'll be able to ring."

"Where are you?" He knew she had not absorbed what he had just said.

"Helga, never mind where I am. You've got to understand something. There's an investigation going on, something really big. Are you listening? There'll be enquiries, questions" – that was the power word; questions. Helga had spent half her adult life being questioned – "about Steve, about me, about you."

"Questions?" The word had penetrated.

"It's to do with this spy case. They're going to find out about you and me."

"Steve already knows." The words came tumbling out. "Steve knows everything. Johnny. I must see you. I *must*. Now."

"Impossible. Helga, do you want to go through it all again, people leaning on you, bullying you?"

"Already I'm going through it all again. Now, not tomorrow." The new note in her voice was an urgency bordering on fear. "You hear, Johnny, now? With Steve. With the children. Steve has told the children."

Oh my God! he thought, torn between the need to be finished with her once and for all and his understanding of what a man like Steve Archer could do if he considered his principles, his public school, varsity, upper-crust clubland principles, had been outraged.

"Helga, I'm sorry. But the best thing I can do for you at present is to keep right out of your way. You must understand that. They

209

may not bother us if we behave sensibly, but they're probably going to tap your phone, ask people about you, even follow you about, though you'll never see them."

She said, quietly, and for the first time he realised that her words were slurred, "He's going to divorce me, Johnny. He's already seen the lawyers." For the first time, he could sympathise with her drinking. It would take a stronger woman than Helga to withstand a righteous and vindictive Steve. The mention of divorce jolted him. Never mind his job; he would lose Sylvie!

"I'm sure he won't go through with it. He's got a lot on his plate just now. We all have."

Quietly, stubbornly, she said, "I must see you, Johnny."

He sighed inwardly, knowing he had lost. "Wait then. Let me think." If they were to meet, the trick was to take precautions even if they were not yet necessary, to think of somewhere where even inexperience could see at once whether it was being followed. He suddenly remembered a time when he had done something exactly like this.

*   *   *

Morpurgo paid off the cab and cut through to his final destination, a small red door in a blank wall at the end of a street that went nowhere. He went down a short, steep flight of steps and into another world. It was still central London, but the change was dramatic. To the left the waters of the canal, still as smoked glass, slid into the blackness of a tunnel. To the right, as he turned along the towpath, it stretched as far as he could see, the chip-age architecture of the Telecom tower standing, at this distance, side by side with the gothic spire and turrets of Saint Pancras on the metropolitan horizon.

As he began walking, the sound of traffic faded, the housing estates of working-class Islington ten or fifteen feet above his head to his right, an exhausted industrial landscape to his left across the water. On the far side of the canal, a disused narrowboat squatted above its mirror image, weathered outlines of once bright lettering spelling out PRINC . . . Behind it, a six-storeyed warehouse, each storey with its access door and hoist, brooded, broken-windowed, over the deserted waterway that had conjured it into existence only to abandon it when barges gave way to the combustion engine and the forty-ton truck.

His view ahead was uninterrupted. As soon as Helga reached

the towpath, he should see her as she, following his directions, would have been able to see any surveillance almost from the moment she left the Underground at King's Cross. He walked quickly, wanting to get this unwelcome piece of business over. Steve was going to divorce Helga. Sylvie would soon know.

He found himself surprised that it should all boil down to that; Sylvie would know. The only thing that mattered was that Sylvie would know.

As to what Sylvie would do, there was little doubt about that, either. Her professional standing, her plans for the future, her self-respect would demand a formal severing of their relationship. She would leave him – no, he decided, he would go – and probably file suit herself. Mr Sylvie Markham would be erased from her private as well as her professional existence.

The towpath passed steadily under his feet. From a crevice in a high brick wall to his right, a self-seeded buddleia hung, flower-heads already visible in miniature. Across the canal a single swan sailed serenely past a female mallard with seven scurrying balls of fluff. No complications for them. In the far distance he could descry a small figure; Helga had arrived, unfollowed.

But it was not Helga; there was something about its progress that said so even at this distance. The explanation came; a jogger, a man in a dark track suit. Morpurgo checked the time. She should have reached the canal by now. Telling her to return home if she suspected she was being followed was probably a tactical error. Nervous imagination might well have substituted for fact.

The jogging man passed him with a nod, intent upon whatever thoughts were passing through his mind. Ahead, a street lamp, only its top visible above the wall, glowed yellow though it was still broad daylight, almost the only assurance that there was life and civilisation close at hand. He imagined Helga, confronted with silence and isolation, panicking and retracing her steps to the safety of traffic and the first available taxi.

A moment later, with a sense of relief, he saw Helga against the background of the distant lock. But again he was misled. A man followed the woman, a dog too. All three came on together.

There was no possibility, now, that Helga would come. He had stopped by a lifebelt mounted on a board. Printed below it, in neat capital letters, was a graffito: IMAGES OF ROBOTS ABSENT FROM BREAKFAST TABLE. In its utter and surrealistic

211

incomprehensibility it was acceptable as a comment. He began to walk very fast, exchanging nods with the man and woman, along the route he had suggested to Helga.

Leaving the canal, he walked fast down York Way to King's Cross Station, fast down the full length of the platform, where clusters of trolleys piled high with sacks of night mail turned his progress into a kind of obstacle race, through the passenger concourse where closed shops and a handful of people served to emphasise an air of late evening desolation. No one – his planning had been theoretically perfect – could have tailed Helga unobserved. He found a telephone.

Before he knew it, he was through to Steve. Instantly, automatically, he started to apologise for a wrong number. Steve interrupted, his voice calm and implacable. "She's not here, Johnny. Would you like to leave a message?"

Crumbling under the pressure of this least wanted of situations, Morpurgo began a muddled statement. Steve cut him off. "I'll tell her you rang when she comes back." And then, as he was removing the receiver from his ear, "*If* she comes back."

*　　*　　*

She had been picked up as easily as a prostitute by a curb-crawler, just an 'Excuse me' by the man in the black leather jacket, leaning toward her through the open window. As she automatically stopped, turning toward him, the other two had jumped from the back of the car.

One of them said, "Get in the car, please, Mrs Archer." The other took her arm. A further moment and the car was drawing away with her sandwiched between the two of them.

The man in the leather jacket said, "Don't be alarmed, Mrs Archer, we just need your help in answering a few questions." The car made a U-turn and went rather fast in the direction of the Angel.

She was horribly frightened. It took her back to another time in West Berlin, after her escape to the West and her first security clearance. She had been walking along the Ku-damm toward the Tiergarten, the ruins of the Kaiser Wilhelm Memorial Church just ahead across Hardenberg Strasse, when a man had jumped from a suddenly braking car to block her path. The worst part, the thing that had stuck in her mind ever afterward, at least ten passersby had witnessed what was virtually an abduction. Yet,

212

fifteen years after the Nazi defeat and the disappearance of the Gestapo, not one of them had said or done a thing. Ten or more faces had gone blank, ten or more pairs of eyes flicked instantly away, ten or more pairs of legs slowed or speeded their pace. She had been consigned to a vacuum of awareness before being bundled into the car and swept away for questioning by people who eventually released her without ever identifying themselves.

In a street of apartment blocks, the car slowed and nosed down to an underground garage. A lift took her through five floors before stopping, delivering her to a short corridor, four doors either side, all closed, not even the sound of radio or television to indicate occupation. The man in the leather jacket knocked at the second door on the right. It was opened almost instantly by a woman with badly styled chestnut hair, white at the roots, and an expression that said: Don't ask me, I only work here. She was shown into a small room with closed shutters and the excessive brightness of overhead fluorescent light.

"Mrs Archer, the person who would like to talk to you hasn't arrived yet. Until then, we'll do our best to make you comfortable."

There were two chairs, a low, round table, plastic-topped, but nothing more in the way of furniture. The table held a pile of magazines – *Good Housekeeping, Vogue, Harper's* – all of them current. There was also a tray with a small dish of savoury biscuits, one cheap, inelegant glass, an open bottle of white wine, German, Schloss Börckelheimer.

She said, "My husband . . ."

". . . knows where you are, Mrs Archer, no need to worry. Please make yourself at home." He locked the door behind him.

She sat rigidly upright, her tension, like toothache partially moderated by a painkiller, establishing itself as a presence to be dreaded less for what it had done than what it was capable of.

In a loud whisper, she said, "But I never drink German wine."

*   *   *

Morpurgo opened his own front door. The first sight to greet him was Epworth, sitting in his, Morpurgo's chair, facing Sylvie in hers. Epworth got up awkwardly. "Mmmm, apologise for calling at an indecent hour. One or two little items that wouldn't wait."

213

Morpurgo suppressed all emotion. "Sit down, sit down. Drink?" Epworth murmured a refusal. Morpurgo took time over giving himself one. Epworth had moved directly into the beam of a wall light. It treated him cruelly, diminishing his already sparse hair, emphasising his soft, almost feminine profile. "In fact," Epworth was saying in his diffident way, "I've really gone as far as I can for the moment. Bad enough to intrude on your working hours, let alone your leisure."

Morpurgo looked at Sylvie. She sat still and silent, her mouth set in a faint and unconvincing smile. To Epworth, he said, "You didn't come to see me?"

"Another time," Epworth said vaguely. He nodded toward the piano Morpurgo had had little time to use during the last week. "Fine instrument. Never managed to master it."

Morpurgo ignored the evasion by accepting it at its face value. "What's your own field?"

"Shawm," Epworth said. "Sometimes I double on crumhorn and bombard. Expect you think it sounds – mmmm – a bit pretentious. You could come along and hear us next week. South Bank, six-thirty to seven-thirty, usual foyer concert." He smiled faintly at Sylvie. "Dare say you might be there anyway, Mrs Morpurgo." Nodding at both of them, he murmured, "Mmmm, must be off. Thanks for your help," released the catch of the door and slipped into the night.

"What was all that about?" He had an uncomfortable sensation of machinery; cold, bright, efficient; working soundlessly.

"One or two things that wouldn't keep." There was something cold and bright about Sylvie, too. She lit a cigarette, rather elaborately, not looking at him. "After all, you did warn me."

"Questions about your private affairs."

"No. Answers, about yours."

"There's more to Epworth than meets the eye. What was he after?"

She blew out smoke, still avoiding his eyes. "He asked me how long I'd known. He was ridiculously apologetic about it."

"Don't be fooled."

"Oh, I won't. I promise."

"What did you tell him?

"That I knew very little. Hardly anything."

"He's not stupid, Sylvie. He won't believe I told you nothing."

"Oh, but you didn't."

Something he could not yet define was about to reveal itself. He would not like it when it did.

"I'm beginning to think we're talking at cross-purposes."

Sylvie looked directly at him at last. "I'm talking about Helga. What are you talking about?"

"He told you about Helga? Just like that?"

"Simply, how long had I known. Of course, the answer was that I hadn't. And, of course, he knew that."

"What did you say?"

"I said, 'How long have *you*?' Of course, he didn't answer."

"It's all over. You might as well know that before we go on."

"Oh, I know. Just as I knew when it began. What do you want me to say? Oh, good, that's that then? I didn't know it was Helga; just somebody."

Oh Christ! he thought; it's happened. "I'm sorry. I don't know what to say. Or what to do. What do you want me to do?"

She stood, crushing her cigarette with controlled, small-scale violence. "Go to hell, perhaps. Is it all over for Helga, too?"

"She knows it's over."

She turned to him, a swift, sudden movement. "That's not the same, is it? You forget, I took her out to supper, the night you ran away from her at my party." She stood motionless, staring at him, her mouth set straight and hard. "Estranged, I gather that's how you described us to Epworth."

He began to say something in spite of having nothing to say. She cut across him. "You bastard," she said quietly. She looked about her for her bag, picked it up and went toward the stairs.

He took her shoulders from behind. "Sylvie, wait. Listen." She not so much slipped as exploded from his grip and, as she did so, kicked his shin savagely. The pain was exquisite. He let his hands fall. She went up the stairs.

He said, "Sylvie, I'm sorry," and then, shouting, "I said I'm *sorry!*"

She turned, halfway up. "You're sorry. I'm glad. Go on being sorry. It'll do you good." She looked down on him. He could feel blood from her kick trickling down the shinbone.

"I owe a lot to you, Johnny, that should give you something to think about. I dare say they think a lot of you in Curzon Street. Dedicated. Single-minded. A nose for putrescence, social gangrene. I've had to look after my own affairs while you made your work your hobby. So when you think I'm not the woman

215

you married, just remember who changed me. You! Pygmalion! Except that you married me first and changed me after. If you don't like what I am now, remember that. And remember that I'm very grateful. So grateful, I'm never going to change back."

Humbly, he said, "What's going to happen, Sylvie? What are we going to do?"

She looked at him in open astonishment. "What are *we* going to do? I know what *I'm* going to do. Move out! Now! Don't ask me if I'm coming back. At the moment I don't even want to think about it."

"You mean," he said idiotically, "it's over between us? For good?"

"Yes," Sylvie said in a cold, clear, utterly unemotional voice, walking up out of his sight. "It's over between us; that's the way it seems. At least, from this side."

*   *   *

The man who came into the room was old-young, almost bald, his sparse hair fine as a baby's. "Good evening, Mrs Archer. I'm sorry you've been kept waiting, you can't be thinking very kindly of us. Unfortunately" – He drew up the other chair to sit facing Helga – "this is all unavoidable, but I do apologise for the – mmmm – inconvenience." On the small table next to Helga stood, two thirds empty, the bottle of German white wine.

216

13

Excursions and Alarms

Morpurgo was just finishing his coffee when the call came. It was Doc Vickers. "Johnny, I think you'd better get yourself down here pronto."

"What's happened?"

"Come and see," Vickers insisted stubbornly.

"Is he all right?" Sattin was dying or dead and the whole thing would blow up in his face.

"Not dead, if that's what you mean. Listen, chum, my advice is to get your skates on and raise the dust. And don't say anything to anybody, not yet." Vickers rang off, having not so much as once called Morpurgo sahib.

As his car, hot and dusty, crunched to a halt, Morpurgo saw Oates waiting for him. "Morning, Mr Morpurgo. Can I have a word, sir?"

"Later, Oatsey. Doc Vickers in the Bin?"

"That's just it, sir." Oates looked more Stalinesque than ever, but also shuffled his feet like a small boy caught in mischief. "Doc reckoned I should have a word with you first."

"To do with Sattin?"

"Yes, sir, in a manner of speaking." Oates seemed unable to look Morpurgo in the face. "Fact is, sir, bit of a mess."

"Go on." A cuckoo was calling from the valley and there was a scent of new-mown grass.

Oates's eyes flickered over Morpurgo then slid away. "Fact is," he burst out, "a bit of a barney."

"With *Sattin*?"

"Yes, sir." Oates appeared to come to a decision. "Bit of a

217

mess, Mr Morpurgo. His face, I mean. Fact is, we were too late, sir. Gilly didn't see no harm and . . ."

The gist suddenly presented itself, appalling in its implications. "Keep out of my way until I want you!" Gilligan was in the day office, head tucked down, pretending to be totally absorbed in filling a plastic bucket at the sink.

"Keys!"

Gilligan handed them over in silence. Morpurgo took them roughly. Whatever had happened, he would hold Oates responsible. Oates dominated the other dentists.

Sattin was in bed. As Morpurgo entered, he turned his head, not so much to look as to show. He had a black eye to end all black eyes, inky dark, with blue and purple shadings. There was another bruise to the right of his chin, complete with broken skin. His upper lip was swollen grotesquely. There would be no chance of healing marks like that before Friday.

But that was the least of it. What struck Morpurgo as stunningly as if he, too, were the victim of violence, was Sattin's expression; rage, triumph, contempt. You're no better, it seemed to say. For all the fine words, you're no better than the rest. It was unthinkable that he should appear in public. Morpurgo slammed and locked the door, his steps hammering down the corridor like pistol shots.

Oates was waiting, Stalin dethroned.

"Why?"

Oates, pure misery, shuffled.

"Come on!" Morpurgo was almost shouting. "Don't you know what you've done? Not just the written rules, the moral rules. There's a difference, a borderline, between us and Moscow. You crossed it! Deliberately! And he knows! Make no mistake, he knows!"

Oates followed him back to the day office. Gilligan, hastily busying himself, moved a little too slowly to hide a bruise on his left cheek almost as colourful as Sattin's. "All right," Morpurgo said. "Who hit you? Sattin?" Something was very wrong.

Gilligan's eyes went to Oates. Oates, with the wooden immobility of a barrack-room lawyer, said nothing. "Pratt," Gilligan said almost inaudibly. "Pratt hit me."

Morpurgo turned to Oates. "Talk! Talk, damn you!"

Oates licked his lips. "It was Pratt's night shift. With Gilly here. Pratt's taken against Sattin, see? Lousy commie scum, that

218

sort of thing. Anyway, Gilly's feeling a bit out of sorts like, so Pratt, he says, why doesn't Gilly take a kip, sleep through the shift? Pratt'll take the night duty and Gilly can do the same for him some time."

Morpurgo was beginning to see it; sleeping through a shift was as heinous a crime as missing a watch altogether. "Pratt set about Sattin, is that it?"

"While Gilly was kipping," Oates said. "Let him have it, not sure when, didn't find out until I came on duty, Gilly was still asleep. Bloody great rumpus, wasn't there? Lost my temper, took a swing at Pratt. Gilly comes running, Pratt's worked himself up into a right stormer, Gilly catches one, that's it. Knocked Pratt cold, didn't I?" Oates looked at Morpurgo directly, now the truth was out.

"Where's Pratt now?"

"Sent him packing. Home, I reckon, wondering what's going to happen to him."

"Who knows, apart from you two?"

"Doc Vickers. Not pleased, the doc isn't."

"You know what you've done?"

"Get him right by Friday, Mr Morpurgo," Oates said without conviction. "Let me work on that shiner, won't be hardly visible by Friday."

Morpurgo gave him a look of such contempt that Oates flinched and turned away.

*   *   *

Epworth was in need of a shave, but otherwise fresh as paint. "Mmmm, well, Mrs Archer, I think that's about it. Thank you for your cooperation."

She had been questioned, on and off, throughout the night, waking nightmare, an endless reminder of things she had spent half a lifetime trying to forget.

She sat motionless, relationship between mind and body somehow distant and indirect, as if everything had happened to someone else, about whom she knew little and cared less. It was how she had felt for months now.

The man in the leather jacket laid a hand briefly and lightly on her shoulder. "You can leave now, Mrs Archer. We'll fix up a car to take you home."

She lacked even the energy to look up. She had come to this

219

place with a feeling of generalised fear, wanting to go as soon as they would let her. Now, so far as she wanted anything at all, she wanted to stay. Any inanimate body, once at rest, tends to remain so.

"Mrs Archer?" The man in the leather jacket looked questioningly at Epworth.

Epworth, gently, said, "Don't you want to go home, Mrs Archer?"

With no sense of surprise, no sense of anything, Helga found that she was crying, nothing dramatic, just a slow trickle of tears that dropped, warm, on her tightly clenched fists.

Epworth said, "Get Olive, will you?" The other man left.

Epworth leaned forward to Helga. His face had assumed an almost vacant look. "Would you like to ring your husband?"

She shook her head.

"Is there anyone else you'd like to ring?"

This time she could barely manage to shake her head.

The middle-aged woman looked as if she had spent a restless night, but that was how she had looked the previous evening. She put two hands about Helga's elbows and lifted. "Come on, dear. A nice cup of tea, then someone will take you home."

As she was led from the room, Helga said, "I think I will go back to Germany," her voice barely audible.

"Mmmm," Epworth said in his vague way, "not possible, not just yet. We have your passport. You'll get it back in due course."

It produced a response. "My passport is at home."

Epworth blinked, turning away. "Your husband gave it to us. Routine, nothing personal."

Her face showed a dull and weary pain. "He has done this, isn't that so? Everything? My past? My background? My . . ." She drew down her upper lip between her teeth and shook her head, unable to finish.

"I think," Epworth said diffidently, "that's something you should discuss with him. And I think – please forgive me if this sounds impertinent, Mrs Archer – I think you should see a doctor and tell him some of the things you've told me. I think he would – mmmm – be able to help."

He nodded at the woman. She persuaded Helga from the room.

"Germany?" the man in the leather jacket repeated. "Where

220

would she go in Germany? There isn't a single member of her family left."

Epworth sighed. "Yes," he said. "I know."

*   *   *

"The plot," Weber remarked, "thickens."

"Durn tootin'," Claas said. "Much thicker and we won't be able to see each other across the room." His heart was not really in the banter, neither was Weber's.

They were leaning on the upstairs bar in the American Club in Piccadilly, occupying a corner and contemplating two untouched Campari sodas. The barman polished glasses at the other end. The only other occupants were a young American and an old American. The old American wore a hearing aid and spoke on the assumption that everybody was deaf. He had a taste, as he was explaining to his companion, for whisky sours made only with Jack Daniel's, fresh-squeezed lemon and one *small* lump of sugar.

"So," Weber said.

"So," Claas reached tentatively for his Campari, then changed his mind. The deaf man, over by the window, said, "Ask your father. He'll confirm."

Claas said, "It seemed like a good idea."

"Seemed to *be* a good idea," Weber corrected.

"But not now," Claas continued, missing the point. "Right now, it seems like one of the lousiest ideas I ever had. My old political science prof would flunk me on content even if I had the style of Henry James."

"If you had the style of Henry James," Weber said confidently, "he'd flunk you on style too. Are you trying to tell me you've got cold feet?"

"Like I was paddling in the Potomac on Christmas morning. Getting colder all the time."

The deaf man announced, "I can pick out Jack Daniel's blindfold from any twenty bourbons you could line up. Ask your father. He'll confirm."

Weber, as wearily resigned as if he were Daedalus watching Icarus pushing at the outside of the design envelope, said, "But we *know*. That's the big thing, Warren, we *know*. And they don't, so we can use them but they can't use us."

Claas, considering the point and his Campari soda, concluded

221

that he preferred the Campari. He drank half of it without tasting a thing. "You think so?"

"I know so. They can't control us, but we can control them."

Claas signalled the barman for a repeat. The deaf man was shouting. "And by golly, that's the way it was, every damn time. Ask your father, he'll confirm." His companion, patient, said, "I'll ask him, sir, but he won't remember. He doesn't remember things like that too well."

Claas said, "Some people want to bring this government down, right? But we only want to bring Delahay down. Well, to me that's like being in a car that's heading for the edge of the cliff with two guys fighting over the controls because one of them wants it to go *clean* over the cliff but the other one only wants it to go *half* over."

"Warren," Weber said seriously, "that is one hell of an awful analogy. We're not fighting anyone. We aren't even in the car. What we have is a steel hawser fastened to the rear bumper that will check that car before it reaches the edge, but so suddenly that the guy at the wheel goes out through the windshield."

The barman put two more Campari sodas in front of them. Weber now had a pair. He said, "Look, put those in a big glass, will you? and freshen up the ice." The barman took them away. Weber said, "No, it's a lousy analogy whichever way you look at it."

"The thing is," Claas said, "neither of us – I mean us and Moscow Centre – know for sure whether the car will *reach* the clifftop, or if it does, whether it will go over, or if it goes over, who it will take with it." Watching the barman return with Weber's double Campari, he said, disgustedly, "Ah, let the thing go over! It's the only way to get rid of the lousy analogy."

"The thing is," Weber said, "I agree about the analogy but not about the rest."

Over by the window, the deaf man said, "Well, ask your father anyway. He might confirm." He looked baffled and resentful, as if what he had testified on oath was Jack Daniel's had turned out to be Old Crow.

Weber said, "Well, kitty should be in among those pigeons all right."

"Yeah," Claas said, "so what will they do, over there in Curzon Street?"

"What can they do? Even if they fix the guy's face, they can't fix his mouth, and won't he know it!"

"You bet," Claas said mechanically. "So Delahay's made to look a monkey. His majority of six vanishes like a crowd on the sidewalk when the cops start taking names. National elections, big swing to the left, Uncle Sam gets marching orders on nearly two hundred tactical and strategic bases. That wild man, Padley, has his Select Committee, the Brit security services, plus us, like as not, gets a press as bad as the one we had back home in '77, '78. President comes down on Director, Central Intelligence. DCI takes it out on a German Frenchman, Kraut Frog has only one guy to kick . . ."

He stopped. Weber was laughing, noiselessly but uncontrollably, slopping the double Campari soda he had been lifting toward his mouth. He fumbled for his handkerchief, shoulders shaking. "Want me to hit your back?" Claas asked hopefully.

"Boy!" Weber said when he could speak. "That is one terrific scenario! Only that's not the way it's going to be, junior. Five years over here and you pretend you don't know how they do it."

"How who do what?"

"Delahay's party. Do you really think they're going to sit around wringing their hands? By tomorrow afternoon the knives will be sharp and the Ides of March just round the corner."

Claas was uneasy. "That's something else. What if the wrong guy tops the poll?"

"What's the matter with you? The Friends didn't go to all that trouble just to get Sattin roughed up. Come the backlash and Security Directorate is in deep trouble. The dirt will rub off on their minister. When the party elects a new leader to take over from Delahay, Merrilees will be a shoo-in and SIS will trash Morpurgo. All we have to do is sit back and enjoy."

"*If* Delahay goes."

"He'll go! Party tradition, when it's a choice between power and a particular leader, that's what *you* told *me*, right? With them, party loyalty means stretching out your neck so they can slit your throat easier. You told me that too."

Over by the window, the man with the deaf aid snapped very loudly, "Ask your goddam father! Ask him if I can't be one goddam ordinary sonofabitch! Isn't anyone in a better position to confirm."

*   *   *

In due course the Knight stirred. "Well, there's only one thing we can do, only one thing left to do." He looked meaningly at Morpurgo.

Oh no, Morpurgo thought, not me! If your thing is my thing, it's a Director-General's thing, perhaps even a ministerial thing. I'll do it if I'm ordered, but the worm never volunteers for the hook.

The Knight sighed, probably divining Morpurgo's thoughts. "That man of yours, Trigg. Think he'd do it?"

Understanding the question perfectly, Morpurgo said, "Do what, Director-General?"

"Stand in, you bloody awful man! Stand in for Sattin!"

"It's an altogether different thing, isn't it?"

"Is it? Why is it? What's the difference?" The Knight, having made up his mind, wanted to be convinced that he was right.

"Standing in for a treff with Kagalov – brief, private, no one but us any the wiser if it hadn't come off. This one?" The full enormity of what they were considering began to make itself plain. "My God! Substituting one man for another in a court of law? A criminal act in itself, but that's the least of it. If it came out, the government would collapse like a house of cards." And yet it was possible, outrageous but possible.

The Knight cupped one hand inside the other and thrust both under his nose, his breathing audible in the ambient silence. "Where is he? Still at the Regent Palace?"

"Strand Palace. I don't know."

"You don't *know*?"

"He wasn't important any more, not until now. Anyway, I don't own him."

"More's the pity. Get him."

"I can't guarantee a thing."

"He'll do it," the Knight declared, as if holding the power of life and death over Trigg. "All right, he may have a price. Everybody does. We'll pay it. Don't tell him that, though. Play on his better feelings." He reached down his bowler, brushed it automatically on his sleeve. "Country threatened, democracy in danger, communist conspiracy, just go on pressing buttons until you find the right one. And get him out of that damned hotel and put him somewhere safe."

Back in his own room, Morpurgo found a message, would he ring Mrs Archer, urgently, at a number he didn't know. She must be crazy! Ignoring the message, he called the Strand Palace. The

224

operator came back to say that no one was answering the room number. He asked for Trigg to be paged. The operator came back again. "Reception says Mr Trigg booked out this morning, sir."

*　　*　　*

The Thames, replete with salt water, was poised almost motionless between the minute of the high water mark and that in which, imperceptibly at first, the tide would turn on itself and take the pent river downstream toward the mudflats of the Kent and Essex coasts. It was a day for tourists, sunlight strewing the normally brown water with shades of green and a million winking diamonds. A tug with a barge was making upstream, aided this far by the inward sweep on the sea. In another five minutes it would have to contest with the river. Sylvie watched the tug. Her mind's eye focused on its bows and, to either side, two foamy sweeps of light like angels' feathers. The fifty mill. lens, she thought, yellow filter, not much below a fiftieth or the foaming water would be frozen.

"Coffee, Miss Markham."

"Sorry. Daydreaming." She smiled and the girl smiled back, placing the tray on the low table. The wall behind her was where, most likely, the flood blow-up would go. Sylvie had leaned it against the naked concrete, ready for the two technicians to hold it up while she made her decision.

Encouraged by the smile, the girl stared admiringly at the blow-up. "It's super. I wish I had your talent, Miss Markham." Sylvie had run through six or seven spools in the West Country, after the February floods. This one was the pick. Most of the scene was emptiness, the almost white emptiness of a totally overcast sky sitting above a pale superfluity of water. From the water rose three trees, naked-branched. Their reflection in the still floodwater yielded a perfect symmetry, so that it would have been possible to turn the picture upside down and obtain the same effect.

"Thank you. It would look rather good on that wall, don't you think?" There you go, Sylvie told herself; it wouldn't look rather good, it would look bloody marvellous! "What about this one? I thought that pillar, over by the circle entrance. You don't think it would be lost when the place is crowded?"

Flattered, the girl said, "Oh no. It's much too strong to be lost, if strong's the right word."

Strong was very much the right word. Two men, walking

225

down a street, foreground to middle distance, the road surface obliquely lighted by intense sunlight so that it presented an etched outline of pavé. Their twin shadows stretched long and thin behind the walking men, but they themselves were all but invisible in the jet blackness, only their upper bodies hinted at by hair-thin strokes of light where the invisible, newly risen sun caught them horizontally. She had walked the village, a crumbling, half-dead hamlet on the Spanish *mesita*, two mornings running to get the series of shots of which this was the masterwork.

"Yes," she said, "I think you're right. It can hold its own."

The girl was suddenly shy. "I'm taking up your time. Your coffee's getting cold."

"Plenty of time. This is just a try-out. We're not hanging until Sunday. Thanks for your help." She watched the girl walk noiselessly away, framed by concrete pillars with randomly textured surfaces. Pictures here, she thought; everywhere pictures.

"Everything all right, Miss Markham?" The exhibitions manager; people were always materialising from this place or that.

"Everything's fine, thank you. I expect you're thinking what an age I'm taking."

He was shocked, a dark-haired, slightly intense young man with eager eyes and a floppy lock of hair that he was constantly tossing back. "Please! Take as much time as you like. It's you who's doing the favour. I just came up to tell you that Sir Peter will pick you up for lunch at about a quarter to one." He looked around him anxiously. "Where are your two blokes?"

"I sent them off for their break. They've been very helpful." She sent him away with a smile. Yes, Miss Markham. No, Miss Markham. Of course, Miss Markham, anything you say. Poor Johnny, she thought. Poor old Johnny. Just when his marriage appears to be set for life, his wife turns into someone he doesn't know, someone he didn't marry.

Her coffee had gone cold. She drank a little anyway, ate a biscuit she didn't want, rather than appear unappreciative, then lit a cigarette and looked at the thick folio of prints which represented her new life. She had feelings; not of pride or even satisfaction; feelings of helplessness, frustration and, finally, a kind of desolation.

She crushed her cigarette, stood up, smoothing her skirt, pushing up her hair with skilful fingertips, paying devotion, in short, to the glamorous, the talented, admired, commended, the married and yet unmarried, loving and yet unloved, unhappy and always crisply elegant Sylvie Markham, who could look, in this vast, deserted gallery – why was an empty theatre always so much more empty than anything else? – at the scattered summation of her status and her talent and see it as secondary, arid, irrelevant.

"Here we are again, Miss Markham," said one of her two technicians as they mounted the stairway side by side. "Got it all worked out, have you?"

*　　*　　*

Morpurgo's knowledge of cricket was limited, but as he looked, briefly distracted from his real purpose, the bowler bowled, the batsman made a stroke and the ball, when he finally located it, was travelling toward the boundary in a direction seeming to bear no relationship to anything that had gone before.

"Nice a glance as you'll ever see," said a well-remembered voice behind him. "Well, worked it out then, did you, sunshine?" Trigg held the inevitable Guinness in one hand, a half-smoked cigar in the other. So far as Morpurgo could tell, his mood was genial.

"Phony Tony steered you here, right?" Trigg went on. "Running it close, mind. Four days I said and four days I meant. Give you a bit of a shock, did it, when you found I'd checked out? Still, you thought of Captain Joliffe. Knew he'd remember. One of my little passions, is cricket."

"Why did you check out? Sorry you got yourself involved?"

"By!" Trigg said, pityingly. "Not too bright, you lot, are you? I didn't *get* involved, sunshine. I involved myself. And if I decide to disinvolve myself there'll be nought you can do about it. No, when I read all about it, give him till first thing Wednesday, I told myself. If he hasn't shown up by then, think again. Now lad" – Trigg finished off his Guinness – "you and me's got to get things settled pretty quick, it's not my style to hang about. Lost your fancy Russian, right? I can read, you know, so long as it's big print."

"Yes." The wormwood bitterness of that particular cup came back to torment Morpurgo. "But Sattin we still have."

"Aye," Trigg said, "but no more need for me to stand in for him."

Morpurgo was tempted to go, now, without another word. Why should he care what happened to a prime minister, a government, a party for none of whom he gave a tinker's curse? He could bargain for terms with his wife; carry her bags, find her taxis, enter full time upon the job of being Mr Sylvie Markham.

A lonely patter of applause signalled the dismissal of one of the two batsmen. "Hardly good enough to get himself out," Trigg commented. "I thought you said your lot never went in for torture."

The shrewdness of the assault almost took Morpurgo's breath away. Trigg read his expression accurately. "If you don't" – He grinned wolfishly – "why can't he go to court then?" He set his empty mug down between them. "I'm not daft, lad. You need me. I reckon there could only be one reason."

"We don't torture," Morpurgo retailed the story.

Trigg listened with the polite disbelief of a hostile judge before delivering Morpurgo's third jolt. "What do you reckon? Was he put up to it, should you think?"

"Put up to it? What?"

"This feller Pratt," Trigg said, displaying the patience of one dealing with the mentally deficient. "Did someone set him up to duff your man?"

He had Morpurgo on the ropes. "Who, for instance?"

"Moscow," Trigg said with his air of persisting in the face of wilful obtuseness. "The KGB or whatever they call themselves when they're at home."

For a moment the plausibility hypnotised Morpurgo. He recovered. "No, it wasn't like that. Just a zealot. We usually spot them in time."

"But not this one."

"Not this one."

"He'd talk," Trigg said presciently. "When he got to court, he'd talk."

"No way of stopping him."

"So you thought you might con me into playing a bigger part, is that about the size of it?"

"Yes."

Trigg grinned, but he was thinking. "If they caught me out. Thought about that, have you?"

"Yes. Not that it'd be my worry."

"Bigger fish? Aye, I can see that. You'd be for the chop though, I reckon."

"I might. That's my worry."

Trigg chuckled. "Not thinking about you, sunshine. Thinking about me." He followed – or appeared to follow – the game for a while. Out of the blue, he said, "Why? Why do you do it, all this stuff?"

"My job."

Trigg made an ambiguous sound. "Using a lie to tell the truth, it'd be. Get caught out, only thing they'd believe is the lie." He was staring at Morpurgo as if waiting for another, more acceptable explanation.

"The lot I work for," Morpurgo said, "and the lot *they* work for are used to getting away with things, so long as they have people like me to do the dirty work. The joke is, they call themselves Us. And they call us Them."

In a tone suggesting that never before in a long and varied life had he heard anything so unbelievably daft, Trigg said, "You *what?*"

"The elite. They're different from you and me. You and me, we're Them. They're Us."

"Us!" Trigg said it witheringly, rhyming the word with a combination of book and buzz. "Them! By! That beats all, does that! So you and me's on the same side, is that it?"

"That's the way I see it. And certainly the way they see it."

"Then we shall have to do something about it, lad, for it's not the way I see it." Trigg raised himself massively. "Where shall we be going? Shall you be using another helicopter? Or is it shank's pony this time?"

Following toward an exit, Morpurgo said, "You'll help?"

Trigg glanced in mock surprise. "Isn't that what you came for? Or have I got it all wrong?"

"No, you've not. I shouldn't ask this, but why? Since you asked pretty much the same question of me."

Plodding steadily on, Trigg said, "Do you know, sunshine, I was just asking myself the same question."

"Did you get an answer?" They were all stark mad, Morpurgo thought.

"Not yet," Trigg said comfortably. "But never you fear, sunshine. You can take it from me that I shall."

*   *   *

Harbutt, a West Country exile with a comforting roundness of speech and manner, suited Morpurgo very well. Quiet, efficient, he barely looked at Trigg as he let them both in, simply enquiring whether they needed anything immediately in the way of food or drink.

"I'd not say no," Trigg pronounced, "to a good cup of tea, two lumps, just enough milk to colour."

Harbutt's bleached blue eyes rested momentarily on Trigg. Faintly smiling, he said, "What I do happen to have brought is a nice pork pie with trimmings."

"In that case," Trigg said, watching him depart with approval, "I'm your man, sunshine." He went to open a window. Three plainly visible electrical leads ran from a fastening that was not commonplace. Trigg confirmed that the other window was similarly equipped. "Prisoner, is that it?" He lowered himself into a big armchair that had seen better days.

"Two reasons for locks," Morpurgo told him. "Keep people in, keep people out."

"And which would it be in my case?"

Morpurgo was saved from having to answer by a ring at the door to the flat. "Afternoon, sir," Harbutt said to someone not yet in Morpurgo's field of view, and then, "Afternoon, Mr Archer."

The Knight was first to enter, his eyes going immediately to Trigg. His reactions were admirably controlled, although he must have been eaten with curiosity. Steve Archer produced a more positive response, only getting his first full view of Trigg as the Knight moved a little aside.

"Good God!" he said. "What's *he* doing here?"

The Knight chuckled and slapped his thigh, an affection employed to express extreme pleasure. "Didn't tell him, Johnny. Pretty good trial run. Right, too, wasn't I? Well, Steve?"

In the meantime, Steve, cool, self-disciplined Steve, stood staring at Trigg as if he were some kind of freak. He nodded without taking his eyes away from Trigg. "It can't be. In which case . . ." His eyes came at last toward Morpurgo. "This what you've been up to? Congratulations." The words were stripped of all feeling.

The Knight was immensely pleased. "It *is* Sattin, what do you say to that?"

Even now, Steve was not entirely sure, and the Knight could see it. "It *is* Sattin," he repeated. "Must be. You'll see him stand up in court on Friday, isn't that right, Johnny?"

Neither Steve nor the Knight, Morpurgo noted, had yet accepted the fact that Trigg was real, human and present, They spoke across him as if he and the chair in which he sat were a single inanimate object. The fact that Trigg was also aware of it gave Morpurgo a certain quiet satisfaction.

"How much am I supposed to know?" Steve asked.

"What you see, old boy, just what you see," the Knight said almost gaily. The interesting thing was that his eyes contained not one scrap of gaiety.

"Which is a bit more than me," Trigg said, deciding to show that he could talk. "Meaning that you can see me, but I haven't seen the other feller. Makes it all a bit strange, does that."

Steve smiled pleasantly at Trigg, not troubling to remove the eternal cigarette from his lips. "Well, comrade, since we're not to be introduced, best of luck for the show."

Trigg nodded coolly. "Come round to the dressing room after, sunshine, but don't forget, booze not flowers."

Still smiling, Steve said, "I'll try to remember," and to the Knight, "I'll run along then. Maybe we could have a word later?"

"Any amount, old boy," the Knight agreed cheerfully. "Any amount," his eyes still at variance with his tone. Steve left.

Morpurgo said, "Your decision, Director-General, but I'd prefer to have Mr Trigg looked after in somewhere a good deal more secure than this."

"Plenty of time for that, Johnny." The Knight pulled up a chair, sat down on it back to front, hands on the high back, chin on hands, eyes on Trigg. "Well, so far, so good, Mr Trigg. This isn't the kind of work where they hand out medals, but we'll find some way of showing our appreciation when it's all over."

"Life exemption from income tax?" Trigg suggested.

To Morpurgo's private joy, the Knight took him half-seriously. "Not quite that, perhaps, but we'll think of something. The country's going to be in your debt."

"I thought," Trigg said, "that the country wasn't supposed to know ought about this."

"Ah, yes, well, it all depends what you mean by the country."

Trigg's eyes widened in dangerous innocence. "Aye, well what I mean is the folk that live in it."

"You're a man of the world, Mr Trigg, so you'll understand, there're times when it doesn't do for everybody to know everything." He turned to Morpurgo. "Johnny, just to keep things

231

shipshape, you might take Mr Trigg for a stroll through the Act."
Favouring Trigg once more with his smile, he explained. "Mere
formality, naturally, but some things we have to do by the
book."

Trigg's look had gone from the expressionless to the un-
fathomable. "Oh aye? Well, seeing as I'm a bit out of my depth
at present, I'd best be guided by you."

"Good fellow. Johnny, you *have* explained everything? A
deception to prevent deception?"

"I think Mr Trigg's got it all worked out," Morpurgo told him
with deliberate ambiguity.

"I'm sure," the Knight said. "So the less said, the better."
Something had adulterated his spurious joy; it was written small
on his face but not so small that Morpurgo could not see it.
"Well," he said, "best be off." He nodded to Trigg as he dis-
mounted from his chair. "Bit of a bore for you, cabin'd, crib'd
confined. Still, do our best to make you comfortable, anything
you like within reason. Johnny, spare me a minute, will you?"

Outside the flat, the Knight, coming close, muttered, "Johnny,
can we trust the man?"

"A bit late to change your mind, Director-General."

"Yes. Suppose so. Bit of a rough diamond, isn't he?"

"Try listening to what he says instead of the way he says it."

"Yes, of course. But I'll feel that much easier when he's signed
under the Act."

"He's not exactly biddable. And a bit old-fashioned, thinks
his word's as good as his signature."

"His word?" For a moment the Knight was prepared to bluster.
Realism prevailed. Trustworthy or not, Trigg had been committed. "Not just thinking of now. There's after."

"I'll have him knocked off," Morpurgo said with malevolent
relish. "The minute we get him away from Bow Street." The
Knight, a splendid example of that traditional, almost endangered
species, English Gentleman, was quite obviously beginning to
think like a KGB thug. "Of course, you couldn't stop there. We'd
have to deal with everybody who knows about Sattin's present
shape, or they'll smell a rat. Oates, he'll have to go. Then there's
Gilligan, Pratt, Doc Vickers. Let's see, Sibley knows about Trigg,
only a kid, has the idea we're all defending civilisation, still, he'll
have to go too, and . . ."

"That's enough!" The Knight, angry, flashing his steel. "He's

232

to sign. Any little difficulty is your problem. We do it by the book." He was off before Morpurgo could raise the question of moving Trigg, let alone pursue his own growing suspicions about that other type of traditional English gentleman, Steve Archer.

*   *   *

Weber and Claas had agreed that they would stay away from the embassy for the remainder of the day, since it was now certain that Security Directorate had discovered just how deep it was in the manure over Sattin's much boosted court appearance. Weber, trapped into saying a formal hello to the ambassador, had joined Claas later, at his home.

So there they were, with Ella Claas temporarily out of the way and Claas making Weber coffee and all the thanks he got for it was Weber saying, in that grey, non-committal voice he used for something devastating, "You're going to love this one."

"Jesus!" Claas had burnt himself on the percolator lid. Sucking at his injured finger, he tried to pour coffee, with the result that not all of it went into Weber's cup. Weber tore off a sheet of kitchen paper and passed it to Claas for the mopping up operation. "What would you say if I told you Sattin will appear before the eyes of the world on Friday with not so much as a blackhead to mar his schoolgirl complexion?"

"Sonofabitch!" Claas said conversationally. "I knew it. I guess I always knew it. I wish I'd gone in the park to fly the goddam kite with the kids."

"No wind," Weber told him. "All that running around in your shape? The best you could hope for would be a coronary."

Claas gave himself two heaped spoonfuls of sugar, pulled up another stool and sat himself close to Weber at the breakfast bar. Stirring busily, he said, "I say we call it off right now."

"You want me to tell you what happened?"

"The Friends screwed it, right? Either that or their boy was caught in the act and it's all the way to Downing Street that the CIA has been found with its fingers in the cookie jar."

"Typical Kraut thinking," Weber said. "Unimaginative, predictable and wrong. You have to let your mind hang loose to come anywhere near this one. Going to give up?"

"You know me, boss. I don't give up even when it's the only sensible thing to do. In some people it's a virtue. With me, it's masochism. Okay, I give up."

233

Weber related the story. In the telling of it, Claas slowly rotated on his stool to stare directly at Weber as if expecting him to shimmer at the edges and turn into a frog. At the end he said again, "I say we call the whole thing off."

"Grounds? We can't just walk away and hope nobody remembers this was so hot that Plans put it out on 'Eyes Only' with a numbered distribution of six copies and an eight hour recall."

"Grounds? Anything. You name it, I'll go along with it. Temporary insanity. The Great Leap Backwards. A sabotaged fortune cookie. Or we could just own up we were outsmarted."

"You think that? Outsmarted? Take your time, it's important."

Claas slid off his stool to amble round the kitchen, which was no marathon since the kitchen was long and narrow, with more built-in cabinets than floorspace. Pausing at the far end, where the wall was decorated with pictures by Sue Ella, he examined them carefully. The art teacher at Sue Ella's expensive private school had told him they showed great ability. To him they were daubs; he knew what he liked.

"Important?" he muttered distractedly. "Sure it's important. Listen, did I ever tell you Sue Ella has this thing against blue paint? Ask her why and she'll tell you, 'I hate it because it's blue and that's why I hate it'. Let me tell you, there's no answer to that." He swung round on Weber. "You really believe this story of a phony ID? Man! there's something about it that pulls me up as fast as that sonofabitch traffic cop in Washington who swore we were doing seventy on the Beltway."

Weber had wandered to the kitchen window, looking down on the small railed garden in the square outside. What he would like to be doing at this time, he told himself, was sitting under a tree in that garden and whittling wood. His grandpa had whittled wood when Weber was a kid in St Louis, sitting on the back porch of a crumbling redbrick house, with the smells of the Mississippi and the old chemical works as much a part of the natural background as birdsong and the scent of fresh-cut grass to the kids who lived out in St Louis County.

His grandpa used to say, "Can't whittle and worry, boy. No shortage of worry, no shortage of whittling wood."

"No, it has to be right, I guess," Claas said reluctantly. "I mean, hell, Pierre, doubles don't grow on trees. I mean you don't just pick up a double when a vacancy shows up. I mean, you don't have a row of doubles just sitting there on the bench, ready for when coach needs a pinch-hitter."

"I get what you mean," Weber said kindly. "What's up, junior? Pressure getting to you? Anyway, I agree. A false identification is hard to take, but any alternative is harder. And no matter how you read it, they've trumped our ace."

Claas was still thinking. "The likeness is so good they really think they'll get away with it? Boy, that must be some ringer!"

"Well," Weber said, looking even more melancholy than usual, "only one thing to do."

"Pull out. Damn, for the rest of my life I'll always be wondering whether it would have worked."

Weber clattered his cup in its saucer. "I called Langley again. Barzelian's sending us a present. No, two. And one of them's two-legged."

"Oh." The semi-jokiness, almost palpably, vanished as the light goes when a storm cloud swallows the sun. "Who? The biped."

"Shlonski. They say the Israelis owe us."

Claas was no longer a chunky little nobody with a snub-nose. The lines of his face were responding to a pull of five or six Gs. "A Mossad hired hand," he said softly. "Shit! And anyway, I sure as hell hate it when it comes to that."

"Is that right?" Weber, too, had grown instantly old. "Funny. The guys we lay it on for never seem to go too much for it, either."

*   *   *

Epworth sat waiting for him in his office, hands neatly folded, like a middle-aged spinster to be interviewed for a vacancy on the clerical staff. "Mmmm, hope you don't mind. I'd be terribly grateful for a few minutes."

Morpurgo gave him a polite, questioning smile. "Ours," Epworth said, "is a very imperfect skill, wouldn't you say?"

Morpurgo made himself go on smiling.

"Mmmm, not a particularly lucky person myself," Epworth continued. Have to go over everything three or four times when a luckier chap might get it right straight off."

Morpurgo made a noise he hoped was suitably ambivalent.

"If you wouldn't awfully mind," Epworth said, "a quick scamper through some of your movements."

Now it begins, Morpurgo told himself.

"The first day. The day – mmmm – Sattin and the Stringers were arrested."

"Go ahead."

"A telephone call, just after you left the Yard. Before your date with your minister."

Placket! Detective Chief Superintendent Placket, crossing the road as Morpurgo left the phone box. "Private call," Morpurgo said. "My deputy's wife. Helga Archer." It would all come out anyway.

"Mmmm," Epworth shook his head gravely, "Sad. Strange how husbands can miss things that are obvious to any outsider."

Morpurgo negotiated the minefield in silence. Which husband? Which outsider? Morpurgo himself and Sylvie? Morpurgo and Helga? Steve and Helga?

"Of course," Epworth said, "depression's so hard for anyone who hasn't had it to take seriously. Inadequacy, unimportance, hopelessness; what does *anything* matter, let alone me? What about the second call?"

Helga. Helga Archer – he should have known – had acute depression! Jesus! Morpurgo thought, don't *ever* underestimate brother Epworth! "The second call?"

"After the arrest. On the way to – I believe you call it Tuck's." Epworth smiled anxiously.

If Epworth knew about the second call, the only person who could have told him was Callow. Taciturn, solid, reliable Peter Callow, Morpurgo's favourite driver, as communicative as your average lamp-post. But the Friends had barely had this investigation forty-eight hours.

"Mrs Archer again. To tell her her husband would be away overnight."

"Distasteful," Epworth said. "This sort of thing. Did she – mmmm – did she blackmail you?"

For the second time Morpurgo had the experience of teetering on the brink of a pit that, a second before, had not even existed. "No. What an extraordinary idea."

"Figuratively speaking, naturally," Epworth said mildly. "The way my wife blackmails me when she wants something in particular."

"Of course." Morpurgo found himself trying to run through

the events of Wednesday, the censor, scissors in hand. "I saw her later that evening. Briefly. I expect you know."

"Did you discuss the Sattin business with her? At all?"

"I may have. Very generally. After it was over."

"Mmmm. But before Kagalov bolted. Where were you after you told Claas you were going to the Yard?" He saw Morpurgo's expression. "Wednesday afternoon, St James's Park. Nobody at the Yard seems to know about it."

Morpurgo remembered. "I told Claas that because I wanted to get rid of him."

Epworth smiled without comment. Liddle, Morpurgo thought. He knows about Liddle. He told Epworth about Liddle. He said, "You do see it's the strongest possible argument for eliminating me from your list. I was saying there was a mole when everyone else was still arguing against it."

Epworth said, "You've read the Stringer interrogation transcripts?" He looked stricken. "I'm sorry. Of course you have."

Morpurgo, in spite of Steve Archer's pointed comments, had left him with the Stringers. So Steve, with Stringer talking his head off, had kept the transcripts to himself. He would say he thought Morpurgo had had enough to contend with. He might well cite the Knight in support. He must *not*, Morpurgo told himself, become paranoid, must *not* suspect conspiracy. He said, "Not yet. Pressure of time."

Epworth nodded sympathetically. "Would it help if I explained?"

"Please." Some sort of balance was tilting in favour of Epworth. Some sort of serpent was twining itself about him.

"Mmmm, well, Stringer talked a lot about the *modus operandi*. Some of it concerned the various ways they communicated with each other."

"Like the small ads in the paper."

"Yes. But apart from the arrangements for the drops and treffs, there had to be an emergency procedure. When to lie low, or even stop altogether."

"Which was used."

"And made you suspicious."

"Yes."

"The signal for lying low was simple and ingenious."

"They always are."

"In this case, a mail order catalogue. If Mrs Stringer got the catalogue through the post, it meant low profile until further notice.''

"And she got it."

"She got it. Which is where you come in." Epworth peeped almost coyly at Morpurgo. "You should be pleased to know," Epworth said, "that you were enormously helpful."

"*I* was?"

"You asked your chap Sibley – what a nice young man, incidentally – to make an analysis of the drops and treffs."

"That's right." So Sibley, that nice young man, had also, already, been drawn into the net and he, Morpurgo, had not even known.

"We pinched the idea," Epworth was saying, "to make an analysis of all the mail Sattin and the Stringers received during the period of your SV." And it's only two days, Morpurgo reminded himself again, since they were authorised to investigate us.

"Mmmm, of course," Epworth said, "we had to check that Stringer was telling the truth about the mail order catalogue first. Really rather simple as things turned out. The mail order company, they're in Croydon, hadn't got Mrs Stringer on their mailing list, which was a sort of clincher on its own. But they did have one of the Soviet embassy staff, a woman we think works in Kagalov's section."

"Sounds convincing."

"We can do better. You know Special Branch took a great heap of – mmmm – junk away from the Stringers' house? Well, it included the catalogue, would you believe? Couldn't re-use the original envelope, of course, date-marked and addressed to the embassy woman. Well, they made a good match, but not perfect, same with the address label. Best of all, the company had brought out a new catalogue. Kagalov obviously didn't know."

"Congratulations."

"Oh, the benefit of hindsight. Your hindsight, really. I expect you'd have got around to the same thing yourself, given time. Anyway, after that, we shouldn't have much difficulty in working back through Sattin to Kagalov. They're on it now."

"Charting all Sattin's correspondence and telephone calls to see if they can find something a little out of the ordinary that ties in with the date Mrs Stringer got her catalogue."

"That's it. Kagalov had a telephone procedure in case of a real emergency, risky, of course, but at that stage it would be – mmmm – *sauve qui peut*. Post was perfectly adequate when it was only a question of caution. Kagalov, or someone instructed by Kagalov, would post the catalogue to Mrs Stringer and – mmmm – whatever it turns out to be to Sattin."

"Ah! Kagalov! You're accepting the fact that someone warned Kagalov?"

"Oh yes, we accept that. Not the telephone, of.course. They know all the calls are monitored. No, we're sure it will be something in the post. Any luck at all, we'll identify it."

"And you think that will tell you who sent it?"

"Oh!" Epworth frowned and smiled simultaneously. "But we *know* who sent it."

"Would it be too much to ask . . . ?"

"The mole!" Epworth said, half laughing. "Who else but the mole?"

Morpurgo released a breath he had held for a long time. "Then you do accept that there's a mole? And you think you'll be able to put a name to him?"

"I hope so." Epworth produced a kind of giggle. "I suppose I should say 'hopefully', like everyone else. And if you hope I *won't* be able to come up with a name, you could say 'hopelessly'." He giggled again, disarmingly.

"Oh, but I do," Morpurgo said. "Hope you're able to name the mole."

"Then, mmmm, tell me this. Who would you like it to be?"

"*Like* it to be?"

"Yes. Or shall I answer for you?"

Morpurgo waved a hand, very attentive.

"One of Us." Somehow Epworth made the capital letter as clear as if it had been written. "Am I right? Upper class? Oxbridge? Public school? The British tradition in moles, one might almost say. And, of course, what makes it doubly amusing is that they hope the opposite. I mean, after all the gibes, going to Cambridge to get a first in high treason, sort of thing, it obviously would be such a *relief* to them to turn up a – mmmm – working-class mole, someone with a red-brick, trade union, Tribune group background. You might almost say they hope it's you. The resident lefty."

239

14

Hits and Misses

"Good, God, Johnny! What's got into you? You put your career at risk by indulging in shenanigans with your deputy's wife and then come here with accusations about Steve being hand in glove with the Friends. Worse, you're practically accusing him of throwing Helga to them simply to get his revenge on you."

The Knight had flushed. His innate puritanism would certainly have been offended by what he called Morpurgo's shenanigans, but was there something else? "Think it through, man!" he commanded now. "Do you think Steve's the kind of man who'd discuss intimate personal problems with anyone, let alone that pack of educated thugs at Century House?"

"You know that Epworth's talked to Steve?"

The Knight, still pink, nodded. Yes, Morpurgo thought, something more than meets the eye here. "And Sylvie? And God knows who else? You, for example?"

"No," the Knight said, so forcibly that Morpurgo believed him. "They have *not* talked to me, Johnny. Not Epworth, not anyone else."

"The Cousins? You must know that the Friends and the Cousins are as close as the two cheeks of my backside."

The Knight's flush returned. He disliked that kind of imagery, which was why Morpurgo had used it. "I know they're close. Their interests are similar, more so than ours." He seemed to arrive at a decision. "After all, Johnny, Steve *was* a Friend. You can't expect him to sever all his contacts. We're all supposed to be on the same side, damn it. Us, the Cousins and the Friends"

"But what they see as being good for our side isn't necessarily good for us. They'd like Merrilees as prime minister."

"Which would be a bad day for us," the Knight admitted. "Trouble is, Merrilees knows how to softsoap the PM. Our Minister doesn't." He brushed his anxieties aside impatiently. "Fortunately, it's of no consequence, since we're the ones who've guaranteed Sattin's appearance in court tomorrow, not Century House. And certainly not the Cousins."

"Have you wondered exactly what Moscow Centre is up to with the TASS statement?"

The Knight looked at him as if he had gone mad. "Damn it, didn't you read that position paper the US State Department circulated last spring? Moscow puts out two thousand hours of foreign broadcasting a week. Eighty-two languages! Three and a half billion dollars a year without even counting the other Warsaw Pact countries! Delahay's every reason to be grateful to us for getting him off the hook."

"It's Trigg," Morpurgo reminded him, "who's appearing at Bow Street in the morning." Like a bull fighter, he was manoeuvring the Knight into a suitable position for the kill.

"Trigg," the Knight hastened to point out, "doesn't exist, not in our world. In Cleethorpes or wherever it is, yes, but not here. Here we only have Sattin. Damn it, Johnny, we would have produced Sattin himself if it hadn't been for that bloody man Pratt."

Metaphorically speaking, Morpurgo exchanged the muleta for the sword. It was not often that the Knight of the Long Knives could be lured to place himself on the receiving end. "Do you think, Director-General, that Moscow Centre would have challenged us to produce Sattin if they knew we'd be able to do it? Or is it more likely that they'd every reason for believing that we couldn't put him on show without proving the allegations of torture?"

"Damn it, man, we *could* have produced him! We were *going* to produce him, the only thing that stopped us was . . ." The Knight came to an abrupt halt, his blue eyes bulging. In a very small voice he said, "The only thing that stopped us was Pratt."

Morpurgo watched a man all but drowning in the swift, silent floodtide of revelation. "We thought the trap was the fact that Sattin's a dying man," the Knight said slowly. "That Moscow had miscalculated, was thinking he'd look much worse than he

241

did. We were wrong, by God! The real trap was sprung after we'd committed ourselves to a public appearance. The real trap was . . ." He pounded a fist on his desk. "Fetch him in, Johnny! Now! Mister don't-know-what-came-over-me Pratt is going to learn what it's like to be at the wrong end of a no holds barred interrogation."

"The running boys should be collecting him just about now. He'll be with us in nice time for lunch."

"Lunch!" The Knight was bristling like a porcupine. He looked wrily, almost sheepishly, at Morpurgo. "I owe you an apology. A mole, alive and kicking! Thank God it's someone from the bottom of the heap, no more gibes at the public school, ruling-class ethos."

Such a *relief* to them, Morpurgo heard Epworth say, to turn up a working-class mole. "Do you think it's likely? A dentist?"

A dentist was, almost by definition, someone whose mind seldom tunnelled beneath the surface, who took things as he found them, considering or being persuaded to consider that everything he did in the course of his unsubtle duties was for the best in the best of the very small number of worlds he saw on offer. The idea of Pratt as a Moscow Centre agent was ludicrous.

The Knight saw it almost at once. His euphoria evaporated. "No, someone else must have put him up to it."

"Someone still unknown," Morpurgo pointed out. "Someone who might know about Trigg. Someone who might be thinking that there's still the best part of twenty-four hours before Trigg stands up in Bow Street tomorrow."

"A second attempt? Dear God, we should have thought!" 'We' Morpurgo noted, wondering if the Knight had been – still, secretly, was – among those who would not consider it an un-mitigated disaster if John Morpurgo, grammar school, red-brick university and trade union movement, should prove to be the subterranean traitor?

"We've got to get Trigg out of London. Wait! Who knows about him? Who knows about him at all?"

"Depends on what you mean by know. The chopper pilot, in theory. Callow, since he drove us from the heliport. But they don't count, not really. Neither of them's seen Sattin, no reason at all to connect him and Trigg. Harbutt, at the flat; same thing, though, never seen Sattin, just another temporary resident, here today, gone tomorrow. You, Director-General."

242

"This is no joking matter."

"And of course, there's me. Unless you count that as a joking matter too." The Knight's eyes flickered. Aha! Morpurgo thought; had his suspicions all right. "Sibley," he said. Knows there's a ringer, knows we've got him on call."

"Sibley's a good lad," the Knight said emphatically. "No doubts there."

"Agreed. And that's everybody. Except Steve. Who's seen them both. And may have shared his information with others." Seeing the Knight begin to boggle, he added, "Meaning the Friends. Or even the Cousins. Not Moscow, I wouldn't go as far as that." He bared his teeth in a grin.

"Now you listen to me! With things between you and Steve the way they are, it seemed best to keep you apart. But he *is* your deputy and you *might* fall under a bus." Or be otherwise removed, Morpurgo thought. "One-man shows are out from now on," the Knight finished.

"You want me to move Trigg."

"At once. And stay with him until he's wheeled before the magistrate tomorrow morning."

"Just one little thing."

"Got to make a flying visit to Bow Street," the Knight was saying. "Squeeze about ninety media people in if they manage to get the extra seating installed in time. About six hundred applications for press passes. As for the bloody public . . ." He stopped. "What little thing?"

"Oates and Gilligan. Doc Vickers, too. They've all seen Sattin since Pratt went over him. They all know he can't appear in court."

"No need to worry about Vickers," the Knight said, slightly patronising. "Pickled his conscience, years ago, one of the reasons he got the job. Oates and Gilligan, hm."

Morpurgo, having achieved the proximity of his objective, was ready to dig in. "I think Doc Vickers and I could take care of things between us, Sattin and Trigg both. Fetch Oates and Gilligan to town overnight, question of checking their statements over the Pratt affair. Keep them here until, say, twelve, one, then let them go back. By that time, Trigg's done his stuff. And Sattin? Just where Oates and Gilligan last saw him, everything as it should be."

"Complete with bruises! You're slipping, Johnny! Story of Sattin at Bow Street all over the media, strong smell of rat."

"Theirs," Morpurgo said brusquely, "not to reason why. We got away with it. Oates and Gilligan both in trouble. Do you think Oates is going to stick his neck out? Do you think he'll let Gilligan?"

"You're right. Got another suggestion. Vickers can keep Sattin heavily sedated for the next twenty-four hours, as near out cold as damnit. When we eventually put him up for committal he won't know anything about tomorrow's little performance." He stared appraisingly at Morpurgo, then nodded briskly. "Yes, my lad, I'll buy that, so off you go and get your Cleethorpes friend shipped down to The Other Place, pdq yes? What about Pratt?"

"All laid on," Morpurgo assured him. "Pratt's going to be looked after by Chief Superintendent Placket. Placket's a dab hand with a soldering iron, so they tell me."

The Knight's head jerked up. Shocked because he didn't know? Morpurgo wondered, or because he doesn't want to? "Since you want me to sort out Trigg double quick, do you think Steve could have a word with Doc Vickers about the arrangements?"

"He's your deputy, Johnny. Whatever you delegate, he'll do. Just tell me what it is, I'll see he gets it."

Having arranged things, as nearly as possible, to his satisfaction, Morpurgo told him what it was.

* * *

"Pull in here," Weber said.

"Not secluded enough." Claas pulled in anyway.

"We aren't going to find a desert island on the London to Portsmouth Road."

Claas manoeuvred the car on to the grass verge. They were within a yard of a wood protected by rusting barbed wire. Traffic was moderately heavy, but moving fast – *shoo, shoo* – rocking the new, hired van a little each time something passed.

"Stop ducking every time," Weber said. "Nobody knows us."

"I'd like that in writing." Claas wrestled with troublous thoughts. "Pierre, this is one I don't like."

"So you keep saying. You're not supposed to."

"I thought this kind of thing was supposed to be out."

"Believe that, you'll believe anything. What's changed is that we have to be more careful. Now, let's see the gismo."

"Look, icing a guy carefully is still icing him."

"Think of it as a preventive operation."

"Is that how Shlonski thinks of it?"

"He's probably iced so many people he doesn't think of it at all. A purveyor of sweet dreams."

"That's why they call him The Sandman."

"Cut it out, will you. I want to see the damn thing."

"It was addressed to me," Claas insisted obstinately.

"That's so you're the one that's. stuck with it if things go wrong, you dummy."

"Oh boy!" Claas commented. "They may not think big, but they sure think dirty. Did you ever think what sort of shit we'd be in if they caught us snooping around here? We're not even supposed to know where it is."

"Hardly worth the bother, a bunch of trees and a dirt road."

"Tell that to Shlonski. Though what the hell he figures on doing in those woods until it gets dark is beyond me."

"Damn right! You have a Mossad agent guesting as hit-man and all you do is bitch. Now, quit moaning and show poppa."

Claas looked at the wood, the road, the wood again. A truck and trailer went by, rocking the van on its suspension. He waited until it was out of sight, then produced a small package that sat neatly on the palm of his hand. He opened it, revealing something chunky, swathed in plastic bubble wrap.

Weber grunted. "Small. Smaller than I thought."

Claas let what was in the bubble wrap slide out. It was a kind of gun, but with differences. The butt was skeletal, with a small metal cylinder incorporated. The barrel was short, fat, and came to a conical point at the centre of which was a kind of needle, hollow like a hypodermic, but blunter and much shorter.

Weber held out his hand. With reluctance, Claas parted with his toy. Weber hefted it. "Heavy. And compact. Come a long way since the days of the cyanide squirter. Let's see the slugs."

"Slug," Claas corrected. Feeling gingerly in the bubble wrap, he produced a plastic capsule, bright scarlet, held it between thumb and forefinger. "One is all we get."

"No second shot if things go wrong?" Weber looked momentarily anxious.

"If the first goes wrong, everything goes wrong."

"Okay, so how do you load this thing?"

Claas retrieved the little gun. "You unscrew this," indicating the cap with a sunken hexagonal head. "You put the capsule in.

The underside of that cap has a hollow needle. It pierces the capsule when you screw it back in. That loads it. When you press this trigger, compressed gas, a zillion pounds a square inch, don't ask me, from this little cylinder, whams the stuff in the capsule down the barrel and through the skin. Barely feel it, just a teentsy prick."

"Instantaneous?"

"That's it. How come you've never seen one of these things before?"

"Too careful." Weber peered at die-stamped, tiny symbols on the barrel. Some were figures, some letters. The letters were in Cyrillic script. "Who put these on? Tel Aviv? Or Langley?"

"Langley. Pointer to Moscow, if anything goes wrong the only thing they'd get." They both knew what would happen in the event of Shlonski's being caught. All Mossad hit-men were equipped with the 'bad tooth', the embedded cyanide dose. But Mossad agents never were caught; it was an axiom of the intelligence community.

Weber was impressed. "Leave any mark?"

"Tiny red dot, goes after an hour or two. Difficult to find if you know what you're looking for. Impossible if you don't. You can shoot it through thin cloth. A shirt, say."

"Elegant," Weber said. "I have a weakness for elegance." His usually melancholy face had a small gleam of pleasure. "Okay, let's move it. The guy should have finished his look-see by now. We can give him that toy and go home."

Pulling back on to the road, Claas said, "Why can't he just be roughed up, the way Sattin was roughed up?"

"You know some way of roughing a guy up in total silence and thirty seconds flat?"

"It would take people a lot less smart than the British to think it was accidental."

"Maybe, but they'll never prove it. What can they do, anyway? When Trigg agreed to cooperate, he walked out of the real world. We're just making it permanent."

*   *   *

Evening and morning papers lay in an untidy heap at Trigg's side. A low table was scattered with playing cards, a half-full glass of Guinness within easy reach. Trigg was tieless, collar unbuttoned, his baggy trousers supported not by a belt but by a particularly wide and powerful-looking pair of bright blue braces.

"Now then, sunshine. I was just wondering when you'd turn up. Fancy a hand? I'm on a winning streak, tell you that for nothing."

"Been on a winning streak ever since he got here," Harbutt said ruefully. "Get you anything, Mr Morpurgo?"

"No thanks. We're moving camp." Harbutt went quietly out of the room.

"My word, sunshine," Trigg said affably. "Take a lot for granted, you do." As always, his vowels, particularly his Us, marched as ponderously through his speech as fat north-country aldermen at a mayor-making, eloquent of his scorn for effete and devious southerners.

Trigg disposed of his Guinness. "And what if I don't feel like shifting?" It served to show how slender was the thread that bound the enterprise together.

Harbutt came back. "Packed your bags, left 'em in the hall. Transport downstairs, Mr Morpurgo?" Morpurgo nodded. Harbutt went out again.

Morpurgo said, "After tomorrow you'll be free to go wherever you please."

"Is that right?" Trigg's sharp gaze rested on Morpurgo, sardonic. "Aren't I free to do that now, then?"

"We're absolutely dependent on your cooperation, I made that clear from the start."

"Aye, sunshine, you did that, and since you're straight with me, I reckon I'll have to be straight with you." He put his hands on his thick thighs and levered himself erect. "Too much to suppose it's another ride in that helicopter? Spoiled me for anything else, has that."

"Nothing so glamorous. A van, North Thames Gas Board."

Trigg hauled himself into his jacket. "When I was a little lad my mam always used to say that if I didn't behave myself they'd come and fetch me away in a van. She'll be right chuff to see it come true." He came very close to Morpurgo. "On to us, are they? Reckoned they might be, all that stuff in the papers. Right, lad, ready when you are."

Harbutt, anticipating once again, stood holding the door open. "Been downstairs and back, Mr Morpurgo. All clear."

The interior of the van was sealed off from the driver's

compartment, the only seating a pair of strictly functional benches. "By heck!" Trigg said as Callow took them up the slope and into the heavy inner city traffic. "Can't you lot afford something a bit more comfy?" Wedging himself as firmly as possible into a corner, he looked at Morpurgo closely. "Well then, shall you be telling me what this is all about sooner or later?"

"Everyone in the know about Sattin will also know that we're holding him outside London, a little place in the country. From now on, everything's going to be done as if you're Sattin."

"Hang on a minute. Everyone in the know? I'd like to think that's not too many, sunshine. And something else, what about those that take care of him? What are they going to make of me?"

Morpurgo explained the arrangements. Eventually, pursuing his own thoughts, he looked up to see Trigg's eyes latched speculatively on him.

"Filling him full of dope, it bothers me, does that. As if you and your lot'd filled *me* with dope, into the bargain." He had not yet finished. "When I was a little lad and used to be sent to have my hair cut, there was a big mirror in front of the chair and another big mirror behind. Sitting in that chair, eight or nine years old, maybe, I could see a whole series of me's, back and front, looking at me and likewise looking at each other. And what I used to think was, how did I know *I* was the real me? What if one of those others I could see, what if *he* thought he was the real me? And what if he was right? Used to give me a right headache, did that. Well, it's somewhat the same with this feller Sattin."

Morpurgo found himself briefly sharing Trigg's vision. In the mythology, to encounter one's doppelgänger was an indication of imminent death. He dismissed the image; what more absurd while being bumped and swayed in the back of a bogus North Thames Gas Board van with a middle-aged rock maker from Cleethorpes! No more absurd, something in him retorted, than the fact that the rock maker, tomorrow morning, would stand before the eyes of the world, charged with espionage and high treason.

"He doesn't know about you, and he never will." Feeling the inadequacy of his response, he added, "And you won't see him. By this time tomorrow it'll all be over, and neither of you the worse for it."

Trigg looked at him strangely. "That'll be for us to judge, won't it? Him and me. Him with a day gone from his life. A bit like playing God, is that, though it may come natural enough to folk like you. Here, what was it you were saying yesterday, at the cricket? Us and Them. Us with ninety per cent of the power, aye and the land and the money too. And Them, the man in the street as the politicians call 'em, as if politicians wafted around on wings like a bunch of pantomine fairies!"

Leaning forward perilously as the van took a sharp corner, he tapped Morpurgo with one thick finger. "Have I got it right, that you and me is Them, honest working lads with corns on our hands and muck under our fingernails? Well, let me tell you how it looks from where I am. Folk like me, *we're* Us" – again he rhymed it with buzz but as if he had borrowed the vowel from push – "and you're Them, sunshine, you and your lot, mucking about with ordinary folks' lives, *you're* Them!"

Unexpectedly, he grinned. "So where's that leave you? I'd like to know. They don't think you're one of them and we don't think you're one of us. I reckon that puts you somewhere between dogs and horses."

There was no malice in it, Morpurgo saw, though if Trigg should display malice, malice he would have to bear, since without Trigg he was nothing. "Sorry if I annoyed you. But Sattin is a spy, when all's said and done."

"Aye," Trigg said ambiguously, "like as not. But the way you treat him – well, in a funny sort of way it'd be something personal to me, so think on, sunshine. Think on. Them that dabble in muck get mucky. Them that start by bending some of the rules some of the time end up bending all of 'em all the time. And them that think they can pull the wool over other folks' eyes want telling that even sheep get used to seeing through it."

Arriving at the gatehouse of The Other Place they found their entry eased by telephoned instructions from Steve Archer, were passed through without the normal obligation to open the van for inspection, and after driving down minor tracks seldom used other than by the housekeeping staff, arrived at the rear entrance to the security wing. Doc Vickers, alerted from the gate, was waiting for them, looming over Morpurgo as he clambered stiffly from the back of the van.

"Day to you, sahib. Why all the hush-hush mumbo-jumbo? Bumbailiffs on your trail? Can't let you . . ." He stopped abruptly at the sight of Trigg debouching from the van like a transshipped hippopotamus. Each temporarily silenced by the appearance of the other, it was Trigg who recovered first.

"By heck!" Trigg said. "Grow 'em tall down here, don't you? What's the weather like up there, sunshine?"

Vickers had begun a series of spluttered queries and expressions of astonishment. "Good God, Johnny? Where on earth . . .? What the devil . . . ? So *that's* what you're up to! Knock me sideways, sahib! *Mubarik!*"

"Do you mind," Morpurgo said, "if we continue this inside? I couldn't give you any advance warning. The number of people in the know is small and hand-picked."

"You flatter, sahib. Good thing the old ticker's sound, drop dead of shock. *Shabash, shabash, Huzoor!*" Salaaming elaborately, he backed inside, thrust out a hand. "Vickers, tuan, regimental vet, retired."

"Brown," Morpurgo said firmly, "Mister Brown from nowhere, least said, soonest mended. Right, let's get on. Steve rang you to tell you what was needed? Everything absolutely clear?"

"Clear as mud, old son, is par for the course in my long experience. Stand Oates and Gilligan down until noon tomorrow, done. No replacements from the duty roster, done. Needleful of dreams for the patient, done, more to come as needed. Get Number 1 in the annexe ready for Sattin, but don't move pending arrival of reinforcements, meaning you, sahib. Ditto for Number 2 here in the Bin, fresh bedroll and toothbrush, so to speak. All done, old Doc flying around like a fart in a colander, first time he's done his own dogsbodying since we lowered the flag in Aden." To Trigg, he said, "One thing you learn in the army, tuan, follow instructions, no matter how bloody silly, yours not to reason why, right?"

"Right!" Trigg said with feeling. "Right you are, sunshine!"

"Sorry," Morpurgo said. "You did say Sattin in the annexe?"

"Very words, friend, or just as good if different. Can't help asking if it's wise, look you. Security in the annexe not as good as the Bin."

"Absolutely right," Morpurgo agreed. "Either I got things mixed up or Steve did. Probably me, I was in a bit of a hurry when I left. Anyway, no harm done. Sattin stays right where he is. I don't want him even half-waking and finding himself in different surroundings."

"Won't do that, old son, take if from me. Another jab twixt now and sunrise, won't even notice if we put him in orbit." Vickers glanced at Trigg. "Annexe not exactly the Ritz, though. Hope Mr Brown isn't expecting caviar and bubbly."

"Bit less hospitalish in the annexe," Morpurgo told Trigg. "No need to swap over until tomorrow. By that time we'll have moved Sattin, got you ready for Special Branch and when they arrive they'll see exactly what they expect. They haven't set eyes on you" – he stopped, smiling – "haven't set eyes on Sattin for a week, and they don't know he's been roughed up."

"Whatever you say, sunshine."

"Want to take a *dekho* at the annexe?" Vickers slid open the drawer of his desk. "Be on the safe side, brought all the keys in here." He selected labelled keys from his collection. "This way, tuan," he told Trigg, and led them down the corridor, turning before the dispensary to unlock the door to the annexe. Another door at the far end required the use of the second of Vickers' keys.

"Where's yon feller, then?" Trigg enquired. "I reckoned you must have half the British Army on guard outside his door."

"Not necessary, friend." Doc Vickers stood aside to let them pass. "No, if we'd gone on instead of turning in here, you'd have come on the patient directly, fast asleep in his little cot and dreaming he's as free as a bird, shouldn't wonder. All the same if he weren't. Once you're on the wrong side of the door to the Bin, you're there to stay and no mistake."

They had entered a long, low wooden building, its army antecedents as plain as those in Soapbox City. A corridor ran down the right-hand side, to its left a row of doors leading into small rooms. Number 1 had a metal hospital bed, a chair and chest of drawers and little else. Its single window looked out at close quarters on a high brick wall running the length of the building.

"By heck!" Trigg was unimpressed. "It's as well this is a one night stand. Wants a bit doing to it, does this, starting with that wall."

"Blast wall," Vickers said. "This was boffin land during the war, tuan, all the brains in the business working away to invent new ways of upsetting Mister Hitler. Powers that be won't put up the money to knock the walls down, so here they stay. Well,"

– he clapped his big hands together gigantically, the sound producing the flat crack of an echo in the empty building – "that's it. What more has life to offer?"

"Guinness," Trigg said promptly. "Can, bottle or bucket, all the same to me. And something to pass the time away, like a colour telly."

"Thought of that too." Vickers triumphantly produced a small pile of back issues of *Reader's Digest*. "Keep you happy *and* make a better person of you, friend, not suggesting there's room for improvement, mind."

Trigg tossed them on the bed. "Booze is all it takes to make a better person of me, sunshine. No booze, no Bow Street." He shed his jacket and settled himself, with a good deal of grunting, on the high, hard-looking bed. "Sooner the better, or I might change my mind."

"Fetch it myself," Morpurgo said. "And see about some grub. I want to be sure you've nothing left to ask for before I turn in myself."

"Oh aye," Trigg said sardonically. "And where will that be? Nearest place with a bar, I shouldn't wonder."

"In that case you *should* be surprised. I'm staying right here."

"Here?" Vickers was more surprised than Trigg. "Didn't tell me that, sahib. No room prepared. Still" – he brightened – "fix something up quick enough over at the mess."

Trigg rolled off the bed, went to the window. "I hope this thing opens. I've no wish to die of suffocation." With an effort, he managed to open the window two or three inches, then a few more.

"By!" Trigg took deep, noisy breaths. "Best air I've come across since I left Cleethorpes. What's on the other side of this wall, then?"

"Wide open spaces, tuan. All things bright and beautiful. Dance barefoot on the lawn by the light of the silvery moon if you don't mind risking rabies."

"Rabies?" Trigg brought his head back inside, incredulous.

"Get it from bow-wow bites, seen 'em run howling across the maidan, temperature one hundred and twenty in the shade, foaming at the mouth, just one tiddy bite from a rabid pye-dog." Vickers grinned. "Course, better class of dog here, tuan, only bite under orders."

"Dog patrols during the hours of darkness!" Morpurgo explained. "No need to worry, they're kept on the leash, mostly walked around the boundaries anyway."

"Have a job getting over that blast wall," Vickers said. "Still, so would you, tuan, so never the twain shall meet, what?"

*　　*　　*

It was somehow typical of Delahay that he should receive the Knight, not in his first floor study, but the White Drawing Room. To the Knight it was an example of his tendency, given the smallest opportunity, to whisk himself away from the public world of Commons, the private one of Cabinet, even the semi-informality of his study next door, in an attempt, absurd, considering his circumstances, to present himself as a private citizen.

Everything was muted shades of beige, providing a background into which Delahay seemed to merge like a fox in the woods of autumn. Or a rabbit? the Knight wondered irreverently.

He was sure he already knew why he was here on this warm Thursday evening, even the second-hand air of central London a little charged with the magic of high and perfect summer. Twentieth-century haruspex, he was required to bring the assurance revealed by entrails and portents. He settled himself at one end of a sofa, leaving the majority of the space for Delahay. Typically, Delahay placed himself at the exact centre of the matching sofa, eight or ten feet away.

"Well now, am I to be vindicated?"

"Tomorrow morning, Prime Minister, the man will go to Bow Street, Special Branch will repeat the charges against him and ask for a further week's remand, which the magistrate will grant. He will then be returned to custody. He will show no signs of ill-treatment, because he has received none." And that, the Knight told himself, having chosen and rehearsed his words with meticulous care, is the entire and unchallengeable truth.

Making no immediate response, Delahay eventually nodded. "You're very confident, Director-General. And very direct. I like people who are willing to stand by their professional judgement. Like them and seldom meet them. One of the most notable characteristics of an expert, in my experience, is his expertness in making categorical statements and then instantly qualifying them."

The Knight smiled. It was a typical Delahayism; mild irony with an inner core of truth.

In a tone of vague interest, Delahay said, "The man refuses to speak, is that correct?"

"It is, Prime Minister." The Knight waited a second or two before realising that Delahay was asking more than his obvious question. "Will he continue to do so when he has an audience?"

Delahay nodded. "The thought presents itself, does it not?" For a moment the Knight could have fancied himself back at Magdalen, victim of his tutor's inquisitorial probings, only too well aware that his thesis was, as an earlier one had once been memorably described, an inverted pyramid of fancy balanced on a needle-point of fact.

"It presents itself, Prime Minister" – hang it, he must not start echoing the PM's phraseology – "but only to be rejected. The man knows nothing either of Moscow's accusations or your reply in the Commons. He will hold his tongue in the belief that he has nothing to gain by speaking."

"Of course. One forgets, so much to remember. 'The world is too much with us.' But there, quotations are for old men and pedants, wouldn't you say?" With no change in intonation, he said, "You see, I should be obliged to go."

The Knight almost missed it, but Delahay was a man awaiting a response. With – to use his own private epithet – Incan obliqueness, the Knight said, "I quite understand, Prime Minister."

Delahay actually laughed. "And if I did, you would soon be sitting there giving your impartial advice to my successor with as much discretion as you give it to me. It's an odd thing but being in my company invariably brings out the diplomat in people, even when they're not normally diplomatic. Do they think, I wonder, that I have a horror of the truth?" He produced his slender smile. "You do understand?"

This time the Knight met him head on. "Yes, Prime Minister, I do. You don't think your party would support you if Sattin spoke out of turn. You're wondering if there's any possibility that he might be persuaded – perhaps given a reason puts it better – to speak out of turn."

"Very direct. And precise. Thank you. My party sets great store by loyalty, but only on loan and sometimes at usorious rates. One hears strange tales, Director-General."

"What sort of tales, Prime Minister?" Good God! the Knight said to himself, the cunning old fox! He knows!

"Oh." Delahay made a gesture as vague as his manner. "Fairy tales, no doubt. Plots. Wheels within wheels." He smiled again. Just as the Knight was despairing of finding a single sufficiently non-committal word, Delahay said, "To be first among equals, as I am privileged to be, is to take a crash course in the art of conspiracy. If some are more equal than others, you may be sure it's only a question of time before the levellers are at work."

He got up. "Thank you for coming, Director-General. Thank you also for your reassuring news. And please thank your staff for their continued good work." He walked with the Knight as far as the door. "I'd give a good deal to be a fly on the wall tomorrow morning. But then, perhaps I should be swatted. And after all" – he held out a boneless hand – "I can stay at home and be swatted in comfort. Do you mind finding your own way down?"

The Knight went slowly and thoughtfully down the two flights of gold-carpeted stairs. Almost at the foot, the prime minister's voice caught up with him. "Sir Hugh, I almost forgot. You'll find Sir Jason in the reception room. Ask him to come up, will you?"

15

Night Calls

Glass in hand, Vickers ventured the nearest he intended to go to a forbidden topic. "Didn't know you were going to stay the night, Johnny. Would have pushed the boat out, killed the fatted calf and that. Better get you fixed up with a room, though."

"No need." Handle this one wrongly, Morpurgo told himself, and he would be stuck with Vickers for the night. "Thought I'd sleep in the Bin, if it's all right with you, don't need anyone to tuck me in."

It was easier than he had expected. Vickers winked, tapping the side of his nose. "Stick with it to the end, right? Perfectly understood, sahib. Only one thing, for charity's sake, don't ask the old doc to keep you company. Getting a bit long in the tooth for that sort of caper. Come along with you after we've sunk another snort or two, give the tovarich his shot, then he'll be more or less out till morning. You can have the cot in the night office, that suit you? Sup up, old son. Time for another noggin."

"Mr Brown's Liffey water." Morpurgo reminded him. "And his supper. Better take them before he broods." When he came back, empty glasses told him that Vickers was a drink or two ahead.

"Everything hunkydory with the tuan?"

"A minor fracas over the little matter of a pint mug, but he graciously agreed to overlook the matter."

From his astonishing sitting height, Vickers looked down approvingly. "Smart chap, Johnny, for a crypto-commie. Cheers, old son." The barman called, "Telephone, Mr Morpurgo."

It was Sibley. "Sorry to disturb you, sir. Thought you'd want to hear straight away." Sibley was young enough to sound excited. "Pratt, sir. He's talking."

256

"Ah." There had been no reason to suppose that Pratt would hold out too long. Familiarity with the techniques was a good solid argument for the reverse.

"Didn't put up much of a show, really." Sibley sounded slightly scornful. "Tried to bluff it out for a bit, but Chief Super Placket knows a trick or two. Soon as Pratt realised that, up went the white flag."

"Don't sound so disappointed, damn it."

"Sorry, sir. The Chief Super had told his missus he might be out all night."

"Okay. What did you get?" He had a very good idea of what they would have got.

"Well, sir, you were right about him. Nothing to do with dirty commies, or losing his temper, either. All done for cash, beat him up, but only on the face and make sure it'll show." This time there was no mistaking Sibley's feelings; contempt; the healthy reaction of the young, for whom corruption, like death, was something that only happened to others, older as well as weaker.

"Not even big money, really, two hundred down, another three after. Mind, they'd got something on him to start with, this woman he'd gone bananas over. Wife doesn't know, natch, *and* he's got two kids, but if you ask me, it was his job he was worried about, not his missus."

Christ! Morpurgo felt like a footballer heinously fouled. A wife and two kids in my case too, my wife, Steve's kids, but I just might keep a job and Pratt won't. Helga, he remembered; he still hadn't rung her, something about a different number. Well, he wouldn't be able to ring her before tomorrow and anyway, Sylvie first, Helga after, that was how it was going to be now. He said, "Ian, what are you trying to do to me?"

"Sir?"

"Pratt gave in fairly quickly; good. He talked; good. It was money, not sadism, very good that, make Sattin feel a lot better if he knew. But there's one thing, trivial, I admit, you haven't told me. Whose money, Mister Sibley? Whose bloody money?"

"Oh, sorry, sir, didn't I say? Yank money."

"Yank money," he repeated.

"Got to give it to you, sir." Sibley's were the tones of one who has witnessed a miracle. "Don't know how you worked it out, honestly. Chief Super Placket, he was so bowled over I thought he was going to kill Pratt. Grabbed his arm, shoved it behind

257

him, you know the style, sir, shouted, 'Don't you make fun of me, sonny! Don't you fucking make fun of *me*!' And there's Pratt, tears running down his cheeks with the pain, yelling, 'It's the truth! It's the truth, so help me, it's the truth!'"

Lost in some remote reach of space and time, Morpurgo heard his voice ask, "Did he say who?"

"Just coming to that, sir." How could Sibley sound so matter-of-fact? "No name, natch, probably false if he gave one, but a good description, plenty of corroborative detail."

"Such as?" Morpurgo could do little for the time being but hang on.

"Well, all kinds of bits and pieces that made sense, got it all on the tape, of course. Where they'd met; first time in a pub south of the river, Trinity Road; second on a river boat, Westminster to Greenwich, contact got off, Pratt came back. Good description of contact, that's what clinched it, really."

"Clinched what?" All he seemed to be able to say was: What? What? What?

"The whole thing, sir. Sergeant Vaisey suddenly says, 'Here, I know that geezer!' Meaning this Yank Pratt's talking about, sir. Anyway, Vaisey starts asking questions and Pratt's giving him the answers, fast, short, didn't want any more arm-twisting.

"Then all of a sudden the Chief Super says, 'Knock it off a minute, Jock,' – that's Jock Vaisey – and gives me the nod to go outside with him. You still there, sir?"

Not giving him any feedback, Morpurgo warned himself. It was hot and airless under the acoustic hood of the telephone. He had perspiration gathering in a droplet at the end of his nose and he was holding the phone, which had a smell of disinfectant, in a sticky glove of sweat. "Yes," he said, "of course. Go on, Ian."

"Sir. Well, this is the other reason I'm ringing. Chief Super comes outside with me, pulls me away from the door and says" – Sibley beautifully imitated Placket; portentous, macho, pompous with juniors – "'No offence, Sibley, but I'm not prepared to continue this interrogation in the presence of a junior representative of Security Directorate. You know why, so better give 'em a bell and see who's available.' Well, sir, knowing you were down there, hadn't much option."

"No. It's all right, go on."

"Yes, sir. So I told him you were out of town, think he knew that anyway, and said, 'Can we wait till he gets back?' Not on your life, sir! Chief Super says no, he's not going to turn off a running tap in case the tank goes dry, but he wants a big wheel from Curzon Street to be present. So I tell him I'll have to call the duty officer and see who's available."

"Quite right." Go on, Morpurgo ordered himself, give him all the credit you can. He'll be there long after you've been given the push, so a bit of encouragement won't hurt. "Who did you get?" He knew what the answer would be.

"Worked out okay, sir; Mr Archer, working late, says he'll come straight over. I give him the drift, seems to know quite a bit already, sir, and he tells me I can go home. So I come straight to the phone, sir, let you know the news." Sibley's voice became confidential. "Didn't want me *or* Sergeant Vaisey any more, sir. Just Mr Archer, the Chief Super and Inspector Garret, I mean, bit delicate, isn't it, sir?"

"Yes, very." He was a fool, looking for KGB footprints simply because it would have made a pretty pattern.

"Mind if I ask a question, sir?"

"Try."

"Well, I'd have bet a hundred to one Pratt had been bought by one of Kagalov's lot. That's what the Specials must have thought, too. I could tell just from looking at the Chief Super's face. So what put you on to the CIA? That's what I wanted to ask. Why would they want to do a thing like that?"

"Ian," Morpurgo said, despising himself for the cop-out, "there are more things in heaven and earth . . ." Yet, now that he was willing to accept the Kagalov link as wishful thinking, he had a feeling that, given time, he might find fact a good deal more logical than fiction.

"Yes, sir." Sibley was unable to suppress his disappointment entirely. "Seems weird, all the same. Like finding the CIA and the KGB on the same side, know what I mean, sir?"

"Hold on to that," Morpurgo said. "You may have got something."

The irony, for once, missed Sibley. He said, "Yes, sir," a crisp eagerness in his voice. Good God! Morpurgo thought, he thinks I've given him a tip. An instant later he thought: Good God! Perhaps I have! He said, "Mr Archer knows where I am, right?"

"Oh yes, sir."

"Any comment?"

"Sir?"

"Never mind. Does he know when I'm coming back?"

"Don't know, sir. Oh, hang on, he said something about you coming in with Sattin in the morning. Is that right, sir?"

"Listen, is that motorbike of yours in order?"

"Sir?"

"You had an accident with it last weekend. Is it in order?"

"Yes, the bike's fine, sir, even got its town wheels back." He could practically hear Sibley grinning. "Reckon I could be out there inside ninety minutes, sir, maybe not much over the hour. Traffic'll have pretty well gone by now."

"I'll be in the Bin. Don't break your neck on the way down. Get them to ring me from the gatehouse."

"Will do, sir."

Walking back to rejoin Vickers, Morpurgo wondered exactly why he had asked Sibley to come. The only answer, he decided, was the fact that he trusted Sibley. And then he saw that he had it slightly wrong. He put it right: In the whole of Security Directorate, Sibley was the only one he trusted; a unique qualification.

"Everything hunkydory, old son?" Vickers, it struck Morpurgo now, had the air of a man who not only has questions he must not ask but answers he must not give. Why should he think that now? Because of Pratt? Why, it occurred to him, had Vickers not kicked up a far bigger stink over Pratt's abuse of Sattin?

"As near right as it's ever likely to be in this business. Tell me, Doc, did you ever wonder about Pratt?"

Vickers' face, amiable, complaisant, the face of one who, like seaweed, has learned to accommodate himself to every change of the tide, altered only a little, and with no great subtlety. "Wonder about, sahib?"

"Ever suspect him of being a sadist?"

"Drink up, friend." Vickers put away his Scotch, virtually neat, and signalled for a refill. He said, "Pratt? No, can't say I have."

"Any views about him at all?"

"Bloody dentist, isn't he? Got views on dentists, sahib, you know that."

"They come under you, don't they? You're required to review them every twelve months."

"Come under me because they're classed as paramedics. Which, by and large, sahib, they bloody well ain't." It was one of the Doc's favourite grievances, he was grabbing for it now,

Morpurgo suspected, as a welcome red herring. Kicking it away before Vickers had it firmly in his grasp, he said, "They come under you, though, like it or not. What sort of reports have you been giving Pratt?"

Vickers' drink arrived. He plainly welcomed the diversion, but Morpurgo, by now, was feeling cruel. "Come on, Doc, not trying to keep something from me, I hope?"

Fiddling with his glass, Vickers said stubbornly, "Personal appraisals are something between me and the subject, plus the Knight. You know that, Johnny, no obligation to discuss them."

"I can pick up the phone and ask the Knight to instruct you to give me Pratt's file. Why not save me the trouble?" Morpurgo had never handled Vickers as brusquely as this before, and they both knew it.

Vickers mumbled, "Rather you didn't press me on this one, sahib. Bit tricky."

"Tricky, shit!" Morpurgo forced his voice back into harness with sweet reason. "Lot of things going on just now, Doc. Pratt has suddenly become important. I'm just the first in the queue with questions."

"Hoohah, that it? *Gurrh-burrh*? Don't like *gurrh-burrh*, old son, never did. Losing temper, general red-faced barney; bad for the old ticker, solves nothing." Doc Vickers, his expression one of purest misery, bowed his head over the glass that still twisted and turned in his fingers. "Golden rule for me, Johnny, whole life through. Look for the heart of the fray, all the ambitious chaps hacking away, head smartly in the opposite direction, what? Far-flung outposts, old Doc Vickers doing his whack in peace and quiet. Don't mind telling you this job was a dream come true, couldn't believe my luck."

He stopped turning his glass and, as if only now recognising it for what it was, drained its contents. "Course, compromise on both sides, got what I wanted, full value in return." He looked anxiously down on Morpurgo. "Got me, sahib?"

"They leave you alone, you don't ask too many questions." It was the only way certain security practices and the Hippocratic oath could rub along together.

"So," Vickers said, finding his empty glass an object of extreme interest, "when I'm asked to accept someone who's not really cut out for the job, someone, not to mince too many bloody words, who's not really even working for the same outfit . . ."

261

"You don't put up much of an argument. Pratt?"

"Pratt."

"SIS plant?"

"Got it."

"Who squeezed you?" He already, did he not, knew the answer?

Vickers gave Morpurgo a look of muted anguish. "Want me to spell it out? Rather not."

Something in his mind sliding home with as little fuss as a key in a lock, Morpurgo said, "Steve. Steve Archer."

Vickers made the most minute of nods. "All on the same side, after all, sahib." He sounded forlorn, despairing.

Steve, Morpurgo knew, had been personally responsible for the positive vetting of Doc Vickers at the time of his appointment. What potentially useful peccadillo or weakness had he turned up? insufficient to constitute a genuine security risk, handy enough to give him leverage in an occasionally crucial area of Directorate activity. A good many things, of which Pratt was only one component, were beginning to make sense.

He punched a fist gently against Vickers' shoulder. "Better out than in, Doc. Safe, too. It's only Pratt I'm interested in." It was, he thought, a humane lie.

"If it was all right with Steve," Vickers said, "it was all right with me. Had to be, make myself plain, do I? Don't believe in asking too many questions, Johnny, leave that to you lot." Something had gone out in him temporarily, some flickering flame of self-respect, on which Morpurgo had had the effect of a blast of cold, untempered air.

Vickers got up, towering above the seated Morpurgo yet looking vulnerable, almost fragile. "Time for the patient's second dose of dreams. Better come and take a shufty."

He lowered his voice to near inaudibility as Morpurgo stood. "Seen quite a bit of Steve of late, matter of fact. Half expected him tonight, don't miss him though. Hope you know what you're up to, sahib." As a warning, not even friendly Morpurgo thought, it was more than he had any right to expect.

*   *   *

"Oh." Sylvie was faintly amused as well as surprised. "You're very well informed. Knowing where to find me, I mean."

"Mmmm, educated guess." Epworth shuffled a little, as if

embarrassed. And so he bloody well should be, Sylvie thought, since it was his deliberately planned revelation on his last visit that had resulted in her coming here.

"Haven't been following you around," he said, "if that's what you mean, Mrs Morpurgo. Oh dear." He looked at her anxiously. "Mrs Morpurgo? Miss Markham? Or even mzz?"

This time she was on the lookout, his sheeplike antics no longer concealing from her his wolfishness of mind. "Mrs Morpurgo will do, thank you very much. Perhaps you'd better come in."

"Just a couple of questions," Epworth said, following her. "If you can spare the time."

"Time doesn't come into it." She waved him to a seat. "Principle does. I have this quaint idea that a wife shouldn't inform on her husband. Or did you think things might have changed?"

"Mmmm, not *quite* fair, Mrs Morpurgo. Informing and giving information are two different things."

"Which of them was it last time?"

He looked at her respectfully. "You're very intelligent. I told your husband so."

"Did he agree? Sherry?"

"Thank you. I thought you must know. About Mrs Archer."

"Medium or dry. No, I didn't."

Epworth was looking distressed. "In that case, I'm sorry. Dry, please. Have you seen Mrs Archer recently?"

"No. Why should I?"

"No reason, I agree. Except . . . do you know where she is?"

"At home, I imagine." She reacted belatedly. "Except what?"

"She's . . . not herself just now, rather worrying."

"She's a jumpy girl at the best of times. And I don't suppose this is the best of times. Not for her" – she looked at him very directly – "or anyone else in this business."

"No. Perhaps, after tomorrow, things will improve . . . I do hope so." He sighed, shaking his head. "In a way it's worse for those who aren't directly involved?"

"Me, for instance? Or am I directly involved?"

"People who don't know exactly what's happening. It sometimes makes things look worse than they really are." He had a positive talent, Sylvie thought, for evading questions.

"It's a funny thing," Epworth said. "Mmmm – in our business we're apt to talk about the intelligence community, the security

263

community." He gave her a wry smile. "It *is* funny, don't you think?"

"Hilarious. Of course, it all depends on . . ."

". . . on what you mean by community." They both laughed a little, yet, after the laughter, the atmosphere was, if anything, slightly less comfortable.

"Community of interest," Sylvie said.

"But not communion."

"Dog eat dog." Sylvie stared at him thoughtfully. "What do you want, Mr Epworth?"

"Would you believe me if I said, to get your husband off the hook?"

"Is he on it?"

"Some people think so."

"Are you one of them?"

He fumbled for something in an inside pocket of his jacket. He looks so . . . so ineffectual, Sylvie thought, so incompetent. Why, then, does he frighten me? Perhaps frighten was too strong a word.

He drew out a cellophane envelope. "Do you recognise this?"

"Yes. Of course. It's mine." She corrected herself. "I mean, I took it."

It was a xerographic copy of a picture postcard. The picture was of a great medieval church tower seen between two others at a steep angle from ground level. What made them intensely, almost theatrically dramatic was that they soared tremendously upward, bright and burning even in black and white, toward a sky with stormclouds of doomsday darkness.

"Seven or eight years ago," Sylvie said. "I was only just beginning, really. Selling to a picture postcard company was something big in those days. Where did you get it? It's been out of print for ages."

"Happened to – mmmm – run across it," Epworth said vaguely. "Of course, something's been lost in the copying."

"Yes and no. I don't use colour stock any more, but that one was taken in colour. It's Lincoln Cathedral, incidentally, I expect you knew. Anyway, in the original those towers are golden, almost bronze. And the sky was blue-black, even some purple. I just happened to be there at the right moment. There was the most tremendous rain-storm, but just before it began there was one minute, not much more, when the sun broke through. A bit like the end of the world, almost horizontal sunlight and the towers burning like torches against that incredibly ominous sky."

Her professional enthusiasm had completely dispelled initial wariness. "Just a minute. I'll show you. I sold the shot outright, I was green in those days, but they sent me some cards. I always keep one of everything, half a professional thing, half vanity."

She was down on her knees, pulling out one of a long row of clothbound volumes. "It's in this one somewhere. Like a journey into the past. I don't do it often, but when I do, I'm always surprised. I think, 'Goodness, I'd forgotten I was as good as that.' Does that sound very conceited?"

She had reached the end of the guardbook, and had gone back to the beginning, turning over the pages more slowly. She stopped at one of them, frowning. "This is where it should be, I'm sure."

"Mmmm," Epworth said, tentatively, "Could it have been taken out? That page looks rather bare."

"Yes, it does, doesn't it?" In the act of agreeing, he saw Sylvie stiffen, "Oh. No. I've just remembered. Managed to damage it, so I threw it away." She closed the guardbook with some force, and returned to her chair. "Would you like another sherry?"

"I really ought to be off." Epworth was already on his feet. "I'll try not to bother you again. Thank you very much for your help." The reproduction of the postcard disappeared inside his jacket.

She was filled, now, with a kind of formless apprehension. "Help with what? You never really said. Where *did* you get that thing from?"

Epworth, a bright, meaningless smile on his donnish face, was through the door. "Can't actually promise, but I just might be able to get you another copy for your collection. Good night," and he was away down the stairs.

Staring after him, Sylvie felt her foreboding fluttering inside her unpleasantly. Epworth had a copy of the postcard. It was reasonable, then, to think that he might also have the original, or where could the reproduction have come from? Where the original had come from seemed, as she thought about it, less and less of a mystery. The real mystery was not where, but why?

*   *   *

Morpurgo watched Doc Vickers go down the crumbling service road in the late evening dusk, heading back to the bar. There was a relationship that would never be the same again. He had forced Vickers into a revelation of personal turpitude. It would always stand between them. It had been between them as he had watched Vickers give Sattin his second injection, so that he had had to force himself to look all the time at Sattin and never at Vickers; so that Vickers, too, had given Sattin a simple intravenous sedative with the overanxious concentration of a new and nervous houseman.

And what now? Nothing, in all probability. Trigg, tucked away in the annexe, was well able to take care of himself. Sattin, the marks on his face less angry but still prohibitive of any public appearance, would sleep, so Doc had assured him, for eight hours. Morpurgo himself might sleep a little, or not at all; it was of no concern to him. There were only two people he was prepared to trust, himself and Ian Sibley, and Sibley should be there within the hour. In the meantime, he was on his own.

He withdrew from its exceedingly uncomfortable lodgement at the back of his trousers the Smith & Wesson hammerless – he preferred guns, on the rare occasions when he needed one, to be simple – loaded the six .38 cartridges, the maximum permitted withdrawal, from his pocket, checked the safety catch to be sure it was on, and slid it back inside his belt. This time it was just in front of his left hip, more accessible but every bit as uncomfort-able. He was not even sure why he had drawn it, let alone brought it with him.

He went down the corridor toward the Bin, passed the dispensary and let himself into the annexe through the short corridor and its two doors. Trigg, apparently absorbed in *Reader's Digest*, barely troubled to turn his head. He was stretched out on the bed, jacket and shoes off, his majestic braces dividing his bulk like a well-tied parcel, a rickety bedside light making the dusk between the window and the blast wall as inky black as full night.

"Bit restless tonight, aren't we? What's up? Bar run out of booze?" Trigg's own supply had diminished considerably.

"Glad when this is all over, that's all." Morpurgo leaned awkwardly against the plasterboard wall with its grubby coating of cream emulsion paint.

"Aye," Trigg said. "No doubt. And yon feller I'm to stand in for, will he be glad when it's all over?"

"I dare say."

266

"You dare say? When it's all over for him, he'll be dead, won't he?"

"I'm not looking beyond tomorrow. Not beyond tomorrow morning, to be more exact. He'll still be alive after that." Since Trigg was just about as far in as he could be, there was no real reason why he should not know a little more. "There's the possibility of an exchange with Moscow, one of ours in return."

"And if he lasts that long you don't care what happens after, is that about it?"

"More or less."

"So he'll never go on trial."

"Wouldn't say never. Doesn't do to say never in this game. But it's quite likely he won't. Depends, these exchanges usually take a little time."

"Might die first? Wouldn't make much difference, so far as he's concerned, would it?"

"Not really."

"By!" Trigg said after considering briefly. "Lot of fuss over nought, isn't it?" He had put down his book. "Or happen you haven't told me everything."

No, Morpurgo thought, happen he hadn't! What, appropriately enough, was still underground, still tunnelling away, was the mole, but now the precise object of the mole's allegiance was in question.

Trigg was doing a little tunnelling of his own. "Bit daft, wasn't it, picking a chap that's dying?" He squinted at Morpurgo through the pool of yellow lamplight. "Doesn't say much for that lot in Moscow."

"Enough problems of my own, thank you, without worrying about theirs. Anyway, they didn't know," Morpurgo said. "Neither did he, come to that. Knew he was sick, of course, but not dying."

"Get off!" Trigg said sceptically. "Near to dying and doesn't know? Don't talk daft!"

"If he'd known it was serious, he'd have seen a doctor. He didn't."

"Dosed himself, then. Some folk can't abide doctors. Our Robbo stuffed himself with indigestion tablets for years because he can't abide doctors. Had to go in the end, though, found he'd got a ruddy great duodenal."

"Sattin didn't take anything."

267

"I see." Trigg pretended to be impressed. "Living in his pocket, were you?"

"Pretty near." Morpurgo gave a general idea of what total SV was like.

"Treffs," Trigg repeated. "That's what you call them, is it?"

"Yes. Jargon word for a transfer of product as opposed to a simple meet."

"Product? What sort of product?"

"In this case, technical drawings. At least, photographic negatives of technical drawings."

"Nought else?"

"No. Technical information. That's what it was all about."

"Saw all that, too, did you? Peering over this Russian feller's shoulder while he was checking it?"

"We're not *quite* that clever." Trigg had to be humoured. "But not far short. We knew exactly what Stringer was marking, what Mrs Stringer was borrowing to photograph. Exactly what was being passed to Kagalov in the treffs."

"Except that you didn't actually see it. Come on, sunshine, I've got a point."

"You've got a point."

"That's better. And the case this Russian feller gave Sattin each time, that'd be empty, would it?"

"Except for money, anything like that. Sattin paid the Stringers."

"Anything like that." Trigg varied between occasional quick looks at Morpurgo and long, pensive studies of the white-painted fibreboard ceiling of the hut. "Happen, then, anything like that could also have been nothing like that? Anything like something else, you might say." Trigg propped himself up on one elbow. "Like say, a bottle of aspirin."

"What?"

"Look, lad." Trigg shook his head gently over Morpurgo's obtuseness. "What I'm saying is that yon feller, Sattin, could have been poorly but not letting on about it. Not wanting to let on about it, do you see?"

"Why? Why on earth want to hide the fact that he was ill?"

"Nay, I leave the fancy stuff to you masterminds. I'm just tinkering with the nuts and bolts. But all right, how about this? Happen him and his boss both knew he was sickening for summat from the start. Happen they saved it up in case he was

268

caught, so they could put out all that taradiddle about torturing dying men and shame you into letting him go. Now, see if you can do better, sunshine."

Sometimes one can find oneself too close to a truth to believe it. Sometimes a complex mind is unable to solve a simple problem. Sometimes deceit is only instantly recognised by those least practised in it.

Morpurgo was like a man brought from darkness to be interrogated under a blinding light. He could sense the questions but not properly identify them, sense answers yet be unable to match them to the questions. What was it Ian Sibley had said, showing Morpurgo his newly completed chart? Blue for drops from Stringer. Or was it green? No matter. Blue for drops, say. Green for pick-ups, Sattin from Stringer's drops. Red for treffs, Sattin and Kagalov. Then Sibley had said – only Morpurgo had been too intent upon the idea of luring Kagalov into a last treff to listen properly – Sibley had said something about treffs with a difference, treffs that *didn't* follow drops and couldn't be reconciled, through the bank statements, with cash moving down the line from Kagalov to the Stringers via Sattin.

Trigg was watching him intently, his stolid, chunky face somehow an encouragement. I was wrong, Morpurgo thought somewhere along a minor network of brain cells; there are two people I can trust; one is Sibley, the other is Trigg.

But what was to be won from Sibley's comments on the unexplained treffs? Patterns? Frequencies? That was it; frequency! He could almost hear Sibley saying it: *six clear weeks before these, it's got to mean something, sir.* And no, it was red for the unexplained, the mystery treffs. Every six weeks there had been a red treff.

Trigg, softly, said, "On to something, sunshine, are you?"

"Bed," Morpurgo said. "Days in bed, no, twenty-four hours. Several times, twenty-four hours in bed. Every so many – six? – weeks?" He looked vaguely at Trigg. "What?"

"Never mind me, lad. Just you get on with it."

"I'll be back. A couple of things I want to check with Doc." He closed and locked Trigg's door behind him, light spilling out through the transom into the dark corridor that smelled of dust, floor polish and pine resin. Locking the connecting doors behind him he went, increasingly fast and without switching on lights, round the corner by the dispensary, across the corridor leading to the Bin, back to Doc Vickers' office. About to enter, he stopped, thinking he had heard a small sound from somewhere behind him. He froze, listening, but it was not repeated; the sort of sound, he thought, that might be expected as a hot day gave way to the chill of a clear sky, so that things that had expanded as they baked had now begun the stealthy process of contraction.

He opened the desk drawer and took out the keys that would let him out through the main building. The scatter of lights from Soapbox City served only to underline the general darkness, velvety, no moon, the sky tacked into place by a hundred thousand stars, misty swathes of radiance draped from tree to tree. In the distance he heard a dog bark; the two guards would be readying their charges for the first perimeter patrol. Toward London, an aircraft, detectable by the wink of its navigation lights, trailed its rumbling cone of sound far behind it.

He found Vickers hunched in a corner seat by the window. A light-tranced moth, ignored, fluttered about the light above his head.

Morpurgo sat down across the small table from him. No one had ever seen Doc Vickers drunk, but there came a stage at which he would adjust his mind to surroundings other than those in which he was to be found. This was his present state, though he returned from it long enough to acknowledge Morpurgo's presence. *"Ek dam, sahib,"* he said thickly. *"Bus. Bus. Jeldi jao!"* Morpurgo knew he was being told to clear off.

"Doc, listen. It's important."

Vickers had resumed his study of infinity. *"Ek dam,"* he repeated, forcing himself to enunciate with a clarity both ephemeral and brittle. *"Bus! Bus! Ijazat hai!"* He returned briefly to English. "Finished, old boy! Bugger off, get me?"

* * *

There are heavy men who can move like light men, noiseless and adroit. Trigg was not one of them. Trigg was of the earth, every lifting of a foot an uprooting, each completed step a foot replanted, moving in a biblical way: a man like a tree walking. But he was silent, the ponderousness of his concentration mastering the ponderousness of his gait.

Waiting until the last trace of Morpurgo's passage had died away, he forced open the window of his room as far as it would go, shifted a chair against it and, tongue protruding a little from his parted lips as an aid to single-mindedness, mounted and slowly eased himself through the gap. One strong hand reached out, locking its fingers to the top of the blast wall. One careful foot established itself on the ledge of the window. His considerable mass rose as lightly and silently as an airship until he could move himself sideways into the space between window and wall. A further levitation took him to the top of the wall, from which, with slow, noiseless dignity, he lowered himself to the ground outside.

He had only the haziest idea of his local geography, but it took him, simply by following the blast wall around three sides of the annexe, to the corridor linking it with the main building and thence to the entrance through which he had passed with Morpurgo and Vickers some little time earlier. It was as far as his imagination had taken him in advance. He knew the door would be locked. He had no idea how he was going to carry out the remainder of his mission.

Not even certain whether Morpurgo's absence would be lengthy enough to get him to his objective, let alone back to his room, and not unmindful of what had been said about guard dogs, he pressed his bulk against the door to make himself as nearly invisible as his girth would permit. The door swung silently ajar under his weight. He wasted no time in getting himself inside. Someone – he reckoned it would be the tree-high doctor, with his vague air of limited competence – had clearly overlooked his duty.

Now he knew where he was. He also knew where the keys were. He was obliged to strike three matches before he found the ones he was looking for. Three on the same ring, two of them labelled, logically enough, ONE and TWO, made it a reasonable bet that the third, tagged H.S. BLOCK – High Security Block was his guess – would open the outer door. About to blow out his third match, he spotted and appropriated a large, rubber-cased electric torch.

Returning to the corridor, he shone the torch briefly. For an instant he had an impression of noiseless movement, but the movement was not repeated. He decided that it had been a movement of shadows caused by the torch. Once again he tiptoed down the passage, mouth open in an unconscious attempt to reduce the sound of his breathing, tongue firmly pressed against his upper denture as a side-effect of intentness. To his faint surprise he found the door to the Bin to be open also. By! he told himself, some of those security fellers wanted a good talking to!

Easing through the gap, he stood quite still, listening. Nothing. He went on, a brief exposure of light directing him to Number 2. There, also, the door was open. Shaking his big head, he shone the torch momentarily through his fingers to locate the bed, made his way to its foot, sweating a little in the warm, still air. Cupping his hand more comprehensively about the lens of the torch, switching it on in a diffusion of pinkish light, he padded around the bed, never taking his eyes from the elongated mound beneath the bedclothes. Speaking very softly to his doppelgänger, he said, "Now then, sunshine, here we are at last."

*　　*　　*

Fish had telephoned to ask if it was okay for Epworth to call, giving the impression that it was important. What could Claas say, except yes?

A matter of some importance, Well, maybe! Epworth, the screwballest kind of guy to be any sort of intelligence operative that Claas had ever come across, seemed to have as his main purpose the prolongation of a rambling discourse on a topic normally as attractive to any senior CIA man as a bouquet of poison ivy.

"I suppose," he was saying in his schoolmarmish way, "you could put it down to lack of cooperation. Or perhaps coordination." Catching Claas looking jaundiced, he said, "Please don't take that as criticism."

"No," Claas said. "I won't," hastily adding, as he in turn caught Weber's eye. "Of *course* not!"

"Though even if all your SV teams had been in the closest contact, I don't suppose they'd have noticed."

"I guess not." Claas steered an imploring look toward Weber, but Weber who, like Claas, was drinking beer from the can, allowed the look to bounce off.

"After all," Epworth pottered on, "even a normal itemisation of the post each of them received while they were under SV wouldn't – mmmm – really have suggested any kind of pattern, would it? A gramophone record, a souvenir paperweight, a reproduction brass rubbing, a picture postcard and so forth. Nothing to connect them without a little luck to start the mental processes working."

"That's right," Claas said. He knew the whole thing off by heart.

272

"And even if one had – mmmm – an inkling of suspicion, the link wasn't exactly obvious."

"Not exactly." Claas steeled himself to be hospitable. "Sure you won't have a beer? Or a shot of rye? Something?"

"No, really. I'm not a great drinker."

Claas grunted because none of the things he was tempted to say would have been polite. "Too bad we're all out of sherry." He poured the last of his can down his throat and fetched another from the fridge; only one, so as to punish Weber, still silent, for his lack of cooperation.

"Of course," Epworth said, "it was easier for us. You had seven subjects to keep under SV. We only . . ." He corrected himself. "Security Directorate had only three."

Seven KGB linkmen who slipped the net in the US, Claas told himself sourly. "Seven plus Kagalov himself," he pointed out. "Kagalov had other people at the embassy do all the posting, different places, nothing to connect with until the birds had flown the coop." He looked curiously at Epworth. "You must be getting some pretty fancy cooperation from Security Directorate to have a complete run-down on all those mail deliveries."

"We have excellent relations," Epworth said. "But, of course, we also had the advantage of Stringer's eagerness to talk, *and* we borrowed Morpurgo's technique to analyse the post; dates, times, nature."

"So given the information about the mail order shot, the rest fell into place."

"Exactly." Epworth seemed determined to have any indication of cleverness discounted. "Of course, the neatest one was Sattin's. A letter addressed to the previous occupant of Sattin's flat, marked: *Please forward.* That's what he did, very promptly, too. Readdressed it and put it in the box at the corner of his own street, right under the noses of the SV team. They fished it out just as promptly for inspection, but there was nothing for them. Sattin had only needed to see it to know he was being told to lie low."

"Smart," Claas conceded wearily. "You have to hand it to Kagalov, a pretty smart operator. Whoever sent the original warning to Kagalov was no dummy, either."

"No. One could be forgiven for thinking it was someone inside the intelligence community."

Claas stifled a desire to whimper. Did this schmuck know who the mole was supposed to be, or not? "Have to know the story of

273

how Kagalov warned his US ring to disband. Back home, that would be a lot of people. Over here? I wouldn't know."

"Quite a number." Weber broke silence at last. "In the intelligence community, that is. Yet nobody in the British SV team spotted the direct link with our own blooper." Weber went through to get himself a can of beer. He called, "Keep talking, I can hear."

"One level too many," Epworth said. "The Post Office special unit at Union House . . ."

"Hey, how about that?" Weber called. "Practically next door to St Paul's Cathedral. Nice touch that!"

"Isn't it?" Epworth produced his little giggle as Weber returned, suggesting rather absurd secrets shared. "Anyway, Union House was intercepting all the mail addressed to the Kagalovs at their house in Hampstead – something Kagalov would take for granted, of course – and they copied the postcard as they did everything else. But it wasn't important until Stringer told us about the mail order catalogue." Again he corrected himself. "Told SD, that is. After that, naturally, *we* were able to say, 'That's it!'"

"Cathedrals," Claas said, "St Peter's, Rome, a disc of choral music. Reproduction brass rubbing from Westminster. Souvenir paperweight from St Patrick's, New York City. Etcetera, etcetera." He emphasised everything heavily to call attention to the fact that this was the second time through the full story.

"Yes," Epworth said. "So we remembered that the picture postcard of a cathedral would instantly put Kagalov on the alert. Which it certainly did. I'm – mmmm – quite sure that if Morpurgo had been less pressed, he'd have spotted it at once. Oh." He blinked and smiled. "Always supposing, naturally, that he knows Kagalov used exactly the same signal pattern in America."

"Sure he knew it," Claas said tiredly. "Heard it from me."

"Really?" Epworth appeared to be momentarily nonplussed. "Well, there you are, too preoccupied with other things. I'm sure he would have come round to it in due course."

"In the meantime," Claas said almost rudely, "find out who sent Kagalov that picture of York Cathedral, right? And you have your mole."

"Not York," Epworth reminded him. "Lincoln. But yes, certainly, we'd have our mole.

*　　*　　*

"Doc, listen." Morpurgo took one of Vickers' hands between his own. "How *do* you treat Hodgkin's disease?" Vickers was as elegantly pickled as plums in brandy. Some question, at this time of night, after being comprehensively dismissed in Hindi. "Doc, I need to know."

Vickers eventually focused on him with the reproachful dignity of a man betrayed. Very slowly, he shook his head. "Don't know, Johnny. Old Hakim Vickers doesn't know anything. Run-down, worn-out, stick-in-the-mud, old has-been of a quack. Losh . . ." He blinked and began again. "Lost self-respect years ago, managed to ignore the fact because of this job . . ." Once again he halted, blinking owlishly. How much, Morpurgo wondered, had he managed to drink between now and their earlier session?

Vickers took a deep breath. "Because," he said quietly but clearly, "this job doesn't require self-respect. Because nobody in this job has any self-respect. Not me. Not you, friend. Nobody. This is a job for creepy-crawlies. Snakes, worms, woodlouses." Vaguely conscious of something wrong, he frowned, eyes narrowed. "Parasites," he said with quiet triumph. "Parasites on the body politic. Crabs, infesting the national pudenda."

He wagged a finger very close to Morpurgo's face. "Know Latin meaning of pudenda, do you? Means the shameful parts. That's me, you, all our lot, British, Russian, American, all live, move and have our being in the shameful parts."

He levered himself upright. "Going to bed, sahib. To sleep, perchance to dream. Going to die, too, no cure for any of us, only paltive . . ." He tried again. "Palliative treatment, treatment between pals, forty degrees proof but no cure."

He put a hand on Morpurgo's shoulder and brought his face close. "Hodgkin's disease. Usually kills young if at all, but no rules, nobody understands properly, see? Best not to be a Jew, or grow up in a small family, be a schoolteacher. Or too well-educated; let's me out, right? Treatment? Chemo . . . chem . . . *drugs*. Radiation too, but mostly drugs. Sish . . . *six* courses of treatment, two injections, weekly intervals, four clear weeks between. *If* brings remission, *three* courses, *four*-month intervals, didn't in this case, right, sahib?"

Galvanised, Morpurgo said, "Are you telling me he had *had* treatment?"

Doc Vickers winked ponderously. "No expert, old son, only

275

pensioned off old hakim, superannuated old quack." He tucked his hands under his armpits, moved his elbows up and down slowly, and solemnly quacked.

"One a week for two weeks, then four weeks, then another two at weekly intervals." Morpurgo recited it aloud, fixing it in his mind. It tallied, didn't it? He needed another look at Sibley's chart. "Any nasty side effects? Would he have to stay in bed?"

"Damn fool if he didn't." Vickers strained to maintain a weakening concentration. "Feel nauseous and so on. Twenty-four hours beddybyes after each injection. Too late, sahib, my opinion." He wagged a finger under Morpurgo's nose once more. "Mush . . . *much* too late. Temporary remission, 's'all, just temporary remission."

He turned toward the door. "Old doc off to climb wooden hill, okay? Sandman cometh, eh? Coals of fire, sahib, socking great coals of fire." With concentrated dignity he walked in a straight line to the door, remembered to duck, almost fell, recovered and disappeared into the star-filled night.

Coals of fire? It took Morpurgo a little while to realise that it was his own head they had been heaped upon. He went back to the Bin a good deal more slowly than he had come. Somewhere down the steep slope of the lawn, toward the southern perimeter, one of the guard dogs was barking furiously. He heard its handler shout it down and silence flowed back in an invisible tide.

The mystery of Sibley's chart was solved, he had no doubt of that. Red for the unexplained treffs, now explained. Chemotherapy, self-administered, with monthly gaps between each pair of injections, a full twenty-four hours in bed to recover from the nauseating side effects. Moscow Centre had forwarded the treatment via Kagalov. Moscow Centre had known of his condition, so had Kagalov, so – must *not* overlook this – had Sattin himself, who, like them, must also have known that any remission would only be temporary.

Without prior warning, the TASS announcement presented itself to him in a very different light. A light that shone, equally revealingly, upon the mole. Or at any rate, the molehill.

Back in the house, he was about to turn by the dispensary when something brought him to an abrupt halt. There was light, faint but unmistakable, coming from the Bin. Feeling for his pistol and only just remembering – Good God! When was the last

276

time he had handled one of these things? – to release the safety catch, he went noiselessly down the corridor.

The door of Number 2 was ajar. He eased it wider open. The light came from a torch held by a figure at Sattin's bedside. He had no difficulty in recognising Trigg.

"How the hell," Morpurgo demanded, "did you get in? You've absolutely no business to be here."

"Happen not," Trigg said stonily. "Nor I wouldn't, if one of your lot hadn't left all the bloody doors open." He made no attempt to move.

Morpurgo remembered how much depended on Trigg. And, after all, it was a natural enough thing that Trigg should want to set eyes on the man who was the cause of so many strange things.

"Sorry, I shouldn't have gone off like that. Anyway, I dare say you've already found out, he's fast asleep and dreaming, and that's the way he'll stay until your own little performance is over."

"Oh aye? My own little performance, is it?" For some reason, Trigg was disproportionately angry. Angry and formidable. "And when will it be time for him to wake up? Day of Judgement? Or happen, sunshine, you don't know he's stone dead?"

It was as if the revelation were some sort of signal for a chain reaction of events. They began with noises back around the main entrance, continued with Morpurgo, gun still in hand, going toward the terrace to investigate and being promptly, violently and painfully seized in an armlock while someone relieved him of his gun. From these and a continuing series of incidents, the one that was to stick indelibly in Morpurgo's mind was the sight of Sibley, a hard-faced Sibley whose eyes met his and moved stonily on, closing the door to the Bin and standing guard while Steve Archer, himself armed, grinned, utterly without humour, at Morpurgo. Chief Superintendent Placket, sharing the general grim satisfaction, backed by Inspector Garret and a Special Branch sergeant whose name Morpurgo could not recall, said, formally, "Good evening, Mr Morpurgo. As you know, sir, I am a police officer and I have reason to believe that you have committed offences under Sections 1, 2 and 6 of the Official Secrets Act. It is my duty to warn you . . . ."

The only thing Morpurgo could think about was Sibley.

16
Trials and Tribulations

"Trust!" the Knight snapped angrily. "Decency! Comradeship! Do these things mean nothing any more?" His face pinched with anger, he presided with the implacable outrage of a judge obliged to be impartial in spite of the conviction that no one on either side had the smallest acquaintance with the truth.

"I am summoned," he went on, "from my bed in the small hours, obliged to endure a long journey by motor car, unable, during that time, to think of anything other than the fact that the crisis which has called me forth is not due to enemy action but a scandalous conflict between senior members of my own organisation. My discomfort made even less bearable by the knowledge that, not content to create havoc intramurally, those responsible have also involved members of another service, the Special Branch, and have actually attempted to have each other arrested and charged with offences under the very Act it is their sworn duty to enforce."

Outside, in conditions of small-hours discomfort, Placket and his sullen inspector huddled together in the little office normally used by the day staff, glowering while Sibley operated a more or less nonstop tea-brewing service. Monitor, his functionary's face chill as an arctic dawn, had been and gone, silently outraged to be instructed to set in motion the logistics of death when death had come and gone without the smallest respect for his authority.

Doc Vickers, remarkably sober considering the nature of his evening, had made an initial examination of the cadaver, announced that a post-mortem would be required to establish the cause of death, after which, eyeing Morpurgo strangely, he had retired.

Now there were four of them in Vickers' small, untidy office, its time-scarred, roll-top desk overflowing with medical impedimenta. The Knight occupied the rickety swivel chair. Morpurgo and Archer had a metal stacking chair apiece. The fourth member of the party had placed himself, ominous and louring as a thunderstorm, on top of an ancient bookcase stacked with battered medical record books.

To begin with, the Knight had endeavoured to persuade Trigg that he should be privately accommodated elsewhere.

Trigg had folded his massive arms much as they were now, as if hugging the very kingpost of immovability. "Bugger that for a game! I'm stopping."

It had given Morpurgo grim satisfaction, the Knight's first real encounter with Eustace Roland Trigg. The Knight, too, was strong-willed. "I'm afraid I must insist. We're dealing with matters touching upon the safety of the realm. I believe you already have some knowledge of Section 2 of the Official . . ."

"Stuff it, sunshine! I'm stopping."

"In roughly nine hours' time," Morpurgo had said, "Joseph Sattin is to appear in Bow Street Magistrates' Court."

The Knight, no fighter for lost causes, knew one when he saw it. "Very well." As grim as a hangman's 'Good morning', he had accepted the inevitable, but was hopeful of conditions. "I've reminded you of the Act. What you hear in this room together with what you already know, you will discuss with no one."

"Happen I won't," Trigg said equably, "happen I will. It'll want some thinking about, will that."

Steve, dangerously quiet since the moment at which Placket, losing his nerve, dug his heels in until the Knight had been telephoned, said, "May as well face it, Director-General. He's Morpurgo's puppet. Cleethorpes may be the back of beyond but these lefties are like vermin. They breed everywhere, even in the sticks."

Slowly, massively, Trigg turned his gaze upon Steve Archer. "By!" His tone was one of reluctant wonder. "You've just insulted me at least four different ways, do you know that?"

"Mr Archer," Morpurgo said, conserving his special knowledge, "consorts with aliens, at home and abroad. Mr Archer sponsors murder. From Mr Archer, simple defamation is almost a relief."

"Jesus Christ!" Steve's brittle self-control had fragmented like

279

a grenade. "He spreads crypto-commie views like a suppuration. He tips off Kagalov to lie low because the game's up, but advises him not to bolt because we'd know he was tipped off. He spins some bloody likely yarn about trapping Kagalov in a final treff, uses his wife and Petröfi to report on Sattin's condition so that Moscow Centre can concoct the TASS statement, gets rid of Sattin and does his best to make it look like natural causes. Now he's inviting you to put this turnip-head in the dock so that he can tell the world media that he's been tortured."

"Do you think," Morpurgo asked, speaking with a deliberate softness, "that Trigg here was put together with some KGB kit? In any case, I think you're in a particularly good position to know that whoever killed Sattin did it because he thought he was killing Trigg."

"By the heck!" Trigg, back on his bookshelf, sat up very straight. "Is *that* why you shifted me? I'm beginning to think I'm in with a very poor class of company, sunshine."

"I'd like to remind you of something, Director-General," Morpurgo said. "Before I came down here, you and I were the only ones who knew I was going to shift Sattin and put Trigg in Number 2. I deliberately asked you to get Steve to ring Vickers and set up the arrangements, so that he would be the third to have information no one else had. What neither he nor you knew was that I changed things around as soon as I got here. Who could have any reason for killing Sattin? We couldn't put him on show, alive or dead. But we didn't have to. We'd got Trigg."

"Are you telling me," the Knight said icily, "that you knew Sattin would be killed?" Morpurgo noted with satisfaction that his eyes had flickered toward Steve Archer before he asked the question.

"No." Morpurgo's self-confidence was growing by the minute. "But I was reasonably sure someone" – He too let his eyes wander toward Steve – "would make an attempt to nobble Trigg. Beat him up, the same sort of treatment that was given to Sattin. I intended to be around to stop him. That's why I had a gun."

"You didn't succeed," the Knight pointed out. "Just where were you when, according to you, the intruder got in?"

"With Doc Vickers. Briefly. And for a very good reason, which I'll tell you about in a minute."

"And you claim that this someone, or whoever was behind

him if he exists, meant to make sure we couldn't produce Trigg in court."

"Exactly. And only one person, you apart, thought he would be in Number 2. A question: who benefits?"

"The obvious answer," the Knight said, "is Moscow Centre. Do you expect me to believe that Steve is working for Moscow Centre?"

"The very question that people asked about Burgess. About Maclean. About Philby, Blunt . . ."

"If you don't stop him," Steve Archer said very loudly, "I will! He's a bloody traitor! Not to mention suborning and seducing my wife, wrecking my marriage, splitting my family. *He's* your bloody mole! That's why he's making smoke, why he's been making smoke ever since . . ."

"One thing at a time." Again the Knight's tone succeeded in bringing a fragile, supercharged stillness into the early morning frowstiness of the room.

"Facts," the Knight said. "I must insist upon facts. It is a fact that Doctor Vickers, on the basis of a first examination, could find absolutely no external signs of unnatural death. It is a fact that Sattin was a man who had begun to die of an incurable malady. It is also a fact that few if any other facts have been put forward in the last hour. Sattin might have died in precisely similar circumstances tomorrow night and no one would be talking of murder."

Painfully aware of Trigg's presence, he made an effort to capitalise on this seemingly reasonable statement. "Mr Trigg, in this business one learns to hypothesise, to throw up possibilities, but one also learns the art of applied scepticism. In both cases, logic is an important tool, but logic can be turned against itself. Logic can be shown to be mere speculation, and thus destroyed."

"And which one are you on at now, then?" Trigg enquired. "Hypothesising? Speculating? Or destroying?"

"A little of all three. We set up a theory. Then we pull it to pieces."

"With bad feeling all round," Trigg said, "like kids with sandcastles. Dad builds a sandcastle for little Tommy. Little Tommy shows how grateful he is by jumping on it. Dad shows how pleased he is by belting Tommy one on the earhole. At the moment I think your problem is too many dads." He rubbed his

281

face, his early morning beard making a rasping sound. "Or too many Tommies."

"Yes," Morpurgo said, smiling a little. "Happen you're right. So if nobody likes the idea of being on Tommy's side, how about a look at Dad? Take Pratt, for instance. Pratt was planted here by Steve's old drinking pals, the SIS. It wasn't sufficient to have a man" – He looked pointedly at Steve – "near the top. They wanted one near the bottom as well."

For the first time the Knight was looking a little unsettled. He was also, Morpurgo saw with ruthless clarity, looking old; tired and old. The Knight said, "No doubt you're going to explain," and Morpurgo also saw that SIS infiltration was not an entirely new idea to him.

Morpurgo was tired of sitting. Vickers' office, very far from cosy, pressed in on them like the walls of a cave, the one suspended bulb creating a cone of inadequate light in which they camped like Indians in a tepee. The atmosphere had become oppressive, stale air made staler by the near presence of death and the close atmosphere of mutual recrimination.

"According to Sibley, Pratt's admitted beating up Sattin because he was paid American money to do it." He glanced at Steve. "Right?"

"According to Pratt." Steve pretended to be absorbed in tossing four or five paperclips on the palm of his hand.

"It was squeezed out of him. By Placket. Using a little force. Is that right too?"

"He hasn't retracted it," Steve said carefully.

"Crap!" Morpurgo could give a little rein to his feelings now, respond a little to the pain he had been repressing. "There was never any need to squeeze Pratt. You already knew who'd paid Pratt to beat up Sattin. You put Pratt on the strength" – He would, in atonement, make no mention of Vickers, though it would probably come out – "and you did it on behalf of the Friends. And when the Friends and the Cousins decided the TASS release was a good way of getting at Delahay, you went along with the idea of making it impossible for Sattin to be shown in public. But you couldn't pay Pratt to do it yourself, neither could the Friends. So they got a helping hand from Claas's people. Then you primed Sibley" – This was when the hurt, real for the last two hours, actually began to surface like the contusions on Sattin's dead face – "to give me that stuff about

Placket making Pratt squeal and you just happening to be working late in the office. Working late, hell! You, Sibley, Placket, the whole lot of you, you'd already set off to get yourselves down here." Sibley, he thought; Ian Sibley; the one good apple in a rotten barrel! It hurt! Jesus, yes, it hurt like hell!

"Johnny," the Knight said wearily. "A minute or two ago you were telling me Steve was a KGB mole. Now you're accusing him of working for the CIA."

"I'm accusing him," Morpurgo said, "of working for himself. He gives things to the CIA, of course he does. And to the Friends. Things like information and his wife."

"You bastard!" Steve flung himself this time, swinging at Morpurgo as he came. Trigg, otherwise motionless, stuck out a treetrunk leg. Steve went down as heavily as a hanged man. The door of the room opened after a quick knock and Sibley looked in. "Tea, anybody?" He stopped, seeing first Steve Archer picking himself up, then Trigg, a dead man risen, on the bookcase.

"Not just now," Morpurgo pushed Sibley out. Through the gap between door and frame he said, "Congratulations, you're learning fast."

Even in the brief moment, Sibley's face showed the archetypal expression of the professional security man; a combination of barely hidden toughness – *'Don't you make fun of me, sonny! Don't you fucking make fun of me'* – disrespect and weary disbelief. "Thank you, sir, I do my best," and then, the mould cracking, in a loud whisper, through the last inch of the gap, "I trusted you, sir. I *trusted* you!" Too late, Morpurgo thought, shutting the door.

"Let me tell you something else," he said. "Ian Sibley who's going to make a first-class counter-intelligence man, did a breakdown of all the drops and treffs and came up with something." He told them about the unexplained drops that no longer were, adding a summary of the chemotherapeutic treatment of Hodgkin's disease.

"Is this getting us anywhere?" Steve Archer demanded of no one especially. His voice was thick with hate. "Sattin's dead, good news for Moscow, bad news for the Friends' man over there in East Germany. Morpurgo's the only one who could have killed him. I can show you patterns, too. I already have."

The Knight ignored him. "Where does this get us, Johnny?"

"This is where it gets us. If the treatment had been successful, if the shots had produced remission, then the pattern would have changed after the sixth pair. A break of a month, then another pair, then a break of *four* months. But there wasn't. Even if he was at the very beginning of treatment when we began SV, he should have reached the four-month interval before we brought him in. He didn't. There's only one explanation."

"No remission." The Knight was beginning to look grey.

"No remission. The thing could only be kept at bay. In other words, terminal."

"Natural causes. He died from natural causes." The Knight offered the alternative mechanically, unconvinced himself.

"So, why didn't they take him out, Moscow Centre? He was going to die. Why didn't they simply fetch him home? It's what we would have done."

"Too late?"

"No. They knew he was sick when they committed him to the operation. They committed him *because* he was sick, incurably sick."

The Knight shook his head uncertainly. "Why in God's name would they do that?"

The answer came from the least expected quarter. "So they could put pussy among the pigeons," Trigg said. "Meaning last Monday's lark."

"Meaning last Monday's lark," Morpurgo repeated. "The TASS statement. British secret police torture dying man."

Disbelief bringing some life back to his voice, the Knight said, "For that? All for that?"

"All for that," Morpurgo repeated. "When they were setting the ring up, maybe even after they'd set it up, they discovered Sattin's illness. Incurable. Alleviate it for a while, yes. Cure it? No. So since he was going to die come what may, why not die for a purpose? For the cause."

No one said anything. "Sattin's business of not speaking," Morpurgo said. "A very proper attitude in a captured agent, even if he talked in the end. But it was nothing to do with attitudes. It was part of a carefully prearranged plan. When he was taken, and you can be sure Kagalov knew when he was taken, they gave it a week, then blew the whistle. At that stage, if things had gone the way Moscow Centre had every reason to expect, we were on a good hiding to nothing. If we didn't put him on view the world would believe the TASS story. If we *did* put him on view, he would have broken his silence and shouted torture at the top of his voice, because he knew all along exactly what was going to happen, when, and in what order."

"A propaganda victory," the Knight said reluctantly. "And a very big one at that."

"A very big one indeed. But don't stop there, Director-General. The propaganda victory would have been only the beginning. No one's in a better position than you to know that."

"The political consequences" – the Knight seemed to Morpurgo to be ageing by the minute – "would have been unthinkable. The Prime Minister totally discredited, forced to resign."

"You're considering a best case," Morpurgo said impatiently. "Look at the worst. And don't forget Joe Padley, MP."

The Knight, still unable, or unwilling, to accept bad medicine at a single gulp, said, "A vote of no confidence in the Commons."

"Go on. Enough government backbenchers outraged to abstain or even go into the opposition lobby."

"Defeat," the Knight said, as if speaking of his own circumstances. "Delahay would have had to go to the Palace. And the country. A general election. Again, defeat."

He looked helplessly at Morpurgo. "Total destabilisation. The other lot in power. With a big enough majority to fulfil the undertakings in their manifesto."

"American bases shut down," Steve said in an ugly voice. "Our own nuclear deterrent scrapped. The British Army of the Rhine, cut to a single division. Or less. Raving lefties wrecking the economy, pulling out of NATO and the Common Market, hellbent on carrying out every last crazy, vindictive scrap of dogma while the roof fell in and the house burned down. Not just the destabilisation of this country; the destabilisation of the whole European alliance, the destabilisation of the whole bloody world."

He made a last attempt to enlist the Knight against Morpurgo. "That's what you can expect from these people. It's why we have the security services. It's why we keep dossiers, why we tap telephones, why we're obliged to go on committing more time, more money, more effort to protect the public from itself." There was bitterness in his voice, but also the desperate earnestness of a man who senses that he is about to lose a case which, in justice, he should win.

"We're not in the business of restricting freedom," Steve said.

"We're in the business of protecting it, which means we have to take some of it, a little of it, away. It also means" – Bitterness was back – "spending more time on the streets than we spend at home, more time checking on what other people are saying than we have for listening to our families. And all the time," his gaze returning to Morpurgo with open hatred, "people like him are in the middle of what we do, as much against us as for us, sitting on the fence so that they can come down on whichever side suits their precious consciences – people like me aren't supposed to have any – at any particular time."

The Knight nodded, his face sagging with the weight of something more than years. "You don't have to tell me how important it is to do what we do. You don't have to tell me the personal price we pay. But in all fairness, I have to point out that it's Johnny who seems to have out-thought Moscow. If it hadn't been for him, we might have swallowed the bait, hook, line and sinker."

Steve laughed, a savage parody of a laugh, angry disbelief. "*Might* have? May still, isn't that a better way of putting it? Out of the frying pan, but into a very hot fire!" He collected the Knight's gaze, than steered it, very deliberately, toward Trigg.

Trigg nodded as if in confirmation, not of what Steve was implying, but rather of some conclusion privately arrived at. "Hit the nail smack on the head, right, sunshine?" he asked Steve, and then, to the Knight. "The way I see it, I reckon I can name my own price. Even then, it wouldn't answer the question, would it?"

"The question? What question?"

"'Can we trust him?'" Trigg said. "Isn't that what you're all asking yourselves? I reckon," he repeated in the profound silence, "I could just about name my own price."

Steve, his face set in a scowl, made a brief sound that said: What did I tell you? The Knight peered at Trigg with open calculation.

"'Can we trust him?'" Trigg repeated. "You want to watch out for me, thought-reading's something we're born with where I come from. Has its limits, mind, only works when we're dealing with someone smart, someone educated, someone who fancies himself a bit. It's had quite a bit of practice since I fell in with you lot."

The Knight pushed himself upright. "You mentioned price. You also mentioned trust. You're right, of course. You could name any price within reason. But unless I'm wholly mistaken, you're not that sort of man.''

"Is that right?'' Trigg said without emotion.

"You know it is, know as well as I do that you can't put trust up for sale. It's like self-respect, you can't buy it, you must earn it. Trust is the mirror-image of self-respect; one's own self-respect is what makes others trust one.''

"Aye,'' Trigg said dourly, "happen so. But which one? I've got to trust you before you trust me, do you see? It takes a lot of trust, does that.''

"Roughly five minutes,'' the Knight began.

"Never mind time,'' Trigg cut in roughly. "You want me to stand up in court and make out I'm Sattin. You want me to deny I've been treated badly. But if I'm Sattin, I *have* been treated badly. If I'm Sattin, I'm dead.''

"But we didn't kill him. Almost certainly, no one killed him. He was sick. He died. You won't even have to say anything. He hasn't said a word since we brought him in. That's known. It can be substantiated. And so there would be no need for you to lie.''

"You can tell a lie without saying ought. That's a thing you should know at your age. The minute I stand up in that court, I'm telling a lie. That's why you're on about trust. Can you trust me to tell a lie.''

He adjusted his mass on the rickety bookshelves. They creaked warningly. "There's another thing. What about after?''

Each of them knew what he meant. No one responded. "You'd have to trust me to stand up in court,'' Trigg said. "And you'd have to trust me to keep my mouth shut, after. Happen that's a risk you'd not be willing to take. Or if you would, happen someone else wouldn't.''

"Oh, come,'' the Knight said rather too quickly, "I think you could trust us not . . .''

"There you go again, trust.'' Trigg bludgeoned him with the vowel. "It's getting out of hand, is this. Each of us asking the other to trust him to be dishonest. To spin a yarn and then stand by it. Well, it needs a bit of thinking about, does that, because if you can trust a man to be dishonest, you'd be daft as a brush to trust him in ought else.''

Determined to come in the instant Trigg finished, the Knight was like a high-diver who, a split second after leaving the board, realises the pool is empty. "Of course, if it's a simple matter of recompense . . ."

"Oh, aye," Trigg said. "And what's the price of trust when it's at home?"

"Name it," the Knight said, and in that moment Morpurgo, for the first time, began to have fears for Trigg's safety.

If Trigg was aware of the unreality of the offer, it showed neither in his face nor his voice. "I'll need time to think that over. Till then, I'll trust you as much as you trust me. How's that suit you, sunshine?" He lowered himself from his uncomfortable perch. "I've no fancy to spend any more time in this place. So since London is where I'm bound to go, I'll go now. And I'll take him with me." He jerked a big thumb at Morpurgo.

"We'll all go," the Knight decided instantly. "Steve, get rid of the Branch. Thank God they don't know Sattin's dead. Advise Monitor that he and Vickers are in charge of the body until arrangements can be made. Johnny, you and Sibley will look after Mr Trigg. Harbutt's still at the flat, call him and tell him you'll all be arriving there. Callow can drive me back."

"Director-General." Steve had brought himself completely under control. "At ten o'clock this morning, that man" – he indicated Trigg – "could speak three or four words and do more damage to this country and its allies than anything short of all-out nuclear war."

The Knight nodded, grey with fatigue. "Agreed. And exactly the same damage by not being there. Do you have any alternative?"

Steve's silence gave him his answer.

*   *   *

The vicinity of Covent Garden was a carefully planned traffic jam. Weber and Claas, their taxi still moving from time to time, but only at a crawl, picked like a couple of vultures at the remains of a subject long since dead.

"You really think they'll put him up?" Claas asked. In one form or another, he had been living with the question ever since the realisation that no one on the British side was going to pass the word that the show had been cancelled.

"No show, no go," Weber said with melancholy patience. "What do they have to lose?"

"Everything. The marks. The risk that he might talk. Hell,

this thing could hardly have worked out better if the Sovs had planned it."

"It won't be the first time brilliant improvisation has stood in for planning. And it won't be the last. The same with the British, the marks may not be so bad now. They may have been able to cover them."

"Without him knowing?"

"Sure, why not? Look, he's on drugs, so they knock him out and paint him up. So long as he's kept away from a mirror, he doesn't know.'

"But if he talks," Claas insisted. "Goddammit, he *will* talk!"

"Call off the show and everything talks. It's a gamble. Say a hundred to one. But the other way? No appearance? A cert, Moscow Centre scoops the pool. Don't put it past the Brits to gamble. Don't put it past them to win."

"Okay, okay, so it's a gamble and there's already been one loser."

"The guy's dead," Weber said sharply. "Accept it, for God's sake!"

"The guy was innocent."

"The moment he agreed to stand in for Sattin he stopped being innocent."

"Oh, look!"

"No, *you* look. You're thinking in ones, Warren. Think in millions! The free world! Our kids growing up in an open society, not a police state."

"Ends and means."

"Crap! If one man's life could save your family, your country, from being nuked to a crisp, you'd strangle him with your own bare hands. And if you had to pull off his fingernails first, you'd do that too."

Claas nodded. "Damn right I would! Sorry."

"Don't be sorry, be glad. You've got a conscience. But better taking out your conscience for a few hours than taking out a country for keeps. I think we're going to have to walk."

They paid off the taxi and started to find their way through increasingly dense concentrations of police and police vehicles, the air alive with the rasp and crackle of police radios. Claas nudged Weber to look up. The skyline was under guard too, no guns in sight, only binoculars, but the guns would not be far away.

They were stopped three times in all before they got within reach of the unimpressive entrance to the Bow Street courts. There, penned at a safe distance like dangerous animals, were those of the media cohorts who had not been able to or would not be allowed to get inside, a strain of directional microphones, a goggle of lenses, a twitchy frustration of pens, pads and pocket dictating machines.

They reached the entrance, to be checked once more and waved on, but being waved on proved to be more or less the same as staying where they were, since the small lobby beyond the door was jammed with other members of the pass-bearing elite. Claas spotted Petröfi a little way ahead. Weber, in turn, drew his attention to the senior TASS representative.

Claas tried extreme pressure on a back immediately ahead of him. Its owner groaned, but otherwise stayed put. "This is where the big shows try out for Broadway."

"Like Poughkeepsie. But they don't all bomb in Poughkeepsie."

"This one will."

They were moving forward again. Someone ahead of them, trapped like a herring in a netted shoal, called, "Hey, Henry! Henry Liddle!" From the opposite side of the catch, a man with prehensile ears and a nose that should have made him top-heavy, glanced across and made a two-fingered response.

"See what they think of us?" Claas said. "We get classed with the press."

"If it bombs," Weber pointed out, "it'll be in front of the classiest audience since Booth shot Lincoln. Quit beefing. It's history and you're privileged to be in it." They began to move. The cause of the delays appeared. Everyone was being searched for concealed weapons. Duly processed, they showed their passes for the last time and were in.

"Hey!" Weber was surprised. "A peepshow! Don't these people know how to stage a smash hit?"

"Done their best," Claas told him. "Quart into a pint pot, there isn't usually this much room." A false floor had been built over the public benches, with rows of steeply raked benches. They settled as far forward as could be managed.

The smallness of the court continued to surprise Weber. The distance from the rear wall to the magistrate's raised seat could have been no more than twelve or fourteen yards, he thought.

Between it and the temporary press accommodation was an area with facing seats and desk space. Behind them again, along either wall, were other benches, all of the same solid, time-polished oak as the panelled walls. Though two of them held a token representation of the general public, the rest of the court, so far as he could judge, was occupied by those, most of them probably lawyers of one kind and another, prepared to risk possible suffocation for the privilege of being present at the first public airing of a *cause célèbre*.

Weber nudged Claas. "There's Morpurgo."

"Listen, does he look worried to you?"

"No," Weber admitted. "He doesn't look worried. Tense, maybe, but not worried."

"You want to know something? That worries me. I know someone round here has to be worried, but I didn't think it was me."

Morpurgo saw Claas and Weber in the same moment that they saw him and let his eyes glide away, coming momentarily to rest on Petröfi. A message passed from Petröfi. Unfortunately, it was in code, and Morpurgo had no key. Again and again his eyes came to rest on the empty seat which, at any moment now, would be occupied by the bulky form of Eustace Roland Trigg, aka Joseph Sattin aka Trigger.

Last night – no, he reminded himself, this morning – he had sat in that small, oppressive office, sealed from the rest of the world in a bell jar of darkness and watched Trigg as Steve Archer, now separated from him only by the taut figure of his Director-General, had said, "At ten o'clock this morning, that man could speak three or four words and do more damage to this country and its allies than anything short of all-out nuclear war."

And in Trigg's eyes he had seen something that smouldered but was bright at its heart. Three or four words, he thought. Three or four words!

On his other side sat Chief Superintendent Placket, his face the face of all those who take nothing in human behaviour as so unspeakable as to warrant surprise. Placket had made the age-old apologia – Pilate, witch-hunter, hangman, soldier – only doing his duty. Didn't come off this time, his saurian eyes had said, but next time, you bloody lefty . . . next time.

Finally Morpurgo, trying to berth his gaze where it would not encounter a disguised enemy or a dissembling friend, saw

Epworth. He was right at the back of the court, standing, in fact, near the door through which, at any moment now, would come the man for whom this stageset had been created and all these people, actors and extras, had been brought together.

Epworth gave a little bob of the head and smiled a little smile. You and I know, it appeared to say. If no one else, you and I know. But there was no immediate possibility of pursuing the semi-telepathic conversation. Someone called, "Stand, please." Everyone stood. The magistrate came in, bowed his head to the court and took his seat. The court subsided. The clerk said, "Call Joseph Sattin, please."

Trigg, sandwiched between two uniform policemen, came through the door to the right. Epworth was no longer visible.

When Trigg and his escort had taken their seats, the clerk, almost conversationally, said, "Will the defendant stand up, please." Given no option by his guards, Trigg stood.

"Your name is Joseph Sattin?" the clerk asked.

Trigg, motionless, stared ahead of himself impassively. Placket, next to Morpurgo, muttered, "Still keeping it up, then?" his reference to Sattin's original refusal to speak simultaneously making it clear that he accepted Trigg as Sattin. He also knew Placket's real meaning, that a private session or two with Placket and a couple of his hard men would quickly have resolved any temporary problem of silence.

The clerk repeated his question. Trigg made no response.

The magistrate, young and with sufficient sense of humour to smile faintly at the impasse, said, "Will the defendant answer the question, please." The court was so still that traffic rerouted around Covent Garden sounded as angry as bees barred from the hive. Trigg himself might, Morpurgo thought, have been standing on the deserted promenade at Cleethorpes, gazing toward an ebbtide that was no more than an occasionally glinting line halfway to the edge of the world.

In the mildest of tones, chiding a wayward child, the magistrate said, "We shall get through these matters a little faster if you will answer the questions that are put to you."

"Big day for the lad," Placket muttered dismissively.

The clerk repeated his question a third time, then looked at Placket. "I take it there is no shortage of witnesses to confirm that this man is Joseph Sattin?"

Placket said, "No, sir."

"Do you so confirm, Chief Superintendent Placket?" the magistrate enquired.

"I do, sir. Perhaps I should make it clear that the prisoner has only spoken once since his arrest. His words were to the effect that that was the only time he would speak."

"So I understand. Is the prisoner represented?"

"No, sir."

"I see. Has he means?"

"I am informed that he has," the clerk said. "But I am also told that they may form part of the evidence to be presented after commital, which means they aren't available at this stage."

The magistrate levelled his pen in the direction of Trigg. "Since this is a request for an adjournment, I will take the opportunity of advising you that unless you make your own arrangements, a lawyer will be assigned to you under the provisions of the Legal Aid Act of 1974. If you are subsequently shown to have sufficient means to pay, you will have to do so. But since you would not be able to choose a lawyer under those circumstances, it really is very important that you should reconsider your decision not to speak."

Trigg continued to study the distant Cleethorpes sea. With another faint smile, the magistrate, careful to speak only to the clerk, said, "It's to be hoped that Mr Sattin's lawyer, when appointed, will explain to him the difference between mute by visitation of God and mute of malice." A low murmur of amusement spread through the court.

"Well," the magistrate said briskly, "we must do what we can. Charge?"

Placket was on his feet. "Offences under the Official Secrets Act, sir. I respectfully request a further adjournment so that the police may continue investigations and prepare their case."

"The previous appearance was at a private sitting, I see, an adjournment of" – the magistrate made play of consulting a document – "seven days, yes?"

"That's so, sir. Respectfully request a further seven days." Placket had the policeman's innate ability to profess himself respectful and sound rather less.

"The question of bail." Once again the magistrate referred to his papers. In the silence, Morpurgo could hear the clatter of the police helicopter somewhere above the court. He saw Trigg's stare lift briefly skywards, and knew precisely why.

"The police opposed bail in view of the gravity of the offences."
The magistrate wagged his pen at Placket. "No objection from
the defendant?" There was a tentative chuckle from the court.
"Obviously not." He transferred his gaze to Trigg. "Mr Sattin,
you have nothing at all to say on the subject of bail?"

Morpurgo wondered whether Trigg realised that, with every
forward step in the judicial process, he was putting himself
deeper in contempt of the court, deeper in opposition to the law.
It was not sufficient that he should not claim to be Sattin. Silence
was a form of perjury. Trigg, beyond shifting his bulk slightly,
made no response.

The magistrate nodded reluctantly, accepting defeat. He looked
toward the clerk.

Raising his voice a little, the clerk said, "Mr Sattin, I have to
ask you at this stage whether you wish to make any statement
from the dock, or give any evidence to the magistrate, or call any
witnesses."

He waited. On Morpurgo's right, tension and apprehension
crackled about the Knight like static electricity.

Trigg said nothing.

"Very well." The magistrate was very brisk now, making up
for lost time. "In the absence of argument to the contrary and in
view of the extreme gravity of the charges, I must rule that the
defendant shall continue to be held in custody for a further seven
days."

It was over. Something drained out of Morpurgo like his
life-blood. He heard the Knight release a small sigh. Trigg's two
policemen prepared to take him out, while a growing buzz of
conversation sprang up all through the court.

"Mr Sattin." The magistrate's voice, high and clear, took the
court by surprise. Morpurgo sat up, his tension regenerated.

"Mr Sattin," the magistrate repeated. "In view of the serious-
ness of your circumstances, I feel it my duty to put one more
question to you, in the hope that you will see fit to answer it.
Have you any complaints about your treatment since your arrest?"

Morpurgo heard a sharp intake of breath from the Knight. At
his other side, Placket, outraged, muttered, "Silly *bugger*! Wants
his backside tanning." A susurration swelled in the courtroom,
to be followed by a silence that was almost painful. Morpurgo
caught a glimpse of Petröfi, high on the press benches, leaning so
far forward as to be in imminent danger of starting a media

avalanche. The Knight, head bowed, hands clasped, might have been and probably was praying. Just beyond him, Steve Archer's face was set in a look of bitter triumph.

Trigg had barely altered his stance since getting to his feet. Now, slowly, he did so, turning to look directly at the Knight, Morpurgo, the ranks of his captors, his stolid face enigmatic. The light in his eyes, Morpurgo saw, was sharply focused; challenging, mocking. This is it, it said, my turn! Did you really think you could get away with it?'

He spoke.

"Have I any complaints about my treatment since my arrest?" The effect of hearing him speak for the first time was a *coup de théâtre*. No one stirred, no one so much as murmured.

"I have been treated," Trigg said, his voice stripped of feeling, accent, class, "as a man in my situation would expect to be treated by people whose way of life, and values, and ideas of what is right and wrong are totally hostile to his own."

The Knight's head sank lower. Placket expelled a deep breath that suggested disgust, contempt. The room was one vast bated breath.

Trigg turned slowly to his left, farther and farther, then repeated the movement in reverse until he had looked at, and been looked at by, every person in the room. The silence pressed cruelly.

Addressing himself to the magistrate, he said, "I shan't be around much longer, but I have no complaints whatsoever about my treatment."

In the following pandemonium, almost a hundred media representatives struggling perilously to vacate their staggered seating and get to a microphone or telephone, all Morpurgo could think was that Trigg, in his exquisitely precise choice of words, had told the truth, the whole truth, and nothing but the truth.

*   *   *

Claas had put on his new Portuguese-British shoes for a second time. After spending all that money, he was not about to junk them. Now he was regretting the decision. "Look at them," he demanded bitterly. "Trampled all to hell." They were among the few left on the raked seats after the press stampede. "Goddammit," he said. "They look like I found them in a trash can!"

"Where," Weber said, not having heard, "do you suppose things went wrong?"

"I shouldn't have bought the goddam shoes." Weber's question registered. "Oh, I'm not sure, but something sure as hell did. Are we going to stay up here all day, or are we going to meet Epworth?"

Weber began picking his way down. "Did that guy look sick to you?"

"Now you come to mention it, no. I'm sick, sick as hell. I never should have bought . . ."

"Warren," Weber said quietly, "start thinking what you're going to say to Head of Plans. Start thinking, period."

Out in the street there was still organised tumult. The plain van that had brought Sattin was inching its way out of the jail yard, surrounded by a dense mass of uniformed police. There were still media men clustered to the rear, hoping to get some kind of a picture.

"They're wasting their time," Weber said. "The one thing you can be sure of is that no one, repeat no one, is going to get a peek at that guy, let alone take his picture."

"I was watching Petröfi," Claas said. "He never doubted it was Sattin. It really rocked him when the guy said he had no complaints."

"I was watching Morpurgo and his knight, also Steve Archer. It really rocked them, too. How do you explain that, junior?"

"How do I explain it?" Claas was picking his way through toward Covent Garden, with Weber in tow. "They weren't sure he would say the right thing until he said it. Which is crazy, because they had to be sure before they could stand him up." Limping along in his scuffed shoes, he said unhappily, "Langley isn't going to like this. Nobody's going to like it. Do we have a Company station in Mali? Or Franz Joseph Land?"

"Where in hell is Franz Joseph Land?"

"I don't know. I'm just thinking I may be about to find out."

"Where is this place we're supposed to meet Epworth?"

"There, right ahead." They reached the Covent Garden shopping precinct. Weber followed Claas in and down the steps.

"Why does he want to meet us, do you know that?"

"Listen," Claas said as they worked their way through the tourists and the stalls of pottery, hand-made jewellery and Indian silks and cottons, "the only thing I know about Epworth is that

296

he keeps what he's got well hidden. There, that's the place. He chose it, so don't blame me." It was a corner refreshment bar. They took a table. There were only a few people there. Claas ordered coffee.

"It was the lookalike, right?" Weber was not so much lugubrious as mourning. "Shlonski hit the wrong guy."

Claas nodded. "What I figured."

"So we lost out," Weber said. "Moscow lost out, but so did we. Delahay won. A triumph for the status quo."

"Morpurgo won too. Didn't he?"

"Maybe. Maybe not. What about – what was his name again? Trigg? – do you think Trigg won?"

"For now, yes," Claas ladled two spoonfuls of sugar into his coffee, "but is now all that matters?"

"It's the only time we live in," Weber commented. "If Trigg talked, he could still bring Humpty down."

"*And* all the Queen's horses, *and* all the Queen's men."

"A lot of the President's men, too, starting with us. Practically everybody except Moscow. Humpty down, Moscow up. Does that say anything to you?"

"I wouldn't sell him any life assurance."

"That's what I mean. Future uncertain, brother Trigg. Here comes Epworth. Who's the character with him? We saw him in the lobby."

Claas looked. "Henry Liddle. Political columnist. Big noise. Pure poison." Claas nodded. "*Ciao*, Henry, Larry. Care for some coffee?"

Liddle, his eyes hooded, face angry, nodded at Claas, then looked at Weber. "Pierre Weber. When do you go back? Don't give me that stuff about taking over London station." He corralled them all with his vulpine stare. "Tell me something. When you're screwed, and you know you've been screwed, and you didn't want to be screwed, does it count as rape?"

*   *   *

"Well," Trigg said, preparing to push himself up from the shabby chair in the flat, "if it's all the same to you, and I reckon it should be, I'll be on my way." The motorcade, following elaborate plans, had gradually dwindled until only the van remained, carrying Trigg, Morpurgo, Steve Archer and the Knight into the underground garage and the care of the quietly efficient Harbutt.

"Ah," the Knight said. "Yes, well, understand your feelings, old chap, but if you could spare us just a little more of your valuable time." He looked relaxed, confident and, in Morpurgo's eyes, silkily dangerous, a tribute to the rejuvenating qualities of success.

"You see," the Knight said, one man of the world to another, "all in all, a great many people had a damn good look at you in the course of that superb – I say it sincerely – that superb performance. What if one of them, just a single one, should come across you again? In the street. On a bus. At a bar."

"How many folk in London?" Trigg asked. "Seven million, last time I heard."

"Only one of them, my dear sir, the wrong one, and the cat would be out of the bag."

"Oh aye?" Trigg was no less composed than the Knight. "In that case, just how long did you have it in mind to keep pussy *in* the bag?"

"We trusted you, dear chap, and you did us proud. Now you must trust us, just for a little while. I promise we shall look after you altogether more comfortably this time."

"Aye." Trigg nodded his big head. "Happen that's what I'm worried about, me not being used to the high life. So thanks very much, but I'll be off. And don't you worry about me being spotted. I'm not staying in London. I've other fish to fry." He winked at Morpurgo. "Fried fish is something I set great store by. Next to rock, that is."

"Seaside rock," Morpurgo explained, making vague pulling movements. "With 'Cleethorpes' right down the middle. Peppermint, pineapple, lemon."

"I see," the Knight said disinterestedly. "But there is a world outside Cleethorpes."

"That's right, sunshine," Trigg said agreeably enough, but Morpurgo, practised by now, saw that the derision lurking in his eyes had come alight, small flames, flickering, feral. "Not that Cleethorpes isn't important, but there's forty-seven other places. Nigh on two hundred thousand sticks of rock is a lot of rock, do you see? So it has to go to a lot of other places beside Cleethorpes."

"Are you telling me," Morpurgo interrupted, astounded, "that that little place on the promenade makes two hundred thousand sticks of rock a year?"

* * *

298

"You know it," Liddle said. "I know it. Screwed. What I *don't* know is how they did it. Yet!" He looked round the small circle as invitingly as the wolf pressing the lamb to stay for dinner.

"Mmmm, maybe you expect too much," Epworth suggested. "After all, there must be a limit to the amount of sensation you can pack into one story."

"Sensation," Liddle said loudly, a public declaration of faith, "is a product with a limitless market. Like the young lady of Ryde who, as you all doubtless know, could never be satisfied, the more you get the more you want. I have an unlimited appetite. So, how did they get a dedicated spy, a man who could have given the Kremlin the propaganda coup of the century – correction, who the Kremlin *knew* was going to give them the propaganda coup of the century, or there would have been no TASS statement – how did they persuade him to stand up and say he'd never been so well treated?" He ravened at them across the table.

"Brainwashing?" Weber had quickly decided not to like Henry Liddle.

"Anyway," Claas demanded. "Why are you loafing around when you should be knocking out your story?"

"I work for a morning paper," Liddle told him. "And I have a rule never to write a story until I've got it. As yet, I haven't got it. Come on! You're the experts. How would you get a Soviet spy to stand up in public and say the opposite to what his bosses expected? Or are you like most experts, full of crap?"

Epworth had apparently stopped listening. "Oh, look," he said, pleased. "I haven't seen any of that stuff in years." He was peering at a confectionery shop next door.

Liddle turned irritably. "Let me know when you decide to grow up. Or maybe you'd like me to buy you a stick?"

"I wouldn't stop you." Epworth giggled. The rock was in an impressive pyramid. A sign said: *London rock. An acceptable present for young and old.* He smiled at Claas. "It should be telling you something."

"Me?" Claas was not sure whether to take Epworth seriously. "What should it be telling me?"

"When I – mmmm – called last night you said you were in trouble over not flying your son's kite in the park. You said you'd had to promise him some candy.

"That's right, I did." Claas turned for a second look at the mountain of rock. "Trouble is, Ella will bawl me out about his teeth."

"Don't be a tightwad," Weber urged. "Buy the kid some candy."

"Well, all right then." Claas got up. "You want some too?" he asked Weber.

"Sure," Weber said, happy to annoy Liddle. "We'd all like some, right, fellers?"

Claas went to buy some rock.

*　　*　　*

Trigg eyed Morpurgo with good-natured contempt. "That little place on the promenade? You don't listen to what's told you, do you, sunshine? Oh, I knew what you were thinking, lad, tuppenny-ha'penny show, tuppenny-ha'penny sort of chap. Here, take a look at this." He got out his wallet, took a card from it and gave it to Morpurgo. Nicely printed on good quality pasteboard, it said:

E. R. TRIGG & SON LTD
Quality Confectioners

The address was in Grimsby.

"Now then," Trigg said, "turn it over."

On the back was a photograph of a modern, single-storey factory building, all glass and steelwork, of considerable size. "Nigh on a hundred people," Trigg said, "shop floor, warehouse, marketing and office staff. More than fifty lines, not counting rock, and still going up. We turn out more rock in a day than t'other place can manage in a month, but I had to wait till the old lady had gone before I could shut it down."

"Would someone be kind enough to tell me," the Knight said in exasperation, "exactly what rock has to do with affairs of state? The safety of the realm?"

"It has this to do with it, sunshine." Trigg took something else from his wallet. Morpurgo had the impression that it was some kind of label, but for the moment, Trigg kept it in his hand.

"Happen you'll remember," he said, "that after you'd snatched me up, so to speak, you dumped me down and left me. Not that I mind being left in the Strand Palace, but it was a bit offhand, all the same. Anyroad, when yon crisis broke, I had a pretty good idea of what'd happened. And as luck would have it, I ran across

300

a feller who was in a position to tell me a good deal more. A feller name of Epworth.

He waited for the Knight to calm down, and for Steve to finish the last of bitter comments on Morpurgo. "Hold on, hold on, it's nought to do with Morpurgo. But I'll tell you this for nothing, yon Epworth knows more about the rock trade than you three put together. And I'll tell you another. He told me, did Epworth, last Tuesday, mind, pretty well exactly what you" – He pointed a stubby finger at the Knight – " 'd be trying on with me right this minute. Now what do you say to that, sunshine?"

*　　*　　*

"Okay," Weber said, "so it goes right down the middle, so let's take a look." He took a stick of rock from Claas, peeled back the wrapper. A label, wrapped about the centre of the stick, fell out and, caught by a stray breeze, wafted gently toward the floor.

"Dropped something." Epworth bent to pick it up and, inevitably clumsy, took some time to separate it from the ground. He came up red-faced and smiling, and gave it to Liddle before realising his mistake. "Oh, sorry." He tried to take it back.

About to relinquish it, Liddle went into shock. His eyes bulged. His jaw dropped. The blood appeared to drain from his predatory nose. He stared at the label as if it were a warrant, signed by the Queen herself, condemning him to be taken to the Tower of London and separated from his head.

"Something – mmmm – wrong?" Epworth asked. "You don't look very well."

Claas recollected he had bought two sticks of rock. Ripping the wrapper from the other, he slid out the label. He and Weber bent over it as one man. "Jesus H. Christ!" Claas said, startled.

"Think so?" Weber shook his head. "Terrible likeness." He looked up sharply, hoping to take Epworth by surprise.

Epworth met the look with his customary air of mild confusion. "May I?" He held out a diffident hand. "I seem to be the only one who doesn't know what's happening."

*　　*　　*

Trigg looked on all three of them with a kind of pitying scorn. "By! I wouldn't have missed this for all the tea in China! I dare say" – He looked at the Knight – "if I was to ask you how long it would be before it was safe to turn me loose, you'd say it again –

301

you trusted me and now it's my turn to trust you. Well, I've never trusted you, sunshine, and I trust you even less now. So me and yon feller Epworth, we put a little scheme together that would help to get me through an awkward moment, and this is it.

"Just about now," Trigg said, hauling out his fat silver watch on its fat silver chain, "that feller Henry Liddle, one way or another, will be meeting up with Epworth. One way or another, and you can bet on it, Henry Liddle will be introduced to a stick of London rock. I *did* tell you, forty-seven different holiday towns, only you wouldn't listen. And when he does, he'll get what anybody gets that buys a stick of Trigg's rock. High quality at a reasonable price, and this." He passed the label to the Knight.

*   *   *

They all tried to get into the telephone box to hear Liddle do his stuff. "No flights? Where is the fucking place, anyway? . . . All right, train . . . Oh Christ! Forget it, I want to get there this afternoon, not tomorrow. All right, I'll use my car. Get a photographer. Get Spink, Tell him to be outside, ten minutes from now . . . Ten, you bastard, ten! . . . What? . . . Of course it's a big story. Correction, it's not a story, it's *the* story, front page banner, all six columns . . . No, I won't, not until I've got it . . . No, I don't trust you. I don't trust anybody . . . I'll phone my copy in and we'll wire the pics . . . Listen, one thing you *can* do . . . Not that, you pimp! . . . No, send someone out to buy a dozen sticks of London Rock. You heard me. Rock!"

"Mind if I say something?" Weber asked.

"I'll give you one second flat. And don't try interfering or I'll break your arms."

"Why do you have to go up there? Isn't the story here?"

"The story *was* here. But at the moment it's where he isn't, not where he is, and if you can't work that out, God help America!"

"Going to stop him?" Claas asked Epworth after Liddle had gone. "He could blow things wide open, right?"

"Blow what wide open?" Epworth asked. "And why would I want to stop him? I'm sure Cleethorpes is a very nice place."

*   *   *

Wordlessly, the Knight passed the label to Steve, who started to say something, changed his mind and in turn gave it to

302

Morpurgo. In small italic script, elegant and slightly old-fashioned, it said at the top: *A quality confection from E. R. Trigg and Son Ltd, Cleethorpes, South Humberside, manufacturers of high class confectionery for three generations.*

At the foot of the label was a signature, chunky, bold, unmistakable in origin: E. R. Trigg.

Between top and bottom was a sharp, well-constrasted likeness, Sunday best smile, of Eustace Roland Trigg.

"What he'll do," Trigg said, as if this were a plan confided to him by the Almighty, "is get up there, fast as he can, see? He knows he couldn't hope to find me down here, me and Epworth are in agreement on that. Meaning" – He gave the Knight a ferocious grin – "he'll take it for granted you'll not let me loose for quite some time, if at all. Which is what I reckon too, or would, if the tables hadn't been turned. So what he'll do is get up there, check I'm not there, how long I've been gone, all the background he can manage, then he'll let fly in tomorrow's paper, remarkable facts about Mr Trigg and Mr Sattin. I reckon the Russians'll do the rest."

Morpurgo saw that the Knight had reverted to his one-in-the-morning self, retribution sitting on his shoulders like the Old Man of the Sea. Steve, in a voice choked with fury, said, "He's right, Director-General. Once Liddle breaks the story there'll be a chain reaction. It won't stop until everything's in ruins."

"Do you know what you've done?" The Knight looked at Trigg hopelessly. "Thanks to you we shall have a new government and the collapse of the Western alliance. Even now, it's too late to stop it."

"Nay, never say die, sunshine!" Trigg was brutally cheerful. "I don't mind letting on it wouldn't worry me over much if you were right, some of it anyway, but me and that feller Epworth, we're not as daft as that. But you must have me back there double quick if you want your chestnuts pulled out of the fire."

A last flicker from dying embers, the Knight said, "*That's* it! You're bluffing. It's all too ridiculous to succeed."

The telephone rang in the corner of the room. "Yon feller Epworth," Trigg said confidently, "calling to say the dog's seen the rabbit and the chase is on."

Harbutt had materialised. "Call for Mr Trigg." He held the phone out.

"Now, lad. What's to do?" Trigg listened briefly before saying,

"Best tell it to the high panjandrum. He doesn't want to believe me." He passed the phone to the Knight. "Yon feller Liddle's on his way. Don't waste time chatting."

"Not just Epworth," the Knight said bitterly when the call was over. "Claas and Weber. All right, they won't talk, but they'll know." He reached a conclusion no less palatable for being inevitable. "Does your conspiracy cover the question of how we get you to Cleethorpes before Liddle? Among his numerous unpleasant habits is an ability to drive very fast, and he has the car to do it."

"How are you going to get me up there?" Trigg shook his head in bemusement over the standards of intelligence in supposedly quick-witted Londoners, though his eyes held a gleam of anticipatory pleasure. "By helicopter, sunshine, how else?"

*   *   *

He was going, Morpurgo kept telling himself as he crossed the Thames on the Charing Cross footbridge, for the music. In the last ten days, music had all but vanished from his life and he had a genuine sense of deprivation. Ahead of him, concrete castles along the riverside, was the South Bank complex. He had the choice of the Royal Festival Hall, the Queen Elizabeth Hall, the Purcell Room, all of which, when work and circumstances had permitted, had given him pleasure. It was a curious quirk of fate that the music he was going to listen to was at none of them, but next door, in the National Theatre. The fact remained; he was going to listen to the music. It had nothing to do with Epworth.

He went down to the Embankment, the serene summer evening gracing it and the river with a blessing of light and tranquillity. As he approached the main entrance he could see the clusters of informal audience through the massive plate glass, some standing, many sitting on the ground. A little nearer and he could hear the music, too. His knowledge of early music was less than extensive, he favoured the late classicists and the early romantics, but he recognised the piece, *Ah, Robin*, a folk classic for almost two centuries up to the days of the Tudors.

Now he could see the ensemble itself and – an unexpected and pleasurable touch – they wore period dress. There were four players, four singers, all men, their colours and costume enhanced by the solid sinuosity of their exotic instruments. Each of the instrumentalists had an alternative instrument at his feet.

Morpurgo would have been hard put to name any of them, but the combined sound was reedy, sweet and in peculiarly apt harmony with the summer night. He circled the crowd to the rear, positioning himself against the blown-up photograph of a group of delicate-sailed Spanish windmills clustered like Quixotean giants in the sunset of a bare-topped hill.

From his chosen place he could observe Epworth at leisure. Epworth wore doublet, padded knee-breeches and hose, with a flat cap of black velvet. The hose were scarlet, the breeches black slashed with purple. The doublet was of deep crimson embroidered with gold. The effect on Epworth might well have been ridiculous. Oddly enough, it was not. It lent him a kind of dignity, the hose emphasising the straightness rather than the thinness of his legs, a pleated white ruff hiding his prominent Adam's apple, while under the velvet cap the lines of his face were humorous with a subtle lacing of intelligence. Morpurgo had long since ceased to doubt his intelligence.

Epworth's instrument was a long cylindrical affair of black wood, curving gracefully upward at the lower end. It was certainly a reed instrument, but which? shawm or crumhorn? And what was the other, not dissimilar but quite straight, in the open case at his feet?

Whatever he was playing, Epworth's fingers, long, sensitive, as Morpurgo had previously noted, moved dexterously over the stops, his concentration total. The counter-tenor, his voice, sweet, sexless and of a marvellous clarity, soared over the accompanying tenor, baritone and bass, lingering and plangent: *Ah, Robin, gentle Robin; tell me how thy leman doth, and thou shalt know of mine.*

The song came to an end, earning enthusiastic applause. From the floor above an amplified voice advised playgoers that the performance in the Olivier Theatre would commence in eight minutes; in eight minutes.

The ensemble launched into something as lusty as their previous performance had been wistful and tender. The singers all but shouted the melody, the wind instruments blared reedily together, the words, though Morpurgo could not catch all of them, were apparently those of a medieval ploughman extolling his ability and his knowledge of the parts of the plough. The effect was tunefully hypnotic.

Looking at Epworth, Morpurgo wondered when he himself

had first come under suspicion. Certainly well before the secret meeting at Number 10 at which the Friends had been given carte blanche to ravage Curzon Street. He was convinced, now, that that had been no more than belated official recognition of what had been going on unofficially for some time. As for the Friends' own interest, it was not, in one sense, hard to understand. They had a fieldman to be exchanged for Sattin. Any mole, Curzon Street or elsewhere, who threatened to endanger the eventual exchange, was in their view as much their concern as Security Directorate's.

But hold on, Morpurgo told himself. The question of the exchange had not arisen until almost the end of the Sattin ring. No mole in Security Directorate could have threatened an exchange that had not then been envisaged, let alone arranged. Question: Why was the SIS already nosing its way covertly through Security Directorate affairs when neither Sattin nor their agent had yet been picked up?

About to abandon it as unanswerable, it represented itself to him in a new light. Who, exactly, so far, had been investigated before and after the arrests? He knew of no one, not even Steve, who would have been another logical starting point; but no, of course, Steve was already on the Friends' strength if not their payroll.

He remembered something Epworth had said to him; if there had to be a mole, he, Morpurgo, would head everyone's list of favourites for the role. Was it he, and only he, so far, who had attracted unfriendly attention? He was inclined to think it was. So the question might be rephrased; why had Morpurgo been elected, in advance, for the post of resident mole? And who had made the nomination?

Once again Steve Archer's name came to mind. Steve Archer, who did not like Morpurgo as a person, did not like him as a type, did not like him sitting in a chair Steve considered his by right. And he had not only seduced Steve's wife – been seduced by, his other self murmured – but, in effect, made it clear to Steve that his marriage, an institution of ritual importance, was a failure, nothing but the crumbling façade of a structure already in ruins. And Steve had kept silence, awaiting a greater vengeance.

Could it, he wondered, be left there? A complex but ancient plot? hatred, envy, revenge? Tempting; not only tempting but reasonable, particularly – he had no illusions now – as it was going to cost him his career. But it would not serve *in toto*; too many gaps. There had to be someone – The Dark and Stormy? Fish? Both and others? – behind Steve. Epworth, his instinct said. Why look close at hand when Epworth was everywhere?

Only the previous morning Epworth, in Morpurgo's own office, had left him in little doubt that he was close to the heart of Morpurgo's own private, unshared secret, yet, at the very moment when he might have delivered the *coup de grâce*, had switched his attentions to the Knight, Liddle and Trigg. But Epworth, Morpurgo reminded himself, was like the Cheshire Cat, his smile lingering on long after its owner was elsewhere.

"Hello," Epworth said at his side. "Pity you arrived – mmmm – when we'd nearly finished. Still" – The Cheshire Cat had rejoined its smile – "I dare say you've plenty to occupy your mind. Excuse me. Just pack my instruments, then we could have a drink." He looked anxiously at Morpurgo. "Unless you're too busy. Or have you been round already?" With that incomprehensible question lingering in place of his smile, he turned away.

"Which one is which?" Morpurgo called after him.

Epworth held up the instrument that curved at the end. "Crumhorn." He pointed at the straight one. "Shawm. Don't have one myself." He bent to fasten a case. "Mmmm, shan't be a tick."

They went up to the nearest bar, Epworth allowing Morpurgo to carry one of his cases. He appeared quite unself-conscious in his doublet and hose. The disembodied voice announced that the performance in the Olivier Theatre would commence in five minutes. All about them, the throng was thinning. Sipping dry sherry with the delicacy of a canary, Epworth said, "Thought you might turn up, first night of the hanging. I brought something for your wife. You can give it to her yourself." Doffing his velvet cap, he took something from inside it. As he recognised it, Morpurgo thought fatalistically: Well, that's it!

It was a colour picture postcard. It showed three medieval church towers, massive, glaring a lurid orange in low-angle sunlight against a blue-black sky shot with purple. Morpurgo turned it over. On the back, printed in a script he knew only too well, was a message. SORRY TO HAVE MISSED YOU. BETTER LUCK NEXT TIME, PETER. It was addressed to Mr and Mrs Yuri Kagalov at their recent home in Hampstead.

The Olivier performance would commence in four minutes; in four minutes. Small queues of ticket-holders were inching into the stalls. "I gathered your wife had damaged her own copy," Epworth was saying. "Had to – mmmm – throw it away. I told her I might be able to replace it."

Morpurgo regarded the card impassively for a few moments more, then tucked it away. "I'll give it to her. When I see her. If I see her."

Epworth looked surprised. "Hasn't she come? It can't be quite the same when the place is empty."

Damn the man! Morpurgo thought irritably. Would he never stop talking in riddles? "The last link in the chain, yes? Me, shackled."

Epworth took a delicate sip of sherry. "Your wife's guardbook's complete again, that's all that matters."

"I was in Doncaster that particular day, not much out of my way to go to Lincoln for the proper postmark. Of course" – Morpurgo looked quizzically at Epworth – "I could have bought any old postcard of the cathedral. Any idea why I didn't?"

Epworth looked deeply embarrassed. "Arrogance," Morpurgo said. "Sheer bloody arrogance, signing my own work, you might say. Didn't expect to be found out. Didn't expect you."

"Mmmm," Epworth said dubiously. "Good rationalisation. Myself, I would have gone for something a *leetle* more elegant, psychologically speaking. I mean, it was your *wife's* picture, the original, so with respect . . . Still," he finished, outrageously, "none of my business."

"So, when are you going to turn me in?"

"But you didn't do anything, not really. Oh, you tipped off Kagalov to lie low, but there was no need. Moscow Centre had the whole thing planned from the moment they found Sattin's illness was incurable. They'd already uncovered our East German field agent, feeding him disinformation. When Operation Bowman had served its purpose they deliberately fed him with material they knew our analysts at Century House would link almost immediately with Stingray. A sort of – mmmm – signal that Stingray was being spied on. We tell you, as they knew we would, and in no time at all you've uncovered Sattin and the Stringers. As soon as Moscow Centre learns that, they pull in *our* man and make an instant offer of exchange." Epworth smiled

308

disarmingly. "How could they know you'd just brought in the very man for exchange? Mole! End of part one.

"Of course," Epworth said as if the thing were already crystal clear to Morpurgo, "the *actual* signal for the trap to be set was Sattin's telling them that his illness wasn't responding to treatment any more. That's when they staked him out as bait. And, of course, though you hadn't the smallest reason to suspect, he already knew exactly what would happen next, and when."

"The TASS statement and so on." The scales had fallen from Morpurgo's eyes.

"But from your point of view, almost everyone's point of view, the only explanation, again, was – mole. From then on, they knew they could rely on the Prime Minister's rivals to – mmmm – set him up for the kill." Epworth shook his head sadly over the iniquity of politicians.

Sadly? Morpurgo thought. Well, perhaps; from this side.

"So you see" – Epworth peeked almost slyly at Morpurgo – "your thinking that there *ought* to be a mole in high office, hence your postcard to Kagalov – stir things up all round, lots of smoke, that was your idea wasn't it? – didn't really matter. And after that, things did tend to get a little out of hand. Moscow Centre playing a deep game. The Cousins playing a dirty one. Not forgetting your Friends. Still" – He giggled amiably, no malice – "no permanent harm done. In fact quite a lot of good. Let's call your own little sin the lefty's revenge, shall we? and – mmmm – leave it at that."

He put down his glass and stood, a comical figure in doublet and hose, and yet not. "Ah, here we are, better late than never. You can both mingle in the intervals and sort of" – Another artless giggle – "*spy* on the audience reaction. Good evening, Mrs Morpurgo. Or ought I to say Miss Markham?"

Astonished, Morpurgo got up. "Sylvie! What on earth are you doing here?" In one minute, the voice said; in one minute.

Sylvie, stunning in a white dress as deceptively simple as Epworth, sighed wrily. "Just when I was feeling a little forgiving. Flattered and forgiving. You really didn't know?"

With a sensation of walking on wall-to-wall eggshells, Morpurgo shook his head. They were alone, the playgoers all departed.

"Look." She pointed behind him.

On the wall above the table at which he and Epworth had been sitting was a photographic blow-up, huge, of bare-branched trees standing on their mirror images in a vast expanse of water. Or were they mirror-images standing on their real selves in a vast expanse of sky? Did trees, he wondered, have doppelgängers? He looked about him properly for the first time. Everywhere his eyes met Sylvie's pictures.

Epworth, cap in hand, said, "Please forgive me, but I really must go. I was so sorry, Mrs Morpurgo, to hear that your Hungarian tour has fallen through." He shook his head. "Petröfi! An undependable little man!"

Looking at Sylvie, Morpurgo said, simply, "I'm sorry. Truly. Oh, Mr Epworth brought this for you." Still looking directly at her, he gave her the picture postcard. "You didn't lose it, but thank you for saying so."

Sylvie looked from him to Epworth. "You've no need to worry about Helga, incidentally. She's in hospital. They found her on the canal bank, somewhere near King's Cross, an overdose of tranquillisers. Fortunately, she was found in time and she hadn't really taken enough, she'd only just been prescribed them." Her voice was devoid of emotion.

"Oh, good." Epworth looked genuinely relieved. Or did he? Was he genuinely anything, Morpurgo wondered.

Overwhelmed by guilt, aware of greater tragedy narrowly averted, he said, "You see? Everything we touch is smeared, so why should I escape? Anyway, Fish and your knight will see that I don't, won't they?"

"Fish?" The Cheshire Cat materialised behind Epworth's smile. "No need to worry about Fish. Fish isn't central to the scheme of things any more. There's been a sort of – mmmm – palace revolution."

"Oh?" Morpurgo was puzzled. "All right, your knight? He's certainly not the type to forgive and forget."

"Oh well," Epworth murmured. "All got to come out some time. You haven't heard the news yet? No? Merrilees has just resigned as Foreign Secretary. For" – Another gentle giggle – "personal reasons. You see, Merrilees *would* insist on you as the mole, based his whole strategy on it. *And* told the PM categorically that Security Directorate would never put Sattin up in court, so your minister won hands down."

Feeling increasingly dazed, Morpurgo said, "Then who *is* in charge at Century House?"

310

Looking more embarrassed than ever, Epworth said, "One – mmmm – does one's best. By the way, how would you feel about changing from gamekeeper to poacher? I fear there'll be some vacancies."

Barely able to come to terms with the realisation that all Epworth's efforts to clear him of a mole charge had been no more than the means to a successful power bid, Morpurgo was mentally on the ropes now. "Me? Move to Century House? Your people would never trust me."

"Your present people," Epworth told him, "don't trust you. Not even the Knight. *He* thought you were the mole, too. That's why he gave you your head. Oh no, I wasn't talking about your coming to us on trust, nothing like that. A strictly – mmmm – practical arrangement."

Watching him leave, scarlet hose, shawm in one hand, crumhorn in the other, Sylvie sighed. "Not trust, a strictly practical arrangement!" She turned to Morpurgo. "Well, Johnny, I might accept it as a starting point for negotiations."

Epilogue

Henry Liddle shouldered his way past the protesting girls on the rock stall and barged through the door at the rear. There were three men in the place, all white-jacketed, white-capped. One, at the far end, where metal vats filled the confined space with the hot smells of peppermint, lemon and pineapple, was stirring with a huge wooden spoon. Another, back to Liddle, wrestled a living mass of white, sticky candy over a table top, one end clutching a suspended hook in its sticky tentacle. The third, surprised, stared at Liddle.

Liddle came farther in, followed by Spink. Spink began to take light readings. "One of you know where Trigg is?" Liddle demanded.

"Who wants to know?" asked the third man. "Private in 'ere, didn't they tell you?"

"Name's Liddle, *Daily Post*, cully. Nothing's private to me. Twenty quid apiece to prove it. Where's Trigg?"

"*Daily Post*?" the third man repeated. "Doesn't cut much ice up 'ere, *Daily Post*, does it, Fred?"

"It cuts none," the man with wooden spoon said. "*Grimsby Telegraph* now, there's a paper that is a paper."

Liddle oscillated his great nose grimly. "All right. Fifty. Cash down." He took out his wallet. "A few to be going on with, Spinky. Close-ups and exteriors later." He thumbed a wad of notes significantly. "Still in London, is he?" He put notes and wallet on the table.

"*Lun*-dun?" That was how it sounded. "And what'd Mr Trigg be doing in London, I'd like to know?" Fred demanded.

312

Liddle's fuse was burning short. "All right. I see you know the game. Final offer, a century each. When did he go? How long's he been there? When did you hear from him last? Hey! For Christ's sake, watch what you're doing, you schmuck!"

The third man, engaged in his solitary combat, had taken a fresh turn over the hook. As he pulled, warm, sticky goo coiled itself lovingly over Liddle's wallet and the scatter of notes he had slammed on the table.

"By! That's done it!" the third man said. "All them mucky notes on a virgin throw. Public Health Inspector'd have something to say to you, yer daft bugger!"

He stopped work and began peeling twenty-pound notes from his throw. Some of them tore as they came. The wallet drew long strings of taffy after it. They settled lovingly on the alligator skin. "No good, Ernie," the third man said to the vat-stirrer. "It'll want scrapping, will that. Twenty quid's worth of good taffy. Here, take one of these notes for damages, Fred."

He rinsed his hands under a tap and began to towel them vigorously. As he turned, Liddle's mouth fell open. "Now, lad," Trigg said, "best clear off before you make any more mischief, or I'll have you for trespassing. London? I wouldn't go to London in this weather if you paid me."

"Can't stand the place, can't Mr Trigg," Ernie said.

"Wouldn't be seen dead in it," Fred added.

Still staring smoulderingly at Trigg, Liddle began to gather up notes. Some of them stuck to his hands, some to each other, some, very determinedly, to the top of the table. "It is your rock that's sold in London?"

"Oh aye, it's my rock," Trigg said. "Sells in a lot of places, does my rock."

"You've got a double down there," Liddle accused. "Do you know that?" He tried to peel a note from his fingers. It tore.

"Is that right?" Trigg said disinterestedly. "Well, they say we all have, somewhere. Look, sunshine, we sell nigh on two hundred thousand sticks of rock a year and it isn't done by standing around listening to daft questions. London? What do I care about London? It's just a market, that's what London is to me." Spink, capping the lens of his camera, went quietly out.

"All right, cully," Liddle said nastily as he prepared to leave. "I'm surprised it's even that. I'm surprised you even know where London is."

313

"Oh aye," Trigg said. "I know where it is, all right. And since you've come a long way to find out, I don't" – he dropped his voice conspiratorially – "mind letting on about something in return."

Liddle hesitated, hope faintly resurgent.

Trigg put down his towel, came around the big metal-topped table, took Liddle by the arm and approached his mouth to one of Liddle's large ears. In a loud whisper, he said, "It's not a patch on Cleethorpes." He pressed a stick of rock into Liddle's hand; lemon.